Mad Boys

BLUE IVY PREP

BOOK TWO

HEATHER LONG

F#ck cancer

Series so Far

Problem Child
Mad Boys
Party Crashers

Foreword

Dear Reader,

Thank you for picking up this book, for taking a chance on a new series. If I'm a new to you author, welcome. If you've read my previous works, hello there, it's good to see you. Mad Boys is book 2 of Blue Ivy Prep, so if you haven't read Problem Child, I would recommend pausing to grab that first as this series needs to be read in order.

Previously at Blue Ivy Prep, KC and Aubrey kicked off their first year at the school to different experiences. While Aubrey seemed to settle in, KC faced friction from the douchebags three. The first, Jonas, a student in all of her classes who stares, says little, and turned her in for failure to help on an assignment when she was pulled away for an emergency. The second, Lachlan, a guy who follows her on runs and takes to ninja kisses following a heated mistaken identity encounter during a Halloween party. The third, Ramsey, is also TA in one of her classes and he re-arranges her schedule so she has to do tutoring. He also kisses her after calling her nothing.

In the meanwhile, KC struggles with the day to day tasks in her larger than life experience including her mother not wanting to leave her "rehab" center, her mother's lover sending her dick pics to send to her mother, gossip and innuendo, bullying from other students, and a cancer diagnosis for her baby sister.

When KC learns the douchebag three are all brothers, she wants even less to do with them. At the end of the year, during parents weekend, Johnny Pound, her mother's aforementioned lover, shows up to support KC and she learned the truth behind some of the douchebags animosity. Not only are they brothers, they are her *stepbrothers*. Her absent father is married to their mother.

Whew. It's a lot, but that's where we were at the end of Problem Child which brings us to Mad Boys.

Triggers to be mindful of: There is some stalking, and I will give a warning for a severe health diagnosis for a side character. An SA is referenced on page and "heard."

If you have read this far, thank you. Mad Boys is the second in a four book series following Kaitlin Crosse as she attends Blue Ivy Prep, an exclusive boarding, prep, and college school for the wealthy and the privileged.

The series is reverse harem/why choose. This means the female main character will not have to choose between the guys in her life. This series is also slow burn, and begins with bullying, secrets, lies, and complicated family ties.

While the first book was told exclusively from Kaitlin's viewpoint except for the prologue, this and future books in this series contain multiple points of view.

Thank you again for taking a chance on this series, I can't wait to hear what you think of KC and the girls. Be sure to join us in my reader group on Facebook where we talk books, book loving, some spoilers, teasers for the future, and bonus scenes. Don't forget to sign up for news and updates on my website to get all the latest news, releases and more emailed right to you.

xoxo

Heather

Prologue

JONAS

"Just fix your tie," Lachlan snapped at me. Mom hadn't let us know they were coming. We probably wouldn't have known if Ramsey hadn't woken us up with the news. Now, he and Lachlan were both glaring at me to hurry.

All I'd done was back-to-back exams, papers, and projects for the last three weeks. KC and I had nearly been paired on a project, but the teacher decided to make them individual. Probably better.

She hadn't spoken to me since the day of the fight. She barely even looked at me. When she did—well, it was like I wasn't there. This morning, however, the music had been posted to my door with the lyrics added. I'd been sitting and reading it, trying to process when Ramsey showed up.

"Jonas," Ramsey said. Oh good, it was time for big brother to tell me what I was doing wrong. Turning away from both of them, I buttoned up my shirt. We never went to parents' day or whatever it was. Mom usually was on tour or in the recording studio. It would be a first for Gibs, too.

Probably because KC was here. I tucked the shirt in mechanically, then retrieved my school tie. It was the last one to survive the school year. The weight of their glares made me take my time. If I hoped they would just go and leave me, I was doomed to disappointment.

Ramsey always seemed to know when I would not show up.

When I slid my feet into my shoes, Lachlan let out an aggrieved sigh. "Finally... let's get this fucking over with so you can go back to moping."

I would have lunged at him, but Ramsey stepped right between us and put a hand to my chest to keep me from going after him.

"Stop being such a dick," Ramsey said over his shoulder to Lachlan. "Antagonizing him is only going to make it worse."

"Whatever," Lachlan said. "Let's just go. You know how she gets if she has to wait too long."

Icy. Impatient. Insulting.

Ramsey shook his head, but Lachlan missed it as he was already gone. "Look," he said, removing his hand when I backed up a step. "I get it, you're pissed at us. Maybe we deserve it. Maybe we don't. But for the next hour, we're going to make nice with Mom and Gibs and be perfect sons."

I just stared at him.

"It's all she's asking."

I continued staring.

"Right, fucking off. Just come on." Not waiting for me, he turned on his heel and stalked out of the suite Lachlan and I had been sharing this year.

Next year I would be rid of him. Lachlan graduated in a week. I had already requested a single. No roommate. No brother. No more backstabbing.

Despite my lack of hurrying, both brothers waited for me before we headed for the dining hall. I kept my hands in my pockets as I followed them. The urge to punch Lachlan buzzed under my skin like a beehive had been kicked over.

He was such a dick

The noise from inside hit like a tidal wave as Lachlan shoved the door open. Ramsey caught it before it could close, and then we were inside.

"There's my boy!" Mom's grin was wider and more open than I'd seen it in a long time. She gave Lachlan a big squeeze before reaching out a hand to me. I wasn't big on—I held my breath as she crushed me to her.

The overwhelming floral spray she favored filled my nostrils. It was *almost* enough to overpower the smell of cigarettes. Mom was smoking again. Didn't surprise me. Gibs smoked. Mom would smoke with him.

"All of my boys." Mom pulled back then pressed a kiss to my cheek before she went to Ramsey. Gibs chuckled as he clapped my shoulder.

"Good year?"

"Yes, sir," I said, shaking his hand briefly. At least he didn't expect much more than a quick handshake.

"Good. Good. Your mother worries." He said it like he shared a confidence. I was aware. My mother didn't worry that much. Gibs, however, had already turned away to Ramsey, and I savored the reprieve. There were too many people in this vast, overcrowded room.

A flash of blue caught my eye and I shifted to see KC staring at us.

No.

Staring at Gibs.

I glanced at him, but he hadn't so much as noticed her. He was focused on whatever it was Lachlan was saying. Lachlan could talk about anything. Mom looked happy about whatever it was.

When I looked at KC again, her expression crumpled before she pivoted and walked away.

Away.

Not to us. The guy she was with hurried after her. I stared until her hair vanished. Should I follow?

Maybe she hadn't known Gibs was coming today? Or did she just not want to see him? Mom said she never returned calls, or cards.

"Jonas, baby." Mom was there pulling my arm. "Come on, we're going out to eat and get real food. Yeah?"

"There's a good steakhouse near the interstate, according to the app," Gibs said as he held up his phone. "Been a while since I had a good steak."

He didn't mention KC. She hadn't known who we were. Gibs wasn't talking about her now.

Should I bring her up?

"Yes, and you boys can tell me what your summer plans are. Gibs and I are..."

I trailed after them, only half-listening. Dinner wouldn't take that long. I'd go see KC after.

Thank her for the lyrics.

Maybe we could talk...

One

Despite being awake already, I let the alarm increase in volume gradually as it repeated the alert that it was time to get up. The louder it grew, the more irritating the sound of chimes became.

Sitting up with a sigh, I picked up my phone and turned it off. It was just after seven. Jonas would be flying back to Tahoe from his father's today. It was why I was getting up early. Lachlan had barely been around through the course of the summer.

As soon as school was out, Lachlan took off to his dad's. Jonas and I came here, to Gibs' house outside of Tahoe, for a break. The plan had been for Jonas to leave to go to his father's for a visit at the beginning of July.

With our mother and Gibs in the studio recording, it was just going to be the two of us this summer. I had two online classes I would be taking. The extra credits would apply toward my degree and keep me certified as a teacher's assistant going into another school year.

June was a tense month. Jonas managed to say next to nothing to me the entire month. Not only that, he locked himself away in his room until I had to get the extra set of keys and let myself in.

A part of me had expected to find him in there hurting himself. Thankfully, I'd been wrong. His fury at me checking on him had been somewhat refreshing. Apathy was a lot worse than anger. Still, his anger where KC was concerned, worried me on other levels.

I had no idea he'd developed such an attachment to her. For that matter, I didn't realize Lachlan had either. They'd carefully edited those moments out of any conversations we'd had.

Then again, I hadn't kept them updated on my tutoring sessions with her or how I'd rearranged her schedule to make sure I could keep an eye on her and help her without tipping my hand.

After scrubbing both hands over my face, I rolled out of bed and then remade it. Neat corners that were even with the sheets and blankets helped relax me. I liked a tidy environment. Lachlan and Jonas both thrived in chaos. I couldn't do that.

Once the bed was made, I checked the messages on my phone on the way to the bathroom. Jonas had sent a message with a time only.

That must be when his flight was coming in. Helpful. I had a couple of hours. There were some news alerts on my phone too. I kicked on the water as I scrolled through them.

Over a dozen featured KC partying her way through Beverly Hills, Los Angeles, and Hollywood. She was the talk of the town. More than one article featured pictures of her dancing. In a couple, she looked almost stoned.

I stared at those pictures for a long time before finally turning off the screen and setting the phone down. In the shower, I ducked under the hot water and let it beat down on me. Kaitlin Crosse could irritate *and* tempt a saint.

Even after telling myself I would turn off the alerts about her, alerts I'd turned on when I found out she was coming to Blue Ivy, I just hadn't done it. Stubbornness? Masochism? Idiocy?

I *craved* information about her, even when I disliked it. Craved knowing she was okay, but I didn't want to picture some other guy kissing her. The fact Lachlan had been wasn't lost on me, or that Jonas was so damn angry about it.

Neither knew about my indiscretions. I'd kissed her. Not only that, I'd *enjoyed* kissing her. I'd enjoyed *her*. Sharper than she came across in the gossip and news stories about her, KC possessed a kind of playful, dry wit that was delightful.

The fact she'd busted her ass to get caught up made lies out of all the reports of her diva behavior. But her mercurial reactions left me stumped. She would go from hot to cold to lukewarm. She dismissed authority, made her own calls, left campus when she felt like it and...

I had to fight the urge to keep from hitting my head on the tile wall. Thinking about Kaitlin Crosse was a dark and dangerous path to pursue. More than once, I'd decided to do one brief check and it would be hours I'd spend poring over the fan sites, the TikTok videos, the Instagram posts, and their personal website where the girls often posted special messages.

The desire to know waged war with the side that said let her go. We might be step-siblings, but she'd made it perfectly clear she wanted nothing to do with us. The fact she hadn't even realized we were brothers grated, however.

We didn't advertise it at school. In the same way we hadn't advertised our new address when Mom and Gibs first moved in together. They spent more time on the road than here, but when they were here, Gibs took the time to talk to us.

He took the time and the energy to ask us what we wanted

to do and how we wanted to accomplish it. He was the reason all three of us got to go to Blue Ivy in the first place. Tuition had been his gift to Mom for as long as I could remember. We'd all started at Blue Ivy in the primary grades and worked our way up.

The only thing Gibs ever talked about with the same kind of joy he expressed when we gave him reports about our years was his daughter, Kaitlin. On weekends when she visited, we were always made to be scarce if we were on summer break. Otherwise, we were at school.

Then Gibs' touring schedule picked up, and she just stopped seeing him. He'd lauded her accomplishments, though. When Torched went platinum, he'd lost his mind. I didn't understand why she stopped coming to see him. Why did she cut ties with a man who clearly adored her and was so proud of her accomplishments?

My own father didn't get me. He did his best, but I pursued more intellectual and artistic avenues and he was an executive in the music industry. He dealt in facts and figures, crunched the numbers. Not that he wasn't proud of me, just...Gibs got KC. They were in the same career. Of course, he understood her.

So why couldn't she understand him?

I was rinsing the shampoo out of my hair when it hit me. I was doing it again. Obsessing about her. That needed to stop before we got back to school.

Twenty minutes later, I headed into the kitchen where Juliet was just sliding a loaf of bread out of the oven. "Good morning," I greeted her as I went straight to the coffee.

A whiff of the bread made my mouth water. Pumpkin bread with honey butter. Jonas was coming home, and Juliet was prepping his favorites.

The older woman gave me an indulgent smile. "Don't you worry, your loaf is going in soon. I just wanted Jonas' to be ready for when he came in. He's been gone so much this summer..." Disappointment edged the words. "Lachlan's barely been here at all."

"I'm sure he'll be back soon." I wasn't, but it sounded better than Lachlan was gonna do whatever he wanted. As he loved to remind me, he wasn't a kid anymore. He was a legal adult.

Downing a mouthful of coffee, I moved over to the butler's pantry, where Juliet had already set up fruit, oatmeal, and scrambled eggs with bacon on the side. A little bit of everything.

Fresh guilt edged me. Juliet was used to feeding all three of us and for the last month, she'd just had me and I simply didn't eat like Lachlan or Jonas.

"Juliet," I said as I carried my plate and bowl back into the kitchen to eat. I could go out to the table but she was in here and I didn't feel like eating alone. "Can I ask you a weird question?"

Wiping down the counter, she gave me a gentle look of reprimand. "You can ask me anything. Just don't expect me to answer everything."

Her smile softened her face. Juliet was in her mid-sixties and ruled the Tahoe house like she was Gibs' mother. It was kind of funny that he would ask her permission to have a party or bring people in. Not even Mom crossed Juliet.

I sipped the coffee to cover my smile. Maybe I should mind my own business. Then again...

"Do you know why Gibs' daughter Kaitlin doesn't visit here?" Maybe it was because of us. That didn't sit well, but I hated the idea that maybe *we* were the reason Gibs didn't get to see his daughter.

"Oh, that sweet angel," Juliet said with a sigh. "She hasn't been here since she launched that band of hers. Have you listened to them? She always had the voice of an angel. Sang every single one of her dad's hits before she was six."

I made myself take a bite of the oatmeal as she wiped down the counters then pulled over a pan that had bread rising in it.

"I wouldn't know any specific reason she hasn't come for a visit. Between her tours and his, they were both just so busy. You know how he is when he's got a new album recording, I'm gonna guess that sweet angel does too and there's always something going on that she has to do."

Juliet gave a little sigh.

"I do miss her, though." A note of melancholy touched her voice, and I felt like an ass.

"Sorry, Juliet. I didn't mean to depress you."

"Not at all, dear. Now eat your breakfast. I'm going to slide this in the oven and check the shopping order. Do I need to send a car to the airport for Jonas?"

"No, I'll pick him up. He wants to try for his license again this year, so I figured I'll let him drive me back." Jonas had a learner's permit, but he hadn't passed the first two driving tests he'd taken. Distraction was a big problem for him.

Distraction and temper.

"Hmm, take one of the sedans," she said after a moment. "They have better safety features."

I didn't laugh. She wasn't kidding, and it wasn't funny. We definitely needed the safety features. Maybe...maybe letting him drive would open up some detente. He'd gotten angry before, but he'd never held out this long before.

Washing up the three dishes I'd used, I left them in the drying rack before heading to the garage to get a car. The airport was an hour's drive down the mountain. On the upside, at least I'd finished my classes, so if Jonas was in a forgiving mood, maybe we could go hiking once he was back.

If not? Well, I had some books to read before senior year started. Senior year in college for me, freshman year for

Lachlan if he decided to go to school, and senior year at the high school level for Jonas.

Once I had the car started, I hooked up the phone's Bluetooth so I could input the address for the airport. I didn't need the GPS specifically, but it would let my mind wander and keep me on target.

It wasn't until I was halfway down the mountain that I realized I'd been bobbing my head, tapping my fingers on the steering wheel, and mouthing the words while listening to one of her albums the whole damn way.

Fuck.

Two

KC

"This is the right hotel?" I checked the information in their email for the tenth time.

"Yes," Yvette said, without looking up from where she sat with her head back. I'd bet all the money in my business account her eyes were closed behind her sunglasses. "Drink your coffee."

"She already finished it." Aubrey punctuated the comment with a yawn, and I rolled my eyes at them. They'd come into town to help Ian and Frankie when I forwarded Frankie's semi-freaked-out email to them.

"All of it?" Yvette frowned, then seemed to focus on me. I paced back and forth, checking my phone for like the fifteenth time. Their flights had landed. Were they running late? Frankie said they'd booked this hotel, but having stayed in my time-share, they might enjoy the house a lot more.

Especially with everything going on in her life. The fact her mother just died. I sent flowers for the funeral, but the chaos at the end of the year and Pen's diagnosis had left me floundering.

"How much caffeine have you had today?" Yvette asked, the French lilt in her voice softening the words.

"Enough," I told her. Sleep had been really difficult.

Really. Fucking. Hard.

I didn't think I'd slept a full night since I discovered Douchebags One, Two, *and* Three were my stepbrothers.

Dicks.

All of them.

Irritating, judgmental fuckers.

Realizing who they were had slotted some hard facts into place. The instant dislike they'd taken to me. The shitty things they'd all said or done. Even the backsliding when I thought things were going well. They knew I was their stepsister and didn't say a freaking word.

Fine.

They could have my father. It wasn't like he had time for me anyway.

"Kait," Aubrey said in a soft voice. She rarely called me Kait anymore, leaning on it when things were bad. Well, she wasn't wrong to use it now. Things were bad at the moment. "You have resting murder face."

"That doesn't look that resting to me," Yvette argued, and I sucked in a deeper breath of air.

Meditation and I did not get along. Nothing helped to take the edge off, and running in L.A. wasn't as easy as it had been in Connecticut. I used the treadmill—a lot—but all I was getting was faster.

A limo pulled into the loop in front of the hotel. It wasn't the first limo to put in an appearance since we got here. The driver opened the back door. At the flash of a familiar blonde head, I bolted for the door.

Following the blonde was one of her boyfriends. Frankie

had four of them, and it was singularly amazing. The one with her was the one she sang with. Like Frankie, Ian was also blond. Excitement poured into my system like an adrenaline dump.

I'd been dying for them to get here and now they were! I crashed into Frankie with a hug that threatened to topple us both. Fortunately, she reacted to keep us on our feet. "You're here!" Granted, I could have been pithier but I was practically vibrating. Looking after Ian and Frankie was exactly what I needed, a distraction *and* something I could actually do to help.

I let go of Frankie so Yvette and Aubrey could greet her. Blowing a kiss to Frankie's boyfriend, I said, "Hey, Ian!" Then I pivoted to face Frankie again, who looked more than a little dazed.

There were shadows beneath her eyes and darkness in them. A darkness I was all too familiar with. Grief could fuck right the hell off to fucksville. "You're so here," I repeated. I don't know which of us I was assuring, Frankie or me.

Thankfully, Frankie laughed. "Yes, we're here. What are *you* doing here?"

"To see you two. Your last email sounded freaked out." It was the absolute truth. There was a lot of freaking out in that email. I'd been in her shoes once, only I'd had a history in the business and some familiarity, not to mention Yvette and Aubrey. Ian was great, but he wasn't us.

"I am not freaked out, I'm fine."

"Freaked out, insecure, neurotic, and emotional?" I countered. So familiar and unsettling. "We totally get it. Been there..."

"...done that," Yvette said and Aubrey added, "Trust us, we have all the t-shirts."

"And the rehab bills." I smirked though Aubrey shot me a look at the joke. "So, first things first, we're old hats at this business, and I needed a break from the East Coast, so we're staying at my mom's place in Beverly Hills. They aren't there right now so it's even better." I glanced past her at the driver who was waiting for them. "Car service or full-time hire for the visit?"

"Car service," Frankie said.

"Fantastic. I got this." I gave her another hug before I made a beeline for the driver, whose name turned out to be Paul. "They aren't going to be staying at the hotel, so you can take their things out to Beverly Hills," I gave him the address. "This is where they'll be. I'm going to give them a ride in our car."

I handed him a hundred; it was the smallest bill I had in my little wallet. He didn't need any persuading at all, and then he was putting their things back in the car.

"Okay!" I hurried back over to them. "Paul is going to bring your luggage out to our place. You're riding with us. Our car is on the other side of the building." It was like I'd downed two back-to-back energy drinks. This was the *best* pick-me-up. Frankie slid her backpack on while Ian picked up their guitar cases. "This is going to be great. Do you guys want help with those?"

"I got it," Ian assured me.

"Great." Time to get moving. We hadn't been seen or hounded, a great thing about L.A. and about hotels like this. Even if you were recognized, people tended to give you a wide berth and respect your privacy.

"Thank you, Paul," Frankie said to their driver as I hooked my arm through hers. "We should probably cancel our reservations."

"Not a problem." It really wasn't. "We can call them from the car. Are you tired? Hungry? Want us to stop somewhere and grab food? We need to take you out to Mackie's." So good. The food there was just the best.

"Later," Yvette said, her French accent lifting the word. "Let's not overwhelm them."

At the pointed look from Aubrey, I grimaced and pivoted to face Frankie and Ian. "I'm not overwhelming you guys, am I? I mean, I know this is a surprise—so like hey, surprise! But I thought it would be easier if you had a quiet place to retreat. Recording a first album is both exciting and nightmarish and we've been there and well—I mean—if you wanted to stay here?"

The couple exchanged one look, and he just nodded before Frankie looked at me again. "You're not overwhelming us, and this is a fantastic surprise. It really is."

"Good." Relief swarmed me. "I felt so bad we couldn't make it to the funeral, and I haven't stopped thinking about you. And I genuinely want to do this for you."

Frankie gave me a smile, a sad one, but it was still a smile. "You don't *have* to do anything. But I really appreciate that you want to."

"Same," Ian added. "Friends are always welcome."

"Wonderful!" I clapped my hands. Definitely not going to bring us down any more than I already had. "Let's go."

Dix laughed as we got everyone seated. I didn't relax until we were back at the house and they were settled in.

Once Frankie and Ian headed off to bed for the night, I told Aubrey and Yvette I was gonna get some sleep. I needed it. A couple of hugs and kisses later, and I headed for my suite. We'd given Frankie and Ian their own wing. Mom had hers, and I had mine. The girls always stayed in my wing.

They used to crash in my room, but as we got older, I'd asked to add rooms for them and Mom hadn't cared. So, I could lock myself in my suite and say I was "sleeping" and they'd leave me be.

Guilt pricked me. Yvette and Aubrey were my best friends. They'd come to help Frankie and Ian, or at least that was their excuse. I got it, they came to help me.

I was fine. However, nothing a little retail and party therapy couldn't fix. At the moment, I didn't want to be reasonable. I didn't want to talk. I didn't want to be comforted. From one heartbreaking scenario to the other, the shit with the boys at school was craptastic, but Pen's diagnosis killed me.

After all, I was the "problem child." I could hardly *hurt* my reputation. I braided my blue hair into a crown so I could pull a wig on over it. Then I changed into dancing clothes.

My phone buzzed with a message from Jackie, right on schedule. Bless Jackie, she never missed a check-in for me.

JACKIE

Pen finished the first round of chemo like a trooper. She was asking about you. Are you still free to come this weekend?

ME

Wouldn't miss it. Make sure to let me know if you guys need anything. Thanks, Jackie.

The next couple of messages were a little more motherly, including one telling me to get some rest, 'cause Bronson had ratted me out for not sleeping.

Traitor.

My next message was to Dix to meet me at the bottom of the driveway. He sent me a thumbs-up. The thigh-high boots were killer, as was the dress that basically was a skirt painted onto my ass and a tank top that didn't quite cover my midriff.

Although once I got going, I'd be hot and sweaty. This was the fastest way to cool off. The dark wig I'd picked out hid my blue hair. If I didn't care about my reputation, why the wig? Dix had asked me that more than once.

I shrugged. I just wanted to dance. Hit the clubs, forget that I was me, forget that my baby sister had cancer, forget that my asshole stepbrothers spent a year torturing me for whatever reason, forget my father didn't want any of his children, even if he couldn't stop fucking every woman who crossed his path.

Forget that I was Kaitlin fucking Crosse.

Forget I was even part of Torched.

I just wanted to *be*.

The doors in my suite opened out onto a private balcony, where I had a table and chairs. It also offered a great view of the western sky, perfect for sunsets and shit.

Hooking a leg over the railing, I climbed down the trellis that had been there since I was seven. I landed on the stone of the patio just behind one of the huge oversized pots that played host to a baby palm tree.

No sounds came from the pool or the house. I followed the garden wall to where I could squeeze out between two of the pillars, and then I was striding over the neatly manicured lawn toward the drive.

This part wasn't visible from the house, just the security cameras. I'd already told Wayne that I was leaving and to keep it from my guests. He wouldn't even tell Mom unless she specifically asked.

Dix leaned against the side of the black Audi at the end of the drive. It wasn't a limo—that was the other thing. Dix went with me to the clubs, got me in, then fucked off to the bar while I danced. When I was ready to leave, he'd take me home.

Fake dating worked just fine to get me inside, and no one asked me for ID.

"Hey, gorgeous," he said, shaking his head. "You are going to cause a riot in that outfit."

I laughed. "No one is going to care. I've seen girls wearing essentially fishnet bodysuits." Honestly, it wasn't about how I looked. It was about losing myself.

He popped open the passenger door so I could slide in, before circling around. Once we were on the road, I glanced over at him. "My friends Frankie and Ian may need a driver while they're here..."

"Long as I'm not with you, I'll take care of it," he said. "Though you may not be able to slip out as much with the girls here..."

"It'll be fine." I wasn't discussing this with anyone. Dix was my key in the door and my driver. Also, having him with me meant I had a tacit amount of security. I hadn't forgotten my so-called Forever Fan. They'd taken to following and commenting everywhere on my social media.

Even when they were blocked, they showed up with a new variation on the screen name. They'd sent some hateful emails after the last time our social media manager blocked him, so I told her to leave it be.

If he wanted to follow me and leave comments, I didn't have to read them. That reminded me, I needed to make a list of solid advice for Frankie. She and Ian had a lot of talent. They were still fresh and new, but I didn't doubt for an instant they would be a hit.

Fame never came for free, so better to know what pieces of yourself you were willing to share and where to draw the line.

"Where are we hitting tonight?" Dix asked as we blended into the traffic bleeding into Los Angeles proper.

"Sammie Bee's," I told him. It was a new club, only opened in the last six months, but it had already snagged a great reputation for hard partying types and the music was supposed to be killer.

"Sammie Bee's it is," Dix said with a sigh. "KC..."

"I'm fine, Dix," I told him, before he could ask. "Just getting some restlessness out of my system."

"Right." He didn't have to believe me.

I didn't care who believed me right now.

The club had spotlights going and music thrumming when we pulled up. A line of people trying to get in stretched around the block. Dix handed off the keys to a valet and then offered me his arm.

Oh yeah, this was going to be exactly what I needed. The doorman knew Dix. So that, along with a couple of hundreds, got us in the VIP line without having to play the Kaitlin Crosse card.

Inside, the music beckoned. I gave Dix a kiss on the cheek and danced toward the floor in the center where the bodies were already writhing together and bouncing to the beat.

Yes, this was exactly what I needed.

Three

LACHLAN

The Mercedes-AMG One prowled over the hills as I drove the PCH on my way toward Los Angeles. It was a longer drive but far more beautiful than the boring shit that was the I-5. Maybe I'd talk myself out of going to see Ace when I got there. The blue-haired siren had taken over my dreams. Now she was coming after my waking hours.

Every-fucking-where I went, there were signs that made me think of her. A woman with blue hair? Yes, I looked to see if it was my girl. The cranked-up sounds of bubblegum pop rock? I stopped to listen.

A resurgence in their popularity had their last album playing on a dozen different stations. Every day, I seemed to find a new one. My phone buzzed, but I didn't pick it up. Not while I was driving my baby.

The car was the best fucking present I'd ever received and one that pissed my mother off to no end. Made it even more perfect, especially since Gibs got it for me. It had almost been enough to make her yell at Gibs. He could take the heat, not that it seemed to bother him at all.

Me, on the other hand? I was in love with the car. I'd seen one during a car show, and I think it was the first time I sprang an erection that had nothing to do with a girl. It arrived on my sixteenth birthday.

Now, my baby went with me everywhere. We drove to school back east, and we drove back. I didn't care if I couldn't drive her much during the school year, I wasn't leaving her behind. Mom would probably sell her when I wasn't looking. Not to mention, out of sight, out of mind. When she didn't see the car, she wasn't pissed about it.

Another message vibrated on my phone, and I scowled. I took the next scenic pull-off and parked looking out over the Pacific Ocean. It was a few hours before sunset, but it would be spectacular out here.

Picking up the phone, I stared at the messages on the screen. Three, back-to-back from Ramsey, one from Jack at school, one from my dad, and fourteen from Payton.

I ignored the last and checked the one from Dad. His message was pretty straightforward. Just thanked me for visiting and hanging out over the summer. He was sorry he had so much work to do that he couldn't afford the off time, but would I like to come back for the holidays?

Rubbing a hand over my face, I debated the message. Sean Nash was an attorney. He worked with several different labels, particularly Gibs'. It was how he'd met Mom in the first place. Their affair was over before the lines even turned pink, but he'd been as involved as Mom allowed him to be.

Ramsey and Jonas struggled with their fathers, but I liked mine. I just shot him back a message that said I'd let him know. The holidays had always been a tough time to see him. Mom tended to get dramatic if I chose to go to his place rather than home.

I debated checking Ramsey's messages, then just skipped it. Although since I was stopped, I did a quick skim of my email on the off chance that Ace had reached out to me. No such luck.

There were a few new stories, including one from the Kissy Kat column, that popped up in my news alerts.

> Guess which singer owns this rockin' bod!

> Kaitlin Cross: Good Genes or Good Doctors?

> Problem Child Turning Heads in See-Through Dress

> Torched Singer Burning Down the LA Club Circuit

The gossip was just that, gossip. Kissy Kat didn't list any credible sources, they just alluded to a few vague ones "close" to a certain "Problem Child." Really annoying. Even more annoying, she didn't list the clubs that Ace had been partying at.

As hungry for knowledge as the news update left me, it also pissed me the fuck off. She was out dancing *every* night? Partying with strangers? On the club scene?

Fuck. That.

I'd never met a girl *more* in need of a keeper than her, and she was out there just shaking her ass for anyone who happened to be present? I dropped the phone back onto the charging pad, then pulled out and got back on the road.

Maybe I should have taken the I-5. I'd already be there. As it was, the sun was just going down when I got into town. I headed for the Bonaventure. Gibs always had rooms there and at one of the Marriott's. They'd been in the studio most of the summer, so I wouldn't have to share.

Once I'd checked in, I started looking up clubs. I could

head out to her mother's place in Beverly Hills. I knew where it was, but she could lock me out there. If Ace saw me coming, there was undoubtedly a seventy-five percent chance she'd head the other way and never look back.

No, I needed to track my siren down while she was out dancing. The idea of her out there dancing with the assholes who frequented clubs—no. All I needed to do was find out what club or clubs she'd picked.

Three days—well, three nights of haunting the latest clubs trending on all the too-hot-to-miss sites. Each night I'd come up empty-handed, so I stalked the gossip sites. Finally, it hit me that I was an idiot and I drove out to her mother's place to stake it out.

The Beverly Hills mansion boasted those fancy gates. Wouldn't keep me out on foot, but at least my Mercedes blended in just fine. I parked just before sunset and waited. My patience paid off in hour three when a car cruised up to the gates, parking just outside them.

I narrowed my eyes at the blonde, who climbed out and circled the car to wait. She appeared out of the shadows from between two trees, just coalescing like some creature of fantasy coming together.

My cock went hard as stone when I got a good look at the outfit she had on...or didn't. A leather skirt hugged her ass and the tops of her thighs. I wasn't even sure it covered her panties —and she better be fucking wearing panties in that. The top was more like a halter-bikini cupping her breasts and leaving everything else bare.

The vibrant blue of her hair was missing under a cap, and she wore a pair of knee-high boots that made me want to strip her out of everything *but* them. The guy who was waiting straightened at her approach.

From this angle, it was hard to see his face, but I didn't have to imagine the lust there. Fuck, lust was strangling my dick, and I wanted to punch this guy in his. He put a hand on the small of her back to usher her in the car.

She was letting him touch her. I flexed my hands on the steering wheel. I gave them a solid thirty seconds to pull away before I followed. It wasn't long before we were in traffic, and I was free to stalk them.

Soon they were pulling up at a club and her guy handed his keys over to the valet before he took her arm and they strutted inside, past the line to get in.

Yeah. Money talked.

I checked my wallet and found more than enough cash. The valet were rushing to get my door after I pulled into the slot. One perk of the car, it more than said I belonged. I handed the guy a fifty and told him to keep it near the door.

Another guy opened the red rope for me without a second glance. Look like you belong and people got out of your way. Once I was in the club, it took me a moment to let my eyes adjust.

I scanned the lower level. The club had four of them. She could be on any one, so I would have to take my time to find her. The hunger I had for a good look at her grew more ravenous with each passing moment.

I found her on the third floor, where the hard rock pulsed the speakers while letting the guitars cut loose and scream out their notes. The music throbbed through me as I cut out onto the floor. Hips swaying and arms up, she held me riveted as she moved.

The night we'd danced at the Halloween party had been a revelation. Of course, she had rhythm, but fuck me, watching her had nothing on holding her or feeling her writhe against me.

My erection grew stiffer, if possible. This was what I'd been missing all summer.

Ace.

The music changed to something a little more classic. Hands came up and began to clap in time to the beat. Oh fuck yeah, I liked this song. Fortunately, the walking dead man who brought her to the club was nowhere to be seen. It didn't look like she was dancing with anyone.

Good. I could savor her before I had to deal with the fucker putting his hands on what didn't belong to him. When I slid up behind her, I sucked in a deep breath of *her*.

Cedar woods. Crisp snow. Just a touch of something citrus with the barest hint of cloves. It transported me back to the woods and the day I threw her in the pond. The fury in her eyes and the impudence had been even sexier than her defiance.

Fuck knew what possessed me to cut her damn bra off, but I'd wanted to see those tits. I wanted to see *her*. No persona for armor or stage makeup. Goddamn if I hadn't seen her.

Once would never be enough.

Her ass brushed my erection. A groan stole out of me as I dropped my hands to her bare arms. "Fuck, I've missed you, Ace."

She jerked at the contact, but I pulled her right to me, hooking an arm around her waist to keep her back to my chest as I followed the hip-rolling booty shake she had going. It was going to drive me mad and I was all in for the damn trip.

When she tried to turn, I allowed it, dragging her up so we were chest to breast, and I drank in the sight of her under the pulsating lights. Sweat gleamed against her skin. The cosmetics were super light, but they definitely didn't hide those stunning eyes of hers.

Even under the strobes of red, flashing purple, green, and blue, I wouldn't mistake her eyes for anyone else. There was only one thing missing... I tugged off her cap and her cascade of blue hair appeared to my delight.

Savage satisfaction flooded me as she glared up at me. Her hands were on my chest and I slid mine to her hips as we moved. Her mouth moved, but the music was too damn loud to make out the words. Fortunately, I managed to dodge her knee and slid a hand right under her ass as I picked her up to rock against me.

"What the hell are you doing?" She all but yelled right into my face.

"Dancing with you, Ace," I answered. The confusion flickering through her eyes wasn't a rebuke at all. I kept one arm banded around her so she didn't get away as I fisted her hair in my free hand.

Her breath against my lips was the drug I'd been jonesing for for the past two months. It had been too long since I had last kissed her. She'd made it fucking impossible those last couple of months of school, but at least I'd been able to see her then.

Need exploded through me as I pressed my lips to hers. I tasted her gasp and for a moment, her tongue tangled with mine. Kissing her was the best goddamn intoxicant on the planet, and I needed *more*.

So. Much. More.

"Stop it," she growled and shoved. This time, I didn't entirely block the knee to my groin. Granted, it impacted more on my thigh. She scowled up at me. "Get the fuck away from me, Lachlan."

Holy shit, hearing her say my name was almost as good as kissing her.

"C'mon, Ace, it's been months..."

"Right." She glared. It was hard to hear her over the music, but I wasn't letting her go or getting separated even as she tried to get away in the crowd. "Not long enough."

She was pissed.

"Look, we didn't know you didn't know..."

At my words, she whirled around. "No? You were just absolute total dickwads to me for no fucking reason whatsoever?"

I shrugged. "Us being brothers has nothing to do with that."

Surprise flickered over her face. "Wait—you think I'm mad 'cause you're brothers?"

"You were pretty damn angry." I was there. Her stare wasn't friendly, but she wasn't running anymore. I invaded her space a little more. "C'mon, Ace. Tell me you missed me..."

"Fuck, no," she almost spit the words. "If I never saw you again, it would be too soon."

Nope. Not the answer I wanted.

I caught her arm and pulled her to me. My mouth crashed into hers and there was no mistaking the heat as she met my kiss with one of her own. Her teeth scraped over my lower lip, then her tongue twined with mine. The raging need in my system was downright fucking painful.

A light flashed next to us, then another and I jerked my head up to see a couple of cameras pointed right at us. They were snapping pictures. I scowled at them, and then pain exploded across my cheek as Ace slapped me. It rocked my head to the side and I jerked my gaze back to her.

Pure fury radiated off of her and she jerked her arm away as phone cameras popped out.

"Holy shit, it's her!"

"Oh, hey, baby," a guy said as he moved up behind her. "Looking for a good time..."

She shoved away from me and it collided her into that bag of dicks. She was already twisting away from him when I slammed my fist into his face. He went down, but she was heading for the stairs.

One of his friends tried to get in my way and I took him

out with a fast uppercut, then down the steps. I could see her blue hair below as she weaved through the people coming up the stairs.

More phones were out. More cameras.

Shit.

She was gonna get mobbed.

Goddammit.

On the ground floor, I had to fight my way to the front. She was out the doors. By the time I got through the insanity, she was climbing into the driver's seat of a car. The tires squealed as she pulled away.

There was more press out here. Lights flickered everywhere.

"Keys," I said to the valet. He handed them over and I gave him another fifty. I was barely behind the wheel when her taillights vanished up the road with two or three other cars following and a motorcycle.

I blasted the horn to get the assholes in front of me a warning before I floored it. She wasn't getting away from me and she sure as hell wasn't going to have to deal with that press by herself.

Despite her erratic driving, I managed to catch up. The fucking asshole on the motorcycle was still trying to snap a picture.

She jerked her car at the last minute and turned around a corner while doing forty-five. She even took it up on two wheels and then down again. The Mercedes followed the curve like a predator on the heels of his prey.

The motorcycle stuck with her, but she'd lost two of the cars. There was still another car between us. C'mon Ace, I tried to urge her. Pull over...

She went around another corner and then right over the curb and down the hill. Metal crunch and glass shattered.

Shit.
Shit.
Shit.

<h1 style="text-align:center">Four</h1>

KC

Douchebag Three was *here*. Not just in Los Angeles but at the club I was dancing in. He was here and he had his hands on me. The shock held me captive for too long. He had time to tug my cap off and then pull it away. The clip holding my hair up popped free and it spilled around me.

Dammit.

It took almost no time before someone noticed me. The hair, as much as I loved it, was too distinctive. I had to get out of here. The whole point of dancing like this was the anonymity. I could get out, cut loose and burn off all the restlessness.

It was so much harder at home. Harder than I expected. Especially...

I pushed against him. No more damn kisses. No more Ace. No more Lachlan. Just no damn more.

Then he said... wait... what? "Wait—you think I'm mad 'cause you're brothers?"

No, that hadn't been my favorite moment, but was he high? The noise level around us climbed, but not so much I didn't catch the first, "Holy shit, it's her!"

"Oh, hey, baby..."

I thrust away from Lachlan and collided with the guy trying to grope me. Lachlan was already swinging, and I ducked away from that fight and hauled ass. I was looking for Dix all the way down the stairs.

He was usually not that far from the dance floor. He'd been amazing about being where I could see him or get to him if I needed reassurance and keeping his distance so I could just let go.

All the way down to the ground floor, I looked everywhere and didn't see him. I pulled out my phone and hit his contact number, pushing my way to the door and trying to ignore the photos being snapped of me. I could always tell the moment someone recognized me.

Dix didn't answer.

Dammit.

I pulled the ticket out of the top of my boot along with the cash to give to the valet. I needed to go *now*. The car was never far, as he always made them park it close. The valet took one look at me and the cameras flashing that came from the other end of the line.

Yep. They knew I was out here.

Fuck.

"C'mon," the valet said, hurrying me to the car. It was parked ahead of a silver Mercedes and I ignored it to slide into the driver's seat. The valet gave me the keys, and I gave him the hundred. He shut the door, and I pulled the seatbelt on and stared at the car.

How hard could it be?

I knew the basics.

I pressed the start button and the engine rumbled to life,

then I shifted into drive and floored it to get away from the building. The car all but leapt like a bucking bronco as I pressed the accelerator. Right, little green lines helped keep me in a lane. Left pedal to stop. Right pedal to go.

I had this.

Lights flashed at me as I raced through an intersection. The lights had been green. Was that a cop? I turned to glance, but another light flashed at me. Goddammit, more press.

My eyes burned from the rapidly changing sparks dancing across my vision. I needed to turn somewhere. I didn't even know where the hell I was. So far, I'd had green lights, which was great.

Sooner or later, I was going to have to stop. I pressed a button on the steering wheel and it asked me what I needed.

"Show me the route home," I said. Hoping that was right. Dix said he'd programmed all the addresses in, and home here would be Beverly Hills.

There were red lights ahead and the car behind me was getting closer, so I turned at the next intersection. There was a sign telling me the freeway was that way. The end of the car fish-tailed, and I fought with the wheel to get it steady even as the car was trying to steady itself.

Yeah, Dix said the car did most of the work, but my heart raced, my palms were sweating, and I couldn't breathe. Too late, I realized the road I was following turned, and I didn't catch it in time before I bounced over the curb and then right down a little hill.

A scream clawed up my throat as the ground went rough below the tires and I bounced down into the woods. I'd tried braking, but the car slid sideways and then came to an abrupt stop against a tree. Everything jerked, and the crunch of the impact echoed inside the car.

Or maybe just inside me. The airbag didn't deploy, but it didn't change the fact that my hands were shaking violently, the car was slammed against the tree, and the headlights were still on.

I hit the power button and then looked for the switch to turn off the lights.

Maybe the press wouldn't follow me.

Maybe...

Lights cut across the road above, and I swore. Okay, get out of the car. I checked my phone. No call from Dix. Man, he was gonna be so pissed at me. But I couldn't be caught in the car. I didn't have a license.

I got the door open, phone and key in hand and nearly screamed when Lachlan appeared.

"You okay, Ace?" Concern etched across his face.

The trembling from earlier redoubled as I glared at him. I was so fucking happy to see him, and I did *not* want to be happy to see him. "Do I look okay?"

"You look gorgeous and in one piece." Did he sound relieved? He glanced up the hill. "But we have company, come on..." He held out his hand to me. "Come with me."

It was like the scene from *The Terminator. Come with me if you want to live...*

Did I want to?

A car door slammed, and there was a motorcycle just there and someone had a camera. Shit...

"C'mon," Lachlan said. "Trust me, Ace. I'll get you out of here."

Not like I had much choice. I clasped his hand and turned my whole body away from the top of the hill. Lachlan's grip tightened on me as he tugged me to him.

"Stay with me," he urged, then started jogging. Thankfully, I could move in these boots, and they didn't have heels on them. He ran and I kept up with him, mostly. We ran across the green belt to where a silver Mercedes sat waiting with the hazard lights on.

"In," he ordered, pulling the passenger door open for me. I slid inside and he shut the door before hurrying around to the driver's seat. He'd barely slid in before he had the car in motion, accelerating down the road... that was some kind of private road. We circled and then raced back up the road.

He barely got his seatbelt clicked in when cars hurried past us, heading to where we'd been.

"You okay, Ace?" he asked, flicking his gaze at the rearview. "Yeah, they've already figured out where you are. Hang on."

Figured out? He cut a corner so tight I almost bit my tongue. The car was smooth as aces though, as he ran two yellows, barely cutting under them before the lights turned red.

I glanced behind us as our pursuers were caught by the lights. But not all of them...

"Motorcycle is still back there and an SUV just ran that light."

Legit ran it. Like up on the curb of the sidewalk and around then down. Were they insane?

"We'll be fine," Lachlan assured me as he shifted gears. We were going faster. I gripped the oh shit handle and glanced at the dashboard.

It read over three digits.

Oh, that was a mistake.

"Lachlan," I said as he turned another corner, barely touching his brakes. The tail of the car slid around, the whole car kind of gliding with the turn before we hit the straightaway again.

My heart and lungs were back there somewhere.

Red lights ahead warned me of stopped traffic, but Lachlan wasn't slowing down. I couldn't breathe.

"Lachlan!"

"We're fine, Ace. Hang on." Except those red taillights were getting closer and closer. At what seemed like the last minute, he cut to the right and followed a ramp up to a highway that I hadn't even seen. There were lights up here, not as many as below, but a lot heavier traffic. While the speed of the car slowed, Lachlan hopscotched his way up the lanes.

At one point, I had to close my eyes. He was making the car fit in places it absolutely should not. I couldn't breathe, and sweat soaked my shirt. The shaking from earlier redoubled and I gripped the oh shit handle so hard, I would probably have a permanent indention.

We left the highway after a couple of miles, and then he was heading through the city, moving at much more reasonable speeds. The traffic could be bad, but at least it was moving. In almost no time, we would be back in Beverly Hills.

"There you go," he said, smugness rolling off him. "Safe, just like I promised."

I didn't throw up, but it was close. As it was, I just ran a hand over my face. The shaking wouldn't stop.

"Thank you," I managed, though the syllables wobbled a lot like I did.

"You're welcome," he murmured, then pulled over to glance at me. "You shouldn't have taken off in the club."

"You shouldn't have just walked up and started hitting on me."

"Ace, the way you were dancing...?"

"The way I was dancing, what?" I dared him to finish that sentence. "I was dancing. By myself. Having fun."

"So maybe I wanted to have fun with you."

"So maybe you should learn to use your words instead of your tongue."

He chuckled. Asshole. "I've missed you, Ace."

"Give me five minutes, and I'll get myself a rideshare and you can go back to it."

The door locked and I glared at him. "Hey, I want to make sure you're all right. You were just in a car accident."

Fuck. "I need to call Dix."

"Who the hell is that?" From concern to fury, the switch was enough to give me whiplash. "That the asshole with his hands on you?"

"It doesn't matter who he is," I told him. "I just need to let him know about the car." I opened the rideshare app on my phone then reached for the door handle. We were in L.A. I could get it from here.

The door didn't open.

"I'll take you home," he said. "You're not calling Dix." He said it like I'd told him Dix was an ax murderer. "Or some rideshare to end up a statistic on the news."

"I'm already a statistic," I muttered.

"Put your phone down," he ordered. "I just said I'd take you home."

"You truly are just an asshole."

"I'm also the guy who just got you out of that whole situation."

"And the reason I was in it," I pointed out. Even if it had been my own stupid fault for trying to drive. My head hurt. My heart was racing. I couldn't decide whether I wanted to throw up or curl into a ball and cry.

Neither sounded appealing.

He growled, then slammed the car into drive and pulled back onto the road abruptly. "You shouldn't be out clubbing, anyway. You weren't old enough to be in there."

"I wasn't drinking, and you're hardly my father, so shove it."

"No, your father..."

I snorted.

"What? I know Gibs, I know exactly what he'd do."

"Must be nice to be so sure."

It wasn't long before I recognized where we were. I was definitely having him drop me off *outside* the gate.

Then I'd call Dix as soon as I got in. Fuck, he was gonna kill me.

"Who is Dix?" Lachlan asked after another brief, albeit a welcome, bit of silence.

"None of your business."

"Boyfriend?"

"See my previous answer."

"Ace…"

"My name is Kaitlin Crosse. You can call me Ms. Crosse. Or Kaitlin—"

"You go by KC."

"To my friends," I fired back. "You and I are *not* friends." I shouldn't even be in his car. It wasn't until he pulled up to the gates that it hit me. He'd driven straight to my mother's place without looking at directions.

They knew where we lived.

Great.

More things they knew that we didn't. I reached for the handle, but he touched my arm. "Ace…"

It was a mistake to look at him. I knew it was a mistake, but the door was still locked. I didn't even get a word out before he cupped my face and slanted his mouth over mine.

Unlike in the club, there was no hesitation here. No distance or gasps of breath. There was just the silken glide of his lips over mine and fuck if it didn't threaten to drown me in need.

The seat belt lock came free, and I slid it off my arm before stretching into the kiss. I leaned over into the driver's seat as he slid back. Our tongues dueled, and little shivers of lightning danced up and down my spine.

I stretched my fingers until they glided over the lock keys on his door. Biting into the pillow of his lower lip, I groaned even as the locks released. Then I yanked backward from him and jerked the door open.

"Goodbye, Lachlan."

I was out and heading for the gate without looking back. "Ace..."

I ignored him, racing up the side into the hedges along the property to find the slot I could ease through onto the other side. I made it almost all the way to the house when Wayne came out, a frown on his expression. "There's someone down at the gate..."

"Don't let them in. They'll go away."

He frowned a beat, then gave me a once over. "Are you all right?"

Was I? "I don't know," I admitted. "I will be." I held up my phone. "I gotta make a call—everything else good?"

"It is," he said, his expression still worried. "If the young man doesn't leave the gate, I'll put a call in to the police."

I gave him a thumbs up. The house was quiet as I crept inside and up the stairs to my wing, then to my suite.

Once I was inside, I sent Dix a message about the car before I collapsed on the bed and stared at the ceiling. My lips were still tingling from the kiss. Tingling that I could feel everywhere.

I thought all I'd wanted was to be rid of them, so why the hell had I missed having that with him? And why did I crave more now?

Dammit.

And damn him.

<h1 style="text-align:center">Five</h1>

JONAS

Everything was packed for school. The new uniforms would be there when I arrived. I kept everything to two trunks. While I was more than capable of flying by myself, Ramsey had booked the same flight with me. Not Lachlan, though. Then again, we'd barely seen him over the summer.

We needed to head to Reno airport soon. We had a layover in Dallas on the way back to Connecticut. I did one last search of the news sites. KC had been in a car accident, or at least, that was what the news reported. It wasn't bad and there were no injuries, but the car had definitely been smashed.

I still couldn't believe paparazzi had been chasing her, even as there had been steady news clips hitting the gossip sites about her out partying. Weirdly, the stories held a similar theme, always highlighting a club she visited *after*. Yet there were no photographs, just "confidential" sources.

The car accident worried me more than anything. Just three lines mentioning it, and the Kissy Kat news blast gave it a paragraph, except it was all speculation. There wasn't even an accident report.

Pulling out my phone, I texted Mom. She didn't like to be bothered when they were in the studio. Gibs didn't need the distractions, but he might not know about the accident.

Someone should tell him, right?

ME

Just checking in before we leave for school, there was a news report about KC being in a car accident in L.A. Thought Gibs might need to know, but I didn't want to harsh the vibe if he's in the zone.

I stared at the message for a long moment then tacked on a *Love you*. It was early, they probably weren't up yet.

"Jonas," Ramsey called from downstairs. "Car is here."

I shoved my phone in my pocket and grabbed the bags with my books, music, and personal items. The trunks were already downstairs.

The car was quiet, our driver didn't say much, and Ramsey left me alone, though he was on his phone. At the airport, we were checked in and through security in no time.

"So," Ramsey said when we got to the gate. "Is this how it's going to be? You saying nothing to me at all? Or only answering in single syllables?"

I glanced at him as I popped open the bottle of soda I'd purchased. "Yes." Then I took a drink before digging a book out of my bag. I'd almost finished it. I could feel Ramsey staring at me from time to time, but he didn't say anything as we waited for them to call boarding.

Sometimes I wondered why he stayed at Blue Ivy. He could have gone to a dozen different universities. He'd nearly graduated at fifteen. He'd been three credit hours shy of completion, but instead of doing it over the summer, he'd just gone back to school with us the following year.

The year after, he enrolled in Blue Ivy's college program. I was pretty sure he planned to teach at Blue Ivy eventually. He was definitely in no hurry to leave the school. I could ask.

But I didn't care.

One more year, and I was out.

Maybe I'd head down to Los Angeles and work on selling my music. Whatever I did, I wasn't doing it with my so-called brothers. I'd barely gone ten pages when they called for us to board.

Our seats were together, but at least it was first class so we didn't have to cram together. As soon as I was in my seat, I checked to see if Mom answered before I put the phone on airplane mode.

"KC was in a car accident?" Ramsey reached for my phone, but I jerked it back. One, he had his own, and two, he could fuck off. I wasn't talking to either of them about her.

Not anymore.

Not after last time.

"Is she all right?" Ramsey stared at me, seemingly unmoved by the fact I glared right back at him. "Cut me a break. Is Kaitlin all right?"

"Yes."

As far as I knew. I looked back at my book, only I didn't see the words. There were still people boarding, and a flight attendant was letting everyone know it was a full flight.

"Look," Ramsey said after a beat, his voice pitched low. It would be hard enough to hear over the rumbling of the engines as they warmed up or whatever it was they were doing. "I get that you're pissed at us. You can continue to be mad all you want, but I'm still your brother, and I'll still have your back."

I didn't scoff, but I thought about it. After that, he left me alone for the rest of the flight. Once we were at the airport, we took a rideshare with our luggage to the long-term parking lot where Ramsey left his car, then we were on our way back to school.

The closer we got to Blue Ivy, the more restlessness invaded me. I was leaning forward, trying to see if she was already here? I didn't know. Even if she was coming back...

Wait, what if she didn't come back? The year before had been her first year. What if she decided it wasn't worth it?

That idea alone seemed to suck all the oxygen out of the car. We were a few days early because Ramsey had RA training to do. He would, once again, be the RA of my building.

Whatever. I didn't care. I could ignore him even better when he was in his first-floor suite and I was in my private one. No Ramsey. No Lachlan.

It would be better.

Twenty minutes after getting to campus, I was letting myself into my own suite. While it still had two bedrooms, I would have it to myself. Ramsey didn't like the idea of me rooming with anyone that wasn't them. I didn't complain or disabuse him of this.

I *needed* the privacy.

My trunks arrived the following day. I had the same suite I'd had to share with Lachlan the year before. Most of the furniture was still ours. It had been thoroughly cleaned, which was nice.

Beginning the first day for seniors and juniors to return to campus, I started staking out the girls' dorm. We had the entire week to get checked back in. If I were talking to Ramsey, I could ask him if she was actively enrolled.

I wasn't talking to him and didn't want to, so I kept it to myself. The weather was nice enough that I could sit outside and read. I found a lot of different spots to watch the girls' dorm from.

Instead of reading, I spent more time on music. I had a tune in my head that wouldn't stop, so I wrote it all out until I'd figured out most of the nuances. I didn't need equipment to test the music on; I could hear it in my head, see the notes even as they played.

On the third day, I went to get my schedule. I ignored most of the kids in line, just keeping an eye out for distinctive blue hair.

"Dekkar," I said to the registrar's assistant, who was passing out the packets.

"C" was in the box next to the one she was digging in. I couldn't make out the names, but I wanted to glance to see if KC was in there.

"Here you go, Jonas," the older woman said with a smile. Her name was Appleby, maybe. I knew her face, but I wasn't great with names. "I hope you have an amazing senior year."

"Thanks."

I was flipping through the folder to find my schedule. I had filled out the classes I wanted before we left in the spring, but I still wanted to be sure.

The music lab was still there for the hour following lunch. That was perfect. I grimaced when I saw Ramsey as TA for the advanced literature class. Well, I should have guessed that. I didn't *need* those credits so I could drop it. I'd totally swapped out of his class the year before.

The class that had KC in it. Maybe I shouldn't have done that, but I hated having Ramsey in charge of anything. I was still skimming my schedule when I bumped into someone and blinked. I'd gotten distracted again.

"Sorry," the girl said.

I opened my mouth, but words failed. I knew this girl. Of course, I knew her. She was Aubrey Miller.

KC's bandmate and roommate.

If she was here...

I pivoted and strode away from her, heading straight for the dorms. Please let her be here.

It would help to see her. If I didn't... maybe I could go back and steal her schedule. I could probably bribe someone. Right, that might be faster. I knew a kid.

I made it to the trees not far from the girls' dorm. There were cars and trucks stacking up in the circular drive in front of it. I looked up Russell's contact, then sent him a quick message asking if he could get me her schedule.

He'd gotten it for me the year before. Not that it worked out. But hopefully, he'd come through with no questions again this year.

I shifted to press deeper into the shadow of the tree as another moving truck pulled up. My phone buzzed but a flash of blue sucked all of my attention.

KC appeared between one of the cars and trucks. She was the best thing I'd seen all summer, dressed in shorts with a long-sleeved sweatshirt tied around her waist, and wearing running shoes with her hair up in a ponytail.

Music whispered in my ear as I watched her circle to the truck where it was open and a couple of movers came to talk to her. She was about to climb into the truck when a guy picked her up by her hips and put her behind him.

The music cut off abruptly with a record scratch. She had her hands on her hips and I could almost imagine her glare as the guy wagged a finger at her then pointed to the trail.

She paced in a circle, then flipped him off and he just laughed at her. Tucking her earbuds in, she turned away from them and headed toward the trailhead.

I knew where they all were; Lachlan ran it all the time. First, he ran to stay in shape for lacrosse, but later, he'd taken to running all year round. Last year...

Now I knew why.

He was chasing KC.

I glanced down at my outfit then at her as she vanished through the trees. I could run, but not dressed like this. Maybe she'd need someone new to run with this year. I could volunteer.

The music began to play slowly again. The notes that had proven so elusive over the last few weeks filled my head again.

KC was here.

She was okay.

My phone buzzed again, and I lifted it to look at the message from Russell. KC's schedule. Good, now I was able to see how many classes we had together. Last year, people had been stupid as fuck about her.

I pocketed my phone and headed back to my dorm. Since she was here, maybe I could leave music pinned to her door. She threw away the note last year, but she'd never thrown away the music.

The door to my dorm thrust open as guys carried their stuff in. But I wasn't looking at the trucks or those guys, I was staring at the silver Mercedes AMG One.

No.

He wasn't supposed to be here.

Pivoting, I came face-to-face with the one brother I could gladly live without ever having to see again.

"Hey, baby bro, miss me?"

"No," I said, then slugged him.

<h1 style="text-align:center">Six</h1>

KC

"**I**'m going to pick up our schedules," Aubrey said as I supervised the moving of our things. Well, supervised was probably too strong a word. Each time I tried to help, Dix got bossy. Including literally picking me up when I was climbing into the truck and putting me on the ground behind him.

"No, ma'am," he informed me in that stern tone without an ounce of humor. "You're still supposed to be taking it easy. I know you said you only had some bruises from the impact, but we're not taking risks."

I rolled my eyes. "Dix..."

"No," he repeated, then pointed toward the running trail. "Go burn off that nervous energy. But you aren't going to be hauling and carrying on my watch." I'd already taken my guitars upstairs, so I resisted sticking my tongue out at him.

"You're not being very nice to me," I told him with a mock pout. He legit laughed in my face.

"I didn't say a word about you totaling my car," he

reminded me. "Or the fact I took that ticket for leaving the scene of an accident."

Guilt raked through me. "Dix...I'm sorry." The words seemed paltry. Even paying for the repairs *and* offering to buy a new one hadn't really put a balm on that.

"Gorgeous, go on. Go run." Almost at once, his stern expression eased. Raking a hand through his sandy blond hair, he shook his head. "You should never have been in that position anyway. Next time, I'll save piss breaks for when we get home."

I winced again. It wasn't until I'd been back at the house for fifteen minutes that he'd called, worried as hell. The yelling had taken fifteen minutes, and when he got to the house at four in the morning, I got yelled at some more.

He had every right to be incensed, but when he was at the house, more than anger radiated off of him... it was fear.

That fear made me feel like shit. Dix had been fantastic the past few weeks, covering my ass and getting me out to burn off all the excess. Then I totaled his car after ducking out without a word to him.

I had my phone. I could have called. Did I call? Fuck, I didn't even remember now. It was all a blur after Lachlan showed up on the dance floor. From the quick excitement to the fury that he would walk up on me like nothing happened.

The feel of him moving with me hadn't helped. Then he pulled off my fucking hat...

Raising my hands, I backed off from Dix. "I'll run. You do this. And Dix?"

"I know," he said, almost indulgently. "I'm the best. Get going."

I grinned, then blew him a kiss as he gave me an exasperated look. "Yes, you are the best and I know you love me."

"Go," he huffed, before turning back to the movers. "And

you boys can button your mouths and get your eyes back in your head."

Walking away, I tucked the earbuds in. They linked to my phone immediately. A message popped up on my screen from Jackie.

JACKIE

Welcome back to school. Focus. Be sure to call us next week and give us all the deets. Pen is doing great. See below…

A photo followed with Pen's sweet face smiling up at me. She was a perfect angel from her light brown skin to her blue eyes and curly hair.

She was showing off four sweet teeth, and it looked like a fifth one was coming through. She'd been teething when I was there the week before. Missing her was a pang in my chest.

ME

She looks great. Will do. Moving in now. Gonna run and get out of my head. Love you.

JACKIE

Love you, too.

Sliding the phone into my armband, I fixed it tight, then fired off the music. The album was the recently cut one by Bound Hearts. Ian and Frankie had *killed* it this summer in the studio and they were out touring for it right now.

I was both wildly proud of them and a little jealous. Not of their album or their success, hell no. Just loved the idea of that first tour. We thought we knew everything when we went out there, but none of us had been ready for the insanity that awaited us as that first album took off.

It helped that their music was so rich with emotion, painting such vivid pictures of their challenges, their loves, and even their passions. At least two of the love songs made me want to swoon. The fact they sang to each other just added to the delicious tension.

They had such an amazing future in front of them. Stretching my arms above my head, I continued my walk to the trailhead. There were kids everywhere. I'd already seen a couple of camera phones pointed in my direction.

The whole drive in, I'd spent the time rebuilding my armor. Aubrey had asked me if I was sure about this. We could go back to online classes or even homeschooling if I wanted. We could certainly afford a private tutor.

But I refused to run away from my personal goals. I didn't know they were my stepbrothers when I chose this school, when I arrived, or even when they started their judgmental bullshit.

No, they were deceptive and kept their secrets, judging me like it was their fucking right. Throw in the ninja kisses? The outright assaults on people in the hallway? On RJ? Just... fuck no.

They didn't get to drive me away. If they wanted Dad, they could fucking have him.

At the top of the trail, I turned my face up to the sun. It was a gorgeous day. The weather was warm, without being hot. The breeze carried the scent of the woods. There was a familiarity that the previous year had lacked...

I was happy to be here.

As soon as the album rolled over to a faster-beat song, I started running. I'd managed a few miles a week on the tread-mill, but running around Beverly Hills wasn't always a good idea. It was part of why I'd started going out dancing at night.

Though after the run-in with Lachlan and the car acci-dent, Dix had been far less on board with indulging my desire. He'd only relented when I let him pick the clubs, and instead of separating, we stuck together. It wasn't quite the same, but at least he could dance and was fun to hang with.

I took the long route around. The trail had been recently trimmed, at least from the look of it. There were no leaves on it, and some of the dips had been smoothed over. A downed tree from the previous year was gone.

Someone had added signs along the trail with miles, and there were a couple that included suggested exercises. They kind of cracked me up, but whatever. It was just nice to be out here running again.

Aubrey had already spoken to Forrest. They'd been talking all summer. I wasn't sure if they were still a thing or not. However, she had sounded happy to hear from him. She also couldn't wait to see him.

That made me happy for her. We had a long talk about the guys and my dad. She and Yvette were furious when I gave them some of the details. They didn't know about the dancing or how many nights, but they did know about the car accident. Hard to hide that when they'd walked in on Dix giving me hell.

Still, they were angrier with the Douchebag Brothers than they were with me. But I'd promised to try and be more open. Being private about family business was something we all understood. It would have helped if we'd *known* they were family. The ninja kisses had been hard enough to explain, but Aubrey called me out on those, too.

What was I angrier about? That he kept doing it? Or that I enjoyed it? Granted, it didn't matter if I liked it. I was the one who said no, and I had cracked him in the nuts for it. But it was food for thought.

For some reason, I'd left Ramsey out of the kissing. It was uncomfortable enough with him being a TA. I wouldn't be seeking any tutoring this year, and if he was a TA in one of my classes this year?

Fuck that, I'd ditch the class and transfer out. *That* would be worth the sanity check.

At the six-mile mark, I slowed to a walk. I was almost around the inner circuit. I hadn't done the outer. It was almost an hour and ten minutes since I started the run. Not quite the ten-minute mile I'd worked my way toward last year. There was time, though.

Sweat soaked through my tank and sports bra, but the moisture-wicking did its job as I walked to cool down and swung my arms. The sweatshirt tied around my waist was a little uncomfortable. But I'd deal with it back at the room.

Hopefully, Dix and the guys would almost be done. Then I could shower and go over schedules with Aubrey. We did actually pick a couple of classes to share this year 'cause that was just stupid last year.

Cutting off the trail, I followed the path made by so many people using the woods for a shortcut to get back to the dorm.

"Hey…"

"Fuck!" I put a hand to my stomach as I barely contained the shriek. Startled, I shuddered as Jonas stepped out from under the shadows of the tree.

Could he be creepier?

"Hey," I said, blowing out a breath. Polite and succinct. Like me, his ink was on display. While I had it on both arms, he only had it on his left. I didn't really have much to say, so I just jerked a thumb toward the buildings. "Gotta go. Moving in."

"KC…" He took a step forward even as I took one toward the dorms. "I heard about the car accident."

"Not surprised," I said with a shrug. "Blame Lachlan. I do."

Shock flickered over his face. "Lachlan?"

"Yeah, your *brother*." I couldn't help but stress that last word. Yes, my irritation was showing, and no I didn't really care at the moment. "About this tall," I continued, holding my hand up above me. "Dark hair. Shit-eating grin, green eyes, and a sarcastic sense of humor."

"I know who Lachlan is," Jonas said. "He was there? When you had your accident?"

I reached up and pulled the tie out of my hair so I could shake it out. The yank on my roots was giving me a headache. Or maybe it was this conversation. "Do you and your brother not talk?" 'Cause I shouldn't have to explain this.

"No."

That— "Wait, you don't?" Fuck. I held up a hand. "You know what, never mind. Forget I asked. It's none of my business. Yes, I am fine. I gotta finish getting moved in."

"Before you go…"

He took another step forward as I backed up one. I'd get annoyed about retreating, only I was trying to leave and he kept trying to shorten the distance between us.

"I'm waiting," I said when he didn't continue.

"I brought you something." He thrust his hand out with a stack of four music sheets. "I was going to pin it to your door. But…your boyfriend…and the movers."

"Boyfriend?" I didn't want to take the music. If I did, it would totally send the wrong message. At the same time, I was eager to see what he'd written. The last few songs he'd brought to me had been amazing pieces. "What boyfriend? Oh crap, Lachlan isn't here, is he? I am not dating your brother."

Curiosity surged through me and I took the offered sheets as he frowned. "Yeah, Lachlan is here, but I didn't mean him."

Jerking my attention up from the music, I frowned. "Why is he here?" Didn't he graduate? Although I managed to not ask that one.

Jonas shrugged. "I don't know. But who is the guy with your movers?"

Pivoting, I glanced toward the big truck where Dix spoke

with a pair of the guys who'd been hauling our stuff up. Most of it was furniture from last year brought out of storage: the coffee maker, updated pieces for our rooms, luggage, and new bed linens. Dix had also insisted on the latest television.

"That's Dix," I said, glancing at Jonas and meeting the sudden intensity in his stare. "He's my driver... part-time bodyguard. And friend." The last I kind of tacked on because Mom used to always tell me that staff was staff, and to never cross those lines, but... I liked Dix.

"So, not your boyfriend?"

"No," I said slowly. "Not my boyfriend. Why the sudden interest in my love life?"

"Are you hungry? Want to get food? Oh, the food court isn't open yet. We can order stuff, though. Would you like to get lunch tomorrow? Or do you go running at this time every day?"

I didn't have time to answer one question before he asked another. To be honest, I didn't think I'd ever heard him say so many words in such a short amount of time.

"No, I usually go running early—before classes."

"How early? Six?"

"Yeah, sometimes. It depends on the weather. Look..." I caught sight of Aubrey coming out to where Dix was. "I gotta go. Don't think food together is a great idea. I love the music, in any case, so I'll see if I can come up with some words. But... you don't owe me anything like food or whatever. So—why don't we just keep this strictly a music thing."

Maybe not even that, but I liked the music.

I waved to him with the sheets, then turned before he could ask me something else and jogged away. His curiosity about Dix was weird, but was he serious about Lachlan being back? And Lachlan didn't tell him about showing up in L.A.?

Blowing out a breath, I slowed down as I got to Aubrey and Dix.

"There's my girl," Dix said, grinning, then he nodded toward where I'd been talking to Jonas. "Run into a fan?"

I shook my head. Yeah, I didn't really want to discuss Jonas with him or anyone else. "No. Are we about done? I'd kill for a shower and some food."

Aubrey laughed at me. "They were just wrapping up."

"Yeah, I'll take care of the movers. You get showered, then I'll take you two out for a senior year kick-off dinner."

I stared at him and I wasn't the only one. Even Aubrey looked skeptical.

"Yes," he told us with exasperation. "It's a thing, now move it."

I saluted, still chuckling, and stole a glance back to where Jonas had been as we weaved through the others coming and going through the main doors.

He was gone.

But one look at the music told me I would see him again.

Probably in classes.

Yay?

I turned that over in my mind as we climbed the stairs toward our room.

"I got our schedules," Aubrey said as she opened the door for us. "Brace yourself. You got Douchebag Two for at least two classes..."

What?

"Shit."

That was definitely not a yay.

Seven

RAMSEY

The sound of alarms blaring jerked me right out of a sound sleep. That and the distinct smell of smoke. Throwing the covers back, I rolled out of the bed. Lachlan was passed out on the sofa in the living room of my suite. The alarms weren't inside, and they were quieter in here than...

Outside. It was another dorm. I often slept with the window cracked until winter meant we couldn't anymore. I grabbed the flashlight, the fire extinguisher, and my phone. "Lachlan," I ordered, flipping the light on. "Up."

"What the fuck?" He groaned as he turned over. His black eye was worse, if possible, but I didn't have time for that at the moment.

"Up, evacuation procedures. Evacuate this dorm and the others..."

"Is that..."

I didn't wait for him to finish the question, I had the door open and yanked the alarm on my way past as I headed out the door. Outside, the smell of smoke was a thousand percent worse.

Students were already coming out the door behind me. "No," I said when they started toward the burning building. That was the girl's dorm. The roof was definitely on fire. Flames licked along the brick as it rolled over the side like a hungry beast in search of a violent meal. "That way." I pointed him away from the buildings. "Fire drill protocols. Stay together."

"Hey," Lachlan called as I angled toward the burning building. The alarms were screaming, smoke was everywhere, and I didn't have time for his questions or explanations.

"Follow the damn protocol," I said over my shoulder, tossing him the flashlight. "Do it and get a headcount going."

Harley was already outside, ordering girls away from the building as they came out. "How many?" I asked. The alarm on my phone indicated the fire department had been called.

"Not enough," she yelled back. "Maybe thirty percent. There are girls on the upper floors."

"I'll go in. You keep on the count down here."

"Ramsey, are you insane?"

I didn't answer, mostly because I didn't doubt the answer was yes. I didn't see any blue hair on any of the girls who'd already appeared. As I climbed the steps, a girl plowed into me, hysterical and in tears.

"Easy, Payton," I told her, trying to ignore the violent tickle cough that was starting to hit. "Go on down there, check in with Harley, and go."

Payton dug her fingers into my neck as she held on. I didn't have time for this. In attempting to disengage her, I nearly dropped the fire extinguisher and then, when she began to scream, I scooped her up and carried her down. Another four or five girls came rushing out behind us.

Once out on the open quad with the others, I set her

down. "Look after her," I ordered one of the other RAs and then turned back to the building.

It looked like something out of a disaster movie. Fire shot out in jets from a couple of the windows. A girl came tumbling down with a scream, and I wasn't the only one racing toward her.

A broken arm would be preferable to burning alive. "How many up there?" I asked, as I scooped her up.

"I don't know." She was sobbing and coughing, so trying to get anything out of her wouldn't be helpful. I carried her back and then returned to the building. This time I made it inside and with the fire extinguisher cleared a doorway to let more girls dash outside, among them the Wideman twins and a few other familiar faces.

Harley descended one of the stairs. She had a girl with her, and they both wore masks yet were also sooty and coughing. "Can't get up to the third floor. Something is wrong with the door..."

"Go," I told her, ushering them toward the door. Then I was running up the steps. It was so hot inside that my skin felt like it had a sunburn, and it was harder and harder to take a breath. I pulled my shirt up to cover my mouth and nose, but it wasn't much.

The door in question had no signs of warping. It wasn't hot to the touch, but it was...jammed. I reached up to grab a screwdriver that had been crammed in between the hinges. There'd be no way to open it from either side.

I yanked the door open and turned my face away as hot air and smoke rushed out. "The door is open," I yelled. "Can anyone hear me?"

"We're coming," a feminine voice yelled. "Need help, Kathy hurt herself..."

I didn't recognize the name as I peered through the haze and the smoke. It was so dense in here I swore my chest burned. My eyes watered and then Aubrey Miller was there with Kathleen Ross. Behind her were three others, including a spark of blue hair. Relief hit as I reached for the injured girl.

"Give her to me," I said. Her ankle was twisted at what had to be an uncomfortable angle. "Downstairs," I ordered as I scooped her up. "Stay together."

There were no arguments as they followed me down. I paused once or twice to make sure blue hair was still with us, but I kept losing her in the smoke. Outside, the cooler air hit like a sledgehammer.

I was coughing all the way over to the quad where the nurse and some of the security staff had set up. I passed them the wounded girl and turned around.

"How many, Harley?" I asked as soon as I found the RA.

"Four...four are missing..."

Four. I twisted, scanning the quad. I'd just brought out three or four. Where...

Aubrey Miller was racing past me back to the building when I caught her arm. "No, stay out. It's too dangerous in there."

"KC didn't make it out. She was right behind me then she wasn't."

Shit.

"Stay," I ordered before running back into the building. The hot air billowing out was suffocating. "KC," I yelled as I took the steps two at a time. "Kaitlin..."

My heart stopped on the second floor where I found my blue-haired menace struggling with a pair of large guitar cases.

"What the hell are you doing?" I tried to wrench one away from her and she held onto it.

"I can't leave them," she said in a voice so raw it hurt my soul to hear it. "I need them..."

"They aren't worth your life."

"Yes," she countered. "They are."

"Give me one," I ordered. "Let's go."

"Don't leave it?" The fact she sounded like she was begging in between coughs rankled me.

"I won't," I said. "I promise. Come on, let me get you and the guitars out of here."

Finally, she relented and I took the larger of the two cases. Then she let me pull her to her feet. She staggered but managed to stay on them. We were descending the stairs together, and she coughed with every step. It was a violent struggle to breathe.

"C'mon," I encouraged her, hating my own raw cough.

The smoke was thick, the visibility low, but I'd already done this route three times. I knew how to get us out of here. She stayed with me, her hand firmly clasped in mine as we made it to the doorway.

If not for how tight she dug her fingers into my hand, I would have missed her wavering and the sudden laxness as she passed out. Guitars, be damned. I turned and got her over my shoulder then seized the guitar to take with us.

Outside, I carried her, nearly dropping the guitar twice. She'd inhaled a lot of smoke; we both had.

"I have it," Aubrey was saying as she pried the guitar from my hand. I kept going, racing KC over to where they had the triage set up.

"She needs oxygen." I put her down, then went back for the second guitar. She'd thought they were worth her life, so I wasn't leaving the damn thing.

When I got back, she had an oxygen mask on. The flashing lights of emergency vehicles strobed through the smoke and the darkness. The sounds of sobbing filled the air. KC still struggled to breathe, even with the mask on. She coughed and kept trying to remove it even if her eyes were closed.

"Don't," I snapped in a croaking voice. "You could suffocate without oxygen right now." Her throat could have smoke damage. Worse, her lungs. I turned away to cough, my eyes were irritated and even my breathing had turned to wheezing.

"Good advice," a paramedic said as he slid in next to me. "Let's get you some oxygen, too."

"She needs a hospital," I said. KC's eyes were red and irritated. Worse, there was a hint of blue around her lips and not just her hair.

"We've got her," the paramedic assured me, before he handed me a mask to put on. The coughing hurt, but the oxygen helped. KC suddenly tried to sit up, her expression wild.

I yanked off my mask. "They're right there," I told her in a raw voice. "Your guitars are safe."

She sagged like someone had cut her strings. The paramedic got the mask more firmly set on her face. He was checking her vitals and then shooting me a look when she grabbed at my hand.

I held my mask in place and let her grip my hand as I watched the fire department get the water hoses on. The building was a loss. Even if they hosed down all the flames, I doubted whatever was left would be remotely salvageable.

"You want to go to the hospital with her?" the paramedic asked. "We're triaging right now. She's breathing, we want to keep her on the oxygen and then we're gonna transport. We have others with more serious wounds who are going first."

"I'll stay with her," I said. "Then yes, I want to go to the hospital with her."

I needed to know she was going to be all right, especially if she was going to make such crazy calls where her life was concerned.

Her eyes were closed again, as she dug her nails into my hand until it felt like she wanted to draw blood. I didn't try to pull away. Instead, I just leaned toward her and said, "I'm here, Kaitlin. I got you. You're going to be okay."

Far too briefly, her eyes flickered open and she focused on me, then they closed again. I had to keep both her mask and mine in place. It wasn't long before Aubrey joined us. She shot me a narrow-eyed look, but I wasn't going anywhere. Neither was she.

When it was our turn to transport in the ambulance, she gripped the guitars then stared at me and the vehicle.

"I'll stay with her," I promised. "Look after those."

"I'll be there as soon as I can," she said finally. "You better damn well take care of her."

I didn't offer any platitudes, but I wasn't going anywhere until KC told me to fuck off herself. It wasn't until I was sitting in the ambulance with a fresh oxygen mask that I caught sight of my brothers. The pair of them stared at me and then at her.

Jonas' expression was one of absolute fear, while Lachlan's bordered on fury. Fuck, they needed to stay here and out of it, but I didn't think they were going to listen. Who knew, maybe it would give them something to talk about that didn't involve Jonas trying to relocate Lachlan's jaw.

KC never let go of me for the whole ride to the hospital. I finally had to take my hand from hers when they wanted to move her to a hospital bed, and they put me in the bed area next to hers. I endured all of the checks while I kept an eye on her.

By the time Aubrey arrived, I was ready to collapse. The news about KC seemed good. Mostly smoke inhalation. They wanted to keep her on oxygen and keep an eye on her throat. Observation for a few hours and then she'd probably be released.

They said pretty much the same about me. I met Aubrey's gaze when she went to close the curtains between our cubicles. Anger was in her expression, but there was gratitude in her eyes.

I understood both emotions. Head back, I closed my eyes and let her off the hook.

A fire.

Fuck, that was close.

Too damn close.

Eight

Eight hours we were in the emergency room of the local hospital. I was out for a few hours of it, at least, that was what Aubrey said when I woke up to her sleeping sitting up next to me. The first thing she did when I opened my eyes was call Yvette. I had a hard time talking with the oxygen mask. I wasn't allowed to take it off, but the croak of my voice wasn't something I wanted to hear again anyway.

"Bitch," Yvette said, her French pronounced as it usually was when she was distressed. "You scared the shit out of me."

I'd apologize, but, yeah, she was a wreck. No cosmetics, her eyes reddened, her nose shiny, and a hint of chap around her lips. It had been a long night for her.

"I wanted to come down, but Aubrey said to wait until we knew whether you were getting out of there."

Was I getting out of here? I glanced at Aubrey as I tried to sit up.

"Hang on," Aubrey said before she set her phone down

and then helped me adjust as she lifted the bed. I didn't try to pull the oxygen mask off. My throat was legit killing me.

Retrieving her phone, Aubrey perched on the edge of the bed next to me. She tucked her cheek to the top of my head. Even with the mask on, the smell of smoke seemed to cling to everything.

"The doctor said he'd have recommendations for us within the next couple of hours."

"How long?" I managed to push the two words out from under the shattered glass coating my throat.

"It's almost six in the morning," Yvette said and I groaned. So much hurt, I also felt scummy. "The fire was at midnight?"

"Give or take," Aubrey said. "We woke to smoke. That was before the alarms started going off."

I was trying to put it together while they spoke. "What happened to the sprinklers?" Yvette demanded. "Weren't those buildings brand new?"

They were...they'd just opened them the year before. I coughed, wincing with every squeeze of my chest.

"I don't know," Aubrey said. "The police came by, and so did campus security." She glanced down at me. "They will want to talk to you when you're up for it. They were being pushy, but TA Douchebag chased them off."

TA Douchebag? Tired swarmed over me. I'd played back-to-back sets for hours and been less tired at the end of the day. "Ramsey..." I croaked out the name. "He—helped."

"He's okay," Yvette assured me before she cut a look at Aubrey. I followed her gaze. Aubrey let out a little sigh, then pressed a kiss to the top of my head. The wrap of her arm around my shoulders kept me grounded, and I leaned into her as much, or maybe more than she leaned into me. "Aubrey said he's right there in the hospital with you."

He was? Before I could look around, Aubrey huffed out a hard sigh. "He's a cubicle over." Her voice was low, probably to not carry. Adding to the surreality of the entire experience, I had on an oxygen mask, and we were surrounded by the sterile environment that wavered between blinding white and fugly green. What was it with hospitals?

I tried to clear my throat, but it hurt. A second attempt brought a nurse into our cubicle. Her smile was warm and almost too friendly. Guilt niggled inside of me, but I was too tired to focus on that particular fact at the moment.

"Hi there, I'm Jesse," she said. "I've been your nurse for the last few hours."

Aubrey scooted out of the way as the nurse checked my vitals. There was an oxygen monitor on my finger, and she got the blood pressure cuff in place.

"The doctor will be in to speak with you shortly, but can you tell me where you are?"

I stared at her for a long moment, then tried to say hospital but the word came out garbled and harsh.

She grimaced in sympathy for me. "That sounds rough. Let's try some ice chips. We can do those in tiny amounts, and I can switch you out to a nasal cannula. Sound good?"

Honestly, anything sounded great if it involved getting something to drink. There was an IV in, and the numbers didn't seem to worry the nurse too much.

While she said it wouldn't take long, it seemed to take forever for them to switch me from oxygen to a cannula. It was easier to breathe, and the ice was ambrosia. Aubrey helped me with the ice chips. Why the fuck was I so weak?

It was hard enough to keep my eyes open. If they were going to release me, I wanted to get out of here. Thankfully, the round with the doctor went easier. He was younger, smiling like he was actually happy to be here, and his eyes held a distinctly sober edge.

He was more than happy with my oxygenation levels. My throat was raw and sore, so I needed to give it all a couple of days. A fact he reminded me about firmly after examining it.

After ordering a few more tests, he focused on me. "We're going to give this another couple of hours. Drink some water, small sips only. Suck on the ice. I'll see about ordering you something cold to eat too in a little while. So far, all your numbers look good. We'll be able to get you out of here soon."

"Thank you," I hacked around the words, grimacing even as they came out.

"Take it easy there, Miss Crosse. That's a valuable voice, and we want to protect it. You should be good in a few days, but we'll want you to check in with your primary physician. If you don't have one locally, come back and see me. My sister is a huge fan."

I didn't laugh, but Aubrey did. "We'll sign any autograph you'd like. Just hearing she's going to be okay is a lifesaver."

"What she said," Yvette declared from the phone. "I'll send something down to the girls once we figure out where everyone will be."

He chuckled. "That's great, however getting better is the best thing you can do for her and for me. Any questions?"

I had thousands of them, just not for him. Not right now. Blood work followed him pretty quickly, then they sent me for more x-rays. More, because they'd done x-rays earlier, but I was out.

The bed area next to mine was empty when I came back. The curtains were open and the bed was freshly made. Aubrey glanced up as they wheeled me back into the bay. "We can get you dressed," she said. "Results will be in shortly. Or we can wait until they actually release you."

I was on the fence about that. We'd sent Yvette to sleep and promised to text as soon as we knew what was happening.

"Where..." I started, but Aubrey made a face and I couldn't blame her. There was almost no improvement in how hoarse I sounded. Maybe I should give my voice a break, at least until my throat didn't feel littered with broken glass. I pointed to her phone, mostly 'cause I had no idea where mine was.

She handed it over and I typed in a message in the notes: *Where is Douchebag Two?*

She glanced at the words then over at the empty area next to us. "He was discharged. They gave him a list of warnings to watch out for, except he sounded fine. Looked more cranky than anything else."

But he's okay?

A gentle smile softened her face. "He's fine. He's still a prick. He also still thinks he's in charge." With a roll of her eyes, she shook her head. "All that said, he didn't hesitate to go into the building not once, not twice, but at least three times that I saw, and he went back for you."

Oh.

"That doesn't mean he gets forgiven," Aubrey said with a sniff, as she leaned back in the chair. "I don't know what he and his pair of Douchebag Brothers will need to do for that, but I guarantee you, groveling will be involved."

I stared down at the phone for a minute, then typed in: *How bad?*

Aubrey's smile fled. "It's toast babe. All of it. Gone. The building, from what I hear, might still be standing but the interior is gutted...our clothes, the computers, the coffee maker..." The last she said with genuine mourning. "They're all gone. We can replace them, even get new pictures printed, but between the fire and the water? Not much is going to be salvageable. Not that we can get in there at all. Sydney texted to say that they're investigating it."

I frowned. *Arson?*

When I held up the phone, Aubrey lifted her shoulders. "I don't know. The sprinklers didn't work. The fire alarms didn't go off when they were supposed to, and it was chaos...maybe it was just a bad accident..."

But she didn't think so. I sighed, then looked around the cubicle.

"Clothes?" At her question, I nodded. She closed the curtains then helped me into what looked like newly purchased clothes. They still had the tags on. When she had time to shop, I had no idea. It was good, though all I could smell was smoke and fire. It was in my hair and my skin. I'd washed my hands, but it didn't chase the scent away.

After an eternity, Jesse came back. "I didn't forget you," she said with a smile as she hustled in. "We're going to get you ready for discharge, but we need to go over some things first. I take it you'll be with Miss Crosse?"

"Yes," Aubrey said, leaning forward. For the next ten minutes, Jesse went over the discharge paperwork with us, including what symptoms to watch for and what constituted an immediate trip back. She also reminded me that I needed to do a follow-up with a primary care physician.

Once she was done, I signed everything. "Stay here for a minute and I'll get the wheelchair. Do you want to bring your car around?" she said the last to Aubrey.

"Calling a ride-share," she said, holding up the phone. "They'll be here in ten." I wish it was Dix, but he'd already gone back to L.A. I'd been so confident I'd be fine—famous last words.

She smothered a yawn while we waited, then, courtesy of Jesse, she rolled me outside via a quiet exit. Apparently, some press had gotten word about the fire. We shoved all my hair up under a hat, but hopefully we could avoid attracting any attention.

Once in the car, we both sagged into the seats. I rested my head on Aubrey's shoulder and she sighed. We weren't heading back to the school. Our destination was a hotel in

Monmouth that was over thirty minutes from the school and forty-five from the hospital.

Privacy.

"We're already checked in," Aubrey said when we got there. She even had two card keys in hand. Wait, that made sense: she set up a retreat zone before following me to the hospital. The fact we were checked in meant we went straight across the lobby to the elevator and then up to the top floor.

Oh, she got us the penthouse. Or what passed for one. When I gave her a look, she rolled her eyes.

"We deserve this, thank you very much, and you need to rest. It's this or whatever they are doing for emergency housing back at the school. Since they already canceled our first three days of classes while they get everything sorted, we have time."

Classes weren't supposed to start for another two days... how much time did they need? Then again, arson, so everything was gone.

A sigh escaped me. All the music I'd been working on. Some photos. Most of it was replaceable.

Most of it.

In the room, I almost sagged again, because my guitar cases were waiting for me.

"I know how much they mean to you," Aubrey said, dropping the keycards on a table. "Go shower. I'm ordering us food, then we're turning on Netflix to binge something before we pass out."

That...sounded really good.

"Phone?" I asked, grimacing at the sound I made. I needed the croak to go away now, but then I was coughing.

"I don't know," Aubrey said. "I didn't see it in your things at the hospital, and we were in pajamas...did you leave it by the bed and only get your guitars?"

I barely remembered the yelling and the chaos. Just the fact I couldn't breathe, I was coughing, the cases were sitting there and I snagged them. Even if it all turned out to be smoke and nothing else, I couldn't afford to lose either of the guitars.

"We'll order you a new one. We can brick the old one then restore the new one from the cloud. I'll text Jackie if you want. I didn't even think about them calling. Go shower... and rest your voice. I'm going to order hot tea with everything else."

I gave her a thumbs-up and headed for the bathroom. There were new clothes on the counter, still with their tags on. Bless Aubrey or whoever she asked to get us what we needed. I was so tired. Images from the smoky hall, pushing on a door that wouldn't open, and the sound of screams filled my head.

Then Ramsey had been there. Douchebag Two had ripped open that door and the smoke moved. The light had cut through the shadows like the scene had been lit especially for him.

I cranked on the water and then looked at my hands. They were cut in a couple of places. Scraped. Bruised. There was a band-aid on the back of my left hand from the IV, and I'd broken three nails.

No idea how I'd even managed that. Time to think about it later. The best part of climbing into the shower and scrubbing was washing away the scent of burnt embers. By the time I rejoined Aubrey, she'd set us up in the middle of the biggest king bed in one of the rooms.

She'd already turned on Netflix and had *Love is Blind* waiting for us.

I grinned. She *hated* this show, but Yvette and I loved it.

"Yes," Aubrey said with a droll smile and patted the bed next to her. "I am the best. C'mon, let's turn off our brains for a while."

That sounded...perfect.

Nine

LACHLAN

The air outside reeked of the sulfur from the fire. Smoke clung to everything. Despite the bright sunshine and the promise of a cool breeze, heat radiated off the blackened brick.

A stack of detritus had begun to accumulate where they'd been carrying out the burnt-out remnants of furniture and electronics. Security was a definite presence, as were the arson investigators.

Students were supposed to stay clear, and they were chasing off the lookie-loos. The investigators were who I wanted to watch. They'd arrived shortly after dawn while the firefighters were still putting out the last hot spots. They'd pushed out a lot of ruined furniture and other debris from the windows.

Frankly, I kept expecting the headmaster of the school to come by to inspect it, right before he passed out. The millions they'd spent on all these shiny new dorms and a *fire* ate one alive in record time.

Record. Time.

"It's so awful," Payton said as she approached me. I was still sipping my coffee when she slid an arm around me, coughing almost "delicately." It was more of a little hack to clear her throat than a real cough. "I was so scared."

Uh-huh. I glared down at her, then focused on the building again. It was hard to tell *where* the fire started. I wasn't any kind of expert, but if they suspected—

"Lachlan, baby," Payton sniffled, running one hand over my chest even as she pressed her breasts up to my side. It wasn't quite humping, but it was close. "I need to feel something else... and you're here..."

"Go get a toy or something, Payton," I told her, extracting myself from her barnacle-like grip. "I'm busy."

"Lachy," she practically whined, then gripped my dick through my jeans. Yeah, if anything, any potential erection shrank from the contact. I hadn't seen her in months. "I need *you*."

"You need a hobby," I informed her, then locked my hand around her wrist. For a moment, I thought she was going to try and wrench my dick off when I pulled her hand away. Instead, she pouted and stomped her feet. "Go away, Payton."

I didn't have time for her, or this. Didn't want it either. Ramsey got back from the hospital an hour ago, he only wanted to shower and sleep. Said he'd give me more info after.

I'd give him another half-hour before I kicked him awake. I needed to know where Ace was. I planned to get him from the hospital and check on her, but he got back before they lifted the blockade on the parking lots.

Smart, the administration was already locking down messaging. The press had been making their way on campus, though. Whether in person or because students were giving them videos, photos, and quotes, nobody was likely to know.

My phone buzzed in my pocket. It took a moment to twist

free of Payton's embrace. The message on the screen needed attention. "Go away, Payton," I repeated, almost absently before returning to my dorm. Jonas stood just inside the main doors, staring at me with those serial-killer eyes.

Baby brother had anger management issues. We usually got a pass from each other. But oh, no, he'd gotten himself in knots over Ace, and now he wanted what was mine.

I felt bad... at first. I'd kept my distance, 'cause he'd been baffled by his own attraction and then he did *nothing*. Right, he had his chance.

Move it or lose it.

Since he wasn't talking to me, I cut past him on my way to Ramsey's suite. I'd planned on crashing in Jonas' free room in his suite. Then our baby bro lost his fucking mind, so Ramsey insisted I crash in his suite. Fortunately, he *also* had a second bedroom.

DAD

I saw a report about a fire on campus. You and your brothers fine?

ME

All good. Ramsey played hero while I was the sheepdog herding kids away. Some injuries, the worst was a broken leg.

As far as I knew. Jonas followed me right into Ramsey's suite and I spared him a look. My right eye was still pretty fucking swollen. "If you came to fight, I'm not letting you get in any free swings."

He snorted as he bypassed me and walked over to the kitchen and opened Ramsey's fridge. He helped himself to the jug of milk, cracking it open before taking a long drink out of it.

DAD

Let me know if you need anything.

ME

Thanks.

Done, I glanced at Jonas. He stared back. For five long minutes, we just stood there in the quiet of Ramsey's suite *staring* at each other.

Right.

I snagged my keys off the counter and lifted a hand toward my little brother. "Good talk."

"Where are you going?" At Jonas' question, I lifted the middle finger in my raised hand to answer before I headed out the door. My car was parked in the closest lot. I got the engine warmed before I was even there and slid right into the driver's seat.

A flash of blonde hair caught the corner of my eye and I locked the doors. Payton was on her way in my direction. She was like a VD that didn't want to go away no matter how many doses of antibiotics I took.

Not looking in her direction, I pulled out and headed for the long drive. One perk to crossing the finish line of "high school" meant I didn't need to sign in and out of campus. Also, classes were all canceled for several days so I had lots of time to sort out my schedule.

A flick of a look in the rearview showed Jonas had followed me as far as the parking lot. Yeah, you get your head out of your ass, baby bro, and we'll go back to talking.

I was done with being the punching bag, especially when I had more important things to do. Nothing salvageable from the fire. No furniture, clothes, books, nothing. When I'd seen Ace, she'd been in pajamas.

She was alive, that was the important part. I headed for town. I needed to get a care package together for her. Running clothes maybe, and shoes. The jacket I'd gotten her last winter was probably in the ashes of the building.

I went all the way to Hartford. Options were good. The first store was fifteen minutes away from opening when I got there, so I went in search of coffee from down the street. News was beginning to trickle out about the fire.

The school had managed to keep a chokehold on it—so far. I doubted that was going to last much longer. It was one thing when students were in shock or trying to wake up. The longer the day went on, the more likely news was going to break.

Ramsey going to the hospital with Ace meant I thought he'd stay with her. Then he came back... sans Ace. He looked like hell so I cut him some slack, but I didn't want to wait for him to wake up.

I just wanted to see her. Maybe make a peace offering.

Two hours later, I had a couple of bags with clothes and at least one pair of running shoes. I was pretty sure I had the right sizes. Ace was athletic and on the terrifically lean side. Her breasts couldn't be more than a b cup. Sweet to hold, but not going to spill out. Her hips were pretty narrow. Nice for gripping. And her ass had just the right amount of curve to it.

My cock was hard as stone by the time I'd picked out everything. I'd debated getting her some lingerie, then I found the sports bra like the one I'd cut off of her.

Yep. Totally got her three different ones. I couldn't decide what color I preferred. So, maybe I'd let her decide. I checked with a friend on campus after a stop at the hospital. KC wasn't there.

Guy worked in administration. He was in his second year at the college and spent a lot of time taking care of records and assignments. It was how I'd found out what dorm Ace had when she first got to the school. Ramsey knew, but he wouldn't say shit.

Asshole.

"Okay, so you didn't get this from me," he said in a hushed voice. "Miller reported they were staying at The Court Hotel in Monmouth."

"They staying under their names?"

"Doesn't say that one way or the other, but I'm gonna guess... maybe not?"

"Double check and text me?"

"You got it."

"Same payment?" While my tone was droll, Guy liked three things... classic vinyl, good weed, and coffee coke. He could never find coffee coke, so I'd been working out a way to buy it for him and I had two cases put aside just for times like this.

"Man, don't make me want to kiss you."

I snorted. "I don't care if you want to kiss me, just don't do it."

He laughed and the call disconnected. Monmouth was a good forty minutes away and it was well after two before I arrived. I stopped at a Coffee Shack and got her the latte she always seemed to order and then doubled it, 'cause I had no idea what the roomie preferred and ten minutes of scanning their fan sites didn't reveal shit.

At the hotel, I carried the bags and the coffee inside, delivered them to the desk, then said who they were for. The cute redhead winked at me. "Let me call up so they'll come down. We can't give out room numbers."

I really loved food service delivery. While she didn't tell me the room number, I didn't miss what she dialed on the phone as I leaned there against the counter. Eventually, she pressed another button and said, "Good afternoon, this is the front desk. You have a delivery, but you'll need to come down to get it. Thank you."

At her apologetic smile, I winked. "Don't worry about it."

Then I moved like my phone had gone off and pulled it out. "Oh, look at that, they just texted."

"Well, we're not supposed to let anyone go up."

"Don't worry, I'll never tell."

I crossed the lobby to the elevators and hit the up button. The hotel was higher-end, very classic and elegant. It really didn't seem to fit her aesthetic but then it also made hiding easier, right?

Since the number she entered was for the top floor, I chose it. Just as the doors closed though, I caught sight of RJ Wallach.

What. The. Fuck.

My good mood shredded all the way up. Had she called *him*? Goddammit. What the fuck was he doing back here? By the time the elevator opened to the penthouse level, I was spoiling for a fight.

I knocked on their door twice. Once gently, the second time with a little more force. No one came to answer. I scowled.

Setting the drinks and the bags down, I dug in my pocket for a pen and then scribbled a note on the receipt. Tucking it on top of the stuff, I backed up and headed for the elevator.

Did I go down? Hunt the little shit down? Or did I stay here and wait him out?

I wrestled with it back and forth, then finally folded my arms and leaned back against the wall facing the elevators. To get to Ace, Wallach would have to come up the same way I did.

If—when—he did, he would find me waiting for him and I had no more patience for the fucker. I'd warned him away from Ace a couple of times now.

Time he learned that I wasn't kidding. The gloves were coming off. He wasn't going to do to Ace what he'd done to Kelly.

No.

Chance.

In.

Hell.

The bruise on my face throbbed, but I flexed my hands. I was ready for him.

RJ Wallach wasn't touching her.

Ever again.

Ten

KC

Aubrey wasn't quite snoring when I left the bedroom and closed the door behind me. I needed water badly, my throat hurt and my nose was runny. Even though I'd scrubbed in the shower, I hadn't managed to get rid of the smell of smoke.

There were a series of messages on the room phone. I got ice water from the fridge, took several swallows, then tested my voice.

Oh. Yeah.

Nope. Not using it, I checked the room voicemails as I sank down into a chair, water bottle pressed to my face.

"Sweetheart," Jackie said, her voice all kinds of relieved. "Thank you for having Aubrey send the message. No, I hadn't heard about the fire and apparently, it's just *now* hitting the gossip sites. Call me when you can." A squeal of sound from Pen made me smile as she half-chanted, "Kay, Kay, Kay."

The next message was from Dix. "I'm getting back on a

plane. I'll be in late tonight." The relief I experienced at the sound of his voice was staggering. "Stay at the hotel until I get there. If you need anything, text my phone. It hasn't hit the news out here yet, but reporters have it. Davina got some calls at the house."

I grimaced. We needed to send a message to Teddy. The last message was from the front desk, letting us know our coffee delivery was here. I glanced at the wall clock. The message was four hours old.

Fuck. *Sorry, Dix.* I pushed up from the sofa I'd perched on and went to the door. Flipping the lock, I pulled it open. There, sitting right by the door, were three shopping bags and a pair of take-out coffee cups. I stared at the latter almost mournfully, but when I picked them up—they weren't cold.

At all.

After getting everything inside, I checked the coffees. They were fresh. Maybe coffee had been delivered hours earlier, but someone had gotten us more. Not for the first time, I wished I had my phone. I tested a sip and sighed happily as I carried the second one into the bedroom.

Aubrey lifted her head to squint at me. Her hair looked as bad as mine, haphazard and definitely sticking straight up in places. I shouldn't have gone to sleep with mine wet, but I could deal with the mess in a bit.

"You got us coffee?" Aubrey said with a yawn. I shook my head, then jerked my thumb at the door. "Someone delivered us coffee. Huh."

I made the "D" letter with my fingers.

Relief crossed Aubrey's face. "I love that man."

Chuckling, I left her to wake up while I carried the caffeine back to the other room to check the bags. My coffee was almost perfect. As much as my throat was still scratchy and sore, the coffee was the perfect balm.

There were running shoes in the first bag. Two different pairs. One was the same brand I normally wore, the second was slightly different with a note that just said, *These are better.*

Weird.

By the time I finished emptying the bags though, I was pretty damn sure these hadn't come from Dix. Sports bras. Moisture-wicking panties. Running shorts, leggings, and sweats—there were two moisture-wicking t-shirts, a tank top, and a very familiar jacket.

It wasn't until I pulled out the last item that a piece of paper fluttered out. Pausing, I knelt to pick it up.

Ace,

You guys were sleeping, I grabbed another set of coffees for you, but I had to go. Will find you tomorrow. Call me.

There was no signature, but it didn't need one. The addition of a phone number had me doing a slow blink. When Aubrey eventually emerged from the bedroom, she studied the note then me.

"So, he's back..."

I nodded slowly. One thing I'd kind of been counting on this year was *his* absence. Maybe it had been a foolish hope. Ramsey practically worked at the school and Jonas was in my grade. Lachlan was supposed to be gone.

Sighing, I sat back against the sofa. Despite who brought the coffee, I'd still finished it. How had he figured out my favorite drink? Aubrey's? Yeah, I wasn't going to focus on that for too long.

It was creepy and... sweet? I tested that last word. Creepy seemed almost too dark and sweet too light. Nonetheless, I legit didn't know what to label his choices. Throw in the fact the man bought me *underwear* and *bras*... and got my sizes right? It was too much.

Aubrey's phone buzzed. She checked it. "Dix landed. It'll

be a couple of hours, maybe more, but he'll be here. I can't believe he got a flight that fast. I don't even want to think what he had to pay to get on the flight."

Me neither. I glanced around our suite then back at her. We needed to...

"I'll call down and get him a room. Then I'm getting us more food. How's the throat?"

I tested it. "Still hurts." It sounded garbled, raw, and frog-gish. It also definitely didn't feel pleasant to talk.

"Honey," she announced. "We're also gonna call Dr. Don."

I made a face. Doctor Don was the physician who'd actu-ally traveled halfway around the world when we'd all gotten sick while in Japan. He'd stuck with us through the Asian leg of our tour, until we headed to South America. He'd also been the one who treated Yvette when she had to have her tonsils out.

He specialized in singers. Aubrey was right. Granted, it hadn't even been a full twenty-four hours, but my voice was instrumental to my work. Maybe I should look at investing my money and being a little more cautious.

While she made calls, I turned on the television. It had been a while since I'd even checked the news for sightings of me. Honestly, I preferred to not know what the press knew or what they were speculating. It was just easier that way.

Jackie indicated there were hints on the gossip sites, but our early evening news—a local broadcast—had the fire at the school as their lead story. Images popped up on the screen, offering footage from cell phone cameras. It was *weird* to see some of it play out on the screen.

It was dark, the flashes of light, the ominous oranges and all the smoke. There was Ramsey... I sat forward as the camera tracked him heading straight inside. He didn't slow down.

Even when he came back out helping people, he rushed back in again.

He was safe. He'd even gotten out of the hospital before I did, but I was holding my breath when he went back inside *again*. Dressed only in what had to be pajama bottoms and a t-shirt, he lost the shirt on one of the trips.

Hand over my mouth, I waited when he plunged back inside. Aubrey was there, and Gentry, as well as Madison. They'd gotten out—and then he was carrying me out. Me and one of my guitars.

"He went back for the other one," Aubrey said when the screen cut back to the anchors. The pair of guitar cases were sitting near the bar. I hadn't opened them, but they were here. "I know how important they are to you, but I'm going to stress to you right now...they are not worth your life."

"Maybe," I forced the word out and when Aubrey glared at me, I shook my head. One of those guitars had been a gift from Dad. It was the first and only instrument he'd ever given me. It had been a gift to him from *his* father. I'd written the first three Torched songs on it.

I needed that guitar. The second one had been the first instrument I bought myself with the money *we* earned from our first album.

They meant the world to me, and I couldn't replace either of them.

Not really.

With a sigh, Aubrey came to sit next to me and wrapped an arm around my shoulders. "I'm with Yvette, you scared the shit out of me."

"Sorry," I whispered but it still came out hoarse. "I couldn't leave them."

"I know," she said with a long sigh even as her cell began to ring—well sing. She answered it without looking. Yvette stared up at us from the screen.

"I've decided that you two need to ditch that school and just come up here to live with me. Or we can go back to California. Fuck it, we can move to France or Australia, just away from that insanity."

"What happened now?" Aubrey asked when Yvette took a breath. "I mean, it's only been..."

I held up all five fingers. We'd talked to her five hours earlier.

"Yeah, it's only been five hours."

Yvette rolled her eyes and glared at us. "That school has been nothing but problems for Kait, and not worth the level of shit you have to deal with in those boys. Not to mention, they're talking about *arson*."

I coughed, but it was Aubrey who said, "They haven't released a conclusive statement about arson, only that they are investigating all possible causes. They don't know what caused the fire and fires suck, but it's not a reason to dump and run."

"I knew you would say that," Yvette practically sulked, but I adored her for being so worried about us.

"We're fine," I promised.

"You do not *sound* fine." Yvette sniffed. "You could finish your degree quickly online, then we could do just about anything else. Or if you really want the "school experience," we can choose a different one without all the baggage."

I sighed. "We could," I said, earning me a startled look from Aubrey. "Although I like this school—even with the stupid stuff." I coughed, then took another drink of water to clear my throat. "Archie used to go here. There's a Grayson building for Frankie's family. I know they aren't here now..."

"But it feels like them." Aubrey groaned then shoved off the sofa when a knock sounded at the door. She left me with the phone.

"I'm worried about you," Yvette said. "Those stupid letters and notes. The emails. Now a fire?"

"The Forever Fan stuff is getting picked up by management." Those letters increased over the summer. They seemed to come from a lot of different locations. Too many. The threats varied from creepy to just weird. "Why would they burn down our dorm?"

It didn't even make sense. Aubrey returned with a rolling table loaded with our food. "Maybe because he kept bitching that we weren't touring."

"Yeah, a fire is gonna hurry me right back into a recording studio."

"Not right now," Yvette said. "And stop trying to talk. You're making my throat hurt."

I smiled at her.

"How about you guys just come up here for a few days while school is sorting things out? Come stay with me."

I would love to, but we had so much to do. Clothes to buy, supplies to replace, and my books... fuck.

Slumping back on the sofa, I made a face.

"What?" Aubrey asked, worry in her eyes.

"My laptop," I said. "I can't remember if I saved that paper to the cloud and all our books." The school liked to give us summer assignments to warm us up for the year.

Her grimace matched my own.

"I'll order your books," Yvette said. "It will give me something to do. You're going to need uniforms and regular clothes. You left stuff here. Want me to send it down?"

That led to a debate about what we needed and when we needed it. Eventually, they made me shut up entirely and write things down.

By the time we finished the call, we had a plan...and it was almost time for Dix to get there. While I normally just liked Dix, right now, I was aching to see him. I just wanted to have a little calm and certainty back.

That would help. Course, we still had to sort out where we

would be rooming. More clothes shopping, uniforms, books, electronics...

I glanced at the running clothes.

More douchebags.

Eleven

JONAS

Three days. Three days after the fire, I caught sight of blue hair ahead of me in the hall. I forgot to breathe for a full minute until she turned and I could verify it was her.

She was back, and she was okay. She and her bandmate were both in uniforms, so they'd gotten those sorted. That was good. I followed along with the steady flow of students into the auditorium. This was the largest of the three on campus. I doubted we needed this much space, except they'd summoned the entirety of the junior and senior classes.

KC's dorm housed maybe a hundred and fifty girls... did we really need a meeting of both full years? When the object of my study settled on the far left side of the auditorium toward the back, I slid into the row a couple behind theirs.

I considered sitting right behind them, but I wasn't sure what to say to her about the fire. All Ramsey had said was she would be fine. I hadn't asked Lachlan, and I was pretty sure I didn't care what he thought.

The hum of conversation rose and fell as people shared distraught stories about the fire, what they lost, or how much they'd "freaked" out when they heard about how bad it was. What happened to...?

Yeah, I didn't care about those people. Tuning them out, I kept my attention riveted on KC as she gathered up her length of blue hair and pulled it into a ponytail. Unlike everyone else, KC and her bestie said nothing.

It was one of the things I noticed about her during that first semester. Well, I'd actually clocked the behavior, the lack of verbal reactions during that first semester. Even in my limited interactions with her, she didn't say much. I thought it had to do with her attitude toward us and toward "peons."

The fact that she'd told me to take a picture that one day, because it would last longer, stood out. Terse, but not unfriendly. Direct, but not inviting me to get closer. It took a while for it to hit me.

I'd made her uncomfortable.

But she didn't talk a lot. To me or anyone else. I had enough classes with her to see her interactions. Her disappearance on our joint assignment had irked me, but I turned her in. The baffling part was that when I tried to make things square, she didn't turn me in.

She did the work, with no complaints, then put my name on it. I didn't deserve the grade. She had the opportunity to get even and just didn't. Her words haunted me...

"Because it was a joint project, and you picked me for your partner." She shrugged like it wasn't important at all. *"I turned it in. It's done. If you have a problem with the research or the video, you had plenty of time to object—or even, you know—show up. But you were too busy doing whatever it was you were doing."*

That didn't make any sense. I screwed her grade. She should have taken the opportunity to pay me back in kind. I would have deserved it. "That's not a reason."

"No." And she glared at me. "That is a reason. It was my reason. You don't have to like it. Hell, you don't even have to believe me. I don't care. Trust me when I say you've beaten the give-a-shit right out of me this semester. It's done, it's turned in. If we fail, we fail together. If we get an A, we get that together, too. You want to be a dick—knock yourself out. I have better things to do."

The spark of irritation in her eyes had almost been worth the confusion. Still, the more I learned about her, the more she didn't fit into any of the ideas we had about her. She wasn't arrogant or stuck-up. She didn't seem to crave attention; if anything, she shrank from it.

The sex tape breaking had left her the butt of every Tom, Dick, and prankster on campus. *That* wasn't her fault. She wasn't in the tape. She didn't release the tape. She didn't deserve the mockery.

Still...until I gave her the music, we had *nothing* to talk about. Or maybe we did but...

"Please, finish taking your seats, ladies and gentlemen. We have a lot to cover." The school's dean—or one of them, since each "school" under the prep umbrella had their own dean—took the podium. "Now, people."

His somewhat nasally voice cut through the crowd's murmurs, gradually silencing them as the chairs filled in. No one sat next to me.

Good.

KC had rolled her head back to stare up at the ceiling and whatever her friend said to her made her smile briefly. Too briefly. Then she turned her face completely away as she focused on the stage.

"Thank you all for coming on short notice," the dean said, giving all of us a look over the rim of his glasses. "I also see dress code being adhered to…” He seemingly pinned a look on the row of jocks who were either still in pajamas or their workout gear. “By most of you. Gentlemen, you four,” he continued with a motion to that row of jocks. “Come see me when this is done.”

The crowd rumbled with laughter at them being called out. Not that it seemed to bother the jocks. Why would it? Prep didn’t make sports any less important. The jocks at the school pretty much got to do what they wanted.

“Now, there have been a lot of questions regarding housing following the incident at Apollo/Volusia One.”

Incident? Burned to the ground seemed to rate more than an “incident.” No one asked me. Movement to my right had me flicking a look over to where Ramsey had come to stand just inside. Dressed in his suit, he looked more like the faculty than an RA. You’d never know he was only four years older than me.

Asshole.

He didn’t seem to notice me. His attention was on the same row mine had been. Irritation scraped under my skin.

“We appreciate your patience as we worked out the best plan to accommodate so many shifts…”

The man droned on in his explanation of how they arrived at their decision. No one cared. They just wanted the information and then to get back to it.

Wait…

What did he say?

“…just because we will be reorganizing current housing assignments to co-ed, this will not change our rules on fraternization or on behavior. If anything, we expect the Blue Ivy Way to be the guiding principle for your interactions. Juniors and seniors, you will also be reorganizing. All juniors currently housed in…”

The groans and the laughter came in equal measure. Co-ed

dorms. It wasn't like we had communal showers. That wasn't the problem. Juniors were all being rehoused out of my dorm to a different one. Yeah, I didn't care.

I wasn't moving. But did that mean KC was moving into *my* dorm?

I couldn't quite wrap my head around the concept. Curiously, I didn't mind it at all, though. If she were in my dorm, it would be easier to—

A shout went up, dragging my attention back to the room. "Are you kidding?" one girl yelled. "You can't force us to share even the bedrooms in the suites..."

It took a moment for what I'd missed to filter back into my brain. Instead of two to a suite, there may be as many as four. Not in all cases, but it was to accommodate the moving of just under two hundred students into a more confined set of spaces.

"The assignments," the dean continued, raising his voice to talk over student objections, "have been made. Log in to your student portal on your phones, and you will find your new assignments. Electronic keys will be accessible via your phones for move-in purposes, then you can pick up physical keys later..."

The number of protests continued to climb, yet the dean didn't appear swayed. Out of curiosity, I checked my phone. Room hadn't changed, nor had the number of students assigned to it.

I glanced over at Ramsey. He hadn't seemed to notice me. If he had anything to do with the assignments, he probably made sure no one else was in my room. I wasn't sure whether to thank him or punch him.

I could do both, I supposed.

Eventually, the assembly was dismissed. Classes would begin on Thursday. It gave everyone present about thirty-six hours to get moved and settled. Students requiring more time would be granted it only on a case-by-case basis.

Oh, and there was a new therapist available to discuss the trauma with them. That was time for me to go. I had zero interest in hearing about anyone coming to talk to us about our feelings. I moved to the back of the hall but kept an eye on KC and her bestie. When they went out a side door, I left through the back and found a way to trail them.

Better to make sure they got to where they were going. A blond guy was waiting for them. KC actually broke from her friend to give him a hug and she smiled for real.

I had no idea who he was, until he turned. She had her phone out and was talking to Dix—that was his name—, then he motioned to where a truck waited in the circular drive.

Rather than get caught staring, I retreated back to my dorm. Yeah, I'd figure out where they got assigned later. I'd just tapped my card key when a familiar, if too scratchy, voice said, "Hey, Hot Shot, can you hold that for a sec?"

I turned to find KC striding toward me. All the words I'd considered saying earlier crumbled. So I just stared and waited.

"Thanks," she said with a flash of a smile, before covering her mouth with the inside of her elbow as she coughed. After, phone in hand, she glanced up at the map on the inside wall.

"What room?" It came out a little breathless, but she spared me a look.

"Four fourteen."

"That's across the hall from me," I told her, then motioned to the stairs. "Want me to show you?"

I was pretty sure she could find the room on her own, but I wanted to help.

"Thanks," she croaked out again with a grimace.

"I have water, too," I said, jerking my thumb to the stairwell.

Her smile was more of a grimace, but she didn't say anything. How badly had her throat been hurt? Was she going to have issues performing? Concern raced like a fire consuming fuel through me. The analogy made me grimace again.

Taking the stairs here meant avoiding going by Ramsey's suite. If Lachlan was there, I wanted to skip dealing with him. We were almost to the top when she paused and glanced down the staircases to call, "Up here."

The sound was horrendous. "You need to stop talking," I told her. "Or see a doctor. That sounds bad." Why hadn't they done more to help her?

"Thanks." The absolute lack of irony as she gave me a bland look was almost funny.

Almost.

"There," I told her when we got to her room. "I'll be right back."

Then I moved to four-eleven, my suite, across the hall from hers. Once inside, I dropped my bag then went to the kitchen. The fridge had been stocked so I pulled out two one-liter bottles of cold water and carried them back to the open door.

"This one," KC was saying to Dix, where she stood by the open door.

"They moved everyone out fast," he commented, and I stared at him where he stood so close to KC. He was taller than her, *older* too. Way too old to be looking at her the way he was. Dislike licked through me. "Okay, gorgeous, park that ass somewhere and rest. We'll get everything up here and get you moved in."

"I can—"

"Do nothing," he told her firmly, then cut a look at me. He lifted his chin. "You have an admirer."

She wasn't the only one giving him a bland look for that.

Older than both of us. Too old to look at her like that. Body-guard? Friend? Was she sure about that?

When KC glanced at me, I held out the water bottle word-lessly. "You're welcome," I said before she could try to talk.

"Be right back, sweetheart," the guy said before he headed for the stairs.

KC stared after him for a minute, then down at the water bottle I gave her. She twisted it open and gave me a faint smile.

"Don't talk," I suggested. "Do you need anything—"

"You have got to be fucking kidding me," a screech cut through the hall, and I flinched. Payton Webber had the *worst* voice, and it didn't matter whether she was getting fucked or trying to fuck someone over, she always sounded so goddamn irritating.

Hands on her hips, she faced off against KC. Behind her were a pair of movers with boxes stacked on a dolly. She glanced at the dorm room, then back at KC.

Oh.

They were going to be roomies.

Oh.

KC's expression blanked and she said nothing, but there had been a fire in those icy eyes before the shutters came down.

This was going to end in blood.

Twelve

KC

Thank fuck for Dix. He handled the overwrought Payton's bullshit so much better than me. Aubrey and I just decided to share a room, and that meant one bed would go into storage and we would share one, or we could just get two smaller beds later. For now, sharing a king wouldn't kill us.

That put us in one bedroom of the suite and Payton in the other. What started as an exercise in just getting everything inside to sort later turned into a sniping argument.

Our choice in sofas was a little pedestrian. Why fabric and not leather? We weren't putting that rug down, were we? She would prefer no dairy in the fridge at all. Also, only organics.

A headache pulsed behind my eye as she kept it up. "You know," Dix said conversationally. "If we stuffed a gag in her mouth and put her in the closet, I doubt anyone would notice."

Snickering, I shook my head. "Trust me, you notice when golden silence hits."

He rubbed my shoulder. "Hang in there."

I did not want to be that diva who demanded a change right after we got assigned to our new suite, but I'd almost take the janitor's closet over this.

"If you're just going to stand around and do nothing, could you at least do it in your room where I don't have to trip over or look at you?"

"Did you have to practice getting your voice to hit that note? Or is it naturally shrill?" 'Cause I'd heard out-of-tune guitars with better pitch.

Eyes narrowed, Payton raised her eyebrows as she straightened and put her hand on her hip. "You sound like the gutter trash whore your mother is... oh wait, I forgot, she's the high-end porn star trash. My mistake."

The smug little smile just put her over the top.

"Honestly, you think 'your mama' jabs are gonna get to me?" Did I like that Mom had that reputation? Of course not. Was Payton getting on my nerves? Yes, she absolutely was. Did I intend to react to every insult involving my parents? Fuck no, I would not.

She gave an airy little sniff. "I'm sure you're used to the view from down there... though I do have to wonder if you and your mother have similar tastes? Maybe why Daddy Dearest prefers the new wife's kids to his own child. Care to comment?"

"Does your ass ever get jealous of the shit that comes out of your mouth?" To be fair, I was genuinely curious. The sudden pink flush to her face amused me. Her nostrils flared and her eyes widened, then the door pushed open, letting in all the sound from the hall.

The volume of sound from so many disparate conversations coupled with the rolling squeak of carts, the thump of boxes, and the steady cadence of feet rushed into the suite like a rising tide.

"Coffee maker is here," Dix announced. "Executive decision time, you need some caffeine." He carried the huge box balanced on one shoulder. The Brevilles were really heavy when boxed up. The fact he handled it so readily impressed me. At the counter, Dix didn't wait for someone to clear away the bags of...whatever the fuck was in the organic sacks, before he shoved it all to the side and in the sink.

"Do you mind?" Payton charged toward him, but Dix barely spared her a look.

"Not in the slightest. You can empty your bags from right there as easily as from up here." Then he went to unpacking the box.

Payton gave him an incensed look. "Do you have any idea who I am?"

"A pain in the ass?" Dix retorted, his tone far milder than the sarcastic look on his face. "Some of us are working, either go coordinate your movers or just get out of the way."

Her mouth opened and closed, before she wrenched her gaze in my direction.

"Don't look at me, I'm fine with you going away and never coming back." Facts were facts. I needed to stop letting her provoke me, cause the hoarseness of my voice might be "better" but my throat wasn't healed yet.

With a little squeal of indignation, she flounced off to her room. The minute her door slammed shut, I rubbed a hand over my face.

"Kill me," I muttered.

"Nope," Dix told me. "I'll have this set up in a minute. Aubrey is heading to the bookstore to pick up all your texts, and the new laptops should have arrived, but she has to sign for them at the mail room."

That was good. We'd ordered them as soon as it hit both of us ours were gone. "Can I help...?"

"No," Dix said, catching my arm and turning me around.

He gave my ass a slap. "Go sit down and rest. You've been over-doing it all day."

I barely felt the pat but I flipped him off before I went and fell on the sofa. It wasn't that comfortable. Not like the old one.

Bummer.

It seemed to take Dix no time at all to get the coffee maker set up. Then the sound of the beans grinding was like heaven. Within a few minutes, he presented me with hot foamy goodness.

"Thank you," I mouthed more than said.

"My pleasure. More to haul up. We're having to take turns with the other movers so we don't clog up the stairs."

I savored another long sip of the coffee. Fuck, it was perfect. Dix even bought the right beans. Maybe Aubrey was right, we should ask Dix to stay for a while. That seemed a lot for someone who lived in California. He'd do it, if I asked, but the chaos of the school year was already a little out of control.

Speaking of chaos...

Coffee on the table, I grabbed my guitar cases and carried them to the room Aubrey and I would share. The closet wasn't really designed for two, but we could make it work. We had on the tour bus.

A knock in the other room tugged at my attention, but I was stowing my guitars first. The murmur of voices—one male and one female—drifted into the room. It sounded like Payton was talking to someone, so I ducked into the bath-room to pee real quick and wash my hands while she was distracted.

I hadn't closed the door to my room so I got there to see Payton practically rubbing against Ramsey, with her arms around his neck.

"You have to do something, Ramsey," Payton half-moaned. Disgust curled through me at the simpering tone pushing up the words. "I need to feel safe and I'm not going to do that having to room with *her*."

"Payton…"

"Please…" She pushed herself into him even as he backed up a step. Neither one of them were looking at me. To be honest, they weren't looking at each other either. Ramsey was trying to get her hands off of him, and he was carefully *not* touching her anywhere but her hands.

The leech, on the other hand, was practically dry humping his leg.

"Imagine," she said. "We get rid of her, then I'm right here in your building…and I'd be so grateful."

I gagged. That was… disgusting.

Ramsey jerked free of her hold and Payton stumbled almost gracelessly. "Do you mind?" she snapped at me. "We are trying to have a private conversation!"

"Is that what the kids are calling it these days?" I shook my head. "Maybe close a door or two if you want to keep it private." I didn't focus on Ramsey or the stiffness in his posture. Course, my disdain lost some power when I coughed. I fought against the tickle setting me off.

I owed him a thank you, but I wasn't doing it now and I wasn't doing it in front of her skankiness. Retrieving my coffee, I detoured the long way around the room to head to the kitchen.

"Ladies," Ramsey said. "We'll be having a dorm meeting this evening in the first floor entertainment lounge. I expect to see you both there…"

"I wouldn't miss it," Payton practically cooed.

I rolled my eyes but fought for a neutral expression as I faced him. It was the first time I'd really *seen* him since returning to school. Yes, he'd gotten me out of the burning building. I had a vague memory of him carrying me out. Of the guitar…

Then nothing.

The last time I saw him, he probably didn't remember. Dad. He and Dad were close. That much had been clear. That also killed any desire to open up a dialogue. "I'll be there." I managed to push those out.

"Good." He frowned. "You feeling okay?"

"I'm great. Thanks." Then because he started it, I added, "You?"

"I'm fine." He gave me a faint, if polite smile. The smile deepened a fraction and it softened some of the harder lines to his face. Had he grown more stern over the summer? Or was it just all the current chaos?

Also, why did he still have to be so hot? Dix arrived, giving me something else to focus on. "More furniture coming up in a minute," he said, before carrying the box toward the bedroom Aubrey and I would be sharing.

Instead of leaving, Ramsey frowned at Dix. Not that Dix gave a damn. He walked out of my room and glanced at me.

"That's not resting." He pointed toward the sofa. "Take it easy."

At the door, he paused when Ramsey stepped into his path. "I'm the RA for this building," he said. "Ramsey Malone. You are?"

Dix didn't even slow down, cutting around Ramsey and out the door. It left Douchebag Two with no choice but to follow him if he wanted more answers.

I blew out a breath, but a hand slapped against my shoulder in a shove from behind. Stumbling a step, I turned to find Payton invading my space.

"You're going to keep your slutty hands off Ramsey," she practically snarled the words in warning. "He doesn't want you. He doesn't even like you. You're just his stepfather's spoiled little bastard. Stay. Away. From. Him."

Flecks of spit landed against my face as she yelled at me.

Yeah...

She raised her hands as if to shove me again.

No.

I raised an arm, using my hand and wrist to divert her shove away from me. It was her turn to stumble this time. She let out a little sound of outrage. Or maybe she just screamed.

I didn't care.

When she whirled around to face me, I slapped her right across the face. The blow made my palm burn and then she charged at me. My coffee cup went flying. Splattering us with espresso, milk, and chocolate.

What a waste. Her slaps landed, but so did mine. I got a fistful of her hair and jerked her around. Yanking her stupid blonde hair, I shoved her forward at the same time. She bounced against the sink.

She fumbled for something in the sink and I dodged the bottle of shampoo she flung at me. It hit the wall with a noisy thud. Then she threw a few more items. I blocked one and dodged another. The third hit my wrist hard enough to bruise and pain shot through my hand.

Bitch.

The water was on in the sink and I grappled with her, twisting her arm in a painful fashion to get her to drop the next item she planned to throw. The sink was filling up with water and I shoved her—face down—into it.

Her screams were silenced for a moment as she flailed and water went everywhere. Twice she shoved back at me and the third time, my hands slipped and she caught me in the cheek with her elbow.

I staggered back. Pain bloomed in my face, but I curled the fingers of my right hand into my palm and got my thumb out of the way.

We'd all learned to jab, hit, and defend ourselves. Just a fact of life on the road. I punched her. It magnified the pain in my hand, but watching her go down was satisfying as fuck.

One moment she was glaring up at me, and then she let out a real scream as she rushed toward me. I never got to make contact because an arm wrapped around my waist and hauled me upward.

Ramsey was between us, he had a hold of Payton, dragging her back as Dix all but carried me to the other side of the room and put himself between me and everyone else.

The others included Aubrey who stood in the doorway, her expression a comical mixture of shock and fury. What startled me was Jonas stood right next to her, the scowl on his face terrifying.

Thank fuck he wasn't staring at me, but at his *brother* and the little bitch determined to hump both of his brothers.

"What the hell is going on?" Ramsey demanded.

"She attacked me," Payton screamed, instantly bursting into tears. "She was going to kill me." Then she threw herself at him and despite the pain in my face and my hand, I just rolled my eyes.

"She's a psychopath," I said without an ounce of her manufactured dramatics. "No fucking way am I sharing a room with her..."

Or anything else.

Ever.

<h1 style="text-align:center">Thirteen</h1>

RAMSEY

Determination, not rage, flooded KC's eyes. The red mark on her cheek promised a bruise, water splattered her shirt, there was coffee on the floor, and the air around her solidified from chaos to almost tranquil.

It didn't matter what happened next, she'd made up her mind. I could read it in the lift of her chin, the professional mask sliding over her face and the total lack of tears and weepiness. Payton, if anything, seemed to grow louder. The fact she sniffled against me was uncomfortable enough. Add in the soaking wet hair and the water trail it created on my clothes just added to the overall unpleasantness. Combine all of that with the total *lack* of dramatic meltdown coming from KC and it was a stark contrast.

"Rooms are at a premium," Aubrey said slowly. "Not sure we're gonna find an empty..."

"I have one," Jonas offered. I wasn't the only one who jerked my gaze to him. Payton sniffled *loudly* and straightened.

"Thank you, Jonas," she said in that tear-soaked voice. "I accept."

"No," Jonas said abruptly and with his characteristic lack of tact. "Not you. KC. KC can stay in my suite. There's a whole empty room there."

Fuck...

I barely had time to process that before Payton started sobbing all over again. The sound was...*obnoxious.*

"Why?" The question came in that husky, smoke-damaged voice. It was hard to believe the sound came from the same person who sang some of the fluffiest pop songs. It also made me hurt for her.

"What?" Jonas pivoted to face her.

"Why are you inviting me to stay?"

Because he was absolutely crazy about her. The crush had been troublesome in the beginning, then downright dangerous as Jonas had grown more and more obsessed.

KC moving in with him was not the best idea. He didn't always handle emotional conflict well, especially when he wasn't sure how he should react. Jonas didn't process like the rest of us. Not normally a problem, but the last year it had escalated into violence...

"If we have to," I said slowly. "KC can stay with me. The RA suites are larger..."

The look KC sent me was not encouraging. The sobs from Payton cut off, she lifted her face. The faint redness to her eyes the only real betrayal of her tears. With her palms, she wiped her damp cheeks.

"Why can't I stay with you?" Payton demanded, genuine hurt in her voice. Payton really needed to stop all of this. It was one thing to be playful, but this was not that. "Then the anti-social bitch can stay here with her bitchy friend."

"Girl," Aubrey Miller said in a flat tone. "Do not drag me into this fight. You will not enjoy my reaction."

"Oh, shut up," Payton snapped. "No one asked you."

"Tell you what," the guy standing way too fucking close to KC said. "Why don't we just press charges and take care of the problem entirely. Pretty sure the school isn't going to let an assault just slide past."

Oh, that had clusterfuck written all over it.

"She started it," Payton shrilled as she pulled away completely. I wasn't the only one wincing at the sound. "She thinks she's so damn precious. But I saw how she was looking at her *stepbrothers*. Makes me think she's a—"

"Payton," I said, my temper slipping. She blinked up at me, all woeful and teary-eyed. "Stop."

The last thing we needed was for this altercation to go public. Payton *loved* a platform. With the fire and the circling press, she'd find one, too.

"Why don't we all take a breath," Aubrey suggested. I hadn't spoken much to KC's bandmate. Her concern, though, remained fixed on her friend. That made sense. KC didn't sound great, even if she looked better than I expected. "Dix...if we had to rearrange some stuff, can the movers stick around to help or do we need to do it ourselves?"

"I'll take care of everything," *Dix* said. If I had to peg him at an age, he was at least a couple of years older than me. Definitely too old to be acting so possessive about KC.

Far too damn old.

But rather than be dissuaded by my look, he kept himself between all of us and KC. His arms were folded, and the intense dislike in his eyes when he glanced at Payton would be troublesome if she weren't being such an annoying twit at the moment.

"Great," Aubrey said, then pivoted to Jonas. "Answer KC's question, please. Why are you offering?"

He shifted his stance, a flicker of unease in his expression as he raked a hand through his hair and then shrugged. "I have the room. She's my stepsister. The school will approve it. Then she doesn't have to deal with Payton and you're still right across the hall."

It was so... *reasonable*. Who was he and what had he done with my hot-headed baby brother? I gaped at him, but Jonas just ignored me.

"There's plenty of room," he told KC. "You can bring your furniture if you want. Most of my stuff doesn't take up the whole suite."

Not that hers did, but he grimaced at the wording. I was right there with him. Payton sniffled again, her tears had evaporated and her expression had soured the longer it went on.

"Fine, move in with your stepbrother," she said. "Maybe Daddy will want to see you then or at least, not forget you the next time he shows up."

"Bitch," Aubrey said, taking a step toward her. "Shut up before I sew your mouth shut for you."

"Did you hear her?" Payton demanded. "She just threatened me."

"Nope," Dix said. "Didn't hear a thing. Maybe you should go see someone if you're hallucinating. It's never a good sign."

That wasn't supposed to be funny, but a flicker of laughter seemed to chase across KC's rather gloomy expression, and I hated that Dix had been the one to coax that expression to life.

Hated him.

Shaking off that somewhat irrational reaction, I tried to focus on what was at hand. "We can look into alternative spaces."

We didn't really have a lot of options at the moment. There were two older buildings closed for renovations, so space truly was at a premium after the fire. Lachlan staying with me was a problem, but Jonas would kill him if Lachlan was in their room so that left...

"Or she can just stay with me," Jonas said. "It really

doesn't involve you." The snap was directed at me, when Payton looked like she was going to say something he just turned away from her. "KC? If you want? I can help move your stuff."

Fuck, this had disaster written all over it.

Rather than answering immediately, KC glanced at Aubrey. The two girls just stared at each other for a long moment, then Aubrey shrugged.

"Not a huge fan either, but I will be right here. It'll be almost like rooming together." There seemed so much more meaning to the way she said that, but I didn't know the possible context or details.

"Temporarily," KC said. Her poor voice. The more she spoke the worse she sounded. Yes, we needed to wrap this up so she could rest. "We will work on alternatives, but I can't sleep in here."

"Let's get your things..." Aubrey said, but KC didn't turn away immediately. Instead, she eyed Jonas.

"Are you sure?"

"Yes." Zero hesitation. "What do you want me to carry?"

That seemed to galvanize everyone. Dix headed for the coffee maker, while Aubrey and KC went to their bedroom and Jonas eyed the boxes. When KC came out with both guitars, I rubbed a hand over my face. They were the reason she'd passed out. The need to hang onto them.

When Jonas offered to take them, she startled me when she allowed it. The hesitation ended. Then she was going back for more things and Dix was carrying the coffee maker across the hall.

"So that's it, she just gets to move in with Jonas? No repercussions?" Payton sounded very unhappy.

"Listen," I told her, pitching my voice low. "Do you really want to start a 'she said, she said' war with her? Right now, you don't have a lot of allies. Let this go."

Shock and outrage chased themselves across her expression before she flounced away and disappeared into her bedroom, slamming the door to mark her exit.

Thank fuck. I didn't want to deal with her. KC and Aubrey passed with bags of clothes and one suitcase.

I picked up a box and carried it over, stepping aside as they exited and headed back to the other room.

Jonas stood in the middle of the sitting room area, arms folded, while Dix set up the coffee maker. The girls came back a couple of times, then another pair of movers showed up carrying a bed that they directed in here.

When Dix finally left, giving me a few moments with Jonas, I turned to him.

"Don't," he said, folding his arms. "I don't care what you have to say, and I sure as shit am not talking to you still."

Rubbing my chin, I shook my head. "Yeah, this isn't an option, J. You need to tell me you can handle her living in this suite. This isn't like being stuck with her in your classes. This is day in and day out. Granted, we might be able to find something else sooner rather than later, but..."

"If I couldn't handle it, I wouldn't have invited her."

Except, he had a huge crush on her and a bad temper where she was involved. It didn't help that all of last year seemed to see him bounce from one unstable emotional island to another. I didn't want him hurting anyone, but especially not himself.

"There's thinking you can and then there's actually having to handle it. You won't have any privacy."

"I have a door." He nodded to his room. "So does she."

I sighed. "Can you please not be argumentative to just be argumentative? I'm worried about you."

"Don't bother, I can take care of myself." Belligerence pumped up every word. "While you're at it, why don't you go get fucked and take Lachlan with you?"

That headache stabbing behind my eye seemed to balloon. "Jonas, I'm still the RA for this building and as such, I'm still responsible for you…"

"And about two hundred plus other students. Maybe more, since they are getting crammed three and four to a room. Go hover over them. I'm not interested in you or anything you have to say."

When the Dix fellow returned, he had a table, followed by another sofa…Jonas had a couple of chairs, but they were for video games. The movers returned with another bed. They didn't have to haul out an old mattress from the second room, because Jonas had never let them move it back in.

Soon as they dropped off another set of boxes, they vanished out the door and down the stairs.

Jonas glanced back at me. "Are you done?"

"No, I'm worried about you. Your temper. Your depression…she's not been great for you." A lot of these problems had started when KC arrived at the school. Intellectually, I got it that Jonas' behavior was not her responsibility, but it didn't change the fact that she affected him.

She affected Lachlan, too. One of us needed to keep our damn head.

"Tell you what, I'm gonna be great. You have nothing to worry about. She might be a bitch, and she might be the worst, but she's way better than you and Lachlan. I'll take a bald-faced bitch over a back-stabbing brother any day."

I winced at the word choice as KC returned. Jonas scowled, then lifted his chin as if determined to own his statement.

She eyed me, then focused on Jonas. "We have a television and so do you—do you have a preference over which one to use?"

"This one is bigger," Dix said as he came in. "He can always take that smaller one to his room."

"Sure," Jonas said.

Raising her hands, KC backed away, then headed to her room. Aubrey followed behind her and then the door closed them in, leaving us with Dix.

I had questions for him, but Jonas cut me off with a look. "Pretty sure you have other people to check on," he told me. "Don't let the door hit you in the ass on the way out."

"Goddammit, Jonas," I swore and he shrugged. "We're not done with this conversation." I paused at Dix. "You have an hour left on campus, be sure to check out with me when you leave."

"Aye aye, Captain Douchebag."

The name gave me pause, and I pivoted to find him working on switching out the televisions and ignoring me. Not Jonas though, his lips twitched.

Captain Douchebag wasn't going anywhere.

Fine, he'd have to talk to me to call me names.

"One hour," I said, then stalked out without slamming any doors. No matter how frustrated I was, I had to demonstrate acceptable behavior and the Blue Ivy Way.

Kicking down her door and checking on her personally didn't qualify for that. Neither did dragging her down to my suite while tossing Lachlan up here or out.

Fuck, this was insane.

Fourteen

KC

After all the chaos, Dix made sure I had everything I needed. He also arranged for a new television to be delivered for Aubrey. When he offered another coffee maker, she turned it down and said she'd hit me up for espresso, 'cause fuck Payton.

I suggested we get "specialty" chocolates made just for the handsy bitch, but Aubrey nixed the idea *for now*. The emphasis on those last two words had made me laugh. Especially when she added, "I reserve the right to change my mind."

Honestly, as much as Hot Shot and his *brothers* pissed me off so much, I'd room with fucking Lachlan before I shared a suite with Payton Webber. I didn't hate many people. That cunt just radiated backstabbing bitch energy.

It was late by the time we got everything transferred over. Aubrey and I divided our time guarding things left behind, specifically so Payton couldn't get anywhere near them.

Thankfully, Jonas seemed to get that, and while we dealt with the room across the hall, he kept her out of his suite.

At some point, Captain Douchebag, thank you to Dix for that name, made himself absent. When I carried in a suitcase to find Jonas alone, I blew out a sigh of relief. He looked up from the notepad he was writing in. I just shook my head at the question in his eyes as I got the last of the things in.

By the time I'd unpacked, put things away, and made up my bed, it was time to send Dix away. We locked up both bedrooms then went out to dinner with him as a thank-you. It was almost ten when he dropped us off.

"Thanks, Dix," she told him. "You were a lifesaver today."

He lifted his chin.

Aubrey gave me a hug and said, "I'll see you tomorrow," before she headed upstairs without me. It wasn't until that moment that it hit me. Last year had been bearable at times because she was right there. My roommate. My best friend. One of the sisters of my heart.

Now?

I was going to be living with a boy. Making a face, I turned to find Dix watching me with concern. The worry flooding his eyes had me lifting my own chin as I shrugged. "It's going to be fine." Even after trying to baby my voice, it still came out gravelly.

"Who are you trying to convince? Me or you?"

"Not sure," I admitted, folding my arms. The front of the new dorm had a great view of the burnt-out husk of the old one. The smell of smoke lingered in the air. There were still floodlights up for the investigators. We'd seen the fire department out there several times during the day, clearing out more detritus. "Is it working?"

"You don't want me to answer that," Dix cautioned, then he leaned back against the car. "I'm sticking closer for the next couple of weeks."

Before I could protest, he held up a hand.

"Hear me out?" The careful phrasing made me swallow my objections.

"Yes."

"Thank you." He nodded to the building. "You have friends here, but you also have enemies."

Payton definitely qualified for the latter.

"Before that..." His expression darkened as he jerked his thumb at the destroyed dorm. "You had Aubrey at your back. Now you have this...punk ass kid."

"Jonas..." Then raised my hands when Dix pinned me with a look. He wasn't done.

"Now, you're separated, granted by a hallway, but it's still separation. You're never going to treat her room as a safe space because of the Queen of the Junior Cunt Society in there."

A laugh escaped me, and I clapped a hand over my mouth as Dix grinned. There was something that edged right on vicious in his smile. Although to be fair, I heard zero lies in what he said.

"That means you will be reliant on your own space more and more. Can you tell me, honestly, that you trust that boy?"

"No," I said with a slow shake of my head. "I have no reason to trust him. Except..." When his expression shifted, I raised my brows. I gave him his turn, so now it was mine. He exhaled sharply then motioned for me to continue. I wished it was more fun to exasperate him. "He didn't have to offer me that room."

As rough as my voice still was, it cracked on that sentence. I wasn't sure if that was the physical damage or the emotional questions I had.

"We're not friends. He's not pretending to be one either." That much was clear. He did *not* like Payton. So maybe it was just as simple as the enemy of my enemy... "He helped me last year... more than once."

"How?" At Dix's question, I shook my head.

"It doesn't matter." I covered my mouth with my fist as a cough escaped.

"That's enough talking," he cautioned. "Aubrey asked me to call Doctor Don. He'll be up here at the end of the week. I told him you didn't want to go into the city, but if this got worse, you *would*."

Translation, he would make sure I would go. Hence why he was staying...

"I'll be thirty minutes away," he pressed on. "Tops. Your new phone will be here tomorrow. I expedited it. If you need any help with the setup, let me know. Otherwise, I'll be back to get you to see Doctor Don, and we'll get all of this straightened out. Don't be surprised if the lawyers reach out to you, too..."

I frowned. "Why?"

"Because you got badly hurt on school property...that's a million dollar plus voice, sweetheart, and there is gonna be hell to pay for that."

Right. I didn't think about that. I'd call the lawyers since I didn't think we should be going after the school. It was a fire. Not negligence. Yes, I'd heard the rumors about arson too, but that didn't make it the school's fault.

"Now, take that gorgeous ass inside." He pushed off the car, then held out an arm. I returned the hug and sighed as he pressed a kiss to the top of my head. "Call me for anything. Think smart and be safe, okay?"

"I promise." I raised a hand before I headed up the steps. It shouldn't have surprised me to find Captain Douchebag waiting just inside. Nor that his position gave him a perfect view out the side windows to where I'd been saying good night to Dix.

Great. RA and stalker. What other skills was he hiding?

"It's after curfew," Ramsey said. His voice was a little

scratchy, but it had nothing on mine. I glanced at the wall clock and then back at him.

Curfew kicked in at ten.

It was five after.

I'd been back on campus and right at the building, just not inside.

Right.

"Not reporting you," he continued, seemingly not interested in glancing at the same clock. "Everyone has some adjustments to make, but rules are there for a reason."

I stared into the eyes of the guy who saved me. The same guy who'd actually gone out of his way the previous year. The teacher's assistant I'd nursed a crush on and tried to thank for all his help...

Yeah, the same guy who ripped into me about being a selfish bitch, all the while hiding the fact he was my stepbrother. No, I had little to say to him, and I didn't want to talk to him. So, I gave him a thumbs-up before I headed for the stairs.

"KC..."

Pausing, I didn't glance back so much as turn my head enough that he could tell I was listening. What was he going to tell me? My hair was against the school dress code? I was out of uniform? Oh, I knew.

Don't lead on my baby brother...

"My brother has his own issues..."

He doesn't need mine.

"I'd appreciate it if you would—" He exhaled and I waited. "Just...use caution."

Glancing over my shoulder, I raised my brows. Caution? For him? Or for me?

Only he was already shutting his door. I studied the whiteboard hanging off of it and his schedule, which was taped below it. RA and TA, not to mention a full-time college student...

Yeah, I didn't know what to do with any of that. Busy life choices weren't an excuse to be a dick.

Period.

Despite the co-ed nature of the "dorm," I'd kind of expected it to be noisier or busier, or maybe just weirder. Instead, it was almost silent as I reached the fourth floor. Maybe everyone else was having a shit week, too.

When I got to the new room, I paused for a second to eye the other door. Aubrey being behind that with *Payton,* of all people, stung. Yes, I'd chosen to move out, but I hated that she was stuck there. Hated more that we weren't rooming together.

Unease prickled through me, and I used the new key to unlock the door to Jonas'—and now my—suite. The interior was dim, with only a single light on the table next to the new sofa. The rearrangement of the furniture set up the room for the new television *and* the previous gaming chairs, as well as the sofa Dix got for me.

It was like my old one. I could curl up in the corner with a heating pad and ice cream to binge-watch once a month and it would be great.

The room was quiet.

Almost too quiet.

There was a faint scent of tacos in the air. Meat, spicy sauce, and the bag on the counter were from one of the local delivery places. Considering we just had dinner, I shouldn't be hungry, but it smelled great. Leaving the bag, I got a bottle of water from the fridge before heading to my door.

A sticky note was posted to it.

The bag of leftovers is for you. Wasn't sure what kind of tacos you liked so three crunchy and three soft. Take what you want. I can eat the rest tomorrow.

J.

Pivoting, I glanced back at the taco bag. He got me tacos?

We hadn't even had leftovers from dinner to bring back. I took a step back toward the little kitchenette. The idea of crunchy tacos was downright heavenly.

Then again...did I dare eat something I hadn't prepared or seen arrive?

I went back and forth on it so much, I almost gave myself a headache. The growling in my stomach would not be ignored so I retraced my steps, opened the bag and took out the three crunchy tacos. Then wrote a note on the little sticky notepad stuck to the fridge.

Thanks.

I posted it to his door before going back into my room. Once inside, I locked the door. I glanced at the bathroom that we would be sharing. I needed to pee, but...well, we hadn't discussed this part.

I peeked inside, but the door on his side was closed. Phew. I locked it then peed before I washed up and got ready for bed. I didn't unlock his side until I was done and heading back to my side of the room.

After devouring the tacos and the water, I went back in and brushed my teeth before crawling into bed. Exhaustion was right there but so were a million questions. I didn't have my phone to listen to for a distraction.

I thought it would take a while, but I passed out relatively fast. Coughing myself awake, I grimaced at the raw feeling in my throat. As much as I wanted to go running, probably not the best idea... yet.

Maybe a long walk, circling the mailroom so I could get my new phone as soon as it was here. For now, I got dressed and headed out to make coffee.

One for me. One for Aubrey. And a third for Jonas.

Hopefully, he drank what we did, because I had no idea.

The light knock on the door alerted me and I was ready with coffee in hand when I opened it to Aubrey.

She gave me a sleepy smile. "This is why I love you."

I grinned, turning to pull the door closed as the door to Jonas' room opened. He walked out, shirtless, running a hand through his disheveled hair.

"Morning," I said and regretted it almost instantly when he jerked his head up. The startled look on his face said he'd forgotten I might be out here. Right... I pointed to the coffee on the counter. "For you."

I toasted him with mine, then closed the door before he could say anything. Aubrey gave me a questioning look and I shrugged.

"Detente."

"If you say so." Then she hooked her arm through mine and we went off in search of food and to wait for my phone.

Fifteen

LACHLAN

Admissions had sent me to the college counselor, who sent me back to admissions. They were getting the paperwork sorted, and in the meanwhile, I got Coach to let me work on training the high school lacrosse team. I couldn't compete on it, but I could kick their sorry asses into shape. The junior class really didn't have anyone to take our places.

I staked out the running trails all week. Classes were officially back on, but there had been no sign of Ace at all. When I asked Ramsey about her, he'd just given me a look.

Fine, keep that shit to yourself. We'd also gotten into it about my stuff in his suite. I cleaned up, but it was never enough for Mr. Perfect. Yes, he got Ace out of the fire, and that definitely deserved some kudos, but he was being tightlipped about everything else.

He wasn't the only one. Weirdly, though, it was like Ace had developed some kind of early warning system. It was like I'd always *just* missed her.

Even the kid at the barista cart just gave me a smirk when I asked about her. No one else attending this school had blue hair. How was she proving so damn elusive? If it weren't so frustrating, I'd be enjoying the game of cat and mouse.

"Are you even *listening* to me?" Payton demanded. The nails-on-chalkboard-piercing nature of her voice dragged me back to where I was seated in the dining hall. I'd taken this spot so I could watch the main doors closest to the Apollo-Volusia dorms. It might be a stretch, but this seemed to be the right spot to catch her.

"No," I said. I'd forgotten she'd even joined me.

She huffed, impatience creasing her face. "Lachy..."

I downed the last dregs of my now cold coffee. "You know, I don't care. I have to go."

"You have got to be kidding me, I've spent the last ten minutes telling you about how horrible that bitch is, and you're just leaving?"

"What bitch?" I focused on her abruptly, skipping the rest of her statement.

"Oh my god, do you ever listen to me?" She threw her hands up and slouched into her seat.

Not if I could help it. But now she'd said one thing that prodded my interest. "What. Bitch." Hand on the table, I studied her eyes and the way the area around her mouth went white as she compressed her lips. The distinct layering of her cosmetics added to the smokey look around her eyes.

It was a little too dark for this early in the day, and I didn't really care, *except* I swore I could smell how much makeup she was wearing.

"The stupid rock star sister of yours who is now shacking up with your brother." Intense dislike rolled off of her.

"She's not my sister," I reminded her. Stepsister, fine. But not actual sister. We had zero DNA in common. Thank fuck, because the things I wanted to do with her were already illegal in some states. Biological relations would make it illegal just about everywhere.

"Whatever," Payton said with a sneer. "When we got reassigned, I was stuck with her and that cunt of a friend of hers."

"And?" I motioned at her to get a move on. I needed the info, not the dramatics.

"And, she tried to kill me."

I stared, fighting the urge to verbally smack her into moving it along. 'Cause, Ace was loaded with all kinds of fire and passion. But she wasn't a killer.

Then again, she had an awesome right hook and a vicious knee. So—maybe a killer. But Payton wasn't dead, so she couldn't have tried that hard.

"You don't believe me." Why did I ever think that pout of hers was sexy? Seriously. As she jutted out that lower lip at me and batted those too-long eyelashes, she didn't turn me on in the slightest. If anything, she just grated on my nerves.

"Didn't say that." I summoned every ounce of the patience I was rapidly running out of. "Just waiting for you to get back to the part about shacking up with my brother."

Payton and Ace as roommates was just all kinds of a bad idea. For me. For them. For everyone.

She held onto her silence for another long moment. Then the faint tremble to her lower lip ceased abruptly, and she sat forward. "All three of us were assigned to the same room. She came unglued and physically attacked me. I can't believe Rams didn't tell you."

I almost gagged at that name for my brother. But I managed to suppress it. Of course, Ramsey didn't say anything. Mr. Perfect would never reveal anything that involved a *private* incident. Especially if he had to report on it. There were nondisclosures involved.

Thankfully, I didn't need to sign that shit.

"So, he saved you?"

"Yes," Payton said, brightening a little. "He really did. Then Jonas...I think you're right about him being a little off, by the way."

Arms folded, I straightened. Not once had I ever brought up Baby J to her, and I wouldn't have.

"His room is right across the hall, and he just shows up while that bitch's pit bull is right there insulting me..."

"Wait, back up... pit bull?"

"Dix?" She made a face. Dix. I knew that name. That was the prick taking her to clubs. What the fuck was he doing *here*?

RJ was one problem. Now I had this Dix?

I fought the need to crack my knuckles.

Payton must have taken my silence as an acknowledgement as she pressed onward. Which was good, because I needed answers.

"*Anyway*, Jonas just comes over and invites her to move in with him. I thought he was going to offer it to me, to get me out of there." Why the fuck would she think that? Jonas couldn't stand her. A point he'd made clear whenever she tried to sleep over in our room.

Thankfully, 'cause it made it easier to shove her ass out the door, but that wasn't here or there. But he invited Ace to move in?

Relief tangled with irritation, but I ignored both for the moment. Now I knew where Ace was. I hadn't even known she was supposed to be rooming with Payton before.

"She agreed. Rams didn't like it either, but neither of them listened, and they just moved all her stuff across the hall. I'm still stuck with her bandmate, but I never see her, so that's something I suppose."

So just Ace and Jonas in the same suite?

Well, well, little bro? Color me impressed. I straightened, picking up my trash. I'd been looking for Ace all wrong.

"Where are you going?" Payton called, but I just lifted my hand in a half-wave after I tossed my trash. I had somewhere to be and it was Saturday morning. Jonas usually had studio time on Saturdays to work on music, which meant there was a solid chance that Ace was on her own.

I had a key to the room from the previous year. Hadn't bothered to turn it in. Planned to share the room again this year when I came back, but Jonas got all butt hurt at the end of last year and it was probably safer for both of us if we weren't occupying the same space.

My girl being there, though... that changed things.

Saturdays on campus in the early autumn term were fantastic. It was still warm enough that everyone was outside. You could find pick-up games. There were horses in the stables on the far side of the campus if you wanted to go riding. The indoor and outdoor pools were still open. Thankfully they warmed both, 'cause warm and warm enough to swim in were two different things.

This was my favorite time of year, usually, but I had a hard time focusing on anything beyond where Ace was and how she was doing. Even the news reports on her condition had been banal as fuck. She was released from the hospital.

That was it.

What the hell kind of report was that?

I held the door for a couple of girls as they came out and then continued inside and up the stairs. By the time I got to the fourth floor, the mixture of female and male voices coming from each of the floors as students came and went was amusing.

Why couldn't they have burned the dorm down last year when I was still a senior? Maybe I could be rooming with Ace.

I damn near missed the last step at that thought. Pulling my key out, I continued down the hall, tapping the card against the door lock and letting myself in.

While I'd been hoping to find her working or lounging in the front room, it was empty. Music filtered out of the bedroom.

My old bedroom.

Oh, that was even better. Ace was sleeping in my room. I liked that. The door to her room was also open. Jonas' was closed, but it was after ten.

He wasn't here. He booked the studio every weekend and vanished for hours at a time. That had to be where he was. It helped that one of his clubs involved musical theory.

I cleared my throat as I shut the door to the hall and made my way across the living room. At the door to her room, I paused at the flash of leg as she danced around on the far side of the bed. She was dressed in an oversized t-shirt that hit her mid-thigh, and while I didn't see any shorts, that didn't mean she wasn't wearing them.

The music was coming from a laptop sitting in the corner. It wasn't her music, however. Hers or the band's. There was a duo singing, male and female. I didn't know the voices...wait, did I?

Leaning against the doorframe, I drank in the sight of her rocking those hips and that ass. The muscles in her legs moved with every step. She seemed... skinnier somehow. She'd always been lean and fierce, but this was different. I couldn't put my finger on it.

"Fuck!" The shout yanked my attention up from her ass to her face, and I barely managed to get my hand up in time to catch the book she'd thrown at me.

"Damn, Ace." I grinned at the text. It was a heavy one. "Nice aim."

"What the fuck are you doing in here?" Her voice crackled like crunched paper. It was definitely not the usual dulcet tones I associated with her.

"Well," I said slowly, as she fisted her hand over her chest.

Maybe startling her had been a dick thing to do, but I couldn't resist this opening. "I came to see who was sleeping in my bed."

Her brows tightened as she twisted to hit the spacebar on her laptop and the music cut off abruptly. Then she stared at me. "This is my room now. And my bed. Trust me, I had a new mattress brought in, along with a brand-new bed. Even happier about it now."

"Ouch." The mock sigh didn't win me any points, so I just carried the flung textbook on governments around the world and set it on the bed. It had to be a couple of thousand pages. "Don't want to sleep in my bed?"

"No," she said firmly, folding her arms and glaring at me. "Get out of my room, Lachlan. Now."

There was something hot about the way she said my name. Even if I didn't like how bad her throat sounded. "You see a doctor about that yet?"

"None of your business," she said, dropping her folded arms to stalk toward me. "Get. Out."

"Hey," I said, enjoying the contact when her hands slapped against my chest. This close, I got a better look at her. I caught her biceps before she could retreat. "I came to check on you."

Her eyebrows climbed.

"Wounds me that you don't think I care, Ace. Didn't I come through for you in L.A.?"

The shock on her face was probably an insult. But if she wanted to make me work for it, well, then I could deal with that.

"I've been worried since the fire, but apparently my brothers are keeping secrets. Didn't know you'd moved in with Jonas, and Ramsey definitely didn't say a word." A fact I'd take up with both of them later. "If I'd known, I'd have been here to see you sooner. How are you?" I rubbed her arms. "Really. And have you seen a doctor about your throat?"

What did one do to make that better?

The stroke of her tongue over her lower lip created a stuttering halt to my thoughts. "Goddamn, Ace," I whispered as I dragged her a little closer. "I've missed you."

A part of me braced for her knee. Worth it, but I'd missed these sweet lips. I'd missed the firebrand in her eyes. I'd missed the bite of her teeth as her mouth opened to me. The connection sizzled to life, and I drank in the taste of her as she went from flattening her hands on my chest to fisting my shirt.

The drag pulled me to her, and I slid a hand up into her hair. It was like silk on my fingers. Her gasp was the perfect accompaniment to the way she met the thrust of my tongue with her own. All the blood in my body went south, but I kept my attention on the kittenish flicks of her tongue as I explored her sweet taste.

Fuck, I'd missed this. Missed her. When she scraped her teeth over my tongue, I welcomed the pain. Even more when she bit my lower lip. All claws and teeth, my girl.

The next bite drew blood and I lifted my head to find her eyes hot as she stared up at me with her face flushed. I waited for the wicked sting of her verbal lashes, but it didn't come.

"Did you get my presents, Ace?" I had to know. I stroked my thumb over the fullness of her damp lower lip and she dipped her lashes.

"Presents?"

"The coffee... the running shoes? The clothes?" I dipped my gaze to her legs. Was she wearing a pair of those panties right now? Oh, the idea tantalized me.

"Hmm," she hummed with a shrug, releasing my shirt. "Were those from you?"

I grinned slowly. She wouldn't even entertain this game if she hadn't got them. "Tease." I pressed another fierce kiss to her lips. "Get that throat looked at, Ace. I can find you a good doc if you need it." The idea of picking her up and tossing her on the bed was right there.

I could slip my hands down and pull away the t-shirt to get a good look. Except she hadn't thrown me out yet, so no need to tempt fate.

"I'll see you in the morning," I promised against her lips, then forced myself to let her go and retreat. It was a stone bitch when every part of my body wanted to be right there with her, but my brain was right.

She wasn't ready to be caught.

Yet.

So, I didn't look back as I let myself out of the room. Nor when I was heading down the stairs.

But I did whistle.

My dick was so hard, I might pass out from blood loss soon. Better to go jack off, take care of it, then have a little fraternal chat with the pair of traitors in my family.

I could imagine that wet lower lip of hers and what it would look like when I painted it with my cum.

Sixteen

KC

After Lachlan's rather unexpected and intense visit, I kept my bedroom door closed and *locked* unless I was fully dressed. I thought about asking Jonas about his brother, but we had this kind of armistice going. I'd found my favorite creamer in the fridge, along with the milk I preferred.

So far, if he wanted to use the television in the front room, he'd asked me if I had plans first. If he was already settled when I came in, he would pause to see if I needed it or wanted it off.

Considering the last time all four of us had been in the same place—well, not counting parents' weekend—he had tried to relocate Lachlan's jaw. An activity I kind of approved of, but either way, I just didn't want to rock the boat.

At the same time, just... what was Lachlan doing here? At the school. He'd graduated and yet he was here. After a consultation with Doctor Don, I was still not running *yet*. He said walking only, no pushing it.

We were babying my throat. Though what did not

running do for my throat, I had no idea. I was restless as fuck and I'd taken to walking, even in the middle of the night, usually up and down the stairs, avoiding Ramsey's floor cause I didn't want to run into him *either*.

The fact he was the TA in two of my classes was bad enough. At least he hadn't twisted my arm into more tutoring.

So far.

But that didn't leave me with a lot of options on discovering why Lachlan was here. Though I might have taken a small amount of pleasure in the idea that he was waiting for me to come running, and I wasn't.

The twins came through for me on that, though. Olivia said he was working with the lacrosse team and had apparently enrolled in all basic college classes. Apparently, the original plan for him had been Stanford. So why was he here?

"Maybe he didn't make the cut at Stanford," Olivia said with a shrug. "No one knows. Just that, according to some of his former teammates, he wasn't planning to come back to Blue Ivy at all."

"He's not stupid," Sydney said, swirling a carrot stick into the ranch dressing. "Not—intellectually, anyway. He's a guy, so that definitely makes him kind of stupid."

Soren and Finley both paused to look at us, but Soren only shrugged. "Definitely a kind of stupid."

Finley snickered, and I had to smother my own smile. "Thanks, guys."

"Look, just avoid the lacrosse field," Olivia said. "We don't have classes with the college, anyway. Even college-level courses are taught in the high school halls. So you can easily avoid him there."

That was nice.

"But he's living with the RA of our building," Soren volunteered. "So maybe avoid that floor, too."

Ugh. I made a face.

Sydney laughed. "Just find some other guy and kiss him in front of him. That usually makes the irritating ones go away."

"Yeah," I said slowly, trying not to think about how my lips were tingling in memory of the kiss he'd planted on me while I'd been listening to the final cuts of the Bound Hearts album.

Their debut was going to absolutely fucking kill. I needed our social media team to do something with it in support. Just hadn't figured out what.

Maybe I'd do some TikTok's lip-syncing to their songs...

Teddy would kill me, but it'd be totally worth it.

My phone buzzed, the alarm reminding me I needed to call Jackie *before* classes. "I gotta run." I was rising and stacking my stuff together.

"I'll get it," Soren offered.

"Thanks."

"Don't forget," Sydney said. "Party this weekend."

"Can't wait!"

Totally planned to forget. Loved the girls. I even liked Soren and Finley. They had a good group. But parties meant Payton would probably be there and I'd sooner pierce my tongue.

"See you guys later!"

Aubrey and Forrest were coming in as I was heading out. She was flushed and her lipstick was definitely gone. I grinned at them and then patted Forrest's chest. "That color looks way better on her."

He grinned and Aubrey rolled her eyes as she gave me a playful shove. "Shut up." Then she sobered. "Everything all right?" Her gaze dipped to the phone in my hand.

"Totally fine, just checking in before classes. Connecting has been kind of hard."

Especially with Jackie's schedule and Pen's course of treatments. I worried about all of them, but Jackie would only let me do so much. I'd actually talked to Davina and she'd agreed to help out with Pen a couple of times a week.

Jackie scolded me, but there had been real relief in her voice, and in Bronson's, when Davina got involved. She was the absolute best, too. Pen would be so spoiled, and I was glad for it.

"Let me know?" Aubrey asked, and I nodded. We were both circumspect about discussing any of this where anyone could hear us. I liked Forrest. Aubrey really liked him. But this was still a need to know, and no one needed to know about my baby sister.

She was too little and too sick to be dealing with press stupidity. I was out the door and had the phone to my ear before I'd gone three steps.

Jackie answered on the first ring. "You have a sixth sense for when my coffee is ready."

I laughed. "If you mean survival skills, then I agree." I spent the next fifteen minutes getting an update. Not that much had changed in the last week. I talked to Bronson nightly via texts.

"You sound much better," Jackie said. It seemed almost surreal that the fire had been nearly three weeks earlier. It seemed like a lifetime and just the day before. "Are you taking it easy? Doing what the doctors say?"

"Yes, ma'am," I promised. "I have another checkup next week. The coughing has gotten much better, and I'm still not singing..." Even if that was killing me. "Cause he wanted me to give my vocal cords a solid rest."

"I know it's hard honey, but it's for the best..."

She wasn't wrong. As much as I wanted to stay on the phone, I had to get to class. The next two weeks followed a similar pattern. Jonas and I developed something of a rhythm. As roommates went, he was pretty quiet.

While we shared a lot of classes, we didn't share the same

schedule. He disappeared on weekends. More of my favorites showed up in the fridge and the cupboards. I also found out that he preferred oat milk, so I made his coffee with that.

It was the little things, but it helped with detente. I preferred the peaceful existence. It would be even more peaceful if Payton accidentally vanished one day, but I supposed we couldn't have everything.

Frankie and Ian's tour looked like it was going well. When Coop called to invite us to the Baltimore show that would "officially" launch their tour and their album, I was down.

"Does she know we're coming?" I asked and Coop laughed.

"No," he said, and there was a smugness in his voice. "It's a surprise for her. Bubba knows. But we want this to be a really special night for her. It's been a tough time."

Yeah. "I know," I said. "Don't worry, we'll be there." I didn't have to guess what Yvette and Aubrey would say. "Just send me the dates."

"Thank you, she's going to love having you girls there."

"I can't wait, Coop," I told him. "Thank you for inviting me."

"Yep. Talk soon!"

Then he was off the phone. I fired off a text to Aubrey and Yvette letting them know. Their answers were unsurprising. Mom was also back in the news—she'd had some meltdown at a club and a very public screaming match with Johnny.

Now she was back at that damn retreat and Johnny was miserable. I felt so bad for Johnny, yet why would Mom go back to the Sunshine Retreat? She wasn't drinking... at least, I didn't think she was drinking anything except the Kool-Aid. Teddy sent me a message about fan mail, and I made a face.

Then again, A Forever Fan had triggered a new review for all our incoming fan mail. If he wanted to talk this over with us, then maybe something new had come in. Despite not having any desire to deal with it, I messaged him back that we would set up a call.

While there were hours left on the West Coast for business, I didn't want to do it today. I texted the girls, and Yvette answered by texting Teddy, along with Aubrey and me.

YVETTE

Can't meet today. Let's schedule for next week?

Grinning, I sent her a separate message.

ME

I could kiss you on the mouth.

YVETTE

I will put it on your tab.

Aubrey just put a thumbs up on Yvette's message. Done, I headed up to my room. Aubrey had a date with Forrest, so I was going to work on some music, maybe some homework... or a movie.

No, I was gonna do homework then music. There was a note on my door. The handwriting was neat and it was addressed just to me. I glanced up and down the hall as I let myself in.

Once in my room, I changed out of my uniform and eyed all the clothes in my closet. It was weird that so much of it was new. Every once in a while, it hit me that I'd lost some of my favorite concert tees in that fire. Including the very first one we'd made.

Irreplaceable.

Shaking off the melancholy, I got changed into something comfy then slit open the envelope to read the letter inside.

Greetings and salutations,

You'll need to head out for rations.

Avoid the hall, or making a call.
It's better to take a walk, then we can talk.
I'll be at a place in the open air, it's beautiful when the weather is fair.
When the surface is calm, you'll find it shimmering yet.
Don't walk too far though, because you could get wet.
If it's after three, then come find me.
Don't worry if you're late, this isn't a date.
Yet.

I read the note three times. It was a riddle, clearly, but it wasn't signed. A riddle and an invitation. The place in the open air? It had to be the reflecting pond. I passed it when running all the time, but who wrote the note?

It wasn't Jonas' writing. That I would recognize, at least now. Not Ramsey. Not that he would send a note like this. I rather doubted it was Lachlan. It was a little too poetic for Mr. Ninja Kiss.

Curiosity niggled at me, so I pulled on my running shoes, took a picture of the note, and sent it to Aubrey. Then I told her I was gonna take a light run out to the pond.

Thankfully, it wasn't in an isolated area. 'Cause with everything else going on, that would be a hard no. Jonas was just coming in as I headed out of my room.

He frowned at me.

"Going for a run," I told him. One upside to the last few weeks, I wasn't croaking anymore. "Not long." Then, because it wouldn't hurt to just cover all my bases, I said, "You didn't leave me some riddle to come find you at the pond, did you?"

He stared at me, then shook his head slowly. "No. Was I supposed to?"

I grinned, and he looked a little startled. "Nope. Thanks. I'll be back."

"But I didn't do anything."

"I know." I saluted him and then headed out. For all that

we were sharing the same space, we were still isolating from each other. I wasn't trying to get to know him, nor was he trying to get to know me.

Like I said, detente. It was working for us. It was a nice day, and I set off at a light run toward the path that wound closer to the administration buildings and the reflecting pond.

The breeze felt wonderful against my skin. Even better was the run. It was just nice to move. I'd given myself a whole extra week past when the doctor said I could resume light workouts. Part of that was babying my voice, and the other part was avoiding Lachlan.

I still did not know what he wanted. Well, besides mind-blowing kisses that should not be fucking hot when delivered by douchebags.

They were all douchebags. Well, maybe Jonas wasn't so much anymore. But they were douchebags. Lachlan was such an ass. Such. An. Ass.

His ninja kisses were also addictive as hell. As I came around the bend toward the pond, I slowed my pace. A figure waited by the pond. He had a blanket spread out on the ground, and a... was that an actual picnic basket?

The sun was in my eyes so I could only make out his outline. Slowing to a walk, I shaded my eyes and then blinked.

RJ?

"Hey, Blue," he said as he faced me, his grin open and almost as bright as the sun. "Long time no see."

Before I could ask what he was doing there, a figure streaked past me and slammed into him, landing both of them *in* the pond.

"You son of a bitch," Lachlan said as they emerged from the water, before he shoved him back under.

la Leçon Gai
107.

Seventeen

JONAS

hree things happened the day KC returned to running. One, I didn't understand. The second, I wasn't sure how to process. And the third? Oh, the third pissed me off.

The third thing? I was pretty sure that wasn't her fault. No, if I had to blame anyone, it would be my fucking brother. It started when she asked me a strange question about a riddle. I'd never been a fan of mind games. Nor puzzles. But suddenly, I wished I was.

The second thing that happened, *she* grinned at *me*... *really* grinned at me. The power of that smile knocked all the breath out of my lungs. It had the power of every ballad I'd ever tried to compose. Memorizing that look, the notes it burst into life, occupied me for more than an hour.

The third thing, however? The third thing was a soaking wet Lachlan stalking her to my door and trying to get inside. She didn't spare him a second look as she slammed the door of her bedroom. He had a bloody nose and a busted lip. His black eye had almost healed.

I renewed the subscription. Dumbass didn't even see me coming. When I tossed him out on his ass, Payton appeared. Gross.

Let her kiss it better. Whatever.

As long as he stayed away from KC.

I split three of the knuckles on my right hand delivering that punch. When KC emerged from her room, she glanced around with a worried frown. "He's gone."

The relief in her exhale wasn't manufactured. She glanced at the door then at me. I'd been working on music, but I didn't hide the sheets. Her eyes narrowed on my hand.

And it wasn't as hard as his skull.

"I'm going to make coffee," she said. "Then I have some work to do...want some?"

"Work?" I frowned. "Or coffee?"

The corners of her mouth curved upward again. It wasn't quite the grin of earlier, but it was definitely fun to see. "I'll save the work for joint assignments if we end up with any."

All of a sudden, I wished we had.

"Coffee, though, is good anytime," she said as she walked into the kitchenette. The coffee maker was like something from a professional coffee shop or stand. She worked it like a pro. There was something soothing about the grinding noise, even if it was loud. Even more was the hum and slurp of the milk. "Jonas?"

The abrupt end of the foaming and her question dragged me back to the present. "Oh. Yeah," I said. "Coffee." Right, she might need more words. "Coffee would be good."

"Coming right up." She didn't ask me what I wanted specifically, but I didn't drink a lot of fancy coffee. So maybe it was easy to figure out what I drank. Or maybe we just drank the same thing. Curiosity niggled at me while she fixed it.

When she crossed to where I was sitting and handed me the tumbler. I stared at the side. It had the Torched logo on it. I hadn't realized that they had that before. Then, the one she'd made me the other time had been in a disposable cup.

"We can use these in the suite because we're not going anywhere," she explained, wrapping her hands around the tumbler like she was cold. Was she cold? Her toenails were a pale shade of blue, paler than her hair or her eyes. Did she pick it out on purpose like that? "The disposable cups are easier."

For her nails? Wait, no for the coffee. "Makes sense." I took a cautious sniff of the coffee before a drink. It smelled almost sweeter than last time. It tasted sweeter. Another sip and I frowned.

The corners of her mouth curved again. "It's the raw sugar, I added it to the top. Just...needed a pick me up."

"Oh." I took another swallow. Definitely sweeter, but it also seemed to make the coffee richer.

"Right, I'm gonna let you work, and I'm going to my room—"

"You can work out here," I offered. "It won't bother me."

"I was gonna listen to some videos while I did research..." But she hesitated. "Mind if I do headphones?"

"No."

Ten minutes later, she was curled up in a corner of the sofa with her laptop, a stack of books on the table, her headphones on and her foot was the only thing about her that moved, keeping time with some beat she could hear.

It was...nice.

We spent most of the weekend the same way. Sharing the sitting room and working, but not really talking. Studio time waited, but I was comfortable here. I grabbed food for her one day. She made coffee a couple of times. We ordered a pizza on Sunday. She paid, and I went down to get it.

Since it had to be dropped off at Ramsey's suite, I just

waited outside the front door to grab it. No sense in giving either of them ideas.

I couldn't really figure out what to say beyond did she need another drink? That didn't really seem like talking. By the time she disappeared into her room for the night, I was still looking for the words.

Why did they have to be so hard?

That night, after I got ready for bed, I heard her guitar. It was soft, but she was playing. I strained to listen if she was singing, but we both kept the doors to the bathroom closed. If I went in, I locked her door. If she was in there, she locked mine.

We communicated without words most of the time. Monday morning, Ramsey summoned me to his suite before breakfast. I walked down with KC, who was in her running gear. I waited for her to take off before I knocked on Ramsey's door.

Unsurprisingly, Lachlan was also at the table in Ramsey's little dining area. He kept his suite way more like an overly tidy little apartment. Yeah, I didn't need to talk to Lachlan. I stared at our oldest brother. "I have things to do."

"Yes," Ramsey said, pointing to the table. "One of those things is talking to us. We're settling this."

"No," I said, folding my arms. I didn't venture deeper into the suite, nor did I sit down. "I have things to do." Yes, I was repeating myself. "If you want to tell me something, just say it."

"Told you this wouldn't work." Smug. Lachlan always sounded smug, even if his black eye was still swollen nearly shut and his busted lip actually looked worse. Maybe I should make his bruised face a permanent feature.

I grinned at the idea.

It made my day better.

Ramsey sighed. "Guys, you two cannot keep up this war."

"Yes, we can," I said in the same breath that Lachlan did. Then glared at him. I didn't want to be on the same page with him. His arrogant smirk was beginning to grate on my last nerve.

Eyes rolling, Ramsey shook his head. "So you agree that you can keep up the war. Well, I guess that gets us started somewhere."

"We don't need to start anything," Lachlan stated. "Jonas' punk ass is gonna be a little bitch until he gets over being butt hurt where Ace is concerned."

"Don't," Ramsey said through gritted teeth.

"She has a name," I stated flatly. "She also doesn't want anything to do with you. Maybe learn she isn't all that into you."

"Except, I've kissed her..."

That statement alone was enough to make me livid.

"...even better, she kissed me back." He stretched his legs out in front of him. "I know when a girl wants me, little bro. You might struggle in that department—"

Ramsey cut me off as I started across the room. "I said don't," he told me, but then swung a look at Lachlan. "Either of you. Keep it up and I'll be the one throwing you out next. Rooms are at a premium and Jonas can't offer you your old one back yet."

Mutiny filled Lachlan's expression, and I savored it with a little vicious pleasure.

"And if you don't get a grip, I will make sure KC is moved *out* of your suite." The warning in Ramsey's tone shut down my triumph. "You know the rules. Anything that upsets your recovery or creates a violent setback and we have to address it."

"She has *nothing* to do with that." I attended my therapy sessions regularly *and* took my meds. In fact, I'd been working on *how* to talk to her for weeks. I just hadn't figured it out yet.

"She has everything—I said don't, Lachlan," Ramsey

interrupted himself as he pivoted to face our brother. "I'm not kidding. I'm sick of this shit between the two of you. Hate each other all you want, but do it peacefully and without a bunch of bullshit insults."

I almost wanted to ask "or what" but I didn't. Not when he was already threatening to have KC taken out of my suite.

"Now," Ramsey said as he yanked out a chair at the table. "Sit down, we're going to talk and lay out some ground rules that you two jackasses are going to follow."

I glanced at Lachlan, who was rolling his eyes at Ramsey. Our gazes locked for a moment and he practically dared me with his raised eyebrows.

"Whatever," I said as I crossed over to take the seat. "Let's make this quick. KC's running and I want to go to breakfast with her."

Lachlan twitched. He started to stand up, but Ramsey pinned him with a look until he sat down. Yeah, he wanted to run after her, but now he couldn't.

That made the next twenty-five minutes of brotherly advice, bargaining, and bullshit tolerable. Especially since I said I wanted to go to breakfast with her. We didn't have plans.

They didn't know that.

As it turned out, Aubrey was waiting for KC when I got back up to our suite. So, I walked down with them to breakfast. While we went through the line together, I left them when they went to join friends. I wanted to find a peace offering for her. One that would say we could be friends, even if we weren't.

It baffled me on what to say or even how to say it. By the end of the week, I was no closer than I'd been at the beginning. The music was done though. I'd finished composing a five minute piece.

The tempo was almost perfect. But it needed something more. I could hear it but I couldn't see the notes. Maybe if KC added lyrics, I'd find it and since we communicated with music so much better than words...

I'd finally decided to just pin it to her door when she came back from—I had no idea where she'd been actually. But she had her phone to her ear. When she saw me, she held up one finger.

"No, I get that, Bron, but I still want to do something." She rolled her eyes in that exasperated way as she slid her backpack off and set it right next to the sofa. Her shoes came off next, but she didn't leave them out here.

Instead, she carried them with her into her bedroom. The fact she didn't close the door all the way meant she was coming back out, so I waited.

"Really?" The huff of laughter took any sting out of those two syllables. "You know, that just means I'll work harder to get it done." She chuckled and all at once her voice just softened. "Yeah, me too. Okay. I'll talk to you later."

Bron. That was a guy's name. I really shouldn't be listening to her conversation, and I wasn't trying. Instead, I just waited as I turned over who was Bron in my head. When she padded back out, she was in shorts and a tank-top.

"Hey," she said. "I picked up the research folder from the library for you."

Oh. "Did I leave it?" Had I forgotten it?

"I guess," she said, as she pulled it out of her backpack. "Soren said you were there earlier and this was on your table after you left."

I took the red folder and stared at it. I'd been color-coding this year to try and stay ahead on everything. This wasn't homework, it was college research. I hadn't made up my mind about going to school yet.

"Anyway," she said. "I want Chinese. Want some?"

"I don't like Chinese," I said absently. "Food poisoning when I was a kid. It just makes me want to vomit now."

Her grimace made me shrug. "I don't care if you get it, I just don't like eating it."

"Tacos?"

"You said you wanted Chinese."

"Not if it's going to make you puke."

That was... nice. "I can go somewhere else. Here." I thrust the music out at her and she took it slowly.

"You don't have to go anywhere else...tacos are fine. Pizza is fine. We could go to the dining hall..." Then she made a face.

"You don't like the dining hall?"

She shrugged. "Everyone is talking about the social this weekend."

"Are you going?"

"I don't know...last year I got paint dumped on me when I went, so maybe not." With that, she flopped down onto her spot on the sofa with the music, her eyes on the page.

"I won't let anyone do that this year." That was totally Lachlan and Payton. I was pretty sure it had more to do with RJ and not her.

Mostly.

Still...

She didn't say anything as she flipped through the music sheets. When she started to hum, I held my breath. Sweat prickled along my back. The humming went on for a lot longer than five minutes...

"That..." I said abruptly. "Go back and do that again."

She glanced up at me. "What?" The slow, almost owlish blink. Had she forgotten I was here?

"That last couple of bars, hum them again." It was a command, but... "Please?"

She backed up a few bars in the music then dropped into a lower octave as she hummed the same passage again.

"Different key." That was what I was missing. "Take it lower..." I eyed the music pages she was holding.

Head tilted, she glanced from the music to me and then handed me the pages back. "Want to change it before I add the lyrics?"

Yes. "Thank you." I retrieved my pencil before I took the other side of the sofa. I erased everything after the first third, then rewrote it, taking it into a lower key with each third until I got to the end.

When I finished, KC got up and went to her room. She returned with her guitar and settled back on the sofa. Spreading the music out in front of her on the table, she studied it for a moment.

I should go.

Then she started to play.

I really should go.

But I couldn't move a muscle as her fingers danced over the strings, giving life to the music in my head.

<h1 style="text-align:center">Eighteen</h1>

My phone vibrated as the messages came in while I was in the shower. I had to get the color depositing conditioner on and leave it while I washed the rest of me, so whoever wanted to blow my phone up would have to wait. I had to be ready to go when the car got here, and that meant stopping by Ramsey's room to sign myself out.

Yippee.

Couldn't wait.

Ten minutes later, with the towel wrapped around my midsection and tucked between my breasts, I ran the comb through my damp hair. The color-deposit would lift the color and I could make an appointment to get my hair redone closer to the holidays.

A message flashed over the screen.

AUBREY

> Car will be here in twenty minutes.
> Overnight bag packed. Grab yours. Train is
> booked. Yvette will meet us and the guys
> are picking us up when we get to Baltimore.

She'd been running point on our plans to attend Bound Hearts official launch in Baltimore. We'd also gotten a hotel for the weekend so that we could hang out. It was a little getaway from home for the three of us.

ME

> I'll be down in 15.

I still needed to pack. But I was sure I didn't need to tell her that. When Jonas knocked on the door, I grimaced. Crap, I hadn't meant to take so long. "One sec," I called. Gathering up what I needed, I unlocked the door and headed for my room. "All yours."

I caught sight of him, hair askew and a pillow imprint on his cheek before I tugged the door closed. It took me all of ten minutes to dress, pack my overnight bag, stow the homework I needed to take with me, and make sure I had my laptop and charging cables.

Purse with ID, credit cards, and some cash was next, and I stuffed tissue, motion sickness pills, and Chapstick into the side pocket before I was heading out to the living room, locking up on my way out.

"You going somewhere?" Jonas asked, from where he stood in the kitchen eating cereal. His hair was still standing almost straight up on top of his head. The sleepy expression on his face faded as he glanced from me to my bags.

"Yep," I said. "I'll see you Sunday night...or if it's late, I'll see you Monday morning. Have a good weekend."

Aubrey was waiting for me downstairs. Big girl panties on, I went to grab the clipboard and knock on Ramsey's door when she said, "Already signed you out. He wasn't there, so I just put in the time we're leaving and expected back."

"Better to ask for forgiveness than permission anyway." I flipped his room and his room's occupants the mental bird. She laughed as she held the door open.

"Impeccable timing," she teased as a car pulled into the circular drive. I grinned. The driver—not Dix, but that was okay—actually got out to put our bags into the trunk before we got in.

"Hey," Lachlan called as I slid into the backseat. "Ace! Where you going?"

"Away," I answered. "Maybe you should try it."

I yanked the door closed and clicked the seatbelt into place. Locked the door, too. Then gave Lachlan a little finger wave as we pulled away.

At Aubrey's snort, I stuck out my tongue at her, and then we both laughed. The school kind of peeled away as we left the campus and got closer to the train station. Bit by bit, I shed Kaitlin Crosse, Blue Ivy Prep student, for KC, Torched band member and singer.

We made it to the station precisely on time and got ourselves up onto the platform with our tickets. First-Class compartments, mainly to be comfortable while we caught up. It was hard not to scream when we saw Yvette. It seemed like an eternity since the last time we were together.

The ride down to Baltimore sped by as we caught up on various news, laughed, and teased.

"Did you ever think we'd miss touring?" Yvette asked when we were an hour outside of Baltimore. Despite the fact we weren't going there to perform, there was a kind of delicious tension to the adventure.

How many bars and clubs had we performed in over the years? Our venues had grown fast, but there was an energy to performing that I'd always loved, and eighteen months of not being on a stage had been both amazing *and* kind of terrifying.

"I did," I admitted.

"Me too," Aubrey said, and Yvette stuck her tongue at both of us. "What? As much as we needed the break, it wasn't like we hated it."

Laughter shook me. "No, we didn't. We were just tired." So tired. No one told you when you made it big just how much work a tour was. How you forgot what city you were in or what day it was. That you lived your life one show at a time and on days when you doubled up—well, you were lucky if you didn't introduce new lyrics to songs because you just went blank on the old ones.

They didn't tell you that hotel rooms all smelled the same and that there are like six carpet patterns. Room service is a luxury that gets old. Or that you should *never* order food you know well and love from one country in a completely different country.

"Not sure I'm totally ready to dive back in..." The musing snagged their attention. "But I do miss—I miss the creating, the recording, the working out new dances and routines."

I missed them. I missed who we were together.

At the same time...

"Graduation is in a few months," Aubrey said like a record scratch, bringing us back to earth. "Let's revisit this then...see if we want to work on a new album."

If we wanted to...

"We should probably talk about it before then," Yvette pointed out. "Especially if this experiment takes you guys to college."

"Maybe." I didn't want to commit to anything. A lot could happen in the next few months. I flipped to the photos on my phone. Jackie had been sending me snaps of Pen with little anecdotes.

There were big tests coming up soon. We'd finally see if the chemo was working.

Fuck, I hoped so. Everyone kept saying the survival rates were good and that the treatment course was ideal. We had good doctors and a supportive staff.

But Pen was a baby and I just wanted her to do happy baby things. My phone rang while I was holding it, and RJ's name popped up on the screen. Yeah, not this weekend. I needed a break from Blue Ivy drama. I still had no idea why he'd sent me that riddle to meet him.

Didn't get any answers while Lachlan was trying to drown him. Lachlan's hot pursuit had been interrupted by Jonas. I should probably have thanked him for that, but the idea that the brothers were fighting was kind of terrible for them.

I loved all my siblings. It didn't matter that we barely saw each other or got time together. Or maybe it was because of that fact, but I made the most of it when we were there. Maybe it would be different if we were together all the time.

Arguably, I talked to Bronson constantly. What had begun as a weekly to bi-weekly chat had become daily texting to calls three or four times a week. We talked even when we had nothing to say.

Speaking of which, I sent him a poop emoji and he responded with rolled eyes and a middle finger. I grinned. Good to remind him that I was around to give him shit.

When we finally pulled into the station, we found almost *all* of Frankie's guys waiting for us, along with Rachel. Oh, I hadn't expected to see her.

Archie Standish, wealthy smart ass with the heart of gold that worshiped the ground she walked on. Jake Benton, the guy was just about as all-American as you could get, from the football player, to the big muscles, to the hot temper. According to Frankie, he led with his fists sometimes. Then there was the birthday boy, Coop Brennen. He'd been

Frankie's best friend since the age of five. He was so easy going and had this golden retriever energy—not that I planned to share that but still...

How fucking adorable was it that all these guys were crazy about her and she was crazy about them? Ian wasn't here, but he would be later when they were on stage. Frankie and Ian were Bound Hearts, and they were the reason we were all here. I couldn't wait to see them perform.

"I got it," Jake said, taking my bag as Archie grabbed Yvette's and Coop grabbed Aubrey's. "You ladies have your hotel plans all set, right?"

"Yes," Coop said. "I told you that. We're all staying at the same place, but they have a different set of suites."

They had a car and a driver waiting. A pair of cars actually; Rachel elected to ride with us while the guys rode together.

"Too much testosterone?" Yvette teased and Rachel snorted. Rachel Manning was a fun, ballsy kind of girl.

"Not as bad as all that, really," she admitted. "But they are losing their minds missing Frankie and it's kind of gotten a little—claustrophobic."

"Awww," Aubrey said and she leaned her head against my shoulder. "Can you imagine being missed like that?"

No, not really. "Did Forrest miss you that much?"

She pinched me and Yvette clapped her hands. "Oh, I want to know this too."

"Don't you start," Aubrey told her with a mock serious frown. "We could start asking about a certain..."

"Pfft," Yvette said. "You can try. But my life is nowhere near as interesting as yours."

"We all pale in comparison to Rachel though." I grinned at her droll look. "Teach us your ways, college girl."

Her sputter of laughter was worth it. At the hotel, we got checked in, had something to eat, then got changed. Yvette had gotten all of us Bound Hearts shirts, and hell yes we were wearing them to the show. It wouldn't be long before we had to be at the club. I swore, I was just *so* ready to see them.

It was hard to express to anyone who had never been in this position, just how gratifying it was, to see someone achieve their dreams. It wasn't about competition. It was about supporting someone to meet the challenges, sharing what I learned to help them accomplish their goals, aware that someday, they would be doing it for someone else.

Based on what I'd learned about Frankie over the past year and a half or so... she was going to be a fantastic inspiration to those that followed her. She'd also truly celebrate their successes.

The truth of how real the excitement was hit when we were shown to our table. The air was electric with it. While the other patrons were happy about the show and getting to see the new band, but this table? Was lit.

Frankie's guys? Rachel? Even Jeremy, the older gentleman who'd accompanied them, was leaning forward in anticipation. The house lights went down as Bound Hearts was introduced. Their band came out first followed by Frankie and Ian. We were all on our feet, whistling, clapping, and stamping our feet.

Frankie Curtis was a sweetheart. The very real shock on her face and the tears in her eyes were so visceral, I felt my own throat clogging. Ian and Frankie's family cared so much, they were here to support them. They showed up.

I was so fucking happy to be a part of this. The music they played *rocked*. They had the whole club on their feet by the end of the first set. I knew every single song they'd recorded. Loved them all, too.

After their first break, we got up and sang with them. It just added a whole new layer to the night, and Frankie's hug was as warm and enthusiastic as she was. As the night wound down, we were going to take off and let them have the time together, but Jake insisted on going out with us and making sure we got into a car.

We'd been recognized. We'd probably hit social media, whatever. I made sure to get a selfie with Ian and Frankie so our peeps could run it, too. For now, it was a wild night and I was almost hoarse again.

At least this time it was from singing and not smoke inhalation.

The rest of the weekend passed in a fantastic blur of late-night room service, ice cream, binge shows, and laughter.

So much laughter.

When we finally got to sleep it was with sides that hurt. Even the train ride back to school was made with a lighter heart. We needed this weekend.

Outside of Bron, Jackie, and Pen, I'd pretty much ignored my phone all weekend. Aubrey and I split up when we were back to go to our rooms, and I hit play on my messages after I grabbed a quick shower and got ready for bed.

Jonas hadn't been in, I didn't think, when I got back. The first three messages were from RJ. The first was an apology for the incident at the pond. I wasn't sure why he was apologizing.

The second was just him checking in to find out if I was angry with him. He was only in town for the weekend, but he'd be back in a couple of weeks. Oops. My bad. I did not see him this weekend.

The third was a little testier.

"I just figured out you were off campus for the weekend. I supposed I shouldn't have just assumed you were waiting around for my call. Probably arrogant of me."

"You think?" I muttered.

"Truth is, Blue, I've missed you and really wanted to talk to you the other day. I left a box for you in the mailroom. Message me when you get it. I'll be back in a couple of weeks.

Maybe we can start over? Chat soon." A pause then. "Missed you, Blue. A hell of a lot."

Then the call ended.

"You didn't ask," Jonas said from the doorway. "But he's a creep."

"Well, hello to you too."

"You can do better than him." The flat intonation made me snort.

"Like Lachlan? I think I'll pass."

"You can do better than him too." He frowned. "Or that is what I would tell you if we were friends. You said we weren't. Still...you can do better than them." Backing up only a step, he paused again. "Welcome back."

"Thanks," I said before he retreated entirely. He nodded, then pulled my door shut.

If we were friends...

Food for thought, I guessed. Wasn't sure we'd ever be friends.

Falling backward on the bed, I stared up at the ceiling. I was too tired to try and figure all of this out right now. Tomorrow's problem then.

RAMSEY

"Heads up," Harley said as she fell into step with me. I was glad to see her return to campus. After the fire, she'd taken a few weeks off to recover. So much lost in that damn fire. The black scar of it was visible every time we left the dorm and there was no missing the lingering smoke smell.

Like KC, she'd had some smoke inhalation issues. Though, as far as I could tell, KC seemed to have bounced back. She sounded better anyway. Her singing voice clearly survived, at least based on the viral videos from their "surprise" nightclub appearance in Maryland.

"The letters are going out." Harley's statement yanked me right back to the conversation. I paused mid-step and glanced at her. Her expression didn't hold an ounce of humor.

Shit.

We were in the middle of the path and the students broke around us, more than one muttering under their breath, but they avoided eye contact. When I nodded past her to where a bench was a few feet off one of the sidewalks, she turned.

"How many? Do we know?"

"No," she said with a shake of her head. "They haven't let that slip since the bullshit that happened three years ago." Back then, Harley had been a senior, and I'd been in my first year at the college-level. Blue Ivy's prodigy. They'd had such high hopes for me to carry their reputation to the Ivy League.

I scrubbed a hand over my face as I scanned the students making their way to their next classes. I had a free period for grading. While the plan had been to get coffee, I might need to...

"I only know they're going out because Melinda and Raquel both got tapped." They were seniors. Melinda was her cousin. Raquel was her best friend.

"Do they know?" I kept that question deliberately vague. No one was close enough to overhear us, but it didn't matter. Knots and Chains required no information sharing outside of the group.

"No." Harley grimaced, then shook her head. "After the shit that went down and the ban on taps for two years, I didn't..."

"You didn't plan on tapping them." Not that I could blame her.

"Nope."

"But they were tapped, regardless." I didn't have to wonder why. "Legacy."

She nodded once. "That means Jonas will likely get tapped this year, too."

Fuck. The last thing Jonas needed was to deal with any of this. He didn't know about the rest of it... "I'll take care of it."

"Ramsey," Harley said, her voice taking on a warning note. "You can't tell him."

Couldn't help him either.

Movement and blue hair pulled my attention. KC had a bag slung over her shoulder and her phone to her ear as she walked. Even with her hair pulled back into a braid, there was a wildness to it. Of course, it was the color, but it was more. Her hair was far too "alive" to be constrained.

Our gazes snagged briefly. Irritation flickered in her eyes and her lips compressed before she purposefully looked elsewhere. I wanted to try and find a way to make peace, but she had zero interest in hearing a word I said.

Maybe I'd pegged her wrong. Maybe we all had. I let a lot of preconceived notions rule my thinking where she was concerned. While she might have been a little unruly and disrespectful, mostly in a playful way, the year before—no such pretense existed this year.

She didn't talk to me at all, given a choice. The few times we'd had to interact for class, she'd been almost coldly polite. Too cool. Almost unfeeling.

That girl? That girl was far more alien than the elemental girl I'd been getting to know.

The one I'd kissed...

Fuck.

"We can't help her either," Harley said in a soft voice as though she was sorry she had to remind me.

"Maybe she didn't get tapped."

Harley snorted, then gave my arm a squeeze before she walked away. Yeah, the chances she hadn't been tapped were slim to none. She was a member of Torched. If they linked her to us, then she was also a legacy. However, the band's reputation and her own ferociousness would speak for themselves.

I pulled out my phone and sent Lachlan a message. He responded swiftly enough that he'd meet me for coffee. I'd have to make up the prep time later. Fortunately, Lachlan didn't keep me waiting.

The fresh bruise on his jaw just made me sigh. At least his

new black eye had begun to turn green and yellow. If he could manage to not ram his face into Jonas' fists anymore, he might heal the rest of the way.

I passed Lachlan his coffee before I nodded to the doors. The sun was out and the temperature was balmy, making it almost a perfect day. That was a good enough reason to be out there.

The paths had cleared with the bell signaling transition between classes had ended and all students should be in class. The quiet in the air was one of the things I savored about the campus, no matter the time of year. There was something about the hum of activity, but it was these moments of profound peace that just soothed something in my soul.

"We just going to walk and drink coffee?" Lachlan asked. "'Cause your message seemed serious."

"The invites are going out." I took a sip of the coffee and waited. While I wasn't looking directly at him, I tracked his reactions in my periphery. Shock rippled over his face and he jerked a little.

"They banned them—"

"For two years," I reminded him. "It's been two years."

He took a long drink of the coffee like he was slamming a beer. Anger tightened his expression until he all but glared ahead of us.

"What?"

"Nothing," he said. "I didn't know they were doing it." It pissed him off. Well, to be fair, I hadn't known they were doing it either.

"We don't really do much with them." We hadn't since the incident with Kelly.

Incident.

I rubbed my face again. The earlier niggling headache blew up into a full-blown pound behind my eyes. This could go so wrong. Most of the members involved had moved on to other schools, or at least other activities.

There were probably only a few of us left who knew the dirtier details. The idea of the pause had been to create a clean slate.

"You going to make me ask?" Warning Lachlan had been one reason to call him out here. The second was a lot more personal.

He quirked a brow at me. "Ask what?"

"Are you going to tap KC?" The minute the question slipped out, I regretted it—the phrasing, if nothing else. Lachlan smirked, albeit briefly.

"We don't discuss the invites," he said. "Just like we don't discuss the riddles or the trials. Everyone is on their own until they make it past the first set of Knots and Chains."

I glared at him.

"What?" He shrugged. "I don't make the rules."

No, he didn't. At the same time, I wanted to tell him to leave her alone. Don't tap her. Let her continue her little experience without the burden of Knots and Chains.

The minute I admonished him to not do something, he absolutely would though. I had a feeling his most recent black eye was directly related to her as well. Since no one reported Lachlan fighting, it was most likely Jonas.

"It's killing you," Lachlan said. "Isn't it?"

"What is?" We were almost to the library. The best way to deal with Lachlan was to not rise to his bait.

"That Ace has a thing for me."

I blinked slowly and glanced at him. "What is the color of the sky in your world?" Because I'd seen KC when she was dealing with Lachlan. Those were not the eyes of affection or interest, unless she was sizing him up for a coffin.

I could get her those measurements. It was like running sandpaper over my nerves. Lachlan never knew when it was too much. He was a bulldozer when he decided he wanted something. Clearly, he wanted her.

"Hey, she's got friends," Lachlan said. "You know, if you need me to fix you up."

I just stared at him.

"Right, I forgot, you never take the stick out of your ass and remember that you're not already a fifty-five-year-old faculty member." He toasted me with his coffee then lifted his chin. "Thanks for this. I actually have to meet with the counselor about classes. They may have worked out a plan for me."

Uh-huh. Right up until he threw a wrench into it. He'd been playing tag with everyone from the administration, and in the meanwhile, they'd enrolled him in three classes to keep him busy. It barely caused him to crack a book.

Sooner or later, his boredom would catch up and then there would be hell to pay. As it was, I headed into the library and used what time I had left to grade papers. The tutoring sessions flew by, though they were not as challenging as when KC was there. Instead of a private room, I met the students out at the main tables near the research stacks.

At the last bell, I nodded to Paul as he packed up. "Thanks, Mr. Malone."

"You're welcome," I said. "You're getting there. Just take your time with the reading and be deliberate. If you find yourself skimming, take a breath and go back one paragraph and start again."

The problem with Paul wasn't his intelligence or even his background. It was his ADHD, particularly when it was a subject he wasn't interested in, or conversely, he thought he had nothing new to learn. That said, the kid was so hungry for knowledge he kind of reminded me of me.

"You got it!" Bag over his shoulder, he was already striding away. It took me a few extra minutes to pack up. I had my own work to do when I got back to the dorm. I also had to do dorm inspections this week.

After disposing of my trash, I headed outside. It was nice enough, I wanted to lose the suit coat and the slacks, but I had enough issues with the faculty and the students taking me seriously when I started TAing that it was just easier to maintain this professional air.

Blue hair stood out like a beacon and snared my attention easily. There was a huge fountain located in the center of a quad. It was turned off in winter, but right now it was flowing and muting some of the noise from the rest of the school. Standing right next to it, KC was laughing at something RJ Wallach said to her.

RJ Wallach.

No amount of telling myself to mind my own business would stop me from interceding. Wallach shouldn't be on campus. I didn't think he was a student of the college classes in Obrecht Hall.

"C'mon," RJ said, nudging her gently. "It'll be fun. Besides, all work and no play will make Blue a grumpy girl."

Did those lines or that smarmy tone work on girls? Really? KC didn't look impressed, but she also didn't look repulsed.

"Miss Crosse," I said as I approached. "A word?"

"Ramsey." RJ turned toward me, and I got a good look at the bruises he currently sported. Well, that might explain who else Lachlan was fighting with. We did not need another run in with the police. "Long time..."

I ignored his outstretched hand. "Not long enough. Miss Crosse?"

Rolling her eyes, KC folded her arms as she paced away from the fountain. "Apparently, *Mr. Malone* needs a word." The way she said my name shouldn't be remotely attractive, but the pointed brattiness amused me.

It was significantly better than indifference.

"Want me to wait?" RJ offered.

"Nope," KC said, turning to walk backwards so she could face him and give me her back. "I have your number. I can call."

"Can doesn't mean will," RJ accused. "Promise me?"

"Nope. Can doesn't mean I won't either. See ya." Then she pivoted to face me. "Are we talking here or do you need privacy to scold me?"

"You think you're funny." Holding onto a neutral expression was a challenge.

"I'm hilarious and I want coffee. So come on..." She set off, and I pinned RJ with a look. His slow smirk increased the friction burn from the sandpaper to my last nerve.

Lachlan should have broken his jaw.

Following KC, I didn't say anything while she ordered her coffee, then waited for me while I placed my order. Then I paid for it before she could.

"I can afford coffee," she snarked at me, and I chuckled.

"I bet you can afford the whole cart. Doesn't mean I can't pay for the coffee."

"Just as long as we're clear that I'm *letting* you, and if we end up getting another cup, it'll be my treat."

"Those are the rules?" I was more curious than anything else.

"Yes."

Turning that over in my head, I nodded then motioned to the outside again. It was too lovely a day. I paused just outside to strip off my jacket, and I folded it carefully and tucked it in the bag. Normally, I'd keep it for professional distance, but it was after school hours.

And distance wasn't something I wanted with KC for this conversation. She watched me curiously as I slung the bag's strap over my chest crossbody.

Pausing, I raised my brows at her. "What?"

"Nothing," she said, then took a sip of the coffee before scanning the area. There were kids flopping out on the grass, and more than one of the male students had ditched their shirts while girls had gone for shorts that didn't meet regulations.

I could give them shit.

I wouldn't.

"You wanted to talk to me," she said, a reminder, and I blew out a breath.

"Yeah, walk with me?" I made it a request rather than an order. I needed to work out how to bring this up to her.

I headed for one of the walking paths that wound away from the academic buildings and into the trees. A lot of the runners favored these paths because they were quieter and they circled the campus, some farther out than others.

"You aren't going to want to listen to me," I intoned. "Based on past experience, I'm pretty sure you're just going to dismiss me out of hand. But I would regret not saying anything and then something happened."

"Okay." The base acceptance felt like a trap, but I went with the face value for now.

"Dating RJ Wallach is a bad idea."

She snorted.

"You don't have to believe me. I imagine me saying anything would be like waving a red flag at a bull. You're going to want to do it even more because I don't like it."

"Why?"

"Because you're obstinate," I said, glancing at her. "Why else?"

KC rolled her eyes then shook her head. "Not why would I not listen to you. *Why* don't you like him? Why is it a bad idea?"

"Does it matter?" RJ Wallach brought up a lot of bad memories. Worse choices.

"Yes. If you want me to think about it. You saying so is definitely not a good enough reason. So, tell me or shut up about who I do or don't date." The flatness beneath those words frustrated me more than the rolling of her eyes.

"You don't really care what I think."

"No, I really don't," she said, leaving the trail to walk up on a rock that looked down a tree-filled slope. "You're a liar."

I blinked. "Excuse me?"

With a kind of careless grace, she spun to face me. The wind tugged at her hair, pulling strands of it loose from the braid confining it. "You're a liar. All three of you are. You knew who I was when I got here. You knew who my father was. You didn't say a word. You played—whatever the hell that was last year and didn't say a word to me."

I frowned. "You were invited to the wedding. If you'd bothered to show up, you'd have met us then."

Her snort was so dismissive it rankled. "I was on tour, and I didn't even get the invitation until after the fact. It doesn't matter. You knew and you kept it to yourself. I didn't even know you douchebags were brothers until Jonas and Lachlan got into that fight. You know what...you could have said something *then*. You didn't."

No. We hadn't. I could try to defend it, but to be honest, at this point... the why didn't matter. Instead, all I said was, "We've lived with your father for years."

"Well, good for you." She saluted me with the cup and guilt stabbed at me abruptly. Had that been hurt in her eyes? "And now I know, so—water under that bridge?"

I sighed. "KC..."

"Oh, no, Mr. Malone. Like I said before, Miss Crosse is fine. You treated me like dogshit, you don't get to just decide everything is fine. We're not friends."

"No," I said, agreeing with her. "We're family."

There was nothing amused about her laughter. It was cold,

empty, and jagged enough to draw blood. "We are *not* family. You just happen to live with my sperm donor. That makes us exactly *nothing*. So, if that's all? I think I need to send RJ a message."

The last was just a dig at me. I knew it was a dig at me. She strode down off the rock, except rather than letting her past me, I wrapped an arm around her and picked her right up. Her chest impacted against mine, and the defiance blazing in her eyes lit a match on the wood chips of my temper.

Nothing could have prepared me for how her lips parted when my mouth fused to hers. Kissing her was the last thing I had intended, but this wasn't just a kiss. It was the activation of an incendiary device.

The rush of her tongue dueling with mine coupled with the rich taste of coffee and sweetness went right to my head. Her cup hit the ground and so did mine. I ignored the splash against my legs as her arms came around me. The press of her breasts through the shirt was a torment.

I fisted that braid, tugging her head back so she would open further. She matched my hunger with her own, the scrape of her nails against my scalp lighting me up.

Dimly, a sound registered. A crack of a branch or a twig. Voices in the distance. A bird song. I was drunk on the taste of her and when I finally dragged my head up, she bit my lip and scraped her teeth over it.

Nose to nose, we stared at each other, panting. The mingling of our breath was a tease. Her lips glistened, her face was flushed, and her pupils huge.

"Don't go out with him," I said. "Please."

She braced her hands on my shoulders and when she tugged a little, I released her hair and then set her on her feet.

Nothing about that kiss had been expected. Not my reaction. Not hers. She touched two fingers to her lips then glanced up at me. "I'll think about it." Her voice came out all husky and tense, but it was so much better than a no.

"Thank you."

"Is that all... Mr. Malone?"

Right. Back to our corners. "Quite, Miss Crosse."

With that, she turned and walked away. The sway to her hips was there, but it wasn't an invitation and she didn't look back. Once she was out of sight, I tilted my head back and stared up at the sky.

Bad idea, Ramsey, I told myself. Terrible idea.

At the same time, all I could feel was the way her lips moved with mine and how fucking sweet she tasted.

Epically bad idea.

Twenty

KC

Autumn blew in with an unseasonable snowstorm that caught *everyone* off guard. I'd slowly been working my way back up to running more regularly —except I varied the times I went out to keep Lachlan from following. I would prefer to hit the trails first thing in the morning, but he'd been lingering near the trailhead so... I switched to after classes. When he figured that out, I went back to mornings.

Thankfully, the doctor gave me the all clear. They'd been overly cautious in my opinion, but they didn't want to risk anything. I was just glad to be freed from restrictions. The ramp up to running daily couldn't come soon enough. The Douchebags Three were making me crazy.

Running let me put my thoughts in order. The cold air nipped at my face as I followed the trail. I hadn't bothered with music today, I didn't think it would get through the chatter in my head. Or maybe it was my awareness of being watched.

Because they were all watching me.

All. Of. Them.

Lachlan seemed determined to stalk me into submission. The fact he'd tracked me down at a club in Los Angeles, and then to my suite, just to kiss me confused the hell out of me. What did he want? The possessiveness wasn't lost on me. 'Course, his fight with RJ was like a reflection from the previous year.

I didn't think it had anything to do with me. RJ just provoked Lachlan. Course, so did Dix. RJ being there was another issue altogether. He'd invited me out on a date, but it was for some kind of escape room thing, and that was definitely not my favorite activity. Course, the riddle invite was kind of cute.

Then there was Captain Douchebag, as Dix dubbed him. He kissed the hell out of me. This *after* he asked me to not date RJ. He even said *please*. I legit had no idea what to do with any of it *or* them. The next time I saw him after the kiss, he acted like nothing happened.

To be frank, neither of them had apologized for the bullshit from last year. Maybe they'd forgotten, but I hadn't. Speaking of bullshit from last year...

Where Ramsey and Lachlan made me crazy, Jonas just flat out confused me. Mostly because unlike the other two, I'd begun to like Jonas. He'd been great as a roommate. It made me nervous when he was so nice.

Unlike the previous year, he actually spoke to me rather than just stare like he wanted to know what was inside my brain. We had developed a kind of routine, and he never wandered into the bathroom when I was in there.

Weird that I found that a perk. Course, I made a point to not walk in on him either. Respecting each other's space came easy. He picked up my favorites, I made sure to order his. At least once a week, we ordered in food and Jonas always went to get it.

I introduced him to some of my favorite reality shows. He showed me how to play a couple of his favorite video games. To be fair, I don't think either of us liked the other's picks, but we tried.

What more could you ask?

I still hated that Aubrey was across the hall and stuck with Payton. Aubrey assured me it wasn't a big deal. They pretty much steadfastly ignored each other. That didn't mean Aubrey didn't keep her bedroom locked, but she also spent more time hanging with Forrest and our friends when she didn't drop in on me and Jonas.

That was something, I supposed.

Thanksgiving came and went. Aubrey, Yvette, and I had debated plans. I headed to California to see Pen, Jackie, and Bronson for the week. They went to see their families to free us all up for Christmas.

We'd already talked about Canada for Christmas. We could go to Banff and ski, or maybe head over to Switzerland. For that matter, we could head south to Maryland. Lots of options, but I wanted an excuse to go away.

There was a pair of notes on my door when I came up the stairs from my midday run—one to me and one to Jonas. The lettering was pretty fancy, but Jonas wasn't back yet. I flew back early so I could have a couple of days for assignments and to look over the latest musical sheets Jonas had given me.

The run had been as much about shaking off frustrations directly related to Pen's treatment as it was my mother's head-long dive down the rabbit hole. She was back at the Sunshine Retreat and taking no calls as she spent time contemplating her future.

I got lunch with Johnny when I was in Los Angeles. He

had no idea what to do about her. She wouldn't answer his calls, either. Trish told me Mom hadn't called before she disappeared back to the retreat.

"Do you think you could…"

"Go back up there and talk her out?" I propped my chin on my hand and raised my eyebrows.

"I was hoping," he said, sadness filling his eyes. "It would be different if I knew what I'd done."

"Johnny, you have to know it wasn't you." It wasn't any of us. "Mom's just…" Did they have a word for Mom? "High maintenance. She's found something that gives her an easy fix of comfort with no responsibility. I don't think she's running away from you so much as her life."

That was as gentle as I could put it.

"So, do I just wait?"

"Well, I'm not exactly the queen of relationship advice. But you don't have to do anything. Relationships should be two-way streets. You can't give everything and get nothing back. It's not fair to you…"

"I don't care about me," he admitted with a prolonged sigh, then motioned to the sushi on my plate. "You should eat more. You're too skinny."

"Don't start." Jackie and Davina had both been the same way. I wasn't eating enough. I was too skinny. I needed to count the calories and make sure I wasn't undercutting myself. I used my chopsticks to pick up a piece of dragon roll. The spicy rich flavor was perfect.

By the time we finished lunch, I'd filled Johnny in on my autumn semester and the fact I wasn't sure about college. The funny thing about Johnny was he was more than just a beautiful face. He was genuinely nice and thoughtful.

"Before you go," he said as we were heading outside. Dix waited at the car for me, and Johnny had driven himself. He handed me a red enveloped card.

"Please tell me this isn't another pic for Mom," I said without opening it. If it was, I'd just deliver it unopened, thank you so much.

Johnny chuckled. "No, it's a present for you, sweet girl. Your birthday is soon. Probably won't see you before next year, so I didn't want to forget."

"Should I wait to open it?" I grinned.

"You can," he said, though a smile flirted with his lips. "But I don't mind if you open it early."

I slit the envelope and pulled out the birthday card. The front of it read *18 Years of Being a Bloody Legend*. I laughed, then opened it up. The interior made me laugh harder. *Now you can use your own ID*.

Johnny had signed it *Love, Johnny.*

Inside was a photo of me and Mom from her first time at the Golden Globes. I must have been all of six in the picture, wearing an identical dress to my mother and our hair was done in the same style.

On the back of it, Johnny had written, "Legends are born *and* made. You're the author of your own story. Never forget."

I blinked back some surprising dampness. I didn't even know there was a photo of this night. I had so much fun. Mom and I had been like besties all night. She didn't win, but it didn't matter. It was one of the few times where she seemed to just enjoy the moment.

Looking back on it, maybe one of the only times.

I gave Johnny a hug and he squeezed me gently. "I don't know where you found this, but I love it. Thank you."

He chuckled, then pressed a kiss to the top of my head. "Trade secret." He winked, then glanced at Dix. "Look after our girl."

"Always do," Dix said with a smile. They shook hands briefly. "C'mon, gorgeous, I think you've already been spotted."

One of the drawbacks of a famous face. L.A. was usually a safer space. Even if I was noticed, most of the locals let me do my thing. Tourists though? Yeah.

"Take care, Johnny."

"You too." He waited until we were in the car before he headed to his own. I had a flight back a few hours later, the redeye to get me back to the East Coast. I crashed as soon as I got back to the dorm, then went out for a run.

I put the note for Jonas on his door. We'd added clips so we could just leave things for each other. I carried mine into the bedroom and dropped it on the bed before I went to shower.

Thirty minutes later, I settled in with pizza, a fresh drink, and my homework. The rest of the night was just—nice. Quiet, easy, and without any interruptions. By the time I went to bed that night, I was feeling good. Ahead on my assignments, lyrics floating around in my head for Jonas' latest song, and relaxed.

I crashed hard. The sun was already up when I woke. My phone had a bajillion messages on it, but I'd left it in do not disturb. I also needed coffee before I went through that many.

The first one that popped up once I had coffee was from Aubrey.

> **AUBREY**
>
> I'll be back on campus this afternoon. Don't look at the articles.

There were a couple from Bronson, too.

> **BRONSON**
>
> You know, I'm impressed at how busy you've been. Based on the press reports, you must have 48 hours in a day. Ignore the h8ters

The haters?

I took a long drink of the coffee before I scrolled past general messages. A couple from our manager. Several from our social media manager. Two from our agent and a third one from the label rep.

What the fuck broke in the press now?

Deep breath, I switched to the news alerts. I had to read them three times.

Problem Child or Wild Child?

Looks like our pop princess didn't even wait for the birthday to start celebrating.

What the hell...?

Below that the first picture that jumped out at me was Ramsey carrying me out of the burning building. His whole attention was on me, his expression fierce. It stirred a vague memory, I thought he might have been pissed about me going back for the guitars.

Maybe?

Problem Child Burnout

Not even one day back on campus and our favorite girl's dorm suffered a massive fire. It burned down, leaving the school to find new accommodations. Thankfully, the injuries were minor, though a rumor had it that the Problem Child's voice might have been compromised. Is this another reason for retirement? And who is the hero here? Neither the school nor Torched's representatives answered our requests for a comment.

The next image was Lachlan and I dancing at the club. Goddammit. It was from the summer and right after he'd yanked my hat off. Another image was him kissing me.

Problem Child Raises Hell on the Club Circuit

Rumors were alive this summer about the Problem Child

and her club appearances. One lucky reader snapped these pics and shared them. Who is the lucky guy? Definitely not the boyfriend, RJ Wallach.

Problem Child Keeping Secrets

The image below that lovely headline was a snap of me and Jonas. I had no idea when it was taken. Clearly somewhere on campus, because we were in our uniforms. I was laughing at something he said. There was also a half-smile on his face. Honestly, it was a great picture.

The one below it had me and RJ from when he'd shown up on campus—that was only a few weeks ago. He was asking me out, and not ten minutes later, Ramsey kissed me.

I rubbed the back of my neck as I kept scrolling down. Never read the articles about yourself. They would only frustrate you. In this case, me.

Problem: Daughter Like Mother?

A picture of Ramsey kissing me. Another of Johnny giving me the hug. A third of Dix with a hand at my lower back to get me in the car.

Not only does it look like the soon-to-be 18-year-old is following in her mother's footsteps, it looks like she might be following her in the sheets.

My jaw fell open. That was *disgusting*.

As seen here, three of the guys she's been spotted with are not only brothers, they're her stepbrothers.

Then the article was off to the races, detailing my father's marriage to their mother. The last few lines of the article made my blood boil though.

Spotted in Los Angeles, with no sign of Mommy anywhere. Problem Child with her mother's lover, the adult film star Johnny Pound. So, not only is she after her stepbrothers, now she's after her mother's lover.

The urge to throw my phone surged through me. At the end of the article, it recommended a linked one.

Parents Group Calls for Boycott of Torched
Do we really want our children listening to trash rock by a girl with no morals?

I threw my phone.

Twenty-One

LACHLAN

The ringing of my phone had me rolling over to stare at it. Only the family rang through the do not disturb. I'd forgotten to change that. Mom's face popped up on the screen as it continued to ring.

Yeah, no. I put it down and let it roll over to voicemail. Flopping onto my back, I hooked an arm over my eyes as I debated going back to sleep. The phone started vibrating like mad. If I didn't look at her messages, I wouldn't be lying when I said I didn't see them. Maybe they didn't come through.

Leaving the phone next to the bed, I dragged myself up and pulled on my running clothes. Ace had been getting clever about dodging me, but the heavy snowstorm meant she'd have to go to the gym.

I warmed up, then headed out and "forgot" my phone on the nightstand. Ramsey stood in the kitchen, his eyes bloodshot and his glasses on. Someone had skipped their contacts today. He gave me a baleful look.

"I didn't do it," I told him as I grabbed a bottle of water out and twisted it open.

"No," my older brother informed me in that too patient tone. "You most definitely did it. So did I."

The last three words came out almost grumpy. Yeah, he'd been caught kissing Ace. "It's not happening again."

He blinked at me. "What?"

"You kissing Ace. It's not happening again." I was a perfectly reasonable guy. She was determined to teach me a lesson and I was willing to take my lumps. My brother could even try to say he didn't know how serious I was... he couldn't say that after the news broke.

Rather than answer me, he just shook his head and turned back to the coffeepot. His phone was going off and Mom's name came up. Ramsey barely even looked at it.

Like me, he skipped sending it to voicemail. "Avoiding Mom, too?"

Ramsey grunted.

"That wasn't a no. If you want to answer it..." I reached for his phone and he pivoted to glare at me.

"Don't you dare," he snapped, and I chuckled, raising my hands as I backed off. "This isn't a damn game, Lachlan."

"Sure it is. We've been reading stories about her for years. This is just the first time we got swept up into it." I didn't actually mind that part. "Wish RJ wasn't in those fucking pictures, or the porn guy."

Or that asshole who had been taking her out dancing. But considering I knew how "accurate" the picture with me was and what they didn't show, it gave me doubts about the rest.

"I don't see her sleeping with her mother's lover," Ramsey said without any prompting. "I also don't see *why* any of it was newsworthy."

"Aww, you embarrassed?" Ramsey didn't date much. Or

when he did, he kept them far away from the rest of us. To be honest, I couldn't think of his last girlfriend.

"No," he lied, then shook his head as he filled his mug. "I just wish that something private could be kept private."

That seemed unlikely.

"And it doesn't bother you?" Ramsey challenged.

Scratching my jaw and grimacing at the stubble, I shrugged. There had been a lot of press that night in Los Angeles. Somehow, the wrecked car stayed out of it, and for that, I was glad. I hadn't liked how terrified she'd been.

"Not a fan." I could admit that much. The idea of staking my claim publicly? I could get behind that. "But, I like it even less that a couple of those pictures came from here on campus."

Putting his coffee cup down, Ramsey picked up his phone. I took a long pull of water as he studied the images. "No one was around when she and I took that walk..."

"What were you walking? Your tongue?"

"Don't be an ass," Ramsey muttered. "I was just trying to tell her to stay away from RJ."

Oh, he had my attention. "That prick was there?" I'd already knocked the shit out of him once. I was starting to think I needed to just bury him. "Speaking of which, why the fuck is he back on campus? He's not going to the college." I'd checked.

"Mentor program."

I stared at him, but he didn't crack a smile or a joke. Scoffing, I shook my head. No way. "For fucking real?"

Ramsey sighed. "Unfortunately. His parents and the dean are close, he needs more counseling and service experience, so he's back on campus to mentor younger students."

That just made my blood run cold. "They aren't giving him any girls, right?"

"Far as I know," Ramsey said with a sigh. "I haven't been

able to find out much other than he is a mentor and he's specifically working with one of the political clubs. But he is trying to get KC to go out with him."

"He has a death wish." One I was more than happy to grant.

"You can't kill him."

"No, I can kill him. I just have to be prepared for the consequences." Currently, I was on the side of worth it, if it meant he never so much as glanced at Ace again. "I will not let what happened to Kelly happen to her."

I couldn't survive it. Kelly…

"Don't," Ramsey said firmly. "Don't go there. We're not going to let any of it happen. This is one good thing about her being Jonas' roommate."

Yeah, he hated RJ too. Course, currently he also hated me—us. "Jonas isn't talking to you, is he?"

Yeah, I didn't expect him to answer that. As it was, Jonas had gone cold as soon as the news broke. Long fucking flights back from Tahoe.

"Go stalk her running," Ramsey said. "That's where you're heading, right?"

"Maybe." But since he didn't want to answer my questions, I headed out to lay my eyes on the beautiful blue-haired menace that preoccupied my waking hours. Even when I should be focused on tryouts for a college team or looking to go semi-pro, I was here…chasing a girl.

The next couple of weeks were interesting. I'd never been the subject of that kind of gossip before. Mom always kept us out of all of it. She blended into the background when they came to see Gibs, and otherwise, she didn't want us spoiled by the spotlight and the ten seconds of notoriety and fame.

Look at KC. The girl had a reputation…

She did. But I had to wonder how much of that was real and how much of it was bullshit.

More than a few students threw me some side-eye. One of the jerks made some crack about fucking my sister and I didn't have to lift a finger, Jonas came out of nowhere and popped him.

When he got called to speak to the dean, I accompanied him. After all, I was a witness and I didn't see anything except Jonas trying to help a guy tripping. His face catching on Jonas' fist must have been an unfortunate accident.

Since it was our word against dipshit's, Jonas got a warning and I got a dirty look.

"Still not talking to me?" I asked when he stalked away as soon as we were outside.

He didn't even bother to lift a middle finger.

"Ouch, baby brother, that hurts."

Still nothing.

My phone rang and I checked it. Mom had been persistent as fuck for days. I don't think we'd heard from her this much in a two-week period since we started at Blue Ivy. It was too hard for her to talk to us on the phone. She missed us too much.

Not Mom.

Dad.

"Hey," I said as I answered. "Everything good?" We didn't talk that much during the week. Most often, I got a call on Sunday nights or we scheduled one. He tended to be busy on the day to day, and if he had a court case? Yeah. He was doing well to remember my name.

"It's fine. I wanted to talk to you about this girl in the news…"

"Ace?" I glanced around the hall, then ducked outside. If I was going to have a conversation about her, I didn't need anyone listening. I didn't give a shit what they said about me, but I preferred to not be weaponized.

"The lead singer of... Torched," Dad said with a question mark at the end. "Is that an actual band name?"

"Yes, Dad," I said, chuckling. "A little too pop for your tastes though."

"Huh," he grunted and the wheels on his chair squeaked as he sat back. I could picture him in his office. He'd been doing legal work for labels for years. But it wasn't for their music, he just enjoyed the work. He preferred a harder, grittier rock. He was one of Gibs' biggest fans. "Regardless, I think you need to think about this before you get too involved."

Get too involved? I paused and glanced up at the gray clouds moving in. It smelled like snow out here. One of my favorite seasons, here or Tahoe. Anywhere that involved the cold.

"Dad, are you calling to give me dating advice?" Because that was just not us.

"Fuck no," he said with a laugh. "I'd be a terrible source. Clearly."

No comment.

"That said, you have plans. A sports career you're planning on building. You wanted to get into the pros and then coach, maybe train... getting involved with someone like—KC—Kaitlin Crosse, is she Gibs' girl?"

"Yeah," I said. "She is. Seeing her has nothing to do with my career choices." Except I was here instead of Stanford.

"That's what you think now. Nevertheless, that notoriety doesn't stop at the concerts or the new albums. It's always there. So is the reputation..." Dad sighed. "I just want you to think about it. This girl already generates a lot of negative press. The fact she's seeing your brothers as well makes her seem a little..."

"Don't say it."

"You have to know how it looks."

"I don't care how it looks," I snapped back. "Don't call her names. You don't even know her."

"Do you?" He didn't challenge me often. "Gossip is cheap. But this many stories? There's truth there. Just don't fall into the trap of thinking you're the guy who is going to change her."

"I'm not falling into anything," I said, even as I caught a flash of blue and turned to track it. Ace was walking with her bandmate and a couple of other girls. They were all laughing as they walked together. Whatever the one blonde was saying, she had KC's total attention. "She's just a girl."

"Yeah," Dad said. "So was your mom. Well, I have to go into a meeting. Be careful, Lachlan."

I didn't really respond but he wasn't waiting for me to answer. The line went dead and I snagged Ace's gaze as she started to go into the dining hall. From this distance, I couldn't really make out her eyes, but I wasn't imagining the question on her face.

It was nice to see her smiling. I didn't get a lot of that. When she paused at the door and raised her eyebrows, I chuckled. Did I want to see her? Of course, I did. But I could wait.

I wanted time with Ace without an audience. And after those pictures? I didn't plan to feed the beasts. I shook my head and a fresh surprise flickered over her expression. Then, because I just wanted to stand there and stare at her, I turned and forced myself to walk away.

I lasted all of three days before I went looking for her. She was just going out for a run, so I walked up to her.

"If you plan on pushing me in the pond, it's frozen, and if you want to listen to my music, I'll share an earbud. But I need to run today." The words came out sharp, but almost shaky. It wasn't my imagination.

"You okay, Ace?" I moved so that I was in front of her.

Scanning the area, I looked for the sign of someone bothering her.

"I'm fine." It was a lie. She tugged her knit cap down. It made something in my chest tight when I recognized the running jacket and leggings. I could ask about the sports bras and panties, but I didn't. "Just—need to run and I don't want to fight."

I wanted to fight. Whatever was upsetting her. "C'mon," I told her, holding out a hand. "I'll make sure no one bothers you." At her skeptical look, I spread my hands. "Not even me. Two-hour armistice, I give you my word. While I might look at your ass, I won't grab it."

The corners of her mouth twitched, but she pulled on her neoprene mask before I could see the whole smile. So I put mine on as well. "Promise?" she asked.

"What's my word worth to you?" Not like I'd given her a lot to trust.

"If you do what you say you will on this run, then it will be worth a little more than it is right now."

Still more. "Lead the way, Ace. I'll be right behind you the whole way. Someone steps out to get in your way, you keep going. I'll deal with them."

She squinted at me, even as she jogged in place. The cold was getting to me too, and it was early. Almost too early.

I never liked her running out here in the dark. Alone.

After one more long, searching look, she nodded then set off, and I was right behind her. I stuck with her for the whole run, monitoring the path for slush or ice. She pushed herself and me.

We were both sweating by the time we made it back and her face was flushed, eyes a little brighter, and her hands were steadier.

Was she jonesing for something? She didn't strike me as the drug type. But I didn't know her as well as I wanted.

Back at the dorm, I continued with my restraint and let her go up the stairs without me. The surprise in her eyes was a little humbling, although her little smile when she headed up the stairs was a worthy reward.

I managed to swing a couple more runs with her. I just kept up my promise to watch her back. Her ass moving in front of me was not a bad sight at all. I also made sure no one bugged her, not that I saw anyone, anyway.

Then again, maybe that was why she'd gone back to pre-dawn runs. No one could see her.

Now I felt like kind of an asshole for crashing her run time. But she wasn't arguing with me, and I kind of missed that part, even if I needed that surprise and disappointment in her eyes to go away.

The next week I focused on classes. Semester finals were coming up, and I had begun to get more active with Knots and Chains. Ace had been tapped. So had Jonas. Ramsey was too tied up running classes to follow up, but I could. The last time Jonas had been tapped...

Yeah, we weren't doing that again either. I went after sponsoring them both. I didn't want RJ trying to recruit her his way. As it was, she'd only completed one trial that they knew of. She hadn't responded to the second challenge.

Maybe she didn't know it was a set of clues, or she didn't care? Did I want her in Knots and Chains? It could be fun. I just didn't want RJ anywhere near her.

She had gone running on her birthday, the day before, with her friend. The girl groaned, complained, and gave me so much side-eye I kept a wary distance.

I had gotten Ace a present, so I headed up the day after her birthday while she and Jonas should be in class to drop off the gift for her. I'd had to order it, but they were custom picks. They were perfect. I'd ordered from them before.

The fourth floor was quiet. College didn't have the same

all day schedule. I did not miss morning, noon, and afternoon back to back to back classes. I let myself in and glanced around the tidy suite. Jonas definitely had taken to picking up after himself. There were no dirty socks on the floor and no trash on the counters.

It even smelled nicer in here.

Glancing down at the little wrapped box, I headed for my old room. The door was locked, but there was—there it was. I grasped the long metal cylinder from above the frame and used it to pop the lock.

Inside, I went to put the present on her rumpled bed when the door to the bathroom opened and she walked out in a towel.

Just. A. Towel.

All the moisture in my mouth fled, and I was pretty sure if not for autonomic functions, I'd probably have died already.

She was...holy shit, she was gorgeous. I'd seen her tattoos before, glimpses of them, but they were on full display on her arms and I wanted to know where else she had them.

I wanted to know everything.

Twenty-Two

KC

Not only was someone *in* my room, behind the door I'd *locked*, it was also the absolute last person I expected to find in my bedroom.

"What the fuck?" It came out halting and stuttered. Jonas, even when he came to talk to me, never came through the door itself. Now, *Lachlan*, Douchebag King of the Damn Ninja Kiss, was standing right there and all I had on was a towel, with another wrapped around my hair. "What the hell are you doing in here?"

"I—" No other sound escaped him. Beyond registering that he was in my room, I hadn't paid much further attention to him. Lachlan swallowed. The sound seemed almost too loud in my room, and his eyes tracked over me like he couldn't decide where to look.

Worse? The scorching heat in his eyes was like a desert wind blowing away all the chills. It was almost too hot in my room now and this was after I showered to chase away the cold. I'd spent too long outside, waiting to hear about Pen's latest scan results.

The chemo *seemed* to be working. "Seemed" being the keyword. They'd had to change their course when the first few rounds had only succeeded in making her sick and not shrinking the cancer.

By the time the call ended, the chill was in my bones and even my feet were numb. I'd sent Jonas a message and asked if he'd grab my assignments for me. It was the first time I'd taken advantage of our roommate situation, and hopefully he didn't mind.

Even boiling myself in the shower didn't burn me up the way Lachlan's eyes were. A shudder climbed my spine and goosebumps raced over my skin. The longer he stared at me, the hotter it seemed in here.

"Lachlan?" I demanded when he seemed to have gone completely mute while he stared at me.

"Ace," he said slowly, dragging his gaze up to lock on my eyes. "Long time..."

"Clearly," I said, hoping for a frosty tone and getting one that came out a great deal more breathless. Fuck. "But why are you in my room?"

"Used to be mine." The flippant response was so him, but then again so was the cocky grin slowly spreading across his face. The last couple of weeks, he'd been a thoughtful prick.

I kind of wished it had lasted.

All good things though...

"It's *not* your room anymore though, is it?" I challenged, fisting my grip on the towel. I wanted to yank the one off my head and snap it at his face. But that would bring me closer to him and right now, I needed every inch of space between us.

"No," he said slowly, the rapt expression on his face irritating and fascinating me in equal measures. Right, no fascination, KC. "It's not, and more's the pity, because it's definitely gotten so much better in my absence."

A laugh escaped with my snort. "Well, look at that, we can agree on something."

Another grin flashed across his lips, and a fresh spark lit his green eyes. The intensity of the mysterious forest was suddenly alive again. And fuck if I didn't want to get lost in there...

No. No I don't. The mental slap didn't do much for clearing out the haze of attraction that just did not *belong* here right now, ninja kisses or no ninjas kisses.

"We agree on a lot more, Ace," he said, taking a step toward me. "What we don't, I'm almost certain we could negotiate. This vibe right here...it's everything." He motioned to the two of us. The excitement in his voice coupled with those scorching looks and the fact he was still between me and the door out of here while I was in a towel just struck a match.

Anger blew through me like a wildfire. The heat burning me up right now had nothing to do with attraction. Where the love and hate coin was concerned, I was far more on the latter than the former. The only thing he was succeeding in doing was dislodging my indifference.

"Let me clear something up for you, douchebag." I eyed him. "This vibe? It's dislike, disdain, and I would imagine *disappointment.* The first two you made clear and the third? Well, let's just say I've been there long enough to earn a permanent address. Now do us both a favor and get the fuck out."

I headed for the closet. I could at least throw on some clothes while in there. I didn't make it two steps before he tugged the towel and it spun me around as he yanked it free. I half-stumbled trying to hold onto it but if I didn't let go, I would have collided with him.

"You ass—" I didn't even get to finish the sentence, because his gaze wasn't on my body. The fact that cool air rushed against me didn't help with the goosebumps or the tightness of my nipples.

Even my thoughts stuttered to a halt at the dark possession in his gaze. Two things happened. I yanked the towel off my head even as he dropped the other one on the floor. Then he was just there, filling the space, taking up all the oxygen and his lips were dangerously close to mine.

"Ace," he whispered. "You're fucking gorgeous."

And naked.

That last thought burned itself into my brain before he dipped his head to erase the few millimeters separating our mouths. I could move, I could have shifted my head. The thought turned to cinders as his lips massaged mine. The touch was just barely there, and his hands didn't land on my skin.

Every other time he'd kissed me, he'd grabbed me and hauled me close. Sometimes it was my face. Other times my body, this time? The only point of contact was our lips. The damp hair on my shoulders and the wet towel between us didn't even seem a deterrent.

The stroke of his tongue seeking access entranced with the delicate, teasing taste he took. I rocked back a step and he followed, like a magnet keeping him in my orbit.

Fuck, this is a terrible idea...

Didn't stop me from parting my lips to suck at his tongue as he plunged it against my own. He tasted like sugar cookies and coffee. Hints of cinnamon and chocolate. Dessert.

Goddammit, he tasted like dessert. I lifted a hand to his head and when my fingers brushed against his face, he pressed a little closer and then I fisted his hair even as he locked a hand on my chin, using his thumb to tip my head back further.

A groan vibrated out of my throat as our tongues dueled. He wasn't trying to take over, but I found myself sinking deeper into the sensual haze conjured by his kiss. When my back hit the cold wall, the contrasting sensations had my hand slipping on my towel.

"Lachlan," I said in the brief respite where he let me get air. The pressure of his body against mine locked the towel in place as I pressed a hand to his chest. To push him away? Pull him closer?

Fuck, I had no idea. The scorch of wanting him seemed to consume me. And I'd never craved being burned so badly.

Curling my fingers into his shirt, I dragged him closer and he slid a hand down my arm, to my side and then to my hip. He left a trail of fire everywhere he touched. My thighs were taut and I ached for more.

"I'm here, Ace," he whispered, nipping my lower lip as he tightened his hand on my hip. "Trying not to—fuck me, touch, but you're so fucking gorgeous."

The towel slid away and then I was locked against him, the fabric of his now-damp shirt a fresh torment for my nipples. I dug my nails into his nape as his mouth fused over mine.

Need ignited in my system like someone poured kerosene on it. I wanted to climb him as he ground against me. The heat in my body was such a sharp contrast to the chill, that I needed both. When he slid his hand down to cup my thigh and lift it, I gasped against his mouth.

The roughness of his jeans against the inside of my thighs and the dampness of my pussy was enough to make me shudder all over again. It was embarrassing, yet I wanted more. He sucked on my tongue as he thrust his hips against mine. Awareness of his erection swept through me as he ground against me. It was almost too much and at the same time not enough.

When he cupped my breast though, it sent an electric shockwave through me and I jerked my head back. The light impact with the wall helped to knock some sense back into me.

I licked my lips as Lachlan stared down at me. The weight of his hand on my breast was a brand. The teasing pass of his calloused thumb over my nipple was a fresh charge that seemed to send a bolt straight through me. Liquid heat pooled in my stomach.

"What are we doing?" I asked in a horrifically hoarse voice.

"Living out my fantasies," Lachlan said, his own lips glistening from our kiss. He rolled his hips, the pressure against my pussy enough to make me close my eyes as he pinched the nipple.

Competing sensations rioted in my system. First kiss. First petting... My Douchebag Ninja was taking a lot of liberties.

"Stop," I whispered, proud that my voice didn't quaver. His hand froze on my breast, and I could almost picture the exact outline from the heat of his palm. He stood there, resting against me, but not moving. "Thank you."

"This is still..." he began and I almost laughed, because it was still too much.

"What are we doing?" I repeated my earlier question and then dragged a hand from his hair to press two fingers against his lips. "Don't say fantasies again because you hated me last year even when you were hitting on me, and I have no fucking clue what you're doing right now beyond trying to drive me mad."

Not that it was a long trip at the moment.

I was pretty sure I'd already crashed into the insanity train head on. I was currently craving more contact, not less, with one of my tormentors and *stepbrothers.*

The guy who lied to me and used what he knew about me against me. A guy who helped to dump paint all over me, ruining an outfit, not to mention threw me in a fucking pond.

Oh, right, and cut my bra off so he could look at my tits. Then there was stalking me in L.A. and finally outing me at the dance club.

The litany of his various comments and actions helped to cool the ardor he'd fanned to life. I swallowed as he brushed a kiss to my fingers.

"This isn't why I came," he admitted. The low, husky quality to his voice promised he was every bit as affected as I was. But was there a camera somewhere? A phone to record us? Was I going to see photos of us pop up somewhere?

"So, you broke into my room for another reason?" Sue me, I was curious.

A corner of his mouth tilted up as he studied me. His hand was still right there, on my breast, but he wasn't moving it. "Pretty sure I had a reason. Fuck knows, I can't think of it right now. All I want is to kiss you again and touch you...and I want to taste—"

Right, I pressed my hand over his mouth this time. Not because what he described was repugnant. No because I was getting a thrill from it and, right now, I needed to let him go and he needed to back off.

Then I should get dressed.

These were all reasonable actions.

I pressed the hand on his chest to nudge him away. "Let me go."

A long sigh escaped him but he took his hands away and fuck if I wasn't suddenly cold for their absence. Even more for when he backed up a couple of steps and the air in the room rushed against my flushed body.

His gaze dipped to my breasts then back up. "Sorry," he muttered as he locked on to my eyes. "I'm a guy and you're..."

"Naked," I told him as I forced myself to stand up straight. "Stay there..."

The sound of the locks giving seemed to tumble loudly into the silence punctuated by our panting breaths. The door to the suite opened...

Jonas.

Fuck.

Fuck.

Fuckity, fuck, fuck.

"Stay," I hissed at Lachlan and then snagged my towels before darting into the closet.

Shit.

As grateful as I was for the interruption and the splash of icy reality, I had some real regrets.

Jonas walking in on this was going to kill all the progress we made.

So much for detente.

Twenty-Three

JONAS

I had KC's assignments and the surprise reading they'd dropped on us. The novel was to be read before the break for the semester and it would be on the final. Gotta love Ramsey tweaking the syllabus. I would bet anything this had to do with KC not being in class. He'd stared at her empty seat more than once.

When he received a note halfway through class to go to the administration building, a certain amount of satisfaction filtered through me. He should never have been kissing one of his students, much less KC. Those images were burned into my brain.

But I'd only kept one and locked it onto my phone behind a passcode. It was the one they'd taken of her with me. I didn't know which dick on campus had snapped it, but the look in her eyes as she stared up at me and her laughter was like a sucker punch of joy.

Were we friends? I wasn't sure. I thought we might be. Then my brothers were kissing her or the press was chasing her. The KC who shared my suite wasn't that "problem child," and I was hating that label.

More, she seemed to *see* and *hear* me. I wasn't less social than Lachlan or dumber than Ramsey. She liked my music, took time to put lyrics to it... she was a dream and a muse. Maybe we wouldn't be friends.

Didn't change my need to protect her. It was unreasonable and bordered on obsession. It had even come up in my sessions, but I refused to talk about her there. The world judged her enough.

Fuck them all.

The door to KC's room was open and Lachlan strolled out like he belonged here. Worry speared through my suspicion instantly. "What are you doing in her room?"

"Oh, look," Lachlan retorted with a smirk. "You remember how to use your words with me."

The distance between us wasn't so great. "You need to up your time with the next black eye?" Because I would be more than happy to deliver.

"Baby Bro, I've given you plenty of leash. Don't try to hit me again. I will hit back."

Given me? I slung my bag down onto the sofa. It was KC's spot, but I kept my focus on Lachlan. "What are you doing in my suite?"

"Does it matter?"

"Yes." I was over this game.

"I came by to drop off something for my girl," Lachlan drawled, possessiveness threading every sentence. "If you really need to know."

"Yeah, I did...and she's *not* your girl."

"You sure about that?" The smirk pissed me right the fuck off.

"He may not be," KC announced from behind him in a

husky voice that vanished when she cleared her throat. "But I am. Definitely not your girl, Douchebag."

Surprise flashed in Lachlan's eyes and his smirk fell away before he spun to look at her. "Ace, you wound me."

"Oh, you need him wounded?" I checked with KC. Her face was flushed and her eyes almost too wide. There was a wildness to her that spoke of unease and I glared at my brother. What had he done?

"I got it," KC said, folding her arms. She was dressed in a plain t-shirt with an open long-sleeved plaid shirt over it and a black pair of pajama bottoms that covered her legs.

Her hair though... was damp.

She'd been in the shower.

She'd been in the shower and Lachlan had been in her room.

"Time to go," KC informed Lachlan. "The door is that way."

She wanted him gone? I was on board with that. I stalked forward. To my surprise though, Lachlan actually raised his hands. "I'm going, Ace. But I'll see you tomorrow for running. Don't sneak out."

Smirk back in place, he headed for the door. I really wanted to throw him out. So, I opened it for him, then slammed it shut as soon as he cleared the door and I glanced at KC again.

Her head was back and her eyes closed. There was a faint bruise on her throat. It looked a lot like a finger mark, or was I just making shit up in my head?

"Are you all right?"

The blue of her eyes captivated me when she opened them. The shade matched her hair, yet seemed wholly its own. Shoulders rising, she seemed at a loss for words. That was usually me, and it just increased my anger at Lachlan.

"I'll be fine... has Lachlan always had a key to this suite?" Confusion filled the question as she focused on me. The intensity in her eyes beckoned me closer. It wasn't the ineffable light from the article photo, but it was like I could feel her gaze viscerally.

"I can request a change," I offered, except... "Ramsey has access to all the rooms. He's the RA for the building, so his keycard opens them all. Lachlan's staying with him." I wanted to apologize for my brothers, but I wasn't even sure where to start with them.

Did she like when they kissed her? Did I want to know if she did? Then again, she didn't want Lachlan in here so maybe she didn't? She grimaced and exhaled a long sigh. I'd figure something out.

It might involve talking to Ramsey.

The worried look on her face arrested me. If I had to talk to Ramsey, then I would. She should feel safe in our room.

"I think I need coffee," she said slowly. "Would you like some?"

"You don't have to make me any." I tracked her progress to the kitchen. "You weren't feeling well..." An idea hit me. "Do you want to show me how to make the coffee you like?"

I'd been careful to not touch the machine. She'd been so pleased when it had been replaced.

"I was just tired," she told me over her shoulder, a flicker of a real smile on her face. "It's been a long day and I had a long call...got cold... and... " She shook her head, trailing off as she seemed to hug herself. "But better now from the shower. Coffee sounds good. So my offer stands."

"So does mine," I said as I pulled off my class coat.

She grinned, really grinned. "Okay. Do you want to get comfortable and then I'll show you how this works?"

I glanced down at my suit and then at her. "Yeah, I'll be right back, and I got your stuff...including the assignment to read *Sense and Sensibility.*"

"Thank you," she called and there was so much warmth in those two words, it buoyed my mood. Lachlan's unwelcome presence had soured the day some, but KC made it better.

Ten minutes later, I foamed my first milk and she wasn't wrong. For all the buttons and controls on this thing, it was pretty straightforward. She laughed when I got a good foamy cap on the first try.

"That's not always easy," she said. "You should be proud. It took me a week to get the right amount of foam, then foam art took a little longer."

"Foam art? Oh, making the pictures in it? You can do that?" It wasn't a big deal, except it was kind of cool.

"I can," she said, before taking a sip of her coffee. "That will be lesson two *after* you master making the coffee without supervision."

I could live with that. "Deal." Now that we had our coffee, I headed over to my bag to get her stuff out. "Did you want to do something? Watch a movie? Order in dinner? Take it easy?" Then again, she'd also missed classes for a reason. "I know you're tired, so if you wanted to get comfortable, I could take care of stuff."

The flow of words spilled out of me in a rush. I nearly sagged from the exhaustion of getting them out. Misty, my therapist, was always telling me to verbalize. But that was a lot of verbal for me.

"That sounds great," she admitted. "But I have homework."

"Me too...we actually have to read that book." I'd instead stick pins in my eyes. "But maybe we could work together? We might be faster, and then we could watch a movie."

A thoughtful look crossed her face as she claimed her corner of the sofa after I removed my backpack. I set her folder and copy of the book on the table. I wasn't sure if she preferred to read eBooks or not. She might. But since I didn't know, I checked us both out copies of the required reading.

"Can we not watch the movies based on this book?" She picked it up. "I mean, not yet. Like watch something fun? Or maybe this is fun for you?"

Putting my coffee on the table in front of us, I tested a smile. It wasn't so hard. Then I dropped onto my seat at the other end of the sofa. "I've never seen those movies. So...I don't know if they are fun."

Which was true.

"I was thinking of an action film or a comedy. Something to just be fun?" I hadn't done much fun since before summer except... I pushed up the sleeve of my shirt. "The last fun thing I did was get my dad to update my sleeve."

Long sleeves was just a habit I had when at school, mostly cause we weren't supposed to show off our tats and I had way more than was legal in most places. But Mom didn't care and Dad did them so...

"Your father's a tattoo artist?" She leaned forward to study the guitar and base he'd finished. It wasn't the only thing he'd finished for me, but I liked the musical representation.

"Yep," I said. "He's based out of Denver now, but he used to be in Los Angeles. He's got a good eye." It was how he'd met my mother. But... yeah, I skated right past that. "He's been teaching me, but drawing isn't my strong suit."

The heart on the side of her hand, the one tattoo I could make out at the moment, had been filled in. I thought it was just an outline before. Maybe it had always been filled in.

"I like those," she offered as she motioned to the banner across the heart covering part of the guitar. "He's got great lettering technique." She set her coffee aside and tugged off the plaid shirt to reveal one of her arms.

Even living together, I hadn't gotten close-ups with any of her tattoos.

"The wildflowers," she said as she extended her arm and there were a lot of them twining around her arm. More, there was a moth, a raven, a moon... so many different elements intertwined with the flowers. There was a rose on her shoulder...a very familiar one. "They're about living life on my terms. Wildflowers—they grow anywhere, in any terrain, and sometimes in the most inhospitable conditions. They'll grow right up through a crack in the sidewalk."

"I like that," I said, trying to memorize the art. She was right, most tattoos had meaning. The rose I'd added to my own did. But... yeah maybe not the time to bring it up. "Is living life on your terms important?"

"People love to consume and criticize celebrities until many budding stars begin to question if they are even built for this life." The comment resonated and there wasn't an ounce of arrogance in her tone. "They've been judging me since before I could talk. Some have been judging me since before I was born." Her gaze went distant. "My parents are...well...yeah you know who they are, don't you?"

It was the first time we crossed the rubble of revelations made the previous year. We hadn't discussed her father at all. Gibs was a great guy; I couldn't admire him more if I tried.

Somehow...I didn't think KC did and I wanted to know why. She traced her finger over the moth.

"This is for them... for being trapped between them forever. Trapped by them and their reputations. Being a Crosse sometimes sucks."

I hated that for her. "Wh—"

Her phone buzzed and then chimed with a familiar tune it played. Someone was messaging and calling her. The noise thoroughly punctured the bubble around us, and she tugged her shirt back on before looking at her phone.

Worry creased her expression. "I have to take this... sorry." Then she was up and striding for her room. The door closing behind her seemed to put a period on the moment.

Caught between her parents. Living life on her terms.

I wanted to know more.

Needed to know.

Twenty-Four

KC

The holidays were rapidly approaching. We were in the middle of finals for the semester. The population at the school swung a wide emotional pendulum between meltdown and slap happy. I'd actually spent two hours talking Sydney down from the idea she was failing everything because she got a ninety on a paper instead of a perfect grade.

I thought *I* was hard on myself. I'd spent half a night and two pints of ice cream in her suite while we talked it out. She seemed in better spirits when she left, and I needed a run from the bloated feeling.

What I thought was just the ice cream proved to be my period, debuting a week early. Stress sucked. The cramps were hell. I had supplies, but I didn't keep them in the bathroom. Jonas and I had developed a rapport, but that was just a little too personal.

The fact it started while I was in class sucked. At least it wasn't still my birthday. I made a dash back to the suite.

Tampons were in the closet, and it took me almost no time to get changed.

I checked two different bags, but there was no Midol in either one. Great, I'd managed to not restock. Stupid, KC, stupid. After checking my tie and pulling my coat back on, I headed back out and down the stairs. I was going to be late to class, but I'd rather be late than messy, thank you very much.

My luck ran out just three steps from the door to the literature class. It opened, allowing one of the administrators to exit the room. Beyond him, I could see Ramsey standing there where he'd been conducting class, his expression neutral if guarded.

"Miss Crosse," the man said...what was his name? Mr. Robin? Robinette? Roban? Something with an R.

"Sir?" I went for polite.

"Don't worry about the tardy or the absence. Neither will be counted against you." The door closed behind him, cutting off my view. "If you'll come with me."

Come with him?

"Am I in trouble?" Academic probation the previous year had sucked, but I'd busted ass all last year and into this one to stay as ahead as I could. I was carrying straight As at the moment, and I had a bet with Bronson I could beat his senior year GPA. So far, I wasn't *winning*, but I wasn't *losing* either.

"Not at all, Miss Crosse. The dean and I have some questions for you. We can contact a parent or guardian if you prefer, so they can be present."

Alarm bells went off, but I re-shouldered my backpack. "I'm eighteen." I was emancipated before then and more than capable of negotiating for myself. We also had a manager, an attorney, an agent, and reps from the label if we ran into issues we couldn't handle. "Although I'd like to keep this brief and not miss my other classes."

"Absolutely," he said, motioning for me to take point. The

walk took us from the academic building to the administrative. With—yeah, I still couldn't remember his name—escorting me, we were in the dean's office in minutes.

"Miss Crosse," the dean said as he stood and extended his hand.

Dean Mayfair shook my hand briefly. "I am sorry we had to pull you out of class, but the board has been meeting and after some serious consideration, I wanted to meet with you personally before we proceed with any action."

Lowering my backpack slowly, I raised my eyebrows as I sat, and he resumed his. My escort did not sit down but stood near the wall like he would be here to witness the conversation but not participate.

Yeah, that wasn't weird at all.

The earlier alarm bells were back and raising a cacophony. "What is this about, exactly?" Because right now, I was wondering if I should be getting an attorney or at least another witness. Business meetings that began with vague premises were never a good idea.

"Straight to the point," the dean said. "I respect that. This is regarding a recent article written about you that included some rather...invasive photographs."

The birthday girl and the stepbrothers bullshit. I said nothing; better to give no comments than confirm anything. He gave me a moment, but I waited for him to finish.

Sitting forward, he opened a file folder and laid out printouts of the online article and all the fun photographs. The last one, of course, was of me and Ramsey, where we were kissing.

Fantastic.

"You have seen this?"

"I have." Admitting to seeing the article wasn't a confession of anything. "I'd recommend against following the gossip sites. They generally have nothing good to say." About anyone, for any reason. Negative news and clickbait were their bread and butter.

"I agree with you," he said, nudging the page with Ramsey and me forward. "Both in principle and in practice; however, this isn't so much about what they wrote as what is depicted in this photograph."

Glancing at the photo briefly, I kept my business face locked on. Neutral and don't commit to anything without verification. So many people thought pushing us around 'cause we were kids when we got started was the way to go, except Mom actually gave me the best advice.

Never walk in like you owe anyone anything. They want you there, so make them earn it.

Right now, the dean wanted answers from me. He'd have to earn them. "All right."

He sighed, then leaned back as he adopted a more sympathetic look. "Miss Crosse, I'm aware that this is probably not the most comfortable of topics, but Mr. Malone is a TA on this campus. He's actually the TA in two of your classes, and he was for one class last year."

The urge to snark at him was right there, but I resisted it... narrowly, 'cause *no shit.*

"You are a student on this campus and, until a few days ago, underage. It would be highly inappropriate for Mr. Malone to pursue *any* relationship with you beyond that of being a teacher's assistant and, I believe, your tutor for some time."

"He was an excellent tutor." Even when he was a fucking dick about it. "He really came through for me last year, pushed me to be better, and challenged what I knew. I didn't really care for it too much in the beginning, however, I think I genuinely benefitted from his help."

A sentiment, I had, in fact, *tried* to tell Captain

Douchebag, except he didn't listen. *Or maybe he did, but whatever, I forgot what an entitled little bitch I can be.*

"I'm very glad to hear this...the concern about this involvement..." He tapped the photograph. "I need to know if he's kissed you before and what happened around this kiss."

Captain Douchebag was in trouble. The too-serious looks on the pair standing here made that clear. "Can you offer me some assurances that nothing I say here will be repeated?"

Surprise stamped its way across his features. "We would never..."

I raised a hand. "Forgive me, but the number of people who have assured me they would never say anything to the press then promptly reported my grades when I was in elementary school have taught me to be wary. You are both bound by a nondisclosure agreement with the school."

He sat back abruptly. "Of course."

"Then let's discuss language with you and the lawyer over there." Because now I knew who he was. Of course, an attorney would be sitting in on this. "Whether or not it covers anything regarding incidents such as this and questioning."

"It does," the lawyer said as he straightened. "It is why I'm here, to ascertain that everything is followed to the letter. Your statement, in full, will not be presented to anyone beyond myself and the dean. We will in turn answer any questions the board asks, but without any details. Your privacy will remain intact."

"And if it doesn't, I can sue you?" Going straight for legal remedies wasn't always smart, but I wanted the lawyer and I to be on the same page. I had my own lawyers, and it would be wise for them to remember that.

My cramps were increasing, and it was definitely souring my mood further. No matter what else happened today, I needed tacos, a heating pad, and some serious chocolate and caffeine.

"While I would prefer that it doesn't come down to that, I can assure you, I will say nothing. If you prefer, I can step out then it will only be you and Dean Mayfair. That said, I would prefer to be present because it allows us to provide a united front to the board."

"Fine," I said, crossing one leg over the other before I sighed. "Question number one, is that the only time he kissed me?"

"Yes." The dean actually looked nervous.

"Not quite, because he didn't kiss me. I kissed him."

The dean blinked.

"He saved my life and my guitars the night of the fire. He got me out when I collapsed. He saved my grades last year...he's not horrible on the eyes. I may have developed... an inappropriate attachment and expressed it." I didn't have to worry about manufacturing a blush, because my face heated just thinking about how truly accurate the crush had been.

Could still be, save for so many factors, including Mr. Ninja Kiss and Hot Shot.

Clearing my throat, I shifted in the chair. "The point is, I kissed him, he pushed me away. Said I needed to be more focused on school and not on dating." Not quite a lie, definitely not the truth. "He told me that I might be a rock star out there, but here, I was nothing. A student and absolutely nothing more."

The dean frowned. "He called you nothing?"

"I suppose when it comes to letting someone down, there aren't gentle ways. He may not have phrased it as that specifically..." He so fucking did. "But the message was clear."

"If you kissed him and haven't before...how did someone snap a picture of it?"

"I don't know. Ask the Tattler or whoever published it. There have been a number of videos and photographs of me published since I've been on campus. Everyone has a cell phone." It was the cost of doing business.

"So, you aren't uncomfortable with Mr. Malone?" the dean pressed.

"No," I said. "At least not because I think he's going to kiss me." There were plenty of *other* reasons to be uncomfortable around him, but I'd handle that on my own.

"Thank you, Miss Crosse. If you would like, we can remove him as TA from your classes." If I would like... Nice ass covering there.

"He's a good teacher," I said, standing. "I would hate to lose out on the expertise because I engaged in a moment of thoughtless stupidity." Backpack slung over my shoulder, I added, "I'm here for maybe one more semester. Don't change his schedule on my account. I won't be going out of my way to kiss him again."

Both men stared at me.

"That's it? I don't need to sign anything?"

The question seemed to shake them out of their surprise. "Of course not," the dean said as he rose. "Thank you for answering our questions. I'm very fond of Mr. Malone, but we do have a code of conduct. For our staff as well as our students." The last he said with a firm eye on me.

"Understood," I told him. "Can I go?"

"Absolutely, go on back to class." He checked his watch. "The bell will probably ring for transition as soon as you're back at the academic building."

I couldn't get out of there fast enough. As it was, the rest of the day seemed to follow that trend. Not terrible, just decaying into uncomfortable territory. Rumors about me going to the dean's office were already circulating. Jonas glanced at me when we met in the hall outside our next class.

I braced for the question or the accusation or something. But all he said was, "Are you okay?"

"What?"

"You look...mad? Sad—off...I don't know the word. Are you okay?" He glanced around the hall then back at me.

"Just...yeah, I'm fine. Did I miss anything in lit?"

"A really boring lecture," Jonas told me before he opened the door. "Really boring."

I laughed. Moments like that helped. When Sydney caught me in the hall after my last class, I wasn't ready for her wide eyes. "Are you in trouble?"

"With?" It had already been a long day.

"The school, I heard you got pulled out of class and marched to the dean's office. Everyone's talking about it, and they aren't sure if you're getting expelled for conduct unbecoming..."

For real? I raised my brows. I'd been at the school long enough to know that I wasn't the only celebrity or in the news student that went here.

"Well, you know, that you were questioned about kissing the teacher." A slow smile creased her lips, then she shook her head and the grin fell away. "Just kidding. Sorta. Mostly. I am not asking you about it now or ever. But there were pictures and you know how people talk."

"Yeah, I do...and I don't care right now. I need Midol, some dark chocolate, and a huge cup of coffee." Because I was on the edge of killing something and I needed to maintain my neutrality.

"Hey," she said with a grin and pulled out a small bottle of the pain relievers from her pocket. "I literally just picked these up."

"You are my favorite human."

She laughed but passed them over, and I dry swallowed two. True to her word, she didn't press me for more answers. But good to know the gossip mill was firing on all cylinders. I couldn't afford to think about it right now, I was already grumpy.

Mr. Ninja Kiss better keep his lips to himself. Today was not the day and I was not...

"KC," a very familiar voice called as I neared the dorm, and I pivoted.

"Johnny?" What the...? I shifted my grip on the backpack and walked to where he was waiting. He wore a lot of layers for being here, but then it was cold and it had snowed. "What are you doing here?"

"Surprising you," he said with an almost sheepish smile. "Davina found out I was coming East to head to the Sunshine Retreat to try and see your mom and she asked me to bring you something..." That was when he pulled the bag out from behind him and I almost squealed.

Davina sent a care package. I could *smell* the cookies and the chocolate and the sugar. I'd bet my savings account she also sent her chicken and dumplings, which was my favorite anxiety food.

After this stressful, shitty day, I threw my arms around him. "You are the best," I said as he returned the hug with a chuckle. "This is exactly what I needed."

"She thought you might, so I brought everything as commanded. If you could put in a good word for me, she promised fudge brownies in the New Year for my cheat day."

I laughed. "I solemnly swear to tell her." I practically hugged the bag to me. "I can't invite you in, but we could..."

"No, no. You have finals and your break coming, I just wanted to deliver it to you personally and make sure you were doing okay." The news article.

"Actually," I told him. "I'm doing more than all right. Call me if you get to see Mom?"

"I will. I'll give her your love, too." Just as long as he didn't deliver it with a dick pic.

Grinning, I gave him another hug. "Thank you again."

"You're welcome."

I waited for him to get in his rental, and I waved at him before I turned to go inside. Davina sent the absolute best treats. Everything she sent was perfect for cramps and PMS. I needed to text Aubrey. We always shared the cookies.

I didn't even make it two full steps inside before Lachlan was just there. "What the hell is he doing here, Ace?" He dipped his head. "And why are you hugging him...?"

He barely brushed my lips with his and I pushed him back. At his smirk, I scowled and then I swung. My fist wasn't Jonas' but it caused enough impact to jar my arm and startle him.

"Damn, Ace."

"Fuck off, Lachlan," I said, then started up the stairs.

"You know...this just makes you hotter," he called after me.

I didn't turn around. "Ninja kiss me again, asshole, and find out."

Twenty-Five

RAMSEY

The past few days had been an exercise in restraint and discipline. The school put me on notice regarding the photograph of my "inappropriate" behavior with a student. I was warned to avoid Kaitlin Crosse and to keep all interactions strictly professional, whether she was my stepsister or not.

Right.

I was to have no private conversations with her regarding the investigation. The dean, my advisor, and the board would be conducting their own investigation. It would be quiet, it would be discreet, and it could result in my immediate termination.

The stomach dropping sensation seemed a permanent addition to my day to day. Jonas still wasn't talking to me, and I had zero idea what he would say if questioned. Lachlan walked around like he was master of the fucking universe and she *belonged* to him and no one else.

Arrogant little shit.

I was forced to keep my distance, while obsession seemed to fuel Lachlan's rather relentless pursuit. I'd had to keep my phone on silent permanently. Our mother's last message had been ominous enough I debated blowing off Tahoe for Christmas entirely.

As far as I knew, Gibs was still in the studio, the latest album had been slow going work. They'd also lost a couple of old band members. Her frustration level had to be high. Either way, I didn't want to deal with her rants about KC.

Keeping an eye on KC from afar was a lot more challenging. If the board slapped me down and fired me, well, I had been the one to kiss her, not once but twice.

Technically three times, but who was counting...

More than once I'd seen the worry on her face as she got off a call. A couple of times, watching her when she didn't know I was there, I recognized the exhaustion that would creep into her expression.

The unnerving part? How swiftly she erased it when others were around. It was like she had to pretend nothing touched her. Her smile was easy and generous. Her attention focused.

But she wasn't sharing her authentic self with any of these people...

The concept baffled me until I came to one truly uncomfortable realization. Why the fuck should she share who she was with any of us? Not when some asshole was just right there waiting to monetize that vulnerability.

Or tear her down when she opened up.

That last one was on me. Because I had done that. Fuck my life.

Lachlan didn't know about the probation, but Jonas figured it out. He'd been watching me with eyes that basically said I deserved this.

Maybe baby brother was right.

Maybe.

I could handle it. I did... right up until the administration and the school attorney pulled her from my class to "talk to her." I was stuck in class with my brother staring me down while she was out there being interrogated.

About me.

This particular invasion of her privacy was on me.

It was my fault.

When she was in my later classes, she didn't say a word to me about her meeting. While I couldn't approach her, I did want to check on her, particularly with how uncomfortable she appeared. More than once, I caught her shifting in her seat and glaring down at whatever we were working on.

What the fuck happened in that meeting?

A message dinged my phone at the end of classes. The dean expected me in his office first thing the next day. There was nothing about arranging to have anyone cover my classes, so—maybe I wasn't fired?

The sinking feeling didn't abate. I hated being in limbo about anything. Despised not being able to control what came next. I liked having a plan, and I liked looking ahead to anticipate potential challenges. Her arrival had always been a rock in the serene pond of my forward planning.

I just hadn't been prepared for ripples to trigger tsunamis. We were coming up on the holiday; if they decided to get rid of me...this would be the time to do it.

Blue Ivy Prep had been my home for almost sixteen years. What the hell did I do if they showed me the door?

The biting cold in the air slapped me in the face as I left the library and headed toward the dorms. I needed to get changed and go to the gym. Maybe an hour on the rowing machine would help.

If nothing else, it could exhaust my brain. My phone vibrated and Mom's face popped up. Fuck... Tomorrow, I promised her mentally. *I'll call you back tomorrow.* I needed answers before I dealt with the fury she was likely going to rain down on me.

None of us had returned her calls. I was guessing about Jonas, but he never did anything he didn't want to do. Lachlan, I knew for a fact, wasn't calling her unless someone made him. And I just couldn't deal with her...

KC stood out in front of the dorm, hugging—was that the porn star? Was he really *here*? Seeing her? Her dark, tight expression brightened so swiftly it was like a sucker punch to the nuts.

Irritation flamed through me. The guy smiled at her like he had the right to be here *on campus* and at *her dorm*, touching her. He was twenty-five? Thirty? Who the hell did he think he was taking advantage of her youth like that?

The only thing keeping me locked into place was the fact if I walked over there it would probably escalate. As long as I had orders to stay away from her...

Fuck.

Still, I kept my gaze on them. He caught me staring and I didn't flinch when he stared right back at me. I wasn't close enough to read his expression, nor did I know him well enough to interpret. But I took a couple of steps forward because I did want him aware that I saw him.

If he did a damn thing to her...

Then he was leaving and she headed for the dorm with the bag he'd handed her. The smile on her face arrested me. All at once, I wanted to be the one who made her smile like that.

I gave it five minutes for her to get clear of the lobby before I continued inside. Lachlan stood there, gazing up the staircase like a madman with a manic grin on his face. It wasn't until he cut a look at me that I caught the fresh redness around his almost healed black eye.

"You should get a tattoo," I suggested, with a nod to his face. "Save you the trouble of getting punched so regularly."

"You're funny," Lachlan said, but his smirk said he wasn't dissuaded. "Getting punched is half the fun." He slapped my shoulder as he turned to head out the door.

Maybe someone had hit him a little too hard, but right now... yeah, Lachlan needed to deal with his own shit. I cast a glance up and then back to my floor. Right.

Tomorrow.

I would find out what I needed to do tomorrow.

And hopefully, I still had a job and a place here.

I kept myself busy for the rest of the evening. Lachlan was conspicuous in his absence, and I was fine with it. The last couple of years of not sharing a room or a suite with one of my brothers had been lovely. I wasn't really a fan of having him as a roommate again.

With most of my homework finished, my grading done, and a half dozen suite inspections completed, I slipped off the tie and the dress clothes to shower. The rest of the night was mine.

Not that I was going to do much more than read ahead for the next semester. We still had to finalize the syllabi so that students would get them before winter break in order to prep for the spring semester.

Contacts out, I actually enjoyed the soft blur of the world. As annoying as my vision issues had been over the years, this was the one time when my need to keep working actually seemed to back off. The soft focus on the world eased the tension of the past day, week, month...

The hot water poured over me and I twisted to let the water beat against my back. I hadn't gone to the gym. I was going to have to set an alarm. Lachlan lived for physical sports and working out. It kept him sane.

I did it because my health demanded it, particularly after my stress levels resulted in a prescription for anti-anxiety meds at fourteen. Competing with students nearly four years older than me for class rank had never been a good time.

My intelligence was my greatest strength and probably the source of my worst experiences. "Yeah, enough with the maudlin bullshit," I told myself and went to work on scrubbing my hair.

Despite the fact I'd need to shave again in the morning, I went ahead and shaved tonight. There was something to be said for cleaning up and making sure everything was in its place.

The scrape of the razor over my jaw and the sound of the bristle being erased settled me. We all had our self-soothing gestures. That was what my psychologist had assured me from the first time I skipped two grades.

As much as I needed the mental challenge, he worried that I wasn't up for the emotional one. In some ways, he'd been right. In others... well, I'd made it. So it didn't matter.

The feel of kissing KC just popped into my head along with the memory of her pressing against me when I lifted her. She weighed next to nothing. Despite the sharpness of her tongue and her wit, she was so fucking soft everywhere.

My dick stirred almost instantaneously. The other reason my nightly showers were necessary. Waking up with a boner was a fact of life, and having wet dreams about a student who was also my stepsister and couldn't stand me was more than a little embarrassing.

Wrapping a hand around my cock, I focused on the way it felt to hold her and I was stiff as a board in no time. It took a little concentration to hold onto the images of her and the sound—the soft little exhales she made punctuated by gasps.

I came in a rush and shuddered. More of my tension spilled off me as I splattered cum against the tile. The water would wash it away. It didn't take me long to finish the shower.

Once I toweled off and brushed my teeth, I dragged on my pajama bottoms and t-shirt. I preferred to sleep in less, but I always had to be ready for someone knocking on the door or needing me.

It was part of the commitment.

The rest of the suite seemed quiet when I shut off the lights and headed into my bedroom. This was my safe space. Organized into neat lines with every book in its place, the bed made, the suits in the closet hung and color coordinated.

The one place I could control. I snagged the e-reader off the desk on my way to the bed. A rustle of fabric and movement froze me in place though. The room was dark, I had the window covered cause even a little bit of light would jerk me away.

Flipping on the light switch, I gaped at a very nude Payton sprawled on my bed. She dropped one leg to the side so I got an eyeful of her cunt and I shifted to pin my gaze elsewhere.

I half-expected her to scream or something. If she was here for Lachlan—note to self, punch him later—she had the wrong room.

"Hey, Ramsey," she said in a whispery voice. "I've been waiting for you..."

Waiting.

For.

Me?

I cut a glance at her again, firmly keeping my gaze *above* her neck. "Pretty sure you mean Lachlan," I said. "This is most definitely not his room."

She rolled up onto her knees and I backed up a step. "I know where he sleeps and that's why I'm here."

"Because he doesn't sleep in here?" How the fuck was I getting her out of this room without a scene? I was maybe hours away from losing my position at the school already. This would seal the deal before dawn.

"I don't want him," she told me, walking on her knees across the bed. Right. She needed clothes. I did a scan of the room.

She'd left a pile right by the door to my room, where I wouldn't trip over it coming out of the bathroom. It irked me that she just dropped them there. I scooped them up and thrust them toward the bed, tossing them at her.

"Get dressed."

"Rams." She practically pouted. "I need you...it's been such an awful year and I didn't get into any of your classes. And I'll be eighteen right after Christmas..."

"Not helping," I said, keeping my voice firm and stern. The absolute lack of interest from my dick definitely helped in the current situation. "Get dressed, Payton. You need to go back to your own suite."

"But..." She pressed against my arm and I kept my hand locked on the tablet. The rub of her nipples on my skin was not what I wanted. "I need you."

Clearing my throat, I frowned at her. "Miss Webber..."

"It's so sexy when you go all teacher on me."

I narrowly dodged her kiss, and the act of pulling my arm away caused me to touch her more. Goddammit. "Payton..."

"Rams," she pleaded, "I need you."

I was doomed.

A knock on my door ended abruptly with Lachlan leaning in. "Hey, I was gonna get—what the fuck are you doing here?"

The last part of that question came out positively hostile, and I'd never been so glad to see my younger brother. I cut a look at him.

"Goddamn, Payton, you're not a whore. Stop acting like

one." Lachlan stalked forward. "Can't you see you're upsetting Ramsey's delicate sensibilities."

Normally, I'd be offended, but he wasn't wrong.

He didn't wait for a response from either of us as he walked across my floor—in shoes, dammit, I'd have to sweep—then scooped up her discarded clothes from the bed. He paused to face us both. "Unless you invited her? And I mean, I don't judge, but trust me when I say listening to her is not worth what her mouth can do."

"You are such a bastard, Lachlan," Payton spat, and the sound of her hand slapping him echoed through the room.

"Hardly news, sweetheart," Lachlan told her dryly. "All three of us are bastards, something you know. Now… take your shit and your cosmetically enhanced tits and get the fuck out of here."

He didn't actually wait for her spluttering to form into syllables as he half-dragged her and her clothes to the door of the suite. Then he opened it, thrust her outside with her clothes.

"Now get lost before I get a squirt bottle to spray you with like the irritating cat in heat you're behaving like."

"You son of a—"

He shut the door, then dusting off his hands before he looked at me. "You should change the sheets. You'll never sleep on those now, and I need to wash my hands."

I couldn't really argue because he wasn't wrong. Ten minutes later, he leaned against the doorframe, watching me put the new comforter on. The rest of the bedding was sacked up to be picked up for laundry.

"You know," Lachlan said in a far more sober tone of voice. "Maybe you shouldn't flirt with the schoolgirls. You couldn't handle it when you were a senior. Granted, you were young, but I heard the rumors and I remember. You shot up that last year. No way the girls didn't notice you."

"We're not having this conversation," I told him as I set the e-reader down on the nightstand. "You also need to stop thinking you're the center of the universe."

He snorted. "I don't need to be the center of everyone's universe..."

"Just Kaitlin's."

Eyebrows raised, he shrugged. "Ace and I get each other. Not sure you'd understand. You prefer the safety of your academic bubble. Real world isn't so friendly, bro."

I frowned.

"But your sex life, or lack thereof, is not why I am here—though if you do decide to tap that with Payton, glove up."

A sigh escaped me. "You dated her for fourteen months."

"No, I fucked her for fourteen months. Payton and I have *never* been exclusive, and I can't stand talking to her ninety percent of the time. She was a casual warm hole in the dark and I enjoyed plugging it."

"And you wonder why Kaitlin wants nothing to do with you?" Did he hear himself?

"Shows what you know about girls. I never lied to Payton or led her on. Not doing it with Ace now, either. But that isn't what I wanted to talk about."

As rattled as I was by her surprise visit, it took me real time to notice the sober expression Lachlan wore. It wasn't snark or sarcasm. "What happened?"

"Initiation is being set for January, and they gave her to RJ."

"He needs to go."

"Yes, he does," Lachlan said as he straightened. "Are you in? Finally?"

Twenty-Six

KC

Finals week was brutal. Jonas and I spent the week mostly ignoring each other—no, not ignoring. He grabbed food one night, I got it the next. We both set up in the sitting room to study or work, but we were able to work in silence.

If we wanted music, we put on earbuds. I ran every morning, but winter storms kept me in the gym. Starting Monday, Jonas followed me to the gym. Surprised, I'd given him a questioning look, but he just put on his headset and walked on the treadmill next to mine.

What amused me was he brought a book with him and had it open in front of him as he moved. He didn't try to engage me in conversation. Instead, he walked and studied while I ran. As odd as it seemed that first day, the next morning, I had a bottle of water waiting for him when he came out to join me.

Lachlan showed up on the second day, too. It amused me

that Jonas claimed that treadmill right next to mine while I took the one on the end, leaving Lachlan nowhere to join me.

His bruised eye looked better, but I had a feeling Jonas itched to give him another one. It was just this little splash of sunshine in the middle of the intense week. I caught Lachlan watching me in the mirror more than once.

I also noticed Jonas glaring at him. It was *almost* comedic, the three of us not talking but looking at each other. It kind of reminded me of a sitcom where the music should get more and more Benny Hill-like.

Right, finals were going to drive me right down the rabbit hole to a mental break. It was coming. I just needed to make it to the last day of the semester before I cracked.

Jackie left me a message each day assuring me Pen was doing well on the new chemo protocol. She'd been sicker than expected, *but*, and Jackie emphasized this point, they had admitted her to the children's hospital.

"I promise if anything changes, you'll know. I will keep you in the loop. They admitted her because they were worried about dehydration and nutrition. Despite not feeling great, she's in wonderful spirits and she keeps playing with the bear you gave her with you singing. Focus on class, keep your head up, sleep, and remember to eat. We'll see you over the holidays."

It was the same message over and over. It helped. It helped a lot. Yvette, Aubrey, and I were planning to do the first week of break in L.A. at my mom's house. She was still off at the Sunshine Retreat and hadn't answered a single call or message. Trish had gone radio fucking silent again. Thankfully, Johnny had let me know he'd tried to see her but no luck.

Poor guy. I felt for him. I wanted to yell at my mom for treating him poorly. And I invited him to Christmas in L.A. if he was out there. He said he'd think about it, and when I promised pie from Davina, he said a firm maybe. Poor dude.

Even with the distractions, there was more gossip and news stories. I ignored them. Fortunately, it looked like Captain Douchebag hadn't been booted from the school. That was good. A kiss wasn't worth his job, even if he was a dick about it sometimes.

In fact, Captain Douchebag stood proctoring our literature final on Wednesday. All the literature classes for this level were taking the exam. The quiet in the room was downright unnerving. Even more, I swore I could feel his gaze every time it brushed over me.

Maybe I imagined it, but I stole looks periodically—yeah that wasn't distracting at all—and each time, he was definitely looking at me.

Not. Helping.

It took me almost the entire time allotted to finish the exam. The fact it included two detailed essay questions made me reread, check, and rework twice. Words were important, and I had a feeling I was overthinking all of this, but I couldn't help it.

Ramsey touched my arm after I turned in the test booklet. "Do you have a minute?"

Did I?

Um...

I shook off some of the sleepy and nodded. "I don't have another final until tomorrow." Awareness of Jonas waiting for me at the door—well, I assumed he was waiting for me, I motioned toward him. "Mind if Jonas hangs out?"

Surprise flickered across Ramsey's face for a moment before he glanced at his brother, then he nodded. "That's fine. I'll be right with you both."

I gave him a thumbs up as I adjusted the strap of my bag over my shoulder. It wasn't my backpack or my book bag, just a standard purse. I didn't normally carry one on campus, but we weren't allowed to bring books or other materials into the tests.

There were other students threading their way out. Jonas caught my arm when I reached him and pulled me to the side just as Payton stumbled and hit the door frame. Fuck, that looked like it hurt. She shot a look of pure venom at me and I rolled my eyes.

Whatever. Apparently, the day I'd been born, I'd pissed in her Wheaties. I didn't care, especially not right now. "Hey," I said to Jonas. "Thanks."

"No problem. She hates you."

"Feeling's almost mutual."

A flash of a smile touched his lips.

"Do you mind hanging out a few?" I hadn't expected Ramsey to need to talk to me, but I also really didn't want to do this alone. For now, it would be better if I limited my time with Lachlan and Ramsey to when we had company.

Safer for all of us.

"Nope," he said. "You don't have to talk to him if you don't want to."

"I know." I pulled the strap over crossbody and then leaned against the wall next to him as the testing hall emptied.

Lot of students in literature. The volume from the hall increased. It was like as soon as you passed through the door, you were free.

Yet, here I was waiting to talk to Ramsey. Why? Fuck if I knew. "It's fine," I told Jonas. "He asked. I don't know what it is, but we're almost done for the semester. Are you leaving Friday?"

"No," he said, with a sigh. "Thursday night. No finals on Friday. Going to see my Dad before I go to Tahoe."

"Cool."

"You?" He eyed me and I lifted a shoulder. "Saturday.

Aubrey has finals on Friday, and Yvette is driving down. We'll fly together to California."

"Spending the holidays—"

"Hey," Ramsey said as the last student left. "Thanks for waiting."

"Sure," I said, facing him. Jonas didn't say anything, but he was right there, like a comforting presence. There was something to be said about how quiet he could be. It irritated me when he would just sit there and stare before. I had no idea why.

Now, I got it. He didn't talk unless he had reason. I could respect that.

"What's up?" Suddenly, I wanted the biggest cheeseburger. Maybe fries and a shake. Oh, chili fries and a chocolate shake. No strawberry. My stomach growled and Ramsey shot me an amused look.

"I won't keep you long if you're hungry."

He wouldn't be keeping me at all, but I kept that to myself. Ramsey flicked a look at Jonas then at me.

"I have a couple of things I wanted to talk to you about. First...thank you."

"For... what?" I was drawing a blank. "We just finished the test with everyone else."

His expression turned droll. "For what you said to the dean."

"Oh." I shook my head. Fuck, that seemed forever ago. "Been a long week or two..." Actually, I didn't even remember when that conversation was, other than it was done. "Yeah, no problem."

Ramsey stared at me, a frown tightening his forehead. "They told me you cleared me for everything. That it was you who kissed me."

"Why don't you shout it a little louder?" I suggested. "People in the hall might not have heard."

"They won't," Jonas offered in a cool tone. "These halls tend to be better about sound proofing for the tests." Well, that was something. "Why did you defend him?"

I turned to Jonas. "I didn't. He said some shitty things and he's had some shitty opinions. I don't need him to get fired because someone took a picture of us and sold it."

"Nevertheless, he shouldn't have kissed you." It sounded so reasonable. "He's always talking about proper behavior, meeting expectations, and not being stupid." Now he switched his attention to Ramsey. "Or does that only apply to me and Lach?"

Captain Douchebag sighed. "No, it doesn't just apply to you two. I would like to say I have a better grasp on my behavior and my impulses." He gave me a damn near apologetic look. "You could have had them fire me. It would have served me right. I broke protocol. I was inappropriate."

I shrugged. "It's done."

Instead of assuaging his concern, he frowned. "But you—"

"Could have been a bitch. Been someone who judged you for a few careless moments? Took some petty pleasure in getting even with you by escalating to having you fired?" I pushed off the wall and moved a few steps away to face them both.

"Yes," Ramsey said carefully. "You would have been right. I know you didn't report me... even when you could have."

"Well, maybe that's just not me. Look... I didn't know you were my stepbrothers. All of you did. I didn't know what I'd done that pissed you off so badly you felt the need to treat me like shit—repeatedly. Now, I do...maybe. Actually no, I don't know. And I'm not asking. I'm too tired for this conversation to go too much deeper. You didn't deserve to be fired by some pompous jackass and his attorney who were desperate to cover the school's ass, even when they've failed repeatedly to keep photos of me from being sent to the press."

I shrugged again. It was impossible to prevent the scrape of hurt out of my voice. I cleared my throat, resolved to shaking it off.

"Then you saved my life... and Jonas gave me a place to stay that doesn't have Payton in it. I didn't know you guys, and you clearly didn't know me." Only what they thought they knew.

Captain Douchebag managed to look more troubled, if possible. "I'm beginning to get that impression." He looked like he'd just sucked on a lemon, too. Truth was rarely perfectly sweet. He rubbed the back of his neck, discomfort radiating from him.

Almost made me feel sorry for him.

Almost.

"That brings us to the second thing."

I lifted my brows.

"Holidays are right around the corner...are you possibly interested in coming to Tahoe?"

Jonas gave a little start next to me, and I cut a look at him, then up at Ramsey. "For what?"

"For Christmas with—us and you know..."

"Your dad," Jonas said abruptly. "But I think Ramsey is figuring out that you and Gibs aren't tight. No one invited you."

"Oh, well, then no. Not planning on Tahoe. I have plans to see my siblings and hang out with my friends, maybe eat a whole pie and then lay on the floor and moan about food babies. It will be great." The more I spoke, the more bewildered Ramsey seemed to become. Right. Time to go. "Anyway, I'm gonna go. Jonas and I were gonna order pizza."

"Yep," he said. "And maybe watch a movie and do nothing."

I laughed. "Doing nothing sounds good."

Ramsey stared at us, almost impassive, like he wanted to

say more. Apparently, he opted against it 'cause he nodded. "I'll take care of the pizza. Text me what you want."

I could afford to pay for myself. But what the hell... "Thanks. Later." Then before we could drag this uncomfortable moment on any longer, I headed for the door.

As awkward as the whole conversation was, it had nothing on Jonas waiting until we had pizza in front of us, ice cold sodas, and a movie up on the screen ready to play to ask me, "Did you tell them you kissed him first because you wanted him to kiss you?"

Pizza slice in hand, I considered the question for a moment. "I don't know," I said slowly. "I don't like bullies. I never have. I don't like hypocrites or overly judgmental jackasses who patronize others. I get that they were doing their job, but they didn't care about me or him. They cared about the school's reputation. So...I don't need him to be fired because he kissed me."

I set the pizza slice down and wiped off my fingers before I picked up the can of soda.

"Did I want him to kiss me? I can't say I didn't think about it last year." If I were being really honest, I thought about it a lot... "That was before he was such a dick about everything... okay he'd been kind of a dick, but he wasn't Captain Douchebag yet."

Jonas blinked. "Captain Douchebag?"

I grinned "Well, you guys were Douchebags One, Two, and Three."

"He's the captain now?" Amusement stole across his face. "Which one was I?"

"Douchebag number one."

He grinned, but it was fleeting. "Why?"

"Cause you were an ass in the hall that day when I ran into you. I apologized and you were all dark brooding stares and cutting comments."

"Oh."

"For what it's worth, I don't think you're a total douchebag now."

"But I'm still kind of a douchebag."

"Yeah, and I'm a bitch." I hadn't forgotten that comment. "Might be why we're doing okay right now."

"But are we friends?" Jonas asked.

"I don't know," I said after a long moment. "What do you think?"

"I think I'd like to be friends," he said slowly, "with you."

"Kaitlin Crosse," I said as I extended my hand to him.

He wiped his own fingers off before he grasped my hand. "Jonas Dekkar."

"Nice to meet you, Jonas."

"Nice to meet you—Kaitlin, or KC?"

"My friends call me KC."

Twenty-Seven

LACHLAN

Connecticut was a postcard for the holidays. Snow blanketing the land, the woods, and just giving it that perfect hush like the whole area just held its breath. So different from Tahoe.

No one ever listened to me when I said there was a visceral difference to the taste of winter depending on what part of the country you were in. I bet the rest of the world was the same. Maybe I'd add that to the bucket list of items I wanted. Taste the snow everywhere in the world.

The drive passed swiftly, if not quietly. I'd never been so glad to have tucked my baby into valet at the airport before we left. Especially as I followed the winding roads back to the school.

My phone vibrated away in the cradle where it was charging, and I just ignored it and the messages coming through. Gaze on the road, I didn't need to worry about what any of them were saying.

Ramsey had tried to intercede. He just didn't have it in

him to stay the fuck out of it. Jonas had been silent, but the look on his face when I slammed out of the living room had been telling.

He was pissed.

Once on campus, the hush trailed me all the way to parking. It was technically just the day after Christmas. I lucked out on finding space on the redeye when my calls to Dad had gone to his secretary. He was at some "retreat" for the holidays.

Translation, Dad was shacking up with a new mistress and wanted to burn off some stress between her thighs before the world went back to work. I could appreciate the idea. Fuck knew, I'd love to be buried between a pair of very specific thighs right now.

Only I had a feeling Ace wouldn't take the edge off me in any way, just make me want more. I wanted her so fucking much right now, my hard-ons were getting permanent zipper imprints from their regularity. I hadn't jacked off this much since I first discovered how good it felt.

With everyone gone, I got to take advantage of covered parking, slotting the car right into a handful of spaces that were available. Leaning back against the seat, I sat there with the car idling.

Maybe I should have gone down to L.A. Jonas and Ramsey had been discussing Ace and Los Angeles, but they both clammed up when I was around. Nice to see my brothers were getting along and unified by something.

Assholes.

Smothering a yawn, I shoved open the door to the car and climbed out. I needed a stretch, then a good run. A long one. After, I'd shower, then try to sleep. The agitation buzzing under my skin had only grown worse on the flight and not better.

I'd even tried listening to Ace sing to get myself to relax. That just left me with another fucking boner.

Obsessed. Absolutely obsessed and I couldn't deny it anymore. I had photos of her on my phone. Some I'd saved from social media and the stupid gossip sites—which I'd also found myself searching religiously. Desperately hungry for any word of her.

It had been ten days since the last time I saw her in person, and it was killing me. The worst part of all of this, I wasn't the melodramatic one. If I could just text her, that might help—but I didn't actually have her number. Go fucking figure.

If Ramsey and Jonas had it, they were not sharing. Once back inside, I turned up the heat in Ramsey's suite. They turned it all down when the dorms were empty to barely warm enough to keep shit from freezing.

Absolutely economical. Absolutely fuck the idea of huddling in a freezing suite. In my room, I dropped my bag in the closet, stripped down and changed into running clothes. Irritation kept me pretty warm at the moment.

Layers for running in the cold were necessary. I needed the moisture-wicking below the jacket to keep as dry as possible while also not inviting freezing too. Once I had my shit on, I dug around for my headphones.

They weren't as fancy as Ace's, but I tended to be tough on mine. The bone conducting type left my ears open for tracking other sounds. Like the familiar slap of a blue-haired vixen's gorgeous steps.

I grunted out a breath. "Stop thinking about her, man." Verbalizing it aloud wasn't helping, not when my dick had already gone hard as fuck. Yeah.

Run.

I let myself out and headed for the trail. The cold was exactly the slap in the face I needed. Pulling the gaiter up over my nose before I started the music, I stared at the messages populating the screen.

MOM

You will answer my calls, Lachlan. How can you choose that girl over me? She ignores Gibs, constantly rejects him, and now you're choosing her over us? How could you?

I muted her.

The vitriol in her messages grew increasingly worse with each one she'd sent. A total of a dozen since I walked out of the house.

Closing it, I eyed Ramsey's message.

BRAINIAC

Tell me you're alive and not wrapped around a tree. I don't care if you're pissed. Be pissed, but be safe.

I sent him a thumbs up. It was about all I could manage right now. Jonas' messages were question marks.

Aww, baby brother did care. I sent him a middle finger. He should appreciate that.

The rest of the messages were from people I didn't give two shits about. So, I didn't bother to look at them. Shockingly, Gibs hadn't sent anything, but he tended to stay out of our disagreements with Mom. Then again, Ace was... Ace was his kid, and they never discussed her when we were all together.

It didn't hit me until this trip. Her name didn't come up once when Gibs was present. Instead, it had waited until he'd vanished to the recording studio they'd built in an outbuilding.

They were seriously behind on the album, and he was not in the best of moods. Apparently, the music wasn't talking to him or something. As soon as he excused himself, Mom launched into us about the gossip, the photos, the fact none of us had called her back—hey, look, all three of us could agree on something—then she started talking shit about Ace.

Ramsey tried to placate. Jonas just left because he didn't do confrontation with Mom.

Me? I did confrontation just fine. Didn't matter who it was. Thankfully, I was going to be nineteen shortly and I did not need nor desire her permission to do fuck all.

By the time I made it to the first mile marker on the trail, some of the rage in my system began to fuel my muscles rather than just make me shake from it. I hit my stride on the second mile and I was flying by the third.

The hush of the air, the crunch of the snow, and the music raised my endorphin levels. The only thing missing was the racing strides of Ace in front of me. She ran like a long-distance competitor with a natural gait and rhythm that was just a thing of beauty. I could picture the muscles shifting beneath her clothes, and I never got tired of chasing that ass.

She'd be back soon and we were gonna talk. Then we were gonna kiss. She could pop me again if she wanted, but there was no way I wasn't kissing her...

After the run, I showered and fell into bed. Exhaustion sucked me right down and I slept for the first time in days. The light scrape of nails over my scalp roused me. Blue hair filled my vision and I lifted my head to find her lying right next to me, one arm behind her head and the other stretched so she could keep caressing my scalp.

"Ace..." I whispered and she smiled at me.

"Miss me?" The fact she rolled onto her side and the sheet dipped to give me another beautiful view of those breasts sent all the blood pounding south to my dick.

"Fuck yeah, I missed you." Didn't even care why she was in here. I narrowed the distance between us. "Planning to punch me again?"

"Would that stop you?" The way she raised her brows made me laugh.

"Nope. Be totally worth it. But don't damage those beautiful hands, I'm sure Jonas would punch me for you."

She laughed against my lips, but I kissed whatever words she was about to say away. The feel of her skin on mine was a revelation. Little nips and bites, followed by swipes of her tongue and we were both groaning. I loved to take over and she usually let me, but there was a demand from her that I'd never experienced.

"Fuck, Kaitlin…" I tested her name out and then her teeth sank into my lip. Blood welled up and I jerked my head up. Three things hit me simultaneously.

I *had* been dreaming about Ace. I *wasn't* alone in bed. The woman in my bed *was not Ace.*

"Did you really just groan that bitch's name at me?" Payton Webber, one of the worst mistakes of my life, snarled up at me. She had one hand on my dick which deflated the minute we recognized who was touching us.

I pushed up with one arm, then caught her wrist in my free hand. She was already tightening her grip and pain flared through me. "Let me go," I ordered as I squeezed her wrist with the same amount of force she was using on me.

With a gasp, she let out a cry before she finally let me go. I was going to have nail impressions in my dick, and I didn't say a word as I rolled out of the bed and then hauled her out of it.

"What the fuck do you think you're doing?"

She stumbled as I let her go once we were clear of the bed itself. I had no idea what time it was. My cock hurt, my eyes were gritty, I had a headache, and for the first time in my life, I wanted to punch a woman.

Fisting my temper, I dragged on a pair of sweatpants then glared at her.

"Since when did you become a fucking prude?" Payton

demanded, one hand on her hip and glaring at me. Her tits were on point and she didn't seem to give a damn that she was naked. Fine, I didn't really care either other than she'd been all over me. "And you never complained about fucking me before. In fact..." She started forward. "I happen to know you enjoyed it."

"Don't mistake enjoying getting off for actually liking you. Fucking you and talking to you? Two totally different things. How did you get into this suite?" It wasn't the first time. "And you'd think after you threw yourself at Ramsey, you'd have gotten a clue."

"Oh, what do you care if Ramsey fucked me," she said with a sniff as I snagged up her clothes.

"I don't, but he has better sense than I do sometimes. Been there, fucked that, not going back for another experience. Now, get the fuck out before I throw you out."

"You wouldn't."

The fact she thought I wouldn't, amused more than irritated. She should remember.

"Yeah, I already have and I don't mind doing it again." When she didn't take her clothes, I put my shoulder into her stomach and picked her right up, then marched to the door to the suite. I didn't exactly throw her down 'cause that would hurt. But the hall had a fucking draft blowing through it and she squealed as I set her down.

"What the hell?" she screamed at me. "Why are you so obsessed with that bitch? Do you think she gives a rat's ass about you? You told me once that she'd never bothered to even get to know you and now what? You pant after her like she's in heat and you are the only one who can satisfy it?"

"Payton—fuck off." I threw her clothes at her, and she only caught one as they bounced off and fell on the floor. "Stay out of this suite. Stay out of my bed. Don't ever fucking touch me again. Or Ramsey, for that matter, since he may not have the balls to tell you he isn't interested but trust me when I say he's not."

"I hate you," she shouted and I shrugged.

"I can live with it."

"You are going to regret this." She dragged up her clothes and clutched them to her.

"I already do."

A sound from the door to the building echoed through the hall. Payton jerked like someone had shot her and I glanced to find the woman of my dreams standing right there with a bag of food in hand that smelled fucking fantastic.

She was back early.

Twenty-Eight

KC

I'd jogged up to the gate to meet the food delivery. Coming back to campus early might have gotten me in trouble except—no one had been around to say anything. If there was an RA who stayed over the holidays, I hadn't found them.

Since I was fine, I just settled in and used the runs to the gate to meet food delivery as a reason to head out. As it was, I'd slept late for my first day back on campus so the exercise would be good for me.

Loaded up with lasagna, ravioli, garlic bread, and tiramisu —because I definitely ordered while hungry, not my brightest move—I ran back up to the building—well, jogged. The run, wreathed in Italian spice, sweet garlic-infused bready goodness, and snow, filled me with a kind of simple peace I'd craved all week.

Seeing Bronson and Jackie had been amazing. They welcomed Aubrey and Yvette, including them in the holiday celebrations with Bronson's rather noisy, extended family on his mother's side.

I'd gotten to meet some of them before, but this time seemed to almost overwhelm me. I was never alone with Aubrey and Yvette right there. Bronson and Jackie had always felt like a home away from home, and Pen—well, I spent every hour I could at the hospital, gowned up and masked, visiting her.

She hated the mask and kept taking it off me. One of the nurses said it was all right, we just needed to make absolutely sure I wasn't feeling off at all. If that meant taking my temperature each time to be in the room with her, I did. I also invested in a clear face mask. It still helped keep it sterile while letting her see my face.

It was almost acceptable to her sweet little eyes. Oh, I adored everything about her from the tight little curls on her head that I worried might fall out and they said would, to the chipmunk cheeks she made when she laughed.

On Christmas Day, Dix drove me to the hospital and came up while I visited with her. He kept a look out while I sang to her and played. She was asleep when I left, and I know Jackie was there regularly, Davina had been coming to see her for me, and Bronson swung by every chance he got...

I hated her in that hospital.

Hated. It.

Leaving the day after Christmas to come back here to think and to plan and to work in the relative quiet while Aubrey and Yvette went to see their families felt a little bit like running away.

Just a little.

Carrying the food toward the building, it still felt a lot like running away. No matter what, though, I'd have to just hate myself for it later. Right now, for the first time in *months*, I could take a deep breath. The leash of lies that had been choking me since the end of last semester had finally let go.

I could breathe.

I needed to be here right now. Just like I'd needed to be with Pen and everyone else the previous week, I needed to be by myself right now. Yvette and Aubrey had both known, hell, they'd known before I had because they hadn't once tried to persuade me to go with them when I said I wanted to do this.

Then I walked in on...a *very* shirtless Lachlan ripping into a very naked Payton in the hall outside of Ramsey's suite. My stomach lurched at the whole scene. Payton glared daggers at me. A momentary touch of pity for her rather unfortunate and humiliating situation died a rapid death.

"What are you staring at?" Payton demanded.

"No fucking clue," I said, her words jarring me out of the shock. Unlike her, I had no desire to film her degradation. "And I don't *want* to know either."

Shifting my grip on the food bag, I turned and took the steps two at a time. I didn't slow until I got to the fourth floor and back inside the "safety" of the suite.

Locking the door behind me, I put the food in the little kitchenette and got changed back into comfy clothes. While some of my peace had been disturbed, I refused to give into the unsettling encounter.

Honestly, if they wanted to play crazy sex games in the hallway while it was freezing cold—I seriously didn't want to know anything about it. That was an uncomfortable image that would likely stick in my head for way too long.

Fortunately, some *Love is Blind*, garlic bread, and lasagna helped to chase away some of the discomfort from that whole thing. When I was done eating, I washed up and pulled out my guitar. The rest of the afternoon, into the evening, I worked on writing a new song of my own. I wanted to write one for Pen.

Or maybe I was writing it for me.

I worked to build the harmonies so the three of us could sing it for her. Whether we ever recorded again or not, trying to sort out all my conflicting feelings on the subject hurt...

Pen was too little to be fighting this battle. Jackie warned me from the beginning this would be tough and I had to deal with my feelings on all of it. It was okay to be overwhelmed and to need a break. That all of this wasn't on me...

She was terrific, and I was so damn glad that Jackie had Pen's back through all of this. She was precisely who Pen needed. Unsurprisingly, Dad had been a no-show.

I made it through the first third. It was going to be balladic. Nothing else was working for me right now. Most people wrote music before they wrote lyrics; I worked the other way around sometimes.

How it worked for me indeed depended on my involvement. Aubrey and Yvette were both way better at the basic music. I heard music, but always in lyrics. I could hear the words before the melodies. Jonas seemed to hear nothing but melodies.

It was kind of sweet.

My hand was cramping from playing and writing. It had also gotten super late. There was no sign of Lachlan or Payton —thank fuck—so I cleaned up, set the music aside to work on the next day, and crashed.

Knocking on the door woke me. It took a minute for me to even realize someone was knocking. The thump was muted; it didn't quite carry through the closed door to my bedroom.

It was definitely dark as fuck in my room, and I didn't even have a nightlight on. Groaning, I sat up. What time was it? The knock came again.

Then again.

Fuck, whoever it was, wasn't going away. I shoved back the blankets and glanced around the room—I needed a baseball bat. After yanking the door of my room open, I headed to the suite door with my phone in hand. I nearly jumped when there was another knock right as I got there.

"Who is it?" I demanded.

"It's me, Ace."

Lachlan.

I stared at the door. "What?"

A soft chuckle carried right through the wood. It was a luscious, dark sound that teased right over me. "It's Lachlan, Ace...open the door."

I debated it. Seriously.

But he didn't knock again or say another word. Finally, curiosity won out over wariness, so I unlocked the door and opened it. Sure enough, Lachlan stood there, dressed in running gear, with his coat and gaiter in hand.

"Morning, Ace," Lachlan said with a smile as he looked me over. I probably had dried drool on my face and a pillow impression on my cheek. I wasn't awake enough to care about that right at the moment. "I figured you'd be up. It's time to run..."

"It's—" I finally looked at my phone. "Five in the morning."

"You always run early," he said, the corner of his mouth curving. "It's been a while, and I thought we could enjoy the run together—there's fresh snow and it's still snowing..."

I twisted to look at our window before glancing back at him. "I gotta get dressed." Then I closed the door, locking him on the other side.

Fuck, I didn't even look at my phone when I crashed. I stumbled back to the bedroom. It didn't take me long to drag on my running clothes and brush my teeth. Fully dressed, I opened the door to Lachlan again. He was leaning against the wall and straightened.

"I'm making espresso 'cause it's too early to be uncaffeinated. Do you want one?" Look, words worked when you got the blood pumping. Thinking could come online as soon as I soaked enough coffee into my brain.

"Sure," he said, another smile flirting with his lips. "Do I stay out here like the abandoned stray or can I come in out of the cold, Ace?"

I snorted. "You are so not a stray." But I waved him inside. I dropped my jacket on the sofa on my way to the kitchen. It didn't surprise me that he followed.

"Thank you," he said with another chuckle. "I think." Instead of looming over me, he settled against the counter while I pulled the shots. I did a quad for me. Dealing with Lachlan was not for the weak.

"You're welcome," I said after I knocked back half of my quad while waiting for his to brew. I could work the machine in my sleep. It gave life and I thrilled to it.

When I handed him the cup, his fingers brushed mine. But he didn't grab my hand or yank me forward. Progress.

"I guess I should thank you, too," I said, after a moment, glancing down at my cup before I knocked the rest of it back.

Closing my eyes, I waited for the coffee to work its magic. Not that it was going to be any kind of instantaneous.

"For what?"

"For knocking," I told him when I opened my eyes and met his gaze. Goddamn he had the greenest eyes. So not fair.

He opened his mouth, and I half-expected him to rattle off something smarmy, but all he said was, "You're welcome. I do know how to listen. And I was raised with manners."

"So, when you're being an insufferable dick, it's a choice?"

The slow grin curving his lips was too damn attractive. "Guilty?"

I rolled my eyes. "Uh huh. Okay... running." I pulled a water bottle out and handed him one before I took a long drink myself. Then I got my stuff and dragged on my jacket before I tucked in an earbud and glanced at him. "Am I going to regret this?"

Honestly, I wasn't even sure what I wanted him to say.

"I hope not," he said, opening the door to the hall and holding it for me. "You good for the wide circuit?"

"Six miles?"

He nodded.

"I can do six miles." My blood was already pumping. "Can you keep up?"

"Try to lose me," he murmured as I passed him.

It was my turn to chuckle, but once we were in the hall I glanced at the door to Aubrey's suite where I presumed Payton was hiding out.

Lachlan didn't say anything until we were on the ground floor and pausing to put on our face masks and hats. I had neoprene; he had a green gaiter that matched his eyes.

"What you saw yesterday..."

"Was none of my business," I told him firmly.

"Ace..."

"I mean it, Lachlan, I don't want to know what you two were doing or—not doing. Just..."

"Payton is the past," he said firmly. "I didn't invite her there or let her in. She showed up; I showed her the door."

I met his gaze, and he was so damn serious.

"She was naked."

"I know, I was asleep and she woke me up like that."

Wait... what? "That's...invasive."

"Do you believe me?" He didn't look away once, I swore he bored right into my soul.

"Does it matter?" I challenged him.

"It matters, Ace."

I pushed the door open and walking out into the dark with the cold wind hitting knocked the rest of the sleep away from my brain.

"Okay."

He followed me as I set out for the trail. "Okay? That's it?"

"You told me. I know. Do I believe you?" I shrugged. "It seems important to you...so I'll accept your version of events. Fuck knows I'm not asking for hers."

I held out my second earbud to him before I raised my phone. "Requests?"

"Whatever you want, Ace. I'm in."

Twenty-Nine

JONAS

The spring term started on Monday, and I got back in on Saturday. I actually spent the last five days of break with my dad rather than stick around Tahoe. Gibs had been too locked into his music, and struggling. That was kind of painful to watch.

Mom was so angry with all three of us. I assumed it was all three, I just dipped whenever her temper spiked. I couldn't deal with her disappointment or her rancor. So, I found other places to be until my planned trip to see Dad. I almost felt bad for leaving Ramsey behind, but he told me not to worry when he took me to the airport.

"You sure?" I couldn't help the skepticism. He didn't like confrontation any more than I did. While I could, and would, just walk away, he would stand there and take it.

"Don't worry about me," Ramsey said, bumping my shoulder with his fist. "Mom—she'll calm down. Just gotta give her some time."

I eyed him. "She was packing Lachlan's room to ship him all his shit." He remembered that, right?

The amusement flickered on his face briefly before he sighed. "Like I said, she'll calm down. Lachlan leaving was probably the smartest move he could have made."

On that, we'd have to agree to disagree. Settling up with Mom rather than leaving her fuming was a better path to peace. Then again, not my problem. The time with Dad was good, he finished up the tattoo I'd done for my brothers, but we added some touches to the definition. I talked to him about another one I wanted to add, although he refused that one for at least a year.

"Why?" I asked, even if I knew the answer.

"J," he said as he paused mid-slice. We were making home-made pizza and the dough was rising for the crust. "You don't add anything about a girl until you are dead certain a girl is still gonna be there. Nothing worse than having a permanent reminder etched on your body if it doesn't work out."

"Fine, give me one year." Cocky? Maybe. But I really wanted to add the image of her eyes. I—loved them. There was just something wholly captivating about them. Darkness and light collided in them and I *never* seemed to grasp what she was thinking.

The mystery alone compelled me, but it was so much more.

"One year," Dad agreed with a nod to the calendar. "I'll do it for you next year on New Year's Day *if* it's what you want."

The rest of my stay had been peaceful, and I finished a second tattoo for him, but I didn't have his gift for free hand art. As long as he did the detail stencil for me to work from, I could do it.

KC was already back on campus, her things scattered over the coffee table when I came in. As much as I didn't mean to pry, I found myself drifting over to look at the sheets of music.

These weren't ones I gave to her. One of her guitars sat propped in a cradle, like she'd just gotten up from where she'd been working to step out. I glanced around, half-expecting to see her exit her bedroom or come in the door.

But the suite was quiet and felt empty. Sitting down, slowly, I folded my arms to keep from picking up the musical sheets. There were easily a dozen, some half-completed.

I could almost follow the flow of music, but there was a disjointedness to it, like she'd skipped around without adding any bridges. After another five minutes passed and I'd read everything I could reach, I picked up a top sheet and straightened it before picking up the next. Then I reorganized them to lie out in the only order that seemed to make sense.

A scattering of lyrics on the pages answered my unspoken question. She was piecing it together. There was a rich sense of narrative to the song. More, she had a very sweet and powerful motif that repeated in lower keys and then climbed back to the original key as the song moved toward a crescendo.

The notes leapt up at me, and I could see where she was going. More, I could see the pieces that were missing. The fragments that would fill in the gaps and build the bridges between hope and sadness, desperation and resignation, as well as the need to celebrate the moments.

It was a really beautiful piece that she was putting together. Fingers twitching, I glanced around the table for a pencil and spun it around in my fingers as I debated the wisdom of messing with her creation.

She certainly hadn't asked me. If she'd been back even for a day, we hadn't discussed our schedules for arriving on campus. I made it ten more minutes, then I began to pencil in the key, the notes, and filled in those spaces she'd been writing around.

I'd just gotten to the last page when the door opened. "I told you not to try running with a hangover," KC said in a sardonic, if amused, tone. "You should have just hydrated."

"I wasn't hungover," Lachlan argued, as he followed her inside. They were both in running gear, faces reddened with hints of chap around their eyebrows. It was a sunny, brutally cold day out there. The fullness of his attention shifted from KC to me as I rose. "Look what the cat dragged in."

My irritation with him evaporated when KC turned around as she pulled off her knit cap and let her long blue hair spill out. It was braided, but the braid's end hit her mid-chest after curling around and falling over her shoulder.

"Hey!" She grinned and that smile beckoned for a response. "You're back."

"I'm back," I agreed, then switched my attention to my brother. "Is he bothering you?"

"Every day," she said with a laugh as she stripped off her jacket and her gloves. "But someone still wanted to go for a run and I needed the break." The whole time she spoke, she narrowed the distance between us and glanced down at the music I'd organized.

Guilt plunged through me as she picked up the first couple of sheets.

"I—" I hesitated.

"You did this?" She glanced up at me then back at the music as she toed off her shoes, but then she sat down. Even the hint of sweat couldn't diminish the sunshine and citrus tickling my nostrils. It had to be her shampoo.

"Probably should have waited for you," I started, keeping one eye on Lachlan who wore a smirk. "Why are you still here?"

"I was walking her back. Campus has been mostly empty and I wanted to make sure she got in safely." His tone was almost snide, and I rolled my eyes.

"She's safe," I told him, folding my arms. "You can go."

"I think I'm fine right here. We've had a nice few days

without you babysitting, little brother. Trust me, Ace has this."

"Don't be a dick," KC informed him. "And Jonas is right, I'm safe. You need a shower anyway." Then she wrinkled her nose, and it was downright adorable. "Me too, for that matter. Which means you definitely need to go."

"Awww," Lachlan protested almost playfully. I shifted my weight and moved to cut off his view of her.

"She needs a shower and you need to go," I told him.

"Or what? You gonna toss me out on my ass?"

"Yes," I said. "Happily."

KC chuckled. "You don't have to throw him out, he's going."

Was he? I raised my brows, but Lachlan let out a long sigh. "Fine, I promised to not be insufferable today."

"No, you lost the bet, which means you *can't* be insufferable today." The ease with which she shifted tones and handled Lachlan worried me.

Raising his hands in a gesture of surrender, Lachlan backed toward the door. "We running in the morning? Or you want a down day before classes start?"

"Maybe," KC answered, but her distracted tone didn't assure me she was listening to either of us.

"Right, I'll talk to you later then." Irritation flared in his eyes as I followed him to the door. But then he jerked his head to the hall with a significant look at me, so I followed him out and closed the door behind us. "Keep an eye on her and don't accept any invitations this week."

I always kept an eye on her. "Why?"

"Wait, look at that, you do know how to use words."

I ignored the little dig and just stared at him.

"You got the invitations." It wasn't a question.

I shrugged. "I threw them out." The stupid secret society thing held nothing of interest for me.

"Ace hasn't."

Shock twisted its grip on my spine. "No?" We hadn't really talked about it. She'd actually clipped one of the invitations to my door. I'd recognized the riddle and the seal. Knots and Chains was a popular rumor. Only members knew who the other members were.

They'd scouted me back in my freshman year. It had been an interesting test to answer the puzzles. Then shit went sideways and all communication just stopped. I guessed they didn't want me after all, or maybe Lachlan got annoyed at them for scouting me.

We hadn't discussed it then. "Why don't you want her to join?"

"It's not about whether she joins or not," he said, keeping his voice low and one eye on the room across the hall. Yeah. The cunt still lived there. Great. I liked Aubrey though.

She was great for KC.

"Then what is it?"

"Find me later," he said. "We need to talk privately. In the meanwhile, keep an eye on Ace and don't let her go anywhere alone."

With that cryptic warning, he stalked off.

I stared after him for a moment, then looked back at the door across the hall. How long had all three of them been back on campus?

Back inside the suite, I glanced to where KC still sat reading through the music. She'd stripped off her sweatshirt in my absence and pulled out her guitar. The fact she was playing when I walked in trapped me in place. I closed the door as quietly as I could and listened.

Then she began to sing the lyrics, sparing me a brief look before dropping her gaze back to the music. Three bars later, I stepped forward.

"Drop it another half-octave."

Her eyebrows climbed as she broke off. Lips pursed, she leaned forward and made another notation, then backed up to the beginning of the transition. When she dropped it that half-octave, I swore it was like she pulled mourning and worry twisted them right up with hope and fear.

It was—perfection and even made my eyes burn.

"Holy shit," she whispered as the last bar fell away. "That's —" She met my gaze. "Thank you."

Running a hand over my hair, I rubbed the back of my neck. "You're welcome. I should have asked before I touched it."

"Maybe." It was neither agreement nor chastisement. "But I've been stuck for three days and you found what I knew was missing."

"It hurts."

Dipping her chin, she nodded. "It definitely hurts." The loneliness I might have imagined, but the melancholy I didn't. Shifting, she put the guitar back on the stand. "I need to shower. I stink. Then we can make coffee."

"I can try to make it for you if you want." She'd been teaching me. I didn't have it fully down, but I didn't get a lot of practice.

"That would be great," she said as she stacked the music sheets together and straightened them. "Thank you."

She was almost at her door when I needed to ask, "KC?"

"Hmm?"

"Is Lachlan bothering you?" Cause if he'd broken in here while I was gone, my brother and I weren't going to talk.

We were going to fight.

"I don't know," she said after a moment, one hand on the doorknob to her room. She'd picked up her shoes and sweatshirt. "I mean, he knocked on the door. So—improvement? We're basically running and that's about it. I'm not going looking for him, but he's been here since right after I got back. So... we run. Usually really early, but he was late today."

"Why don't you just tell him to fuck off?" She was more than capable of doing it. I'd heard her—more than once. She could tell me to fuck off, too. It was part of what I liked about her.

She laughed, pushing the door open to her room and setting the stuff down on her bed before facing me again. I'd followed as far as the door but stayed out of her space. The sound of her amusement flooded me with warmth.

In all those pictures, she'd been kissing my brothers, but she'd *smiled* at me. Smiled and laughed. The rich, throaty sound of her laughter right now reminded me of that and made me want to just wrap up in that musical sound.

"None of you listen to me," she pointed out. "None of you."

"I do," I protested. Granted, it had taken a while. But I did listen.

"You do now," she admitted after a long moment. "Will it last long?"

The doubt should have stung, yet the reality was right there. We'd all judged her last year. We'd all...done a lot of shitty things—some shittier than others. But I liked that we'd become friends this year.

"Can't know until we try. I can go running with you if you want. Make sure Lachlan leaves you alone." Kind of like I had at the gym over the last couple of weeks of the fall semester.

KC studied me, a faintly puzzled frown on her face. "But he's your brother."

Discomfort shifted through me. All I could hear was Mom ranting about us choosing KC over her and Gibs... over family. So yeah, Lachlan was my brother. He, even more than

Ramsey, had known about my interest in KC last year and it didn't stop him from chasing her.

From tormenting her.

From *kissing* her.

"He is my brother. But I want you to be my friend."

"Brothers are important," KC told me as she came back to the door to face me. "I'll never ask you to choose between us. No one should."

"Brothers aren't that great." I shrugged. Lachlan was annoying as fuck, and Ramsey could be such a control freak at times.

"I wouldn't trade mine for anything in the world." She grinned again. "Lachlan's a dick, but he's still your brother. Don't give up on him."

"I'll think about it," I agreed, grudgingly. "Go shower. I'll make coffee."

Her smile flashed to life again. "Thank you."

I retreated to let her close the door, and it wasn't until I was at the coffee machine that it hit me. She wouldn't trade her brother for anything in the world?

What brother?

<h1 style="text-align:center">Thirty</h1>

KC

"I vote we hire someone else with a stamp to do this," Aubrey said, as we hauled the crates into my suite. We weren't going to her suite to do it.

"We did hire someone," I reminded her, grunting to get the door open. It opened despite my struggle, and I nearly toppled into the room. Jonas saved me from landing on my face as well as catching the crate of letters so I didn't dump them.

He kept an arm around me for a beat until I was steady, before taking the crate fully.

"Thank you," I said, grinning and leaning into the door to hold it open for Aubrey. "We're going to kind of take over the sofa and table...unless you're studying."

With a nod, he set the crate next to the coffee table, then took Aubrey's and put it next to it. "It's fine," he said. "No homework this weekend."

"Lucky you, I have a paper to write still." I made a face. "Be right back."

He followed us to the hall. "There's more?"

Aubrey groaned. "Yes, unfortunately."

"I'll help."

She shot me a look and waggled her eyebrows. I mouthed *shut up* and she smirked.

"Thank you, Jonas," I said with another warning look at Aubrey. She just threw an arm around me and laughed.

"He better behave," she murmured. "Or I'll stab him with a spoon."

"He's fine," I hissed at her. "We're friends now."

"You can be friends all you want, and I can still stab him with a spoon if he's a dick."

Three steps down and in the lead, Jonas paused to glance at us. "She's right, she can stab me if I'm a dick to you."

Aubrey blinked, but a hint of a smile touched Jonas' mouth.

"But only if I'm a dick to KC." He looked at Aubrey pointedly. "You don't get the same considerations."

"Noted," Aubrey countered. "I'll be watching out for my friend."

"Me too." With that firm nod, he continued down the steps. Aubrey glanced at me then made a face and I laughed at her.

Fifteen minutes and three trips later, my quads were hating me for the stairs, but we had all of the crates up here.

So. Many. Letters.

"Next time, warn me and I'll get a hand truck."

"Hopefully, next time won't be so many." I flopped back on the sofa. I'd already run six miles before dawn with Lachlan. Jonas met us when we got back with coffee for me and a smirk for Lachlan.

It was kind of funny how much Jonas was sticking it to Lachlan. I should probably discourage it, but frankly, I was enjoying Lachlan *not* getting his way. I'd cut out my tongue before I admitted to missing the brain melting, panty burning, and toe-curling ninja kisses.

Since that day in my room, he hadn't kissed me once. Good? Bad? Honestly, I had no idea. Lachlan seemed to be growing more human each day, and I liked it.

But I wasn't sure that I *should* like it.

"You realize this is more than last time, right?" Aubrey prodded me to move so she could sit down. With a grunt, I sat up and stared at the stacks of mail.

I wasn't the only one. Jonas eyed the crates like they were going to explode or something. "So you get this much regularly?"

"Eh," I said. "It varies. We've always tried to answer the mail ourselves, especially the handwritten notes and stuff."

"Yep," Aubrey said as she dropped onto the sofa next to me. She wasn't in any more of a hurry to dive in than I was. "Problem is, they held back on everything since the fire, and I think we just forgot to ask."

"Nope," I said. "Didn't forget. Totally avoided."

She laughed and bumped my shoulder. "Then it's your fault we have this many."

"Yep, we should fire me."

"Nope," Aubrey said. "Cause then I'd be stuck here without Yvette to help, and I'm not asking Payton Fucking Webber."

I snickered. "Oh come on, she'd die if she got to read our fan mail."

It probably wouldn't be *actual* death, unfortunately.

"Pretty sure she'd just spit on it," Aubrey said. "Go make coffee, and then we're going to divide up the crates and dive in. I've got an idea…"

Rising, I glanced at Jonas who still seemed to be studying the mail like it might bite him. "Want some coffee?"

"Not right now," he said. "But I'll order us pizza and drinks. 'Cause this could take hours."

Us.

"Planning to help, Hot Shot?" It was a joke, but the intense way he looked at me erased the humor.

"Yep, unless you don't want me to."

"I don't mind if you help at all, in fact...I'd appreciate it. But it can be boring."

"Then we turn on a movie or something if we get bored..." So practical.

I grinned. "Pizza sounds great. Aubrey—"

"Prefers white sauce to red on her pizza. She also likes chicken and mushrooms."

Yes, she did.

"And spinach," he said after a moment. "The weird stuff."

"It's only weird if you don't like spinach," Aubrey retorted. "But that sounds amazing. Thank you."

"Welcome." He glanced at me. "Same thing as always?"

Since I could eat practically any kind of pizza and apparently so could Jonas, we'd gotten into the habit of ordering one vegetarian and one meat lovers. I grinned. "Yes, please."

"Are you going to drink soda?" He glanced at Aubrey. "Or do you want the fancy water stuff?"

"It's just fizzy water and it's not that fancy," Aubrey replied with a nearly indulgent smile. "But I think I'll need caffeine so get a couple of the two liter bottles?"

"Okay," he said as he pulled out his phone. "I'll be right back." Then he vanished into his room.

As soon as the door closed, Aubrey hopped over the sofa and joined me in the kitchen as I ground the coffee. "Who is he and what did he do with the douchebag?"

To be fair, she wasn't wrong to question it. The last few months had been kind of a revelation, if a hard-earned one, considering the fire. If we hadn't ended up being roommates, I didn't think we'd be anywhere near this comfortable with each other.

At all.

Still, I laughed. "He's working on it." Tamping the grounds took a minute, and I waited to until the shots were brewing before I reached for the milk in the fridge. "I think we're really becoming friends."

Aubrey stared at me as I filled the little silver pitcher.

"What?"

"You're becoming friends... with one of your stepbrothers?"

I shrugged. "He's my stepbrother 'cause his mom happens to be married to Dad. It's not like we knew each other before the school or anything."

"Still your stepbrother," she pointed out. "He still lied to you."

They all had. "I know," I reminded her. "I have not forgotten any of it. Not the hate or the way they treated me..." The paint. The kisses. The degrading speech. Irritation scraped under my skin. "But Jonas and I...we've been talking and we're working on the friendship thing."

"Doesn't change what he did."

No. It didn't. "I can't hang on to hate forever. And I didn't hate them...or I didn't before I figured out what they were hiding." The steamed milk was next. "He asked if we could be friends. He's been a huge help, and he offered me this place, plus he's been kind. For the most part."

"Okay, you work on being friends with him, and I'll watch them like a hawk. I still want to stab them all with spoons and make them pay." The ferociousness in her tone made me smile.

"That's 'cause you love me best," I said, bumping her hip as I poured the foamy cap into place on her coffee.

"Yes, I do," she said, lifting the coffee cup. "I don't like fuckboys who go out of their way to hurt others, especially not my best friend. They're just lucky Yvette isn't here. They'd never sleep again..."

We made faces at each other and then burst out laughing. Yvette would go for more than pranks. She could be downright cruel when provoked. Then, she had lots of practice from dealing with all the people from her parents' world.

Just, pissing off Yvette was a mistake.

I finished with my coffee when Jonas emerged with a couple of notebooks, sticky notes in six different shades, and a stack of pens.

Wiping the coffee machine down, I tracked Jonas' progress over to the living room. He set his stack on the coffee table before he reached for a crate and lifted it to sit next to the notebooks and sticky notes.

"Do you have a system?" Jonas asked, looking at us.

"Usually, we just each take a crate and start working. Some just want signed pictures. Some want actual notes. We kind of read them all to see what they need and then we answer them."

"All of them?" His eyebrows climbed.

Shrugging, I claimed my coffee to walk over to where he studied the crate. "All of them."

"We like responding to the fans that took the time to do this. Emailing or tagging on social media is super easy and fast. We appreciate them, too," Aubrey said. "But the kids that take the time to write these? They deserve an answer. The creepy dudes deserve paper cuts on their nostrils."

The corners of Jonas' mouth dipped at the mention of creepy dudes.

"You take the good with the bad. Management also went through a lot of these before they sent them over." The envelopes were all slitted, having been opened, read, and then sent on.

Our "Forever Fan" had triggered new protocols. Though I had to imagine the guy was just a creeper.

"And," Aubrey said as she joined us and slid off her shoes before walking them over to set them inside the door to my room. "I think we should finally concede to the stock response for some of these. "

When I opened my mouth to respond, she held up a finger.

"I know you hate it. I know you prefer the handwritten responses. So do I. Being farmed out to assistants is never fun. However, I think we're getting an ungodly amount of mail these days. We can still respond to some of them, but the generic requests can get generic responses...you know?"

Sighing, I studied the crates as I chewed my lower lip. "So we do what?"

"We sort," Jonas said. "We make three stacks...one that's generic for generic responses and those go back into a crate to be sent wherever. The second stack will be the 'might be generic, might be personal.' You can decide when you're done."

"And the third will have all the ones who need a personal response. We can start on those today and get as many done as possible. Did you pick up more band pics when you were in L.A.?"

"Yeah," I said. "Yvette signed a chunk of them, so we'll use those first. Let me grab them." I headed for my room.

"Perfect."

"How do you determine what needs a personal response?" Jonas asked.

"We read the notes," Aubrey explained. "It's easier to show you, 'cause sometimes it's just having a feel for what they're saying."

Fifteen minutes later, we'd found examples of three different kinds of those that needed personal responses, a couple that were just straight up generic. Then a third that we were so-so on.

"Okay," Jonas said. "You two do responses. I'll sort. Anything I'm not sure on, I'll put in the second stack and you girls can check it when you run out of personal responses."

He checked his phone.

"Pizza will be here in fifteen. I'll go down and get it once it's here. I told Ramsey to be on the lookout for it." With that, he set his phone aside and literally picked up one of the crates and turned it upside to dump everything out. In fact, he dumped out three then set up the crates with sticky notes on them and went to work.

"He's kind of bossy," Aubrey said idly as she took one of the "needs responses" and signed one of the pictures before writing a note and sliding it over to me.

I took a sip of coffee as I studied him. All that intensity he used to focus on me with such baffling force was now on the letters.

And he was fast. He opened, skimmed, and sorted.

"I don't mind it so much," I murmured when Aubrey elbowed me and I made a face at her.

"Clearly," she said, then grinned.

An hour later, we'd made a real dent in the "needs a personal response" and had a huge stack ready to be mailed out, one full crate to go back to management, and more waiting for us to tackle after we ate. As it was, the pizza tasted incredible and so did the soda.

Jonas was searching for a movie while Aubrey threw out some helpful suggestions, and it was just—nice.

Really nice.

Even if my fingers ached from the signing.

Maybe we really were becoming friends. Granted, he had a long way to go with Aubrey, but he'd get there.

Not that I thought he cared all that much. Thoughtful,

smart, and talented. He was also dedicated as hell. By the time we called it quits for the day, we'd done most of it. We had a handful of responses to write out, but we split those up to do the next day.

Then Aubrey claimed the remote, and I ordered out for the Chinese. "What are we watching, Jonas?"

He scrubbed a hand over his face. "What?"

"It's your turn," I told him as I filled in the order on my phone. "You let me and Aubrey watch *Love is Blind*, so what do you want to watch?"

With a snort, he twisted to look at the television. "There were more episodes...we can watch those if you want."

"See," Aubrey said. "Now you're just sucking up."

"Maybe," he agreed and I nearly snorted soda out of my nose. "But I don't see how any of those couples end up together. Like... ever."

"Oh, you have got to watch *Move It or Lose It* with us next..."

Bless him, he asked, "What's that?"

Thirty-One

RAMSEY

"Why am I supposed to be watching her?" Jonas demanded of Lachlan who sat on the sofa in my suite, legs stretched out with his feet on the table. At least he'd taken off his damn shoes this time.

"Just watch her," Lachlan said. "She has enough shit to deal with here. You're more likely to punch first and ask questions later anyway."

Our younger brother eyed Lachlan like he was about to make good on that statement. "Jonas," I said, pulling his attention toward me. "You know there are clubs on campus and…"

"And the stupid Knots and Chains people." He made a face. "I've had four invites so far."

Lachlan sat up and I sighed. "Why didn't you say anything?"

"Secret society?" he drawled, then popped the lid on the soda he planned to drink. "Remember? Besides, you're both in it, so I figured you'd know."

I didn't laugh, but I thought about it. Lachlan scrubbed a hand over his face. "How did you—you know, never mind. You know about it. Great. They are trying to recruit Ace into it. Don't let her take off on anything that might be a 'secret' meeting or a quest."

Jonas wasn't the only one staring at Lachlan. Arms folded, I leaned back against the counter. Classes ended thirty minutes earlier, and Jonas came down after he walked KC back to their room. The pair had been thick as thieves the last few weeks.

To be honest, I wasn't entirely sure how I felt about it. Not with his past issues, his history of internalizing everything, and the violent explosions of temper that burst out randomly. As much as I'd worried about them sharing such close proximity, she was good for him.

Maybe.

My feelings on it were complicated.

"Exactly how is he supposed to know if she is going off on a 'secret' anything?" The point of a secret was she wouldn't tell anyone.

Right?

A headache thumped behind my eyes as Lachlan snorted. "Just follow her."

"That's your style," Jonas countered. "Surprised you aren't out in the bushes right now."

"Is she outside?" Lachlan snarked and I rubbed my face. "'Cause if you let her leave on her own, it won't be my bruised face we're dealing with."

Jonas grinned, though it was not a friendly smile. "I'd like to see you try."

"Enough," I told both of them. The tone did what no amount of words ever could. While the pair of them had often sniped and bickered over the years, I rarely fought with them if I could help it.

"He started it," Lachlan muttered.

"I'll finish it, too."

Kill me. "Enough," I repeated, and they both glared at me. While Jonas' expression was more sulky than heated, Lachlan was pissed.

"You and I both know—"

"We do," I said with a slice of my hand. But Jonas didn't and we weren't bringing up Kelly, the set-up, *or* the fucking fallout in front of him. RJ's choices that day still infuriated me. While Lachlan had taken great pleasure in exacting some kind of revenge over the years, it would never be enough.

While I'd never punched the asshole myself, I had a feeling if I ever let go, I might not stop. I understood where Jonas got his temper from, because I had the same one.

"What do you know?" Jonas demanded, glancing back and forth between us.

"Just tell me Ace is in your suite," Lachlan said, without answering his question.

For a moment, a very long moment, I thought Jonas might keep the answer to himself, but he sighed. "Yes, she's working on answering a few fan letters they didn't get to last week, then we're going to get dinner at the dining hall before we meet Aubrey back at the suite to finish this last season of *Love is Blind*."

The absolute bewilderment over the last item on his verbal list was the only thing arresting the sudden surge of—jealousy? Envy? Irritation? The label defied definition at the moment.

"What the fuck is that?" Lachlan asked. "What do you mean, finish?"

"None of your business," Jonas told him. "You just keep doing whatever shady shit it is that you're doing."

Glaring, Lachlan stood up and I sighed. "Jonas, stop provoking him. Lachlan, sit the fuck down, and shut up. You did start this."

That earned me two glares. I'd love to blame KC for this schism that seemed to be ever shifting between the three of us. While blaming her might be the easy out, the simple truth was, we'd *always* argued. Friction had always been a problem for us. Despite how close we seemed in age, we just—we were just vastly different people sometimes.

The simple truth right now was our problem boiled down to one blue-haired siren. Lachlan definitely had a thing for her. Jonas' crush had been evident from the beginning, not counting the fact he confessed it.

And me? I had no business looking at her at all. Especially not after she saved my ass with the school when she didn't have any reason to cut me so much as a break. I tried to thank her, and she'd shrugged it off.

I couldn't tell if it was because she was really indifferent or just uncomfortable. Frankly, the more I got to know her, the less I understood, and it disturbed me. I'd been hard on her. Harder than I would have been with any other student.

We only had a few months left until KC and Jonas both graduated. Then... what?

"Look, Jonas," Lachlan said with a sigh in a far more reasonable tone than he'd even attempted earlier. "I know you have questions. We all do. Right now, I—" He shot a look at me. "We want to keep RJ as far away from Ace as possible. He's bad news and she doesn't need the issues."

"He hasn't been near her."

"Not totally true," I said, and Jonas scowled. "Granted, I haven't seen him since the day I asked her to not accept his date. Nevertheless, I also don't know what else is going on, and I've been keeping my distance."

"I haven't," Lachlan said and I rolled my eyes. "He's on campus, I've seen him a couple of times, but he refuses to go near her when we're around. So we just need to keep that up for at least another three weeks."

Initiation.

"And you're not competing for a spot?" I checked with Jonas again. Arms folded, he just rolled his eyes in answer. Yeah, he was not a joiner by nature.

"If she does, I will," he said. "I'll talk to her about it. I've seen the invitations, and she put a couple of them on my door when they came."

The admission added sandpaper to the tension in the room. Lachlan scowled and cut a look at me. Did we tell Jonas the truth now? Or keep it to ourselves as we had for the past two years? He had no idea how involved in that whole nightmare he'd almost been.

I preferred it that way, especially considering how concerned I was about the fallout to his mental health. Lachlan grimaced. Yeah, he couldn't argue the last part, so I just shook my head once.

"Let us know if anything changes," I said rather than let Lachlan push him. If he demanded Jonas stay out of it, he'd be all in. If we kept pushing, he'd want to know why, and if we didn't tell him... he would find out.

As disconnected as he often "appeared," he wasn't an idiot. Given a question he wanted to be answered? He'd find out on his own, no matter how long it took.

"Please," I tacked on the last word. Then because we needed a change of subject, I asked, "Have you heard from any colleges?"

"Nope," Jonas said and I frowned. "Didn't apply to any, either."

What...? My phone played a familiar note that had Lachlan and Jonas both standing abruptly. I didn't even have to look at the screen to know it was Mom.

"Gonna go," Jonas said with a half-wave, and he didn't wait on us to say anything before he was out of the door. Just as that door closed, so did the one to Lachlan's room.

Picking up the phone, I sighed as I stared at the screen. As much as I wanted to send it to voicemail, I hit answer. "Hey, Mom." I even made it sound natural. Good for me.

"Ramsey, baby," Mom said, exhaling a long breath as ice clinked in the background. There was an almost electronic hum. I'd bet they were at the studio and she'd stepped out of the recording booth to get a drink. "You answered."

I winced. "The last couple of times I was in class, Mom. You didn't leave a message, so I just assumed you were calling to catch up and not a big deal." I crossed my mental fingers at that lie.

After Lachlan's Christmas walkout and Jonas going radio silent as soon as he headed to his dad's, I'd been stuck with trying to soothe her ruffled feathers *and* her temper.

Neither had been successful. I'd tried to talk to Gibs a couple of times, because if he'd seen the pictures—and I had to wonder if he had since he hadn't said a word to either of us —he might want an explanation.

"I know you're busy," she said, reproach in every syllable. "I count on you to look after your brothers. You know that, right?"

"I know, Mom, and I'm doing my best." Now would not be the time to mention that Jonas hadn't applied to any colleges. How the fuck I'd missed *that* I had no idea. However, I needed answers before I mentioned it. I went to get a drink and changed the subject. "How are you and Gibs doing?"

"Much better," she said. "I think he finally broke through the block. We just finished recording a new song, and it's probably the best thing he's ever done." The absolute gush in her voice brightened her right up. "I've been so worried, and he's been so frustrated. But the song is just... honestly, Ramsey, wait until you hear it. This is so much more like his classic stuff, only stronger, you know?"

"Sounds great," I said. "I know he was distracted over the

holidays." Yeah, that was a word for it. Mom guarded every single interaction to keep us from making it worse. Considering how annoyed she'd been about...

"Well, something has to be good. There's another series about you boys in the Tattler." The scolding note was back. "A detailed expose about all three of you, and it looks like they tried to interview your fathers."

That was news to me.

"Mom, you gotta stop reading the gossip sites. You know nothing good comes from them." I needed to take my own advice. We all did. The more I got to know KC, the more I recognized just how much bullshit was out there.

"How else do I get updates? You boys aren't calling me back. Lachlan's been a ghost since he left, and now even Jonas doesn't answer my text messages." The mournful note grated on me. "His birthday is coming and...you boys are all so grown now."

"Mom...it's been crazy here. Jonas is in his senior year, and you know how tough that is. Lachlan's in college classes, and he's been working with the Lacrosse Coach and the team. They're picking up drills this semester 'cause the season is coming..."

"That makes sense, I suppose," she said, the ice clinking as she took a drink. "I just—I miss my babies, and I don't like fighting with all of you. With that girl there..."

"There are lots of girls here, Mom. Speaking of which, I need to go..."

"Speaking of which?" Her voice climbed to a hint of a shrill note. "Is *she* there?"

"What?"

"You know who," Mom said, her tone going quite unfriendly.

"No, Mom, she's not here. No one is here. I'm by myself, and I have some grading to do and classes of my own to prep for tomorrow." I had one more year and I'd be graduating college, too. If I stacked my classes right, I might be able to graduate early.

"Oh."

"Yeah, anyway, I gotta go. I'll let them know you were asking after them. Talk soon, and good luck with the rest of the album. I'm sure it will be great." I hung up before she could say anything else and groaned. The earlier headache had redoubled in force.

On the list of problems we had right now, this one went lower on the list. I turned over the rest of the issues on my list. Jonas not applying to college was at the top, along with the situation in Knots and Chains.

While I was still stumped on the latter, I had to wonder if KC could help with the former.

It would give me another reason to talk to her...

Thirty-Two

KC

"How do you break up with a girl nicely?" Bronson asked when he answered the phone. It was a cold, damp day on the campus, with rain having washed away most of the snow and turning the area muddy. Course, it would be frozen by the next day.

"That's how you say hi?" I'd just left the library. Aubrey and I had both set up there to work on research papers. Mostly because I needed out, and neither of us wanted to deal with her roomie. When Forrest swung by to talk to Aubrey, I'd left them the study room for some privacy.

"Hi, K," he said. "How you doing? Good. Great. Busy with school? Yeah, I get that. More press drama? I know, I know, we just have to ignore it. Fantastic, now that we're caught up on you, can we switch back to me?"

A snort of laughter escaped me. A blonde ahead of me pivoted like she'd suddenly decided to change directions, and I braced—nope, not Payton. Good.

"Sure," I said to Bronson. "Let's talk about you." The girl

hurrying back to the library shot me a shy smile, and I nodded to her. Then I had to pretend I didn't notice her stumble and half-squeal.

"You're my favorite sister," Bronson informed me, a chuckle underscoring the words.

Weirdly, I hadn't seen Payton since the day Lachlan dumped her naked ass in the hall. I wasn't sure if I should be grateful or worried about that fact.

"For the moment," I countered, and he laughed for real.

I hurried through one of the open areas to avoid getting too wet, then slowed when I got under cover. At the moment, I was loving being outside. I was also a little worried about Aubrey. She hadn't talked about Forrest much over the last few weeks. That didn't have to mean anything. We'd all been busy.

Still...

"How do you break up with a girl nicely?" Bronson asked and I really couldn't help it. He opened the door.

"No idea, I've never broken up with a girl. I can ask Aubrey when she gets back." I grinned.

"Bitch," he said, almost groaning as he laughed. "KC, help me out. I like Diane, I do, but it's just not working for me."

"Okay, tell me why it's not working. Not sure I can help, but maybe I can give you the right words."

"She's—great, but she doesn't have any passions. Most of the time she just wants to do what I want to do, or she wants to go to a movie, and that's it. We hang out, we talk—sometimes we make out—"

"You can keep the graphic stuff to yourself. I'm still dealing with the scars of my mother's relationships, thank you very much."

He snickered. "Right, the point is—she's nice, really nice and... that's it. Maybe it's 'cause of all the crap with Pen or the fact that I'm getting ready for college and I think I really do want to go for law school...I need to focus on the here and the now and not..."

"Is she your friend?"

The long exhale of his breath came out in a rush. "Am I an asshole if I say no?"

"No," I said, glancing over the wet quad. Usually there were people out here, even in the snow, but the rain tended to chase people inside. We were almost at the end of January. February was right around the corner. Then spring and... "Sometimes we want to like people and we can't, no matter how hard we try. Sometimes we don't want to like them at all, but we can't stop thinking about them."

The Douchebags Three flashed across my mind's eye. Although, Jonas didn't really qualify as a douchebag as much now out of the three of them. Not anymore.

"Attraction is just weird." It was my turn to sigh. "But for what it's worth, if she's not someone you consider a friend and you're not enjoying the time with her—then maybe just tell her the truth. I don't know if there is a nice way to break up with anyone. In my experience, break-ups are usually loud and involve copious amounts of alcohol and shouting—sometimes we burn their clothes."

Bronson sputtered. "When did you burn someone's clothes?"

"I was seven?" I was trying to remember. "Might have been eight. It was during pilot season 'cause the guy she was dating was up for a pilot and apparently banging his co-star on the project. I think we pretty much burned all of his clothes 'cause Mom was pissed..."

It was such an odd memory to dredge up. Like I had the feel for the texture of the situation, but not the details.

"Oh, he was banging his co-star in our pool house." I'd walked in on them. Damn. How did I forget that?

"You know, that's some weird shit, right?" His droll delivery just made me smile.

"Yep, I do. But hey—love me, love my weird shit and damage."

"Deal," he said with a sigh. "All right, I'm gonna call Diane and see if she wants to get food. Then I'll talk to her."

"Good."

"Yeah?"

"Yeah, breaking up over the phone or text is shitty. Granted, my experience is all second-hand, but...I think it's shitty. So go you for being a good guy."

"Shh," he said, chuckling. "I have a rep to protect."

"Pfft."

"Shut up," he said, still laughing. "I'll talk to you later?"

"Yep. Good luck and give Pen a hug for me."

"Will do. You gonna be free for a video call this weekend?"

"I'll make time."

"Sounds good." Then he was gone and I sighed as I stared out at the rain. The new course of treatment had been going well... that's what they said. Well. We couldn't expect changes overnight and she was still spending more time in the hospital than out of it.

Everyone sent me updates, Davina, Jackie, Bronson, and even Dix. He'd gone to take her some toys for me, because her favorite sloth toy had gotten nearly ruined when she'd been sick. It took time to hunt it down, but we found one exactly like it.

We got a dozen to make sure we had a backup if we had the same problem. Dix had sent me a picture of her cradling the new sloth.

I scrolled to that image on my phone and grinned at her happy little face. Some of her hair had begun to fall out. Not a lot, but it was noticeable how it had thinned around her pigtails. Jackie discussed getting it cut just to make it easier for her while she was in the hospital. It was hard to get her hair braided properly with everything else.

Tracing my fingers over her face, I sighed, then closed out of that and glanced at the gray, gloomy, rapidly darkening sky. Yeah, I was gonna go take a shower and then order takeout unless we had leftovers to heat up.

Oh, we might.

The walk to the dorms left me soaked despite my hurry. Aubrey and I had used an umbrella earlier, but I left it with her. No biggie. I was cold, but I could warm up in the shower. Inside, I got the wet off my shoes and shuddered before I jogged up the steps.

I didn't know if it was the rain or talking to Bronson about break-ups or thinking about Pen, but the whole day just seemed—darker somehow. Shaking off the melancholy, I shifted my backpack before I unlocked the door to let myself in.

The light in the kitchenette was on, but we always left it on. The whole suite felt quiet and shadowed—empty. Maybe Jonas had stuff to do after classes, too. I checked my phone to see if I had any messages from Aubrey before I set my backpack down.

A faintly funky smell tickled my nostrils. I frowned. Did we forget to take out the trash? I diverted to the little kitchen area. I never had to remember it 'cause Jonas took it out like clockwork almost every day.

Honestly, it was a really nice thing to do and after a while I stopped thinking about it. When I opened the drawer with the little trash can in it though, it was empty with a fresh trash bag in it.

What the hell was that smell?

I checked me, just to be sure, then loosened the tie of my uniform. It wasn't laundry, that had been picked up, so whatever it was, I'd find it after I showered. Hopefully we didn't shove a food package under the sofa or something.

That happened to me once and I didn't think I'd ever get over finding the fuzzy, desiccated remains of what I thought had been a microwavable burrito.

Just nope.

I went to unlock my door and it pushed right in. I flipped on the light and stared.

The room was—trashed.

The funky smell hit me full force. There were shredded books on the floor. All of my clothes had been dragged out of the closet and they were in tatters...it looked like someone had just got scissor happy. There were pictures scattered along with papers amongst the ripped books.

The smell? It was coming from the bed. The pillows had been ripped up. The sheets and the comforter had been ripped and the stuffing flung everywhere.

Right in the middle of all of it was a pile of shit. A legitimate pile of shit. There were also print outs and magazine clippings. I had my phone fisted in my hand as I stared at the photos of me and the douchebags. In each one, they had their faces scratched out.

The smell and the damage...it was awful.

It was also creepy as fuck. Backing up, I began my retreat and then froze. I had two stands in my bedroom. One for each guitar. The cases were in the closet.

One of my guitars was still there with every single one of the strings cut and the fret board looked awful. Tears clogged in my throat. But the second guitar...

The one Dad gave me.

It was gone.

I swung my gaze around at all the destruction. Where was it? Why wasn't it here?

What if they destroyed it, too? The strings could be replaced and I could fix the fret... but if it was gone.

My eyes went hot. The smell was making me gag, and I pulled the phone up to dial security as I made it to the sitting room. Something hard hit the back of my head. It was like slamming into a wall if I'd been falling. As it was, I pitched forward and my phone went flying as I tried to catch myself.

I managed to get my hands out, hitting my knees hard enough to jar my teeth. Shoes entered my periphery, but I couldn't get my eyes to focus and I tried to lift my head when another blow crashed into me and the world went black.

Thirty-Three

LACHLAN

"So why no college?" I asked as I followed Jonas toward the stairs. I'd "run into" him coming out of the music hall where he'd been using one of the studios. I'd had a lecture one building over, and I'd only had to wait fifteen minutes for him to emerge.

The shift in his schedule to be around for Ace on the weekends hadn't been lost on me. Nor the fact that Ace typically went to the library to study with her best friend right around this time.

He paused at the first step to stare at me. Eyebrows raised, I waited for him to shake his head and climb the steps before I continued after him.

"Don't want to go," he said, and it was so grudging, it kept me from actually smirking that I got him talking. "Kind of like you."

"Eh, I am going to college." At my protest, he glanced over his shoulder at me.

"Here...you're taking basic bitch classes here rather than Stanford where you could be working on going pro or at least training in sports therapy."

"Always time for that later." Shrugging that off was easy. I busted ass to get into Stanford. I had a plan. The plan might be shifting, but I still had one.

"Then same," Jonas said.

"Same that you'll go later?" We were on the second floor, and a girl I barely recognized detached herself from another grouping to head toward us. Yeah, nope.

"Same as in always time for it later," Jonas said, then paused as the girl cut between us and the stairs.

"Hi Jonas," she said, her smile almost nervous and shy— except her eyes weren't. Head cocked, I glanced from the brunette to my brother then back. She caught my glance and licked her lips.

Still a no from me. As weird as it was to have girls living in this dorm, this was weirder.

Instead of saying anything, Jonas just stared at her.

"Do you have a minute?"

I could predict his answer. In three, two...

"No," Jonas said, sidestepping her and continuing to climb the stairs.

"Oh, I was..." She hesitated then looked at me since she was now between us before she twisted to glance up at my brother. He hadn't turned around; if anything, he'd paused only to let her finish the sentence. "I was kind of hoping you'd go with me to the Fire and Ice Party."

Huh. Forgot that was coming. Maybe I could coax Ace into going. With her blue hair she'd look amazing as an ice princess.

Not turning, Jonas said, "No." Then he continued up the stairs, not waiting for her to say another word. It was both hilarious and sad. The girl turned wide eyes on me. Her cheeks were red and flushed, and there was a hint of tears in her eyes.

"He's not very big on verbal," I told her, more out of pity than anything else.

She sniffed. "I don't suppose..." Her hopeful look pretty much flushed my sympathy right away.

"Sorry, I'm taken." I gave her a little salute and then followed my brother up, taking two steps at a time until I caught up with him. "Okay," I said, picking up the thread of our interrupted conversation. "What do you plan to do, if not college?"

"Might study with my dad for a while."

"Why don't I believe you?" It wasn't a taunt, but I was curious.

"'Cause you're an asshole?" Jonas said in a tone so damn dry it made me laugh.

"While you're not wrong, pretty sure that's not why I don't believe you."

He almost cracked a smile. The fourth floor was at least quiet. Most of the noise from downstairs muted the higher we climbed.

"Are you going to keep chasing KC?" Jonas asked abruptly.

I slid my hands into my pockets. They were still a bit chilled from outside. Most of the time, I didn't take more than the jackets we were required to wear with our uniforms and it was enough.

"I run with Ace every day," I reminded him.

We were almost to his door, but he paused to stare at me.

"You live with her, J, you should be able to talk to her—I was under the impression you'd gotten past the verbal blockage though..." I glanced behind us. "Maybe not."

"She's my friend, Lachlan." There was a warning layered into that sentence.

"Is she now?" I raised my brows.

"Yes. I protect my friends."

"You think you have to protect her from me?" Fuck, that actually stung. "What the hell?"

"You don't listen. You and your friends dumped paint on her." He was ticking the items off on his fingers. "I heard about you throwing her in the pond. You were hunting her down and kissing her constantly."

"That was—"

"What?" Jonas met my hostility with absolute ice. "You knew who she was, just like I did. Just like Ramsey did. More —I *told* you I liked her."

"You said you *could* like her."

"At the beginning of the year, and then I said..."

A sigh ripped out of me. "You said a lot of things."

"I said, 'you know...she surprises me. A lot.'"

I barely remembered that.

"Then I said, 'I like her. For real.'" He continued to stare at me.

Fuck. He had said that. "And you asked me for advice."

"Kissing her wasn't the advice I thought you would offer," Jonas continued.

"Kissing her had nothing to do with you," I said, locking my gaze on his. "Not one damn thing."

His expression tensed, but I didn't flinch. Kissing Ace had never been about Jonas. He was the last thing on my mind. I couldn't even pinpoint *why* I wanted to kiss her the first time beyond just getting in her face and after that...

"You're an asshole."

"We established that," I told him lightly. "Now, are you opening the door or am I?"

"You remember this *isn't* your suite anymore, right?" But he was already pulling out his keycard.

"Yep, it's why I offered to let you do it." The fact the

comment earned me another glare that devolved into rolled eyes just amused me. Jonas could be salty all he wanted. I'd kind of missed his comments to go with the sour looks.

He opened the door and a funky smell rolled out to greet us. No way Jonas forgot the trash. He had a sensitive nose and noticed it even when we bought the damn bags with odorizer in them.

"What the fuck—" Jonas' question snapped off like ice cracking and I pushed in past him. Ace was on the floor, sprawled, and the copper scent in the air was blood.

"Call Ramsey," I ordered as I crossed to where she was laying, face down. She was still in her uniform. She even had her damn shoes on. "Ace?"

I dropped to my knees to ease her over. There was a small puddle of blood on the floor; more of it spilled down her too pale face and stained the icy blue of her hair. There was too much of it.

"C'mon, Ace," I said, putting a hand to her lips and the first wash of breath against my fingers sent relief spiraling through me. I wanted to get a look at the wounds.

"What happened?" Ramsey was there, just a touch out of breath. I didn't doubt he'd run up the stairs.

"No fucking clue," I told him. I wanted to check her skull, and find where the hell the blood was coming from. "We might need an ambulance."

Wouldn't the school shit on that? After all the negative press generated by the fire, having a student assaulted on campus...

The idea of someone just hurting her sent a red haze over my vision. "We need to find fucking RJ, too." I knew that motherfucker was up to something.

"Here." Jonas was there, thrusting a towel at me. "We need to stop the bleeding." His face had gone ashen.

"Easy with her," Ramsey ordered when I shifted my grip to take the towel.

"What do you think I'm doing?" I snapped. I had her resting against me and I didn't give a fuck about the blood on my jacket. Soon as I knew she was all right, I'd be adding RJ's blood to the pattern. Son of a bitch had his eye on her like he had on Kelly. I should have done fucking more.

She was definitely still bleeding and not moving. How long had we been here?

"We need to time this. I don't know how long she's been out already."

"Fifteen minutes," Jonas said, and I tracked to where he was holding her phone. "Maybe." The screen was locked but a call failed notice popped up with the contact for campus security.

"Son of a bitch." The only thing keeping my temper in check was the towel I had pressed to her head. If I lost it, I could hurt her.

"This is Ramsey Malone, RA, Apollo-Volusia Four. We have a security incident on the fourth floor. I need campus security and a paramedic. We have an injured student."

She was more than just an injured student. Not for the first time in my life, I appreciated Ramsey's grounded calm as he took over.

"We need to notify administration, and I need the fourth floor locked down," he continued, and when I glanced at him, I found his gaze fixed on Ace. Unlike the three of us, Ramsey wasn't in his uniform. Instead, he had workout clothes on, t-shirt with the sleeves cut off.

He'd probably been lifting weights in his suite. He hated going to the gym. He'd gotten too much shit back when he was a fourteen-year-old senior or whatever. Weird how those memories drifted up from the ether. We'd been at the school then, too. Granted in younger grades, but I'd seen the crap he'd taken.

One of the reasons I made sure no one was in a position to *ever* give me that kind of shit. More than once, I'd gone after some of his tormentors. Nearly got kicked out of the school for it, and Ramsey ripped into me for risking my admission to the school.

"Holy shit," Jonas muttered, and it pulled both my attention *and* Ramsey's to where he stood in front of the open door to her room.

Ramsey crossed over to look inside. I wanted to see but I wasn't moving. "What the—" He glanced back at her then at the room again.

"What?" I demanded.

Jonas turned his ashen-face to me. "Someone's trashed it —there's even shit on her bed." He pulled out his phone to snap a photo then another, and finally a third before he came to me. "I'll hold this," he said, putting his hand over mine on the towel. I eased my fingers out from under it and then took the phone.

The images were a horror story. The room had been completely trashed. Clothing torn and destroyed. Books shredded. Paper everywhere... and the words "problem child" followed by "bitch" in all capital letters had been scratched into the wall over the bed.

The destruction was impressive and terrifying. The door pushed inward and I snapped a glare at it as security entered a step behind the pair of paramedics. They made a beeline straight toward me.

Jonas surrendered his spot as Ramsey moved to talk to greet security. Ace was still out when the paramedics had me move. Handing her over was one thing, but I didn't move from being right there with her. Neither did Jonas. We tracked everything they did even as Ramsey went to show security her room.

"Is there any chance she could have done this herself?" one of the security guys asked.

"Done what herself?" Aubrey demanded from the open door, then she was across the room and I had to block as her gaze zeroed in on Ace. "What the fuck did you assholes do this time?"

Thirty-Four

KC

"**I** don't give a fuck who found her, she's *my* friend," Aubrey sounded *pissed*. "She's more than that. She's my sister *and* we have medical power of attorney for each other."

I was going to kill whoever made her this angry. My head *hurt*. The sound of her aggravated tones, pitched perfectly to carry, were a repeated punch to my brain.

"You don't *have* to like it." Oh, Lachlan was here.

"Shut up," Jonas said. "She knows more than we do right now."

"*Stop*," Ramsey's tone was bullish and aggravated. The intensity in his voice dragged at me. "This isn't helping anyone. Let them do their jobs."

Let who...

There was an increase in pressure on my left arm...blood pressure cuff? What was going on? I wanted to look around but opening my eyes took forever, it was like they were glued shut.

"Pulse and respiration are good. We've got an ambulance on the way…"

I didn't know their voice, but I didn't want to get in an ambulance. Hadn't I already ridden in one this year? No, wait that was last year.

"I'm not feeling any movement to the bone. This is good. We won't know if there is a fracture until we do x-rays…"

Right. *Open your fucking eyes.*

The first things I saw were the cool blue of Ramsey's gaze, laser-focused on me. Well, all the Ramseys really. Was he a trio now? My stomach rolled as I tried to blink and get the dancing vision to meld back into one super Ramsey…

A laugh escaped me and that sound alone made my head hurt so bad, I swore there must be something stabbing into my skull itself.

"Kait," Aubrey said, tears creeping into her anger-soaked voice. I tried to move my head and nearly blacked the fuck right out. "I'm right here, don't do that—" She appeared in my line of sight, the line of her mouth going tight.

"No ambulance," I managed to say. Or at least I hope I said that cause my tongue felt almost too big for my mouth. "No press."

One would grab the other. I didn't want either.

"Don't get any ideas," she warned, taking my hand in hers.

The other one was trapped and I couldn't move it. Warm fingers gripped both hands, and I slowly shifted my gaze to where Lachlan sat, my other hand firmly in his. The haunted forests were on fire tonight, fury ablaze in his green eyes.

I tried to swallow, but that just made the pain in my head redouble as my vision blurred again and there were three Lachlans.

Yeah, I wasn't sure I could handle three of them.

"Miss Crosse?" A voice I didn't know pulled at my attention and I frowned as I tried to focus on an older man, light brown hair that was receding, clean-shaven, and dressed in a suit and tie. He reminded me of the guy cop on the show with Mariska Hargitay. Only with far less scowling.

"I don't know you," I said after giving myself a few breaths to get the spinning under control. Mouth breathing was awful, but something smelled awful. I really hoped it wasn't me.

"Probably not. My name is Murray Creglin, I'm head of the security here at Blue Ivy Prep."

"Awesome." I tried to sit up, 'cause having so many people looming over me while that smell kept randomly assaulting me was not my idea of a good time.

"Easy," Aubrey said, putting a hand on my shoulder.

"Hang tight, Ace. The ambulance is almost here."

Yeah, no ambulance.

"Miss Crosse." I focused on the security guy—Creglin? Wasn't that the guy from that show... "We need to ask you a few questions. The police are also going to have questions for you."

"Head hurts," I said. Wait, why did my head hurt? The destruction in my room trickled back into place along with the filth on the bed itself. "My guitar is gone."

"We have your guitar," someone else said. There were too many people in the room. But great.

"You sure, they hurt one and took the other...someone took it...not even sure how they got in."

"Have you been having any issues here at the school? Any threats?"

"No, not really..."

"Well, there was the fire," Aubrey said pointedly, but she wasn't looking at me. No, she stared at Creglin. She was definitely in fire mode. Oh man, I hope she and Forrest hadn't broken up. "There have been a few other issues, but our management team has handled it."

"We'll want to talk to them," Creglin said. "Now we checked the door. The electronic lock records someone accessing it but not the number of the keycard."

"It had to be a master then," Ramsey said. "All the RAs have masters."

"How you got in before," I said, flickering at Lachlan. "Not the first time you tried to sneak up on me."

"Hey." His expression tightened as a wounded note crept into his voice.

My eyes were fluttering close. "Hardly the first time you went after me."

"Mr. Nash," Creglin said. "Maybe we should step away and have a conversation." There were more words, but my eyelids were too damn heavy.

The next time I opened them, I was in a hospital room. Fuck, I hated these places. Aubrey sat in the chair next to the bed, scrolling her phone and she leaned forward as soon as I twitched.

"You are in so much trouble." Naked worry filled her expression. "I have to get the doctor—don't move."

Wasn't really planning on it, but she didn't leave me alone. As soon as she was out the door, Jonas was in. We didn't really have time to talk, because there were so many people filling the room.

A doctor. A nurse. Someone else. They were all talking, and my head thudded so bad.

"You do have a concussion and you have lost consciousness for some time twice, we're going to keep you here for at least twenty-four hours..." Around and around it went. The concussion had been serious, but x-rays showed my cranium was intact. They had not identified the weapon yet.

The cops were here.

Fun times.

Twenty-four hours later, Jonas and Aubrey walked with

my wheelchair-borne ass to a private entrance where a privately driven SUV pulled up.

My head still hurt, but I hadn't passed out again and I didn't want to throw up anymore. Good times. Neither Aubrey nor Jonas would leave, and Aubrey was *seething*, even when I thought things were going well.

It wasn't until we were back on campus that Jonas said, "I called Ramsey; he's making sure the hall is clear, and Lachlan will clear the stairwells to get you upstairs. Ramsey said you can stay with him if you're not up for the stairs."

Yeah. No.

"I'll be fine going up the stairs." If I wasn't, I'd fake it until I made it. "What did the police say?"

"They cleared Lachlan," Jonas told me.

"Cleared him of what?"

"Of being the sack of shit that broke into your room, wrecked it, and hurt you," Aubrey said. "So instead, he's just the guy who assaults you on the regular while being a fucking liar —"

"Aubrey," I said slowly and she held up a hand.

"No, Kait. You can accept them at whatever word you want, even Jonas here. He seems to have at least developed a fucking clue." Yeah, she was *pissed*. Two Kaits. No KC. No babe. Dammit. The heat of her anger seemed to make the pulse of my headache intensify. "The lies? The assaults? The stalking?"

"I know." I squeezed her hand. "They didn't know I didn't know."

"I don't *care*," Aubrey stressed that last word with enough force to make it leave a physical imprint in my soul. "They know how to use words. Whether they realized you knew or not, *they* knew." She wasn't staring at me, but at Jonas.

"Leave him alone," I said. "Jonas—"

"She's right," he said abruptly, and he might have moved

except I put my free hand on his. "We knew. We should have said something—I did. I did the first day we met, but you threw the note away."

Note? What note? Was I forgetting something like he gave me a note?

"The day we met," he said, shifting in his seat so I didn't have to strain to look at him. "In the hallway not far from your room."

"Yeah, I ran into you...and you were kind of a dick."

"You told me to take a picture..."

I winced a little. "Oh...yeah..."

A faint smile touched his lips. "I left a note on your door to introduce myself...to tell you if you needed help...you could ask me."

Confusion filled me. "There was no note." I would have remembered that right.

He shrugged. "There was a note. You crumpled it up."

Crumpled...

We were pulling up to the dorm, and it was a lot later in the day than I realized. Actually, I had no idea what time it was. Aubrey had my phone and wouldn't surrender it. Ramsey strode down the steps to the car and opened the back door before the driver could get out.

I had to let go of Aubrey so she could climb out, and then I was next. Jonas held onto my hand until I had to let him go and Ramsey was right there to help me out. Even though it was gray and overcast, it also seemed really bright.

"Welcome back," he said as he steadied me. "Lachlan says there's no one between us and the fourth floor. He'll also cover it and move up ahead of us to get rid of any stragglers. You good for stairs?"

I honestly had no idea. "I think so?"

He held onto my arm as he guided me toward the steps into the dorm. "You can stay down in my—-"

"Thank you," I said. "Really. Just—I'd rather go up to my own space and just...I'm really tired."

"Okay, let's get you up there then." All three of them moved. Aubrey hooked arms with me, but I nearly missed a step by the time we got to the second floor, so Jonas traded out with her. Ramsey stayed firm on my right and didn't back off.

Once we made it to the fourth, I was flagging hard. My head weighed so much. Lachlan stood in the middle of the hallway ahead of us. His hands were in his pockets, his expression dark as hell.

It probably had something to do with the cops questioning him. Once we were inside the suite, I started toward my room. The door was still open and... fuck, I forgot what a wreck it was.

"Take my room," Jonas said as he came up next to me. "We'll take care of this tomorrow...I would have, but I was at the hospital."

"You don't have to..."

"I can sleep on the sofa," he insisted. "Take my room before you fall down." It was very bossy.

We could get a hotel, but I was tired. "I'm with Jonas on this one," Aubrey admitted. "I'll stay over here, too. I'd say stay in my room, but Payton is over there, and I do not need to be arrested for murder."

That almost made me smile.

"But we're up here now and you're safe. No one saw. That's something. The ambulance is already in the news. I'm sorry. We tried to dial it back...I called Teddy. He'll take care of it, and I need to call Yvette before she shows up here ready to go to war."

That was a good point. Fuck, if it was on the news...

"It's all right," she soothed. "I called them, too. It's fine." I almost sagged in relief. "Let's get you in here, and I'll go grab us some clothes from my room."

"I have shirts—" Jonas offered.

"Thank you," I said. "You guys didn't have to do all this." The more I thought about it, the more I kind of wished we'd gotten a hotel, and at the same time...there was a strange comfort present here with my three douchebags—well, two point three. Jonas wasn't a full on douchebag anymore.

It was strange going into Jonas' room. I did not know what I expected to find, but it was... comfortable. A lot like mine had been. The comforter was black, but the sheets were dark navy. There was a keyboard in the corner, and I stared at it kind of blankly as Aubrey hustled me over to the bed.

"Grab your pillows," I said softly to her, and she glanced from me to the pillows on the bed. "He's sleeping on the sofa. If I remember right, mine were all gutted."

Cupping my face, she frowned. "How's your head?"

"You want the truth?"

"Yes," she said firmly.

"Hurts," I admitted. "And I feel like we just played back-to-back sets at the Garden."

"Jonas?" No sooner did she say his name than Hot Shot showed up like he'd straight teleported into the space. "She needs to sleep now. You said you had shirts?"

Oh, that was a plan. As curious as I was, I didn't want to dig around in his stuff.

"Yes." He turned away. A drawer opened in the closet, and he came back with a dark gray shirt that was so soft that when it touched my hands I kind of wanted to hug it.

"Thank you," I told him.

"Hungry?" he checked and my stomach rolled.

"No." I'd managed a little food at the hospital. Anything to get out of there. "I just need sleep."

"Then sleep. I'll be out there, so no one is getting in here."

Some of the tension crushing me collapsed at the assurance. As soon as he was out of the room and the door closed,

Aubrey helped me out of the hospital gear and into the shirt. My head was still tender. I also had stitches—and a new haircut that I'd have to deal with at some point.

I was too damn tired to worry about it right now. "The cops are going to want to talk to you again," she briefed me as she tugged the shirt over my head. "I'll get your clothes sorted. I also had management send them the stalker emails and letters—especially after the pictures that were left on your bed."

"Okay."

Once I was under the covers, she pulled them up and tucked me in. "I'll be right back."

I was already floating off. My eyes were glued shut, but I could still feel the weight of her regard.

"What stalker emails?" Lachlan demanded in a really loud whisper. Or maybe he wasn't whispering.

"None of your business," Aubrey snapped. "You won't leave her alone?"

"I won't. Want the door closed or open?"

"Open until I get back. Her eyes are still unfocused."

"If you want our—"

"I don't want anything from you," Aubrey cut Lachlan off. "Don't mistake convenience for forgiveness. You've all been assholes to her, and I don't give a shit about your reasons. That's my best friend, so I'll be taking her side in everything even when she won't. There is always someone out to make a buck off her name or her parents, and the fact you used that against her makes you no better than the rest of the world..."

"I just want to help her," Jonas said, though the others were silent and guilt stabbed at me. Aubrey was scared and she was angry. I needed to get up and—do something.

"Then look after her and I'll be back in five minutes. Maybe less."

I was losing the battle for staying awake.

"She's taking the next three days off," Ramsey said. "So are you, Jonas. Stay with her. I'll make arrangements for excuses and assignments..."

"I'll..." Whatever it was Lachlan was going to do faded out and would have to wait. The thud of my headache rocked me to sleep.

Thirty-Five

JONAS

It didn't take Aubrey long to get some things and come back. Ramsey actually went into the hall to make sure no one interrupted or tracked her. She came back with a pillow, and I wasn't sure why until she handed me the extra from my bed. KC was asleep on mine.

In my bed.

That left an unidentifiable feeling settling in my chest. When I stared at the pillow, Aubrey sighed and shot a look behind me before focusing on me. Yeah, I know my brothers were still here. For once, I didn't mind it. They weren't going to let anything happen to KC either.

"She didn't want you to sleep on the sofa with nothing," Aubrey told me in a low voice like I needed the explanation. "Do you have an extra blanket? Or can I grab one for you in here?"

"This is good," I told her. Then... "Thank you."

"Wasn't me, I don't care if you sleep hard." The sharpness in her smile and the hint of a smirk gave her away. The expression and the reduction of rancor in her voice when it came to me versus my brothers. It was weird to be the one someone liked more than them. I didn't usually care if someone liked me. Still didn't...

Except, the moment that thought crossed my mind, my gaze tracked to KC where she slept. I liked being friends with her.

I liked that she liked me.

"Okay," I said, nodding to where KC was. "I'll be out here. No one will bother her."

She met my gaze, and for the first time, I thought maybe we got each other. If not peace, then armistice. To be honest, I hadn't thought much about Aubrey Miller at all.

"Good," she said, bracing a hand against the door before she pushed it almost closed before she added, "Thank you." Then it shut silently before the lock engaged.

As much as I wanted to stare at the door like I could see KC through it, I needed to talk to my brothers. Pillow in hand, I faced them.

Lachlan leaned against the back of the sofa, arms folded, chin down to his chest, and a brooding look on his face. Like I had been, he stared at my closed bedroom door. The air around him was electric with unrepressed fury.

Ramsey was closer to the door, but his attention seemed more targeted on the door to her room, which stood open. "You guys should go," I said. "I'll stay up."

No way I could sleep.

Lachlan cut a look at me and straightened. "I'll be back up at six. You want anything? Food? Coffee?"

I could use KC's coffee maker, but that seemed wrong if she wasn't up to enjoy it. "Food. Whatever."

He nodded. "Don't let anyone in."

While I had no intentions of doing so, I didn't argue. For

all his jerky movements as he yanked the door open to the suite, he didn't slam it behind him.

"The cops were pretty brutal," Ramsey said, pulling my attention to him. "They talked to him for hours, and they want to talk to him again."

Did I feel bad for him? Maybe.

"She wasn't wrong about what he did."

"He didn't say she was." Ramsey surprised me with that. "But he also didn't answer in detail. His father also sent an attorney over."

I set the pillow down on the sofa. The smell in here hadn't improved in all the hours of our absence.

"Don't forget your meds," he said in a softer voice, and I sighed. But before I could respond, he raised his hands. "Not getting on your shit. But the last twenty-four hours have been brutal."

And I had missed my meds the night before 'cause we were at the hospital. "They're in my room."

"I have extras downstairs. Want me to bring them up?" I must have taken a beat to answer because he said, "I can grab food for you, too. Have you eaten?"

"Maybe." I really didn't remember. "Aubrey let me stay with her when she had to take a call from Yvette. She also brought back some snacks from the machine."

Pretty sure I ate one of those. Maybe.

"Right, I'm getting you food and meds. If you need anything else..."

"You have any candles?" The smell was just beginning to grate.

"I think so, if not, I'll grab some for you tomorrow."

He was already at the door when I said, "Thanks, Ramsey."

After he left, I walked over to the door to her room. The

mess...the bed sheets and destroyed comforter were gone as was the shit—but the smell lingered. It was... disgusting.

"Don't mistake convenience for forgiveness. You've all been assholes to her, and I don't give a shit about your reasons. That's my best friend, so I'll be taking her side in everything even when she won't. There is always someone out to make a buck off her name or her parents, and the fact you used that against her makes you no better than the rest of the world..."

Aubrey's words echoed inside my mind as I lingered in the doorway. Ramsey didn't take long to return. He brought me a grilled ham and cheese sandwich that he'd made, along with a bag of chips. It was so reflective of the kind of meal he made when I was younger that I stared at him.

"Whatever, just eat it," he told me, the corner of his mouth kicking a little higher. But there were deeper shadows under his eyes, and he hadn't shaved. That was unusual for him. When he left, I carried the food and the meds into the kitchen.

I ate on autopilot, then took the three pills, washing them down with a deep drink of water. After I drained the bottle, I cleaned up my debris, then wiped down the counters.

Turning, I faced the room. There are signs of the paramedics, campus security, the police, and more throughout the room. I was surprised at the lack of crime scene tape on the door to her room, but the school probably hadn't gone for that.

Was that why they'd taken the bedsheets and stuff? Evidence maybe. After sacking up the trash in the sitting area, I made a point of wiping it all down before I headed into her room. It was hers, so she'd probably want to decide on what to do with stuff.

But the mess was just...too much. The photos with our scratched out faces were also gone. I began a mental list of what was missing. Sorting the room's debris into manageable piles, I put all the shredded clothing that didn't look remotely salvageable into one bag.

It was all of her uniforms. Every. Single. One.

Even the ties had been cut. The shoes in her closet had also been stabbed. Repeatedly.

The more I uncovered the damage, the more disturbing it grew. There were three t-shirts that she might be able to wear. The dirty clothes were gone, so maybe when the clothes came back from the laundry there would be more.

I tackled the papers and shredded books next. A song had been torn into several different bits of paper. I recognized some of the bars. I gathered as much of it together as I could. Maybe I could tape them back enough for her to recover the missing pieces.

It was the middle of the night by the time I finished sweeping, wiping down, and collecting the damaged pieces together. There were a few photos that seemed to have escaped her attacker's wrath.

One of her guitars was missing. Had the police taken it, too? I'd made a list of everything I thought was missing, but she would have to check it. The three photos that survived the assault included one of KC as a child. It had to be; we all knew what Jennifer Crosse looked like. She was very glamorous.

The writing on the back said, "Legends are born *and* made. You're the author of your own story. Never forget."

It wasn't KC's writing.

The second photo was of her and a guy I didn't know. The dark-skinned dude was tall, at least next to KC, and wore a pair of glasses. They were making faces at each other, but there was no mistaking the affection in her eyes for the guy next to her.

I hated him.

Who was he? Why did he get to make her smile?

The back said *we could have been in a condom.*

What did that mean? I glared at the photo again.

The third photo gave me far more pause. It was her with another dark-skinned child, this one tucked right up to her chest as she cuddled the baby.

A baby girl?

I flipped the picture. *My little rock star. My sweetest Pen.*

My.

The repetition set off alarm bells.

Was this...?

I stared at the images again—one at a time.

KC looked like her mom. A lot. But she didn't have blonde hair anymore—KC didn't anyway. It was always blue. The baby had KC's eyes though.

Did she really have a baby? Was that what she kept so carefully guarded?

I kept going back to the back of it and what it said: *My little rock star.*

Pen.

So many questions.

I went back to the picture of KC and the guy. I'd never seen him in the news with her and on none of the gossip sites. Was he the father?

Despite the curiosity consuming me, I stacked the pictures together and set them carefully on her night stand. There had been a board in here with pictures pinned to it, but that was in pieces.

Leaving her room, I retreated to the sitting room and a new drink. Sliding an earbud in, I turned on a podcast and went to work sorting out the shredded pieces of music. I got most of her song back together. Four of the five pages were there, and I got them mostly intact, but I couldn't find the fifth or it had been turned into so many little pieces it was unrecognizable.

I grabbed a soda and finished most of it as I pieced

together some assignments. Some notes—they didn't make any sense, but there were lyrics jotted down. I recognized the need.

One of the last pieces I reconstructed was a Knots and Chains challenge. I had one similar to it: the riddles and the scavenger hunt would identify the where and the when.

The riddles worked out to something happening in roughly ten days.

The night of the Fire and Ice Party.

Was that what all of this was about? An initiation gone wrong? For all that they were a secret society, I'd heard about some of the insanity to do with them and their initiations. I'd been tapped once, but it ended up going nowhere.

Then nothing for two years, until this one. Now they were after KC, too. I had a few of the invitations in my room. I hadn't cared about it, but maybe I should.

My eyes were sore and gritty when the clock hit five and Lachlan texted me.

LACHLAN

Running. Then bringing food. How is she?

I stared at the message for a long moment, then answered.

ME

Sleeping

I'd heard nothing from them all night, so I hoped that was good. It had to be—Aubrey was too protective. I stared at the stack of papers, the few I'd been able to save. Then I thought about the damage to her room and the photos in there.

If she had a baby while on tour, or even on one of their breaks, they could have hidden it. Maybe that was why she came to school? She needed time to heal?

Twice I glanced at my phone and debated hitting Gibs'

contact and calling him, but twice I put it down. Should I call him? Would she want me to call him?

I didn't think so.

After another hour of staring, I tried her mother's apartment in New York. The number was actually written on one of the pieces of paper.

Five minutes later, I stared at my phone. KC's mom was in rehab.

Again.

The lady didn't call it rehab, she said a retreat, but that was what most people called rehab.

How long had she been there? The press hadn't said a word, so maybe they were keeping it quiet?

I was still chewing on that question when Lachlan texted that he was there.

So. Many. Questions.

I flicked my gaze to the taped-together pieces. But only one I really wanted an answer for—who hurt her. I wouldn't leave enough of them to be put back together.

Thirty-Six

KC

"Hey," I said as Jonas snagged my backpack before I could even stand. He'd been my self-assigned personal escort everywhere since I returned to classes. Aubrey had gone back thirty-six hours after I got out of the hospital, more because I made her than anything else.

"Anything after this?" he asked as I stood. I still had to take my time and not rocket to my feet.

"No," I said, checking my phone. My head was still sore, and I had a checkup the following day. "I don't think so." I scanned the list. "We have a make-up test Saturday morning at the testing center—two tests." Jonas, like me, had missed three full days of class, and he hadn't returned until I did.

"We can study tomorrow evening," he said. "If you need it."

"What about you? Are you ready?" I smoothed down my jacket and made sure I had the umbrella before I followed him toward the hall.

Jonas shrugged. "Mostly. It's not that hard."

I hid a smile because he wasn't being arrogant at all. He meant it exactly how he said it. The work wasn't hard, nor was the material.

"Good, when I want to double check stuff, you'll be my guy."

A hint of a smile touched his lips while he waited for me to set the pace. I'd definitely been doing better, though it had taken forever to get the headache to go away. Running was still not a hot idea. I'd made the mistake of pushing it.

I'd puked five minutes later and ended up missing three morning classes because of the blinding headache. So, now, baby steps were the name of the game. Jonas acting as escort helped a lot.

No one collided with me. I didn't have to balance my bag on the stairs. If I needed to take my time, I did. Whether I was going up or down the stairs, he was right in front of or behind me to keep me from falling.

"Want to grab food on the way back?" He waited until we were downstairs to ask. The rainy days had turned frigid again, and the snow blanketed the campus. It was kind of picture perfect.

"We can order food when we get to the room." I didn't really want to go to the dining hall. It was so loud there, and Jonas never relaxed when we were there. "Don't ask what I want," I continued, hiding a smile as he frowned. "I don't know yet."

Though the desire to have a nap was strong.

"Jonas?" A girl I didn't recognize called to him as we stepped outside. There was still a steady flow of students leaving the academic building.

He paused in front of me to stare at her. I had to bite the inside of my lip as he didn't respond verbally to her, at all. But she had snagged his attention.

Poor thing looked so nervous, I thought she might faint.

Sympathy swelled inside as she darted a look at me then back to Jonas. "The Fire and Ice Dance—"

"No." He didn't wait for her to finish or say anything else, just cut her off before motioning to let me know it was okay to keep moving.

Her entire expression fell, and her cheeks flushed deep pink. "I already asked him," I told her, taking the heat for his rejection.

"Oh," she said, then winced. "Sorry, I didn't mean..."

"Nothing to be sorry about, he is pretty cute." Which was an understatement. Hot Shot had always been good looking, even when I thought he was a dick.

She laughed, but her blush deepened and she hurried off. Turning to Jonas, I found him staring at me now. Only instead of the blank look, he seemed—puzzled.

It wasn't until we were walking again that he said, "Why did you tell her that?"

"Because she was embarrassed," I said. "It didn't hurt me to say I'd asked."

"Because I'm cute?" His mystified tone endeared him even more.

"No, though you are definitely easy on the eyes." Then, because he still looked confused, I said, "Can I hold your arm?"

It was as much to stay steady on my feet as to narrow the distance. He offered his arm immediately, and I tucked my hand against his elbow. Closer, I could talk without worrying about someone following us, hearing me so clearly.

"It's hard to ask someone out. Even harder to do it in front of someone *else* and then have the person you were asking out tell you no."

He seemed to turn that over in his head. "Do you want to go to the dance?"

The slight pivot on subject caught me flat-footed. "I don't

know," I admitted. The latest riddle quest was sending me to it, and I'd kind of thought about it before...

"You got the hidden invitation." It wasn't a question. Did that mean...? "Yes," was all he said by way of confirmation.

By unspoken decision, we waited until we were back in the suite before continuing the discussion.

"What do you know about them?" He ducked into his room, but he left the door open so I could talk while I headed for the coffee maker.

"I didn't even know it was a *them*. I haven't really thought about it much. Except that the first set of riddles took me out to the pond where RJ was waiting." That was surprise enough. "Then Lachlan showed up and I never found out what it was about."

"It's a secret society," Jonas said as he padded back out in a dark t-shirt and pajama bottoms.

I'd just finished pulling the shots when he motioned to the coffee maker.

"I'll finish if you want to change."

"Thanks." I headed for my room. We'd made progress all week restoring stuff here, though I'd literally had the old mattress taken and a new one brought in. I just couldn't bring myself to lie on it after the shit.

Just—no.

"And a secret society?" I called. Like Jonas, I'd left the door open. He couldn't see me where I changed just like I couldn't see him. "For real?"

"Yes," he said. "It's a stupid, dated tradition. They're called Knots and Chains."

That was—a weird name.

Casual clothing options were limited. I hadn't bothered with buying more just yet. Aubrey loaned me a couple of outfits, and I still had two of Jonas' tees. I dragged one of them on right now; it was super soft. Sleep shorts fit on under it.

"And they're like a real secret society? All Skull and Bones?"

"Yep," he said and if he followed it with anything, I didn't hear it over the milk steaming. I slipped into the bathroom to empty my bladder. After, I checked my appearance in the mirror as I washed my hands. You couldn't quite see where they'd had to shave part of my head to do the stitches.

I'd give the doctors credit, they'd been careful. But I also had to keep my hair loose to cover the missing chunk. If I could make it through the rest of the semester without another disaster, that would be great.

I paused on the way through my room to stare at the empty guitar stand. It was a very real, physical pain for my guitar to not be there. The second one had to be re-strung, and apparently Lachlan had taken it to get it fixed.

He'd even left a note to tell me where it had gone. That was almost sweet. Beyond that, he'd been a ghost. Outside of classes, I hadn't seen Ramsey either. Though his attention rested on me so firmly in both classes I had with him that I could feel the echo of the weight even now.

With a sigh, I left my room. I hated that empty stand. When I'd reached out to the cops and campus security, both denied taking a guitar, so the one Dad gave me was just —gone.

That... *hurt.*

Jonas held out the coffee to me as I returned. The latte was practically perfect. "Thank you... you're getting good at this."

"You're welcome." Not for the first time, he waited until I settled on the sofa before he joined me. Only this time, he brought over a blanket. "It's a little cold for shorts."

"I'm out of actual pajama bottoms," I admitted with a sigh. "Aubrey wants to go to town to get some but I just—I have bought two full wardrobes this year. I almost hate to buy more."

"You could order some," Jonas offered as he sat at the other end of the sofa. "I'd loan you mine, but they wouldn't fit."

"Well, if they had drawstrings," I said, trying to keep it light.

"Ramsey's have drawstrings," he said after a minute. "I don't like them. But he's too tall."

He didn't offer up about Lachlan and I didn't ask. "Maybe I'll go shopping next week."

"I can go with you," he offered. It wasn't the first time he offered something like that. Where I went, so did Jonas. I hadn't missed how he and Aubrey made sure I was never alone in the suite, or between classes, or pretty much anywhere.

They'd become my unofficial guardians. It was very sweet.

"One thing at a time," I said before taking a sip. "What do you know about Knots and Chains?"

"They are the only secret society on campus; they don't allow others. That's why there are no fraternities or sororities for the college students."

"So, no Greek societies?"

"Nope."

"Knots and Chains has been here since the school opened. I think it started as something for the legacy of the school's founders and their hand-picked successors. They have a reputation for being a political force, but also good for business and careers. If you're in Knots and Chains, doors open."

I wouldn't point out how weird that sounded, considering the name of it.

"Every year they tap a handful of students. No one knows the criteria, just that you have to be tapped by someone in Knots and Chains to be considered, then you have to unravel the knots and unlock the chains to get in."

I frowned. "Okay, that's weird."

He grinned, a real one flashing over his face as he laughed. I hadn't seen much of these smiles.

"What? You don't think it's weird?"

Instead of answering, he looked thoughtful as his smile faded. "I guess it is weird." He sobered. "It's also dangerous. I was tapped a couple of years ago... If you aren't a part of them, you aren't supposed to know about them."

"Clearly," I responded when he glanced at me. "The whole 'secret' part of the name. Is that how you know them? You're one of them?" But if he was tapped a couple of years before, why was he getting invitations now?

"No," he said with a shake of his head. "I was tapped. Didn't make it to initiation."

"Is it something you can tell me?"

"I'm not sworn to secrecy." The blunt answer made me grin. "They tapped me. I was pretty sure I had been. I knew what it was, and I solved a couple of the riddles, followed the clues, completed the tasks, but then... nothing. The messages stopped after the Bonfire of the Vanities party."

"What happened?"

"I don't know all of it. I think that was the night I was supposed to be formally in, but maybe I didn't do it right. I didn't really care. I just—didn't know."

"Well, they sound like they suck," I told him, savoring the coffee and the company, if I was being honest. The idea of a secret society was kind of fascinating, mainly since it didn't involve discussing all my issues. "I don't really have time for secret societies or any more strange things happening. Not with *everything* else."

"They are the ones who decide when to stop asking," he told me. "You have to be careful..."

"I haven't done all of them," I pointed out, "and I don't really feel like it now."

"If they send you another and you decide to do it—I'll go with you."

"You don't have to," I said. "You've been doing a lot already."

He didn't shrug it off though. "You shouldn't do it alone. Did Aubrey get tapped?"

I opened my mouth, but all at once I wasn't certain. "I don't know. I haven't mentioned my invites to her—wait... you said you have to be tapped by someone in it?"

A single nod was my answer.

"If RJ was there...does that make him one of them?" To be honest, other than a few abortive attempts, I hadn't really seen RJ. The last time was probably the day Ramsey asked me to not date him and stay away.

"Wallach isn't a good guy."

"Well, clearly you and your brothers agree on him." Which, I guessed, should tell me something. "Lachlan all but attacked him and threw him in the pond. Apparently, he likes tossing people in the water."

"Good," Jonas said, sitting forward. "Don't go clue hunting without me?"

"Since you asked so nicely," I said, then closed my eyes. I was exhausted.

"How much homework do you have?" Jonas asked.

"Not as much as I expected. I don't know what Ramsey said to the teachers, but they've all gone light, despite the idea that they never cut anyone breaks."

He didn't comment on that last part but reached for the tv remote instead. "Take a nap, then we can eat. I'll watch something and keep you company if you want."

Not waiting for me to say yes or no, he searched through the apps and pulled up an entirely different reality show. I hadn't seen this one before. He pressed play and then put his feet on the coffee table while he opened one of his books.

Curled up, I rested my head against the sofa cushion, aware of Jonas reading while the show lulled me. It was ridiculously sweet of him.

"Jonas?" I flicked a look over to find him watching me. "If I asked you to go to the Fire and Ice Party?"

"You already did," he said. "I said yes."

"Cool," I said, hiding a smile as I snuggled into the blanket. "Wake me up in an hour if I fall asleep?" I did have some homework to do.

Thirty-Seven

RAMSEY

KC and Jonas were both in the testing center. I'd finished two of my own tests and had moved to a research station when they came in. While she seemed—better wasn't the right word—steadier, she was still too pale.

I didn't like it. I didn't like how she moved gingerly, every step careful and deliberate. The natural grace and elemental energy that populated her steps absent, to be replaced by marked hesitation and uneasiness.

What I would have once labeled a brash, larger-than-life personality that served as the core of her fierce approach to life seemed to have been hollowed out following the attack. It concerned me almost as much as the fact she'd been assaulted in the first place.

Nothing that happened the previous year seemed to slow her down. The fire had been a blow, but she'd rallied. This? I hated this. I hated even more the rampant climb in Jonas' watchfulness. He wasn't sleeping. Not as much as he should be, and he'd become a fixture at her side.

I couldn't say I blamed him. Keeping my distance was killing me. There had been another report to the administration. This time, the complaint about harassment included both Lachlan and Jonas. This is on the heels of Lachlan being questioned by campus security *and* the local police.

The angle I had to seeing through the wide glass window of the testing room let me see her as she dipped her head to work on the test. Jonas was seated behind her next to the wall, but with one desk between them. The position was smart; he could see the whole room in front of them.

I could monitor anyone coming or going. Since Jonas needed to focus on his own tests, I told him I'd be here. The school hadn't said anything about *who* filed the complaint, but they had to investigate it.

A second offense for me. One more and I would automatically lose my TA status for the rest of the semester. I'd still be a student, but I would also have to surrender my RA post as well.

The threat had rung in my ears, but it wasn't preoccupying me. I pulled up a secure browser and put it in anonymous mode so it wouldn't track my searches or record them in the history.

Something the girls said the night KC came back from the hospital preyed on the back of my mind.

Stalker emails and notes.

Stalker.

Couple that little revelation with Aubrey Miller's assertion about the constant media attention and photo sales, and I couldn't put it aside. Any of it. The photos sold to the gossip sites about me kissing KC, about Lachlan, the others with her and Jonas.

Most of them had been taken on campus.

Administration had not been happy with the first viral video from the campus. They could only crack down so much. The more privileged the student, the less likely they were going to face real consequences. Stern advice, firm requests, and even some genuine pleading were policy.

Until it came down to one student's power and prestige versus another's. Then the lawyers came out. KC's family attorney, alongside one from the label, had begun to exert pressure. It was the primary reason I insisted that Lachlan call his father.

Gibs paid for our schooling, but it was Sean Nash who was the Blue Ivy Prep legacy. He had smoothed the way when Mom wanted to send us to private school. Making sure all of us could attend the same academy kept us together while she was on the road.

Pulling off my glasses, I pinched the bridge of my nose. The search window had populated with dozens of news stories about Torched. Over the top of the computer, I stared at where she focused on her test.

She twirled a pencil with her fingers like a drummer, caught in stop motion, getting ready to play. The faint blur around the edges softened everything about her and the soft gasp of sound she made when our lips collided echoed in my head.

Not helpful.

Turning my attention back to the screen, I started skimming each story. Headlines like *Problem Child or Party Girl?* I just scrolled right past.

Intruder Arrested on Crosse Estate, Beverly Hills

That headline leapt out.

Man Caught Boarding Tour Bus for Torched In Phoenix

Another one.

Kaitlin Crosse Getting Extra Security for Alleged Stalking

The article tones varied between snide condescension and

wild speculation. From unnamed sources to the even more vague: *rumor has it*, didn't illustrate what was going on effectively.

Jennifer Crosse Security Says Stalker Won't Leave Her Alone—Despite Restraining Order.

Alleged Crosse Stalker Caught Masturbating on Camera Violating Multiple Legal Orders

Crosse Stalker Arrested and Charged With One Count of Felony Stalking

These all seem related to her mother, but they were all sick —and not the same person. Son of a bitch. The more I read, the more disturbing the picture it painted.

After another check on KC and Jonas, I continued my deeper dive. I did searches on KC, the members of her band and pulled up online blogs, tweets—TikTok's and threads on discussion boards that ranged from the ridiculous to the terrifying to the obscene.

Threat Management Unit Investigates Alleged Stalking by Disturbed Woman

While the band wasn't mentioned by name, KC was. Multiple grainy photographs showed a woman appearing all over the Crosse property in Beverly Hills. There were more articles about increasing security in the area, police patrols, and...

I jerked upright at the next page of articles to come up as I followed links deeper and deeper.

Nude photos.

There were *nude* photos of KC—no, fuck, it was her mother.

Rubbing my eyes, I needed brain bleach to scrub the image away. While she wasn't actually nude, the string bikini she was wearing was just a suggestion of cloth over her breasts and there was nothing covering her ass.

Yes, her mom was a looker and had done plenty of nude

scenes in movies—but yeah, I had zero interest in looking at these...

I was about to click away when a comment caught my eye.

Think the mom is hot? Look at the daughter. Best tits and sweet little ass. Bet she is still a tight fit. What I wouldn't give to...

It pretty much degenerated into much worse in the comments. The depraved and at times fucking disturbing comments included threats against each other, and with even more against KC.

The fact there were even deleted comments removed for violating the site's terms for harassment spoke volumes for the shit they'd left up.

What was wrong with people?

Aubrey hadn't been kidding about the threats. There were no campus security alerts for it. But those might be kept quieter... then again, the fire set at the dorm was still being investigated as *arson*. Administration was trying to keep it quiet, but I'd been called in three times to answer questions.

Alleged Teenage Mom Baby Drama for Torched Singer

Hitting the link, I stared at the photo of KC snuggling a baby at a children's hospital just outside of Los Angeles. The photos were blurred, like they'd been taken through windows and distortion cut into the clarity.

I'd recognize the blue hair anywhere.

The article didn't go into any depth, just discussed the baby's age and speculation on date of birth... right around when Mom and Gibs got married.

I sat back in the seat abruptly. Lifting my head, I locked eyes with her. Surprise flickered across her expression as I stared at her. Was that why she hadn't come to the wedding? There was no such thing as truly private. They'd still been on tour then, maybe. The dates seemed to line up...

But there were a few days missed due to illness. Not always

attributed to KC, just illness. Some pregnancies didn't show—Mom barely did with Jonas. At least until the end…

Summoning a smile for her, I put a pin in that line of research. It was *one* little click bait article on a site that just didn't scream journalistic integrity. At the same time, I scrolled back to the photo.

Blurry and out of focus or not, there was no mistaking the affection on her face as she cradled that baby. The bottoming out of my stomach didn't help.

Was I fucking disappointed? Or… the reaction made no sense and when I stole a look back at her again, KC wasn't looking at me, but she did seem to be staring off into the distance. If I had to guess, she was in the zone. I'd seen her do it plenty of times when I was tutoring her.

The laser focus, the ability to immerse herself in the work, and more—the way she processed it. The combination of keen intelligence and creativity captivated me.

Kaitlin Crosse was nothing like I expected. Vulnerable and uncertain one moment, powerful and confident the next. The intense pendulum swing from maturity to playfulness to—such intense melancholy.

Every facet demanded I rethink every fact I'd ever accepted about her. From the day I heard she was coming to the school, I dreaded the inevitable conflict. The reminder that she didn't want us or Gibs in her life.

But that hadn't been present…

Well, it hadn't before the previous spring semester. Was that really on her?

No.

Fuck. Shutting it all down, I leaned back in the seat and drummed my fingers against the desk lightly. Was someone stalking her on campus? Was that what this was? Or was it all some kind of cosmic coincidence?

Prior to her attendance, Jonas, Lachlan, and I rarely if ever discussed her. Outside of wishing she'd forgive Gibs for his sake, for whatever reason she was cutting him out of her life.

When she was younger, it made sense. Her mother probably encouraged it. Mom thought less of Jennifer Crosse than she did her daughter. Mom, who'd been there for Gibs through everything. Where his family couldn't be bothered, Mom put him first.

Was he flawed?

Yes.

But he tried. He tried for Mom. For me. For Lachlan. For Jonas. He connected with Jonas on a level none of us could.

When the door to the testing room opened an hour later, letting KC and Jonas out, I pushed up from my seat. I still had way more questions than answers. I also hated how exhausted she seemed. It was like someone had drawn her skin too tight over her bones.

"Hey," I said as they turned to me. Jonas kept glancing at her, always seemingly aware of her every step. "All caught up?"

"Yeah," KC said, lifting her hair with careful motions as she slid her bag over her shoulder and then crossbody. Her stomach growled and the sound seemed to echo in the silence. "Mostly just tired."

"And hungry," Jonas supplied the last, and they both grinned at each other. The brief flashes of their smiles settled some of my disquiet.

"You know what," I said as I rose and put my notebook back into my messenger bag. "It's Saturday and I'm clear until tomorrow morning. Let me take you guys off campus to eat and just get away from all of this."

I needed it. Jonas needed it.

My younger brother cut a look at KC who stared at me with so much tiredness in her eyes, I wanted to just take them away for the weekend. Take her away—I shoved that thought right back into Pandora's box and locked it.

This wasn't about anything more than looking after my brother and my *stepsister*. Someone should be taking care of her.

"We can grab Aubrey, if you want," I continued, and KC shook her head.

"We can ask, but she has a date." That sounded promising. "What do you say?" She glanced at Jonas. "My gut was to just say no and go back to get some sleep, but…"

"Yeah," Jonas said with a slow nod. "It sounds good." Then he looked at me. "Think we can go to Jack's Escape?"

I snorted. I probably shouldn't. "We can—it's a drive."

"What's Jack's Escape?" KC asked. "And should we get coats?"

I motioned them to the door. "It's kind of an indoor theme park, laser tag, bowling, pool, video games, and more pizzeria. The food is crap, but the games are fun."

Jonas grinned for real. It was one of his favorite places, despite the chaos.

"It'll be fun," he said. "Long as none of the kids puke."

KC laughed, genuinely laughed, as we headed out of the testing building. Jonas fell in at her side and I walked on the other. It was still early enough in the day, but it had begun to snow again.

"Do you bowl?" I asked, more curious than anything else.

"Yep," she said. "We learned how to do that for a video. It's way more fun than I thought."

"What about pool?" Jonas said, and it was the most animated I'd seen him in a while.

There was a sly smile on her lips and I shook my head. "Yes, she knows how to do that, too. Okay, ten minutes, get into some comfortable, warm clothes, grab jackets, and meet back here. I'll sign you both out."

"Ramsey?" KC said as they turned to the stairs and I glanced at her.

"Yeah?"

"Are you inviting Lachlan?"

I hadn't planned on it. Still, I quirked my brows. "Want me to not?"

She lifted her shoulders. "Just—wanted to prepare if he was going too...you know what, just ignore me. I'll be back." She started up the stairs, but Jonas glanced at me with one hand on the banister.

"Go," I told him. "I'll deal with Lachlan."

How? I wasn't sure yet. But I'd figure it out.

Thirty-Eight

KC

A FEW DAYS LATER...

"It's not good news," Bronson warned, his tone gloomy.

"Don't think that way," I cautioned. It was snowing again. The campus really had taken on a magical winter wonderland appearance. The Fire and Ice Dance was around the corner, and I had a date. "You heard what Jackie said the same way I did."

"When did you become the reasonable one?" The grumble in his voice made me laugh. Nothing about the vandalism in my room or the assault had made it into the media. Even the ambulance visit barely registered a blip on the radar.

The school actually honored the NDA. It meant I could keep Jackie and Bronson from worrying about this. Davina knew, but she promised to keep it to herself. As had Dix, but he swore one more incident and he was moving to the campus and they could fucking try and remove him.

Where I would typically just argue against it, I had to admit the ferociousness in Dix's tone had been as fierce as Aubrey's defense. Even the guys had become my shadows. Jonas was always there. Lachlan and Ramsey were also always around. I couldn't seem to get more than a foot outside my room before I had one of them there.

The twins had taken to checking on me more frequently. The softer rumors going around campus had been tolerable, but everyone seemed to know *something* had happened even if they didn't know what.

Thankfully, it was just me and Aubrey making our way between buildings. I'd tucked a knit cap over my head to keep it warm. The constant company forced me to be more cautious about the calls with Bronson or Jackie about Pen.

"It had to happen some time," I teased him. "But Jackie said the doctors were never going to make us promises about everything. They have to look circumspect and doubtful. We just have to rely on the tests to give us answers."

"I hate this shit," he muttered, his voice dipping. "I hate that everything is wait and fucking see."

"Me too."

The silence stretched out between us as Aubrey and I just walked.

"Tell me something fun? Or good?" Like me, Bronson sometimes just needed something to hold onto. A positive thought or moment. Something that said we were going to be okay. "You guys hitting the studio after you graduate?"

I cut a look at Aubrey. What we were doing after graduation was still up in the air. I'd been writing again, but after the wreck of my room? Yeah, I hadn't really managed the music as much. Jonas had been trying to help. He really had.

Unfortunately, each time the urge to write hit, the absence of my guitar sucked my muse dry. I had written damn near every song with it. Every. Single. One.

It was like someone had cut off my hand.

"We're debating it," Aubrey said when my tongue wouldn't unglue it from the roof of my mouth. "Though I think a vacation is in order. Yvette and I want to kidnap Kait and run away for a month or two. Maybe we can disappear into the mountains or to a beach and write a new album."

That sounded heavenly. I threw her a grateful smile and she winked at me while hooking her arm through mine.

"That sounds fun. Don't disappear too far away though." It was his turn to caution me and I grinned.

"Don't worry," I said, still smiling. "You'll never lose me. I'm like a bad penny..." The next few words clogged in my throat as we rounded the corner, nearly colliding with Ramsey. "I always turn up."

Bronson chuckled even if my smile faded. "Good. Talk soon?"

"Promise," I murmured, we ended the call and Ramsey glanced from me to Aubrey then back.

"Can we help you?" Aubrey asked when he still said nothing. No amount of warmth could chip the ice in her cool tone.

"Just coming to check on you," Ramsey said, searching my expression with his blue-eyed gaze. He'd been doing that more and more. I'd catch him staring at me, a lot like Jonas used to, with the most enigmatic expressions. "You girls were late making it back."

Aubrey's eyebrows raised. "Protective I get, but you might not want to tell us you're tracking how long it takes us to get from point A to point B."

"We took the long way," I said, before tucking my phone back into my bag. "Something up?"

Please say nothing is up. While I'd been stumbling around trying to get my equilibrium back, I'd gotten a little too used to him—well, to all of them really—being around. If that didn't set off alarm bells, I didn't know what did.

"No," he said, almost gently, and hot on the heels of the worried convo with Bronson, relief spilled through me. "Nothing like that. I just wanted to make sure you—both— got back all right."

The hesitation wasn't lost on me. "Thanks."

"Are you both still going to the dance?" I really couldn't read his tone on that one. I kept forgetting about the dance, but Jonas and I were going together if we went. I still needed to put together an outfit for it.

"Tomorrow," I said. "Maybe—depends on how I feel." How Jonas felt too. To be honest.

"Let me know if you need anything," he said, stepping aside so Aubrey and I could continue.

"We got it covered," Aubrey informed him, that chilly tone dipping to another layer of frigid. I shot her a curious look but kept my questions to myself until we were at the room. Jonas wasn't in the suite and Aubrey hesitated...

"You have a date," I reminded her. "And I have some writing to do..." Jonas had set sheet music on my door that morning and it was the first time he'd given me any since everything went down.

While I might not succeed, I really wanted to try.

"I can cancel," she said, leaning against the doorframe.

"You can, but I don't want you to." I set my backpack down. "Really, you and Forrest haven't seemed—"

"In sync?" Aubrey shrugged. "I don't know. He's focused on what he needs to do and so am I. I like him, but I'm not changing my life for him."

"Is he asking you to?"

"No," she admitted, then frowned. "He's not asking for anything, really. It's just..." She shook her head as one of our neighbors passed. Melanie? Melody? Mindy—her name was Mindy. She lifted her chin, but she didn't say anything. She also had on a headset and was dressed to workout. As soon as she disappeared, Aubrey shrugged. "I don't know. We're eighteen. He's great. But he has plans and so do I, and you know… he might end up just being that guy I dated for a year."

"Then go date him," I said. "Go have fun with him and don't worry about me." At her bland look, I raised my hands. "I'm locking myself in. Then I'm gonna play with some music and see what I can get done. I promise to make sure someone is with me if I leave."

"That doesn't make me feel better," she said. "You know that, right? This year has been brutal for you and I hate it."

"I know." It had been brutal for all of us. Yvette was on the warpath. "I'm sorry…"

"Pfft, you have nothing to be sorry about. I just—I feel like each time I look away, you might not be there when I look back." Emotion clouded her expression and she gripped my hand. I squeezed hers back. "That's unacceptable. You know that, right?"

I crossed my heart, then hugged her. "I'm not going anywhere without kicking and screaming."

Her groan-filled laugh dragged over me. "That doesn't help."

"Yes, it does," I teased as I leaned back. "Now, go have fun with Forrest. We've had enough gloom this week. I'd love to hear some good stuff."

Studying me, Aubrey squeezed my arms. "Promise not to go off alone? Not even to run in the snow and the quiet to get your head together?"

Yeah, she knew me. "I promise. If I need to run, I'll go to the gym and I'll see if Jonas wants KC-watch."

"The answer to the last is yes," she said with a smirk.

"Go away now," I said before she started and she chuckled, even if she looked pointedly at my door. Withdrawing, I closed it and waited until I heard her door close on the other side before I leaned back against the door and sighed.

I hated being separated from her, and at the same time, she was right there. A note from Jonas was pinned to my door.

Have to meet with my adviser. Couldn't change appt. Be back by dinner. Text if you have to go somewhere.

Below it, he'd written his number.

All this time and we'd never exchanged phone numbers. Then again, we didn't have the most conventional of relationships, even for a friendship. I put his number in my phone, then fired off a message.

ME

It's KC. Got your note. Making sure you have my number too.

He answered with a thumbs up on the message, but nothing else. Then again, he was meeting with his adviser. I carried his note into my bare-bones room. The idea of decorating it for anyone else to trash or burn just didn't sit well with me.

The note also reminded me of the fact he'd left me a note that first day of school and I had no memory of it, at all. Did I not just see it? I didn't remember throwing a message away from him. Maybe I did? The only one I remembered possibly tossing was the note from Sydney, cause she said she'd…

Oh shit, had there been two notes? It was like the memory of it was right there, just vague and uncertain. Kind of like the rest of me. Guilt raked through me. Jonas seemed to believe me, but it made me wonder. Was it as simple as a miscommunication that kicked off all the shit?

Or was it more?

Did I care to keep digging at the old wound or should I just let it close?

By the time I'd changed and made coffee, I still hadn't come to a decision. I set up in the living room, periodically checking my phone for messages. Aubrey sent one with a picture of herself dressed for her date. She looked awesome.

Said they were going off campus to eat and then to a movie. I wished her luck. She deserved every good thing that could happen to her, I just wished that the thing with Forrest wasn't a source of anxiety for her.

The lack of guitar hit me again as I sat down and then I glanced at the space beneath our coffee table. Jonas had pulled out an electronic keyboard and set it in the living room for me. I didn't even know he had it, but he said he played with head-phones on most of the time.

Setting it on my lap, I played through Jonas' song a few times, just getting a feel for the music. It was halting and jerky. I liked piano. I could play keyboards. I could play a lot of instruments, but the guitar—

Frustrated as tears burned in my eyes, I put the keyboard aside and scrubbed at my face. I hated that it was gone. What if I never got it back?

A knock at the door jerked my head up and I frowned at it. Rising, I glanced at the bat Jonas had hung on the wall near the door. Moving closer, I kept my hand off the doorknob before I said, "Who is it?"

"Hey, Blue," RJ called in a loud whisper like he wanted me to hear but was also keeping his voice down. "I'm here to pick you up."

"For what?" I checked my phone. There were no messages from RJ on it. We hadn't spoken in weeks. Hell, I hadn't even seen him,

"You know what for, you finished the last puzzle."

The last puzzle—so he was part of Knots and Chains. "I can't." Jonas wasn't here and we were doing it together.

"Come on, Blue," he said, his tone coaxing and warm. "You finished all the plays, but there's one step left..."

"Look," I said, straightening. "RJ, I'm not—"

"It's okay, Ace," Lachlan's voice shocked me. "You can open the door."

Yanking it open, I stared from Lachlan to RJ. "What the hell are you two doing together?" Had I actually entered the *Twilight Zone*?

The corner of Lachlan's mouth curved upward and the shadows inhabiting his haunted eyes eased. "C'mon, Ace, you know you wanna know. It'll be fun."

I did want to know but...

There was something about the way he looked at me. He *wanted* me to trust him for some reason. I cut a look at RJ who wore a cocky smirk. It was like they'd body swapped or something.

And that thought just creeped me out.

"Give me a sec," I said, shutting the door. Opening the message to Jonas I told him RJ and Lachlan were here for "it." Should I go or not?

He didn't answer.

Fuck—did I go? Or did I wait?

Blowing out a breath, I waited an agonizing five minutes for an answer, any answer.

"Ace," Lachlan said. "We need to go now."

Dammit. I stared at the phone with no response from Jonas and not even a note that said he'd read it yet. Babysitting me wasn't his job. Lachlan was here.

Jerking the door open, I found the pair of them glaring at each other, but all at once their expressions changed as they focused on me.

"What do I need to wear?"

Thirty-Nine

LACHLAN

When Jonas texted to say Ace would be on her own, and he was stuck, I'd read the message three times before I sent a response.

ME

And you want me to go look after her?

JONAS

Do I need to text Ramsey?

Oh, hell no. I had this.

ME

Just checking.

Avoiding Ace was not my favorite activity, but nearly six hours of police interrogation, the arrival of the attorney Dad hired, and Dad's cautions on the phone... yeah, I'd taken a step back. Maybe I could see what was going on better from a distance.

Ramsey was fucking infuriated that we'd *all* been reported, even Jonas, for harassing a female student. The alleged harassment involved the suggestion of sexual battery, but the student in question had not gone that far.

They also wouldn't tell us who it was. The school intended to protect the so-called victim from any kind of retaliation. Yes, Ace had definitely called my ass out while she'd been foggy, unfocused, and concussed. Called me out and thrown me under the bus.

I still had the tire tracks to prove it.

The problem was—

I hit the top step of their floor, turned the corner and then just *paused*. Who was standing in front of the suite door but RJ fucking Wallach.

Dressed in slacks, a button-down, and a jacket, he looked like he was picking her up for a date. A heady amount of violence thrummed through my system as I strolled down the hall to where he'd begun to knock on the door.

Amusingly, RJ seemed less than situationally aware but then movement at the door across the hall had me shifting my gaze. The door definitely moved, closing almost softly. What the fuck was Payton up to now? That had me flicking my gaze back to RJ just as Ace's voice floated through the door.

"Who is it?"

The corner of my mouth kicked up. Good girl. Don't just open the door.

"Hey, Blue," RJ said in a mock whisper. What an ass. Blue? How fucking original was that stupid goddamn nickname? I'd like to cram the whole syllable down his throat until he choked on it. "I'm here to pick you up."

"For what?" Skepticism rifled the words and I had to bite back another smile. Even more because RJ *hadn't* noticed me yet. I owed McCallum a case of booze. The initiations were coming sooner than the Fire and Ice Dance.

"You know what for, you finished the last puzzle." The smug amusement scraped over my nerves.

"I can't." Good girl. Don't accept fuck-all from this asshat.

"Come on, Blue," he said, his sugary tone vomitous. "You finished all the plays, but there's one step left..."

"Look." Anger populated that single word. Yeah, she was never coming out of there, and I fucking approved. "RJ, I'm not—"

Unfortunately, I needed her to say yes now, but I wouldn't let her take a single step without me there.

"It's okay, Ace." RJ whipped around like I'd stabbed him. Sadly, I hadn't. "You can open the door." Yet.

The speed at which she opened the door massaged some of the raw spots left by the interrogations. "What the hell are you two doing together?"

There was my girl. "C'mon, Ace, you know you wanna know. It'll be fun." Didn't she look adorable all dressed to stay in...

Locking my gaze on hers, I urged her to trust me. I had her back. C'mon, Ace. Do it.

"Give me a sec," she said, shutting the door.

"What the fuck are you doing here?" RJ demanded in a low voice that wouldn't carry, and I smirked at him.

"If they didn't tell you then, I don't see the need to enlighten you."

RJ's expression darkened as he glared at me. Yes, the rules were the rules. Didn't mean anyone had told me to be here, but the beauty of it was, he couldn't ask to verify. So, suck it up jackass.

This has been a long fucking time coming. Hands in my pockets, I fisted them to keep them there and not beating him black and blue.

He didn't answer.

"Ace," I said, holding RJ's eye contact until he looked away. "We need to go now."

When the door opened once more, I met her gaze and smiled slowly.

"What do I need to wear?"

Good girl.

Fifteen minutes later, I strolled with Ace and RJ toward McMillan building. A/V classes, equipment, and sound-proofed studios were there. Aware of her attention swinging back to me in repeated suspicion, I caught her eye and winked.

"What are we doing?" she leaned in close to me, her voice a soft whisper. Lifting an arm, I settled it over her shoulders and tucked her closer. It was just starting to get dark. The clouds overhead, the rapidly declining light, and the blanket of snow over the campus gave it a kind of ethereal feel.

"Trusting me," I told her and tried not to take her wrinkled nose and skeptical frown to heart. I'd told her from the beginning to stay away from this piece of shit. It might have taken her a while to listen, but tonight she'd understand why.

Everyone would.

I was done playing games with RJ and his family. The school covered shit up once. Good luck with shutting this down.

RJ kept shooting me looks. His discomfort satisfied a very primitive part of me. But he didn't understand just how bad this was going to be for him. I *let* him unlock the building and hold open the door.

I kept myself firmly between him and Ace. Once we were inside, I also paused to let him take the lead. His huff before he stomped ahead added another cherry to the justice sundae I was about to serve this motherfucker.

When he paused ahead of us, Ace slowed and I stopped with her. Then he held up a blindfold.

I snorted.

"She won't need that."

"Rules," RJ reminded me, smirking.

"I don't care about the rules," Ace said, beautifully defiant. "I'm not putting that on."

"Then we can call it a night right here."

Oh, this was the hill you want to die on, asshole? I stared at him. *Really?*

"Works for me," I said, giving Ace a squeeze. "I'd rather spend time with Ace without you, anyway."

A scowl wiped away his self-satisfied bitch expression and he glanced at Ace. "C'mon, Blue. You can do this. We'll both be there. Nothing will happen you don't want anyway..."

She stiffened under my arm. I expected her to pull away, so I tucked her closer then pressed my nose to her hair like I was taking a deep breath.

Her sharp little elbow dug into my side, and I met the heated look in her eyes. I couldn't help dipping my gaze to her lips. This close with the sweet scent of her filling my nostrils, all I wanted was to kiss her until the rest of the world faded away.

Unfortunately... "Tick tock, Blue."

"She has a name," I growled. The damn near triumphant look in RJ's eyes should have warned me.

"Do you prefer Ace then, Blue?"

I was going to kill him.

"Oh my god, if you two wanna go make out with your fists, you can do it without me." She yanked herself free of me and I glared as she snatched the blindfold out of RJ's hand. "I'll put this on, and you have exactly sixty seconds to get a move on or I will leave, clear?"

She was going to do it? It took every ounce of effort to wipe away my shock when she pivoted to face me. The dare in her eyes sparked a very real passion I'd been keeping a leash on.

I wanted to do more than kiss her... "Atta girl, Ace," I said instead. "Such a good girl for me."

The fact she rolled her eyes did nothing to diminish my pleasure at her cooperation. She pulled the blindfold over her eyes, and I stepped right up to her and took over tying it before RJ put a finger on her.

Frankly, at this point, if he even looked like he was going to touch her, I'd have to kill him.

I met his gaze over her head as I smoothed down her hair. Then dipped my head a little lower to press a soft kiss to her lips. She didn't gasp, but there was no mistaking the swift inhale of breath as I nuzzled her lips. The scrape of her teeth was a warning, even as she put her hands to my chest. I caught them then tugged her closer.

"Don't worry, Ace," I murmured. "I have you."

RJ's scowl darkened, but I just smiled as I tucked her securely under my arm again, then raised my brows. Go ahead motherfucker, say something.

I dare you.

Instead of issuing a verbal complaint, he pivoted on his heel and stalked off ahead of us.

"Stay close to me," I told Ace as I set off to follow him. She hooked her fingers through one of the loops on my jeans. The contact sent a ridiculous surge of lust right through me. Ahead, RJ paused to glare and I nuzzled a kiss to her ear.

With her eyes hidden, he didn't bother to disguise his jealousy.

Good. Suck. It. Up. Ace was mine and I wasn't fucking sharing with anyone, least of all his abusive ass.

"No matter what happens," I said against the shell of her ear, not bothering to resist the temptation to trace the whorls with my tongue. She gave the most delicious little shudder. "Stay with me."

"You already said that," she complained in a breathless tone.

"Hmm, I did, didn't I?" I pressed a kiss to her lips once more before I straightened. Time to get this going. She clung to me as I followed RJ down the dimly lit hall to one of the a/v recording studios.

Soundproofed.

Just like last time.

Once inside, no one could hear us.

The interior had been set up for some video project or other. The presence of a bed, roses, and candles were probably just staging. Once RJ secured the door, he turned to face us.

Now...I just had to wait. I had one arm around her and my free hand in my pocket. The remote was right there. I had to resist the urge to stroke the buttons.

"Blue," RJ said. "You have solved all the puzzles and riddles. Proven that you are clever and witty. You have freed the knots, but to unlock the last chain, I—" He paused a beat. "We have one more riddle for you."

"Yippee." Ace was so droll I had to grin. "You're also out of time."

Not that she'd tried to pull the mask off. Yet.

RJ took another step toward her. "What disappears when you say its name?"

"For real?" she asked and shifted under my arm. Whether she meant to press closer to me or not, I wasn't sure, but I just hooked my arm around her tighter to pull her back to my chest.

"You learn everything after this," I promised her. "Just one more question."

Her absolute huff of impatience was downright adorable. "Silence."

RJ blinked, shock stamping across his face. What, did he

think that particular riddle was hard? Probably a good thing the dick had money, 'cause he definitely didn't have brains.

"Congratulations," I told her. "Welcome to Knots and Chains."

"That's not how this works," RJ argued. "There's still initiation..."

"Oh, right." Clicking my tongue against my teeth, I shook my head. "Almost forgot." With that, I tugged the tie on her blindfold free as I pressed the remote.

Sound blasted from all sides.

"I have to do this?" Kelly asked from the recording, but I didn't take my gaze off RJ as his whole body stiffened. His gaze jerked off Ace to the screens on the wall.

It had taken me time, but I'd found the recordings. The cocky mother fucker thought he'd erased them. The problem was—nothing was truly gone once it hit the internet.

"Yes," RJ said in a coaxing tone. "It's the rules. Every initiation is different. When I did it...I had to keep it up for hours and please four different women."

"Oh," Kelly sounded so crestfallen and it took everything I had to *not* look at the screen right now. Just the sound of her voice was enough to put me on edge all over again.

"It's going to be fine," RJ continued, soothing. "You'll love it. Trust me. All you have to do is take every one of us... the blindfold will be on so you can just pretend it's me if you want."

"Every one...?" Her voice trembled. "How many?"

"Does it matter?" RJ asked. "You know I can make it so good for you baby, trust me."

My fingers dug into my palms as I played it out.

"Turn it off," RJ ordered. Because the video skipped ahead and there was slurping and sobs. The slurping turned to choking and then the sobs grew more pronounced.

"It hurts..." Kelly pleaded.

"It's okay, baby," RJ said on the recording. "You're such a good little whore for me. Fuck, look at that hungry cunt—four cocks have filled you up and you want more don't you..."

"I—" The word choked off as another cock was shoved down her throat. Then it was just skin slapping, wet sounds as guy after guy fucked her. It lasted an eternity.

Ace shook against me, but I kept her right there. RJ had this coming. He and his recruited band of fuckboys had fucked Kelly until she couldn't stand.

When it was over, they'd left her covered in cum and walked away.

The videos hit the school the next day—all edited, of course, to just show her and cock, nothing else.

This video was different, however.

"Turn it off," RJ yelled as he charged at me. I pushed Ace behind me and caught his fist. My fist was already colliding with his face as he went down.

"Can't take what you did?" I said to him. "Or did you forget how you left her? What you did? How you sent it out? You told her she had to do it —"

"She could have said fucking no," RJ yelled back at me. "If you knew how to fuck a girl, maybe she would have. But I made sure she got off." As if to prove his point, there was another scream, only this wasn't one of passion, it was anguish. "Your brother would have too if he'd fucking showed up on time."

It was that sound that had killed me when I'd found her.

I hit him again. And again. And again.

When he was on the ground, bloody mouth and nose, staring up at me. "She killed herself, you son of a bitch. She killed herself because of what *you* did. Then you covered it up with your family's money, just like you do everything. Now you want to add Ace to your little list of conquests?"

I snorted.

I'd kill him first.

Killing would have been too easy, though.

Killing wouldn't hurt as much as this.

He let out a yell, blood spraying from his mouth as he charged me. A minute later, the door slammed open, and the cops were there.

It was glorious. They took him down like the perp he was, rather than a wealthy little fuckboy. He was shrieking at me as the cops put him in handcuffs.

RJ wasn't getting out of this one. I was still grinning when I faced Ace. She was safe.

Then her hand collided with my face so hard, I tasted blood in my mouth. The slap rang my bell, literally, and I blinked as I stared at her again.

"Ace—"

"Fuck you, Lachlan." She glared at me, her eyes almost incandescent. "Fuck you right to hell and back."

Then she was gone.

KC

The sound of that girl sobbing was like a ghost in my ear. The minute it started, all I'd wanted to do was look away. But I couldn't. RJ's reaction had been so intense, but it had been the rigid stance of Lachlan's body wrapped around mine that kept me in place.

"She killed herself, you son of a bitch. She killed herself because of what you did. Then you covered it up with your family's money just like you do everything. Now you want to add Ace to your little list of conquests?"

She killed herself.

Those words played on an endless loop long after the cops finished, following a brief questioning. They had way more questions for Lachlan. Questions I kind of wanted answered too. After the police walked RJ out to a black and white car in handcuffs, dozens of students were out there with their phones in hand.

For once, the viral video from campus wouldn't be me. Or at least, it wouldn't only be me. The administration showed up, along with their attorneys. It was a scandal. The rumor mill lit up so fast there was no mistaking the speed because I had a message from Aubrey before I even made it back to the dorm room.

AUBREY

WTAF?

YVETTE

What happened?

Jonas was on the path of leaving the dorm when I got there. He swept his gaze over me from head to toe. Ramsey was a half-step behind him, looking considerably angrier.

"I'm fine," I told them. "I just need to go upstairs, and I need a shower and..."

To forget. That poor girl.

I didn't think I'd ever forget it.

"Go," Ramsey told me, his gaze moving behind me. "There will be press on campus soon. Stay out of sight. I'll make sure they fuck off."

I really didn't care about the press right now. While I hadn't been that cold when I went out, I was freezing now. Awareness of Jonas following me up the stairs helped chase some of the unsettling feelings away.

Payton was standing in the hallway when I got up there. Her smirk held so much venom I wanted to punch her.

"Don't look so happy," I told her as I got to the door of the suite Jonas and I were sharing.

"I guess being a whore is something you're used to," Payton countered.

"You're projecting," I said, pushing the door in. "And I wasn't the one who got arrested."

Her whole expression shifted. "What?" Except Jonas stopped her from coming any closer.

"Go away," he told her. "Now."

"Don't talk to me like that." She darted a look at me. "Who got arrested?"

I didn't answer, just went straight to my room. Jonas' soft knock on my open door pulled me around as I toed off my shoes. "I need to shower," I told him. "And I need to think."

He nodded. "I'll be out here."

Before he turned away completely, I blew out a breath. "Jonas?"

He looked at me again.

"Thank you."

One nod. "Do you want food?"

"No," I said. Even if I should eat, I was pretty sure I'd puke. If it weren't late, with cops everywhere, I'd just put on my running clothes and run until all the thoughts melted away.

I might still do it.

It wasn't until I'd chased away the chills and let the tears streak down my face in the safety of the shower that I answered the girls.

ME

I'm fine.

Filling them in took a little longer, and I stood in the hot and steamy bathroom while I told them everything.

AUBREY

Forrest and I are coming back to campus now.

YVETTE

Holy shit.

AUBREY

Forrest said he'd heard rumors but no one had proof.

He HEARD rumors???????? WTAF??? Why didn't he tell us when that asshole was trying to date K?

The fact I could practically hear Yvette's shrieking fury pulled a smile from me.

I'm okay. Jonas is here. I'm safe in the room. Just gonna try to sleep. Tomorrow is the dance.

They didn't answer immediately, but I could imagine their faces. For once, I was glad they weren't here to see how my hand was shaking.

Before you ask. I want to go. This—I need this shit out of my head.

I didn't think there was enough brain bleach on the planet for it. Honestly, I'd rather have seen more dick pics from Johnny or something than this.

She killed herself.

It wasn't just the words, but the agony in Lachlan's voice when he said it.

I promised to check in with them, and Aubrey said she'd text as soon as she was back on campus. When I made it back out to the sitting room, Jonas had coffee waiting, and pizza, and there was *Love is Blind* cued up on the television.

Bewildered and more than a little touched, I blinked at him.

"You don't have to tell me," he said.

"But you heard." It wasn't a question. At his nod, I said, "I hit Lachlan."

"Good."

At that a flicker of a smile chased across my lips. "About tomorrow…"

"You don't have to go." He waited for me to curl up into my spot on the sofa to pass me the blanket. He'd already cleaned up the work I'd had spread out earlier and it was stacked neatly.

"I want to go," I said and he straightened, surprise on his face. "If you still want to go with me."

He frowned. Then glanced at the screen before he looked at me again. "I want to go with you."

"Then we go." Wrapping my hands around the hot coffee, I took a sip and let out a ragged sigh. It was so damn good. "I even got a dress."

I'd had Davina send me one from my closet there, but it would be perfect. It had come a couple of days earlier. I just hadn't really thought about it.

"KC?" Jonas perched on the sofa. "Are you okay?"

"Nope," I said with a slow shake of my head. My hands were still shaking and even white knuckling the cup wasn't helping. "But…I will be."

He frowned, but then offered me the remote. I turned on the show and tried to drown out all the noise in my head. The whole situation was so fucked up.

So. Fucked. Up.

Stepbrothers. Stalkers. Serial rapists. Because I hadn't missed the bed in the room that RJ had taken us to, or the blindfold, or the indication that what had happened to Kelly was something he wanted to do to me.

No, I hadn't missed any of that. And as much as my palm still stung from slapping the shit out of Lachlan, I couldn't imagine how he sat on that tape right up until that point.

Why hadn't he turned him in sooner?

I shuddered, then dragged my attention to the screen. Jonas sat with me all evening, but bless him for not pressing any questions. He even hopped up to let Aubrey in. Forrest was with her, but he didn't come inside. Instead, Aubrey just crawled onto the sofa with me and curled up under my blanket.

Then it was the three of us watching the show. We were almost out of episodes, but it definitely helped. I even managed a slice of pizza before Aubrey and I went to bed. When she insisted on staying, I didn't argue. We even talked to Yvette for a little while before sleep swallowed me whole.

The next morning, I started working on a plan. After graduation, the girls and I were going to write another album if they were both still in. If they wanted to keep up with the break, maybe I'd work on a solo album. The last couple of years had already been hard, and I didn't know what they wanted to do yet, but we'd figure it out.

Normal life?

Yeah, I think I'd rather go back to knowing where all the knives were and that trusting people was a mistake. At least there, I knew what to expect.

"I forgot you even *had* this dress," Aubrey said, with a wild note of admiration. I glanced at her over my shoulder. She'd just finished zipping it up for me and I glanced down again. Ice blue, the dress went with my hair really well. The one-shoulder style with side ruching was actually one of my favorite dresses.

When we'd been nominated for a Grammy, I wore it to the ceremony. The hammered satin was fully lined and fit like a glove. It would leave my arms bare and on display, but school party or not, I didn't give a crap.

The dress felt good to wear and looked good, too. Pivoting, I faced Aubrey, who grinned. "Definitely the hottest ice ever."

"Let it go," I deadpanned. Her whole expression transformed as her eyes widened and a laugh exploded out of her.

"You did not."

I spread my arms. "Sure, I did. Besides...I'm feeling very empowered."

"You look empowered." Her soft laughter gave way to a teasing smile. "But for real, you look amazing."

She'd helped me with my hair, fashioning it into an updo that hid the missing chunks.

A pair of silver drop earrings and a bracelet were my only accessories along with a pair of pale white ankle boots.

"So do you!" She was done up in a red dress that looked smashing with her darker coloring, not to mention she had a ruby red lipstick I didn't have a hope in hell of carrying off. "Forrest coming too?"

"Yes," she said as she slid her heels back on. "We're sticking with you and Jonas tonight." Before I could protest, she ducked into the bathroom to check her cosmetics. "And don't argue with me. I swear, every single time I take my eyes off you, something goes fucking screwy."

"I wasn't going to argue," I said and her skeptical look made me laugh. "I wasn't, I'm just glad Forrest will be there so I can interrogate him, too." With a wink, I pivoted to head for the sitting room with Aubrey hurrying after me. "Don't you dare..."

Jonas and Forrest were waiting for us in the sitting room, both in suits, and I did a double-take at Jonas. He was in an actual suit. It was white on white and looked...amazing. There was even an ice-blue tie that he fidgeted with.

The guys hadn't been talking. If anything, it looked like they'd just been waiting in silence. Forrest whistled as Aubrey sauntered over to him after shooting me a *look,* and I bit back a smile that turned into a full blown grin when Jonas held out a single blue rose.

"Thank you."

"You're welcome," he said. "You don't have to take it with you but—I thought you should have one tonight."

I pressed the soft velvet of the blue rose to my nose and took a breath. The perfume was light and sweet. "I'll put it in water." It was so perfect as it was, I didn't want anything to happen to it. When I caught Aubrey's eye she gave me an indulgent smile and I crossed my eyes at her which in turn made her stick out her tongue.

The guys both chuckled and I hummed my way over to put the rose in a glass with some water. It looked perfect next to the coffee maker. I checked the trembling in my fingers as I turned back to find Jonas waiting for me.

"Is it okay if I tell you I like the dress?" The question pulled another smile from me.

"Yes," I told him. "Wolf whistles are also acceptable."

He nodded.

"I really like your suit, too. You clean up nice, Dekkar." If I hadn't been watching him, I might have missed the hint of red that touched his ears as he raked a hand through his hair. As sweet as that was, I gave him some privacy to glance at Aubrey and Forrest.

"Right," Forrest said. "Let's get you ladies to the party."

He opened the door, revealing Lachlan standing there with his hand raised to knock—the Douchebag King himself. I braced myself for whatever bullshit he was about to say when he gaped at me. Then Aubrey cut off his line of sight and slammed her knee right into his crotch.

I wasn't the only one who winced, because he was in no way braced for it and he went down gasping for air. Stepping over him, she glanced back. "Now it's a party."

Forty-One

JONAS

Words had never been my strong suit. They failed utterly when KC exited her bedroom wearing the ice blue dress. I didn't know anything about clothes, but it looked amazing on her, or maybe she just looked amazing in it. Her arms were on display and I'd gotten a good look at a few of her tattoos over time.

So many hidden stories in there. Stories I hadn't gotten to ask her about her. Were any of them for the baby? Or for the guy? Each time I thought about it, I swallowed the questions again. Her reaction to the rose chased away any concerns about going to the dance.

I didn't usually go to these things. I didn't like them. Too many people and too much noise. However, KC wanted to go and I wanted her to smile. She'd been—off lately. Sadder somehow.

Losing her guitar. The attack. The destruction of her things. I understood.

But Lachlan taking her to the confrontation with RJ? There had been no mistaking how upset she was the night before. I hadn't seen my brother since she came back, and I hadn't wanted to leave her.

Then Aubrey dropped Lachlan with a very well-placed knee that would have made me wince if he didn't deserve it. She stepped right over his prone form and I followed, offering KC a hand to help her.

"Damn," Forrest said as he followed us and amusement speared me. Was this his first taste of how fierce these two were? It made me curious about Yvette.

Downstairs, I helped KC into her jacket. Ramsey was out of his suite signing out students heading for the dance. His gaze lingered on KC, the worry in his eyes familiar to me.

"Staying on campus?"

"Yes," Forrest answered for all of us. "The plan is to be back before curfew."

"It's extended tonight," Ramsey told us, flicking a look at KC. "Don't cross campus alone. Try to move in groups. They've also set up a path to get around the heavier snow."

The Fire and Ice Dance was taking place in the old Blue Ivy Manor. The house that served as home to the original headmaster had been donated by the family who'd owned the estate. Now it was just kept for historical significance, fundraising events, and things like this dance.

"Jonas?" Ramsey said as we turned to go. I glanced at KC and she gave me a little smile.

"I'll wait." She squeezed my arm before she followed Forrest and Aubrey outside, leaving me in the foyer of the dorm building with my brother.

"She's waiting in the cold," I reminded him.

"Just wanted to see how she was doing?"

"She looks great." If he wanted to know anything else, he

could ask her. I wasn't going to be a spy for either of my brothers. Oh, that reminded me... "Lachlan came up. Aubrey dropped him on his ass. If he doesn't come down, you might want to scrape him off the floor."

Head back, Ramsey sighed. "Right. Go, have fun. Check in when you get back."

"Sure."

Aubrey and KC were laughing as I came out, and Forrest almost looked grateful to see me. The cold air frosted against my cheeks. I didn't bother with a coat, we didn't have that far to go and the suit was pretty warm.

When I offered KC my arm, she threaded her arm through mine. Forrest and Aubrey took lead and we followed them. It was an interesting contrast, Aubrey was fire and KC the ice.

"Everything okay?" KC asked as we walked. There were other students heading for the dance just like we were, but we were strung out and moving in our own groups.

"Ramsey just worries," I muttered. "Brothers suck."

Her laughter made me smile despite my irritation with Ramsey and Lachlan both. "Brothers aren't that bad." Then she tilted her head thoughtfully. "Well, maybe some are."

It was the second time she brought up siblings. "I didn't know you had any brothers."

The corner of her mouth quirked upward. "I didn't know I had three stepbrothers."

It was my turn to laugh even as my neck heated. "I know that now."

"Me too." She grinned and her eyes flashed.

"Feels weird," I admitted.

"Agreed." Then she waited until we passed through one of the buildings before resuming the thread. "I actually like having a friend more."

"Than a brother?" Curiosity shuttled through me.

"Maybe."

The smile took any kind of insult out of it and just increased my desire to know more. "What about a stepbrother?"

"Seems hit or miss to me, so I'll definitely go with friend there."

I could live with that. The manor was lit up when we got there. The ice theme outside took advantage of the snow. They'd added ice sculptures of horses, birds, and even one of a prince and a princess.

KC burst out laughing when we got there, then she and Aubrey insisted on posing with each sculpture. I was happy to take the pictures of her, but she insisted we join. By the time we made it inside, she was shivering a little. I checked her coat, then pulled her deeper into the building away from the entrance.

Fire wasn't hard to find in here. Between the red cast lights, the throbbing beat of music, and the faux "fires" set everywhere, it was like dancing in an outer circle of hell. Not that I knew much about the dancing, but KC didn't hesitate to pull me out there.

The throbbing beat of the music was familiar. KC moved so fluidly, I wasn't sure I could keep up. Then she caught my hands, and where she guided, I went. The next couple of hours flew by with us pausing to get drinks, or once when the girls needed to go to the bathroom.

I followed them as far as the door and waited for them just outside. Forrest had drinks for us when we got back. Leaning against me, KC sipped her water and watched the dancers with her eyes half closed. When the music shifted to a slower, sweeter note, Forrest and Aubrey drifted back out to dance.

"You want to go back out there?" I offered, but KC tilted her head back and shook her head.

"Tireder than I thought," she admitted. "Sometimes, I can

just get out of my head with the right music and the dancing... kind of reminds me of being on stage without all the pressure." She made a face, then shook her head a little. "Yeah, I know, poor little KC..."

"No," I said slowly. "Music makes more sense to me than people."

"Sometimes," she said. "It's just—easier to be when the music is playing. Dancing is an escape. So is running, and this year has been crap for that."

"Do you want to run more?"

"Yeah," she answered slowly, her eyes going distant. "I need to burn the energy. I'm so used to a tour schedule, and we were always on the go, two sets every night, sometimes three. To go from that to nothing is a bit jarring. Even with homework thrown in."

I'd never thought of it that way. Not at all. "I've never done a tour," I admitted. "Mom has. She goes on tour with Gibs all the time."

The minute I brought him up, I regretted it because her expression shuttered a little. Talking to KC had gotten easier and easier. Then I bring up someone she doesn't want to talk about.

Part of me wanted to ask more questions. Find out why she was so mad at him...

The rest of me wanted to leave her alone. She'd had enough grief this year.

"What Aubrey said about your stalker..." The shift in subject wasn't subtle, but I swore she almost looked relieved for it.

"The problem with being a celebrity," she said as she lifted the water for another drink, "is everyone thinks they know you better than they do. Stalkers fall into the same category, but most of them are harmless."

"You got hurt." That wasn't harmless at all.

"We also don't know if it was a stalker," she countered, the distance appearing in her eyes again. "That—I don't know what it was. I wish I did. I wish I knew where my guitar is."

"I wish you did, too. The other one will be fixed soon, right?" Maybe I could find her an acoustic guitar. I had a pretty good allowance and I barely ever touched it.

"It will be... but it's not the same." The music changed and she turned to face me. "You still want to dance?"

"With you?" Because I didn't care about anyone else. The shift of her stance pulled her away from me and I was already missing her.

Water finished, she held out her hand. "Yes, with me. Slow dancing can be fun...but it means more touching."

Heat flushed my face this time. "You noticed I didn't know how to dance."

"You dance really well, Hot Shot," she said with a wider smile.

Embarrassed, but pleased, I put my hand in hers and let her pull me out onto the dance floor. The slower music was different, I didn't recognize the artist and I really wasn't listening to the words, not with KC pressed up against me and her arms around my neck.

"You can put your hands on my hips," she said. The satin or silk or whatever the fabric was made out of, was soft under my hands. I kept the touch light, but there was no escaping how close we were.

The soft feathering of her breath against my chin distracted me almost as much as the press of her to my chest. Everything about KC was soft, and warm. She lifted her head and held my gaze all the way through the song, and when it segued to another slow one, she rested her head beneath my chin.

I could have floated out here forever. When the music

changed tempo though, she didn't flow away, just danced right up next to me and I kept an arm around her waist for when she wanted to dip.

The third time I swung her back up, her hand pressed to my shoulder as her gaze locked on mine. I don't know how long we hung there but one moment we stared and the next our lips connected.

The kiss lit me up as her mouth opened to mine. Soft, silken, electric, and the throb of the music seemed to match the rhythm of my heart as it thudded out a base note for how she tasted.

I'd kissed exactly three girls in my life. The first one had been Natalie Porter in fifth grade. She'd kissed me on a bet. It had been gross.

The second was Melissa Tarrington in sophomore year. She'd been really sweet and kissing her had been... weird but not unpleasant.

Kissing KC was like fireworks on the fourth of July while eating the hottest wings on the planet. I was burning up and dazzled at the same time. When I lifted my head, she opened her eyes to stare up at me then dipped her gaze to my lips again.

Hers were shiny, and pink, damp from the kiss and she tasted a lot like more. I wanted the hot burn of her on my tongue, and I wanted to feel the way her breath changed. I flattened a hand against her back, the pound of her heart the tempo I wanted to follow.

We flowed apart as the music changed again, but her eyes were shining and her smile was even wider. The next time there was a slow song, she nuzzled a kiss to my chin and then I stole another from her lips.

It was how the rest of the evening passed, Aubrey and Forrest had slipped out earlier, but KC and I stayed until it was almost midnight. Then our walk back to the dorm was slow. We held hands, traded little kisses, but no words. KC didn't need words from me.

We were almost back to the dorm when my phone went off with a news alert. I only had a handful set, usually about Mom and Gibs, so I pulled it out and stared at the screen. It was a video.

KC leaned against my arm. "Someone send you something?"

"It was uploaded," I told her. Maybe I should just watch it later.

"I don't mind," she said. "He is your stepfather."

So she had recognized the screen, and I hated Gibs a little bit right now because there was a shadow passing over her eyes, diminishing the soft glow of the earlier light.

"Go on," she teased, almost playful. "You know you want to." And was she being playful to make it easier for me?

With a sigh, I hit play. It was a video from a concert. Were they on the road again? I honestly didn't remember. They'd been working in the studio at Christmas.

Then suddenly the camera zoomed in on Gibs where he stood on the stage with a guitar strapped on and a wild smile on his face. "Glad to be out here tonight and I've got a little something I want to share with all of you thanks to one of my favorite kids...Jonas, man, this is for you."

The first three notes vibrated out of the phone, and I recognized it instantly. Where had he gotten that? I jerked my gaze up to KC and all the light was gone. The animation in her face had disappeared behind shutters and her smile vanished.

The look on her face crushed me. The apology she was desperately owed seemed glued to my tongue, and my mouth wouldn't work.

"So... you gave it to him." The song I'd written, the one

she'd put the lyrics to and Gibs was singing them with such passion it would totally be a hit. "Cool."

Then she just walked away and didn't look back at me once.

Forty-Two

KC

Friends.

We'd become friends. Or at least, I thought that was what we were doing. Even Jonas seemed to behave like we were. When I did the lyrics for his song, I never asked him what he was planning to do with it...

Then Dad called him one of his kids.

One. Of. His. Kids.

That hurt way more than it should have.

His singing *that* song in particular only served to dig fingers into this fresh wound. At the end of what had been a fantastic night, and with my lips tingling from the kisses I'd shared with Jonas, I had no idea what to do with the burn of that revelation.

Jonas seemed surprised. I didn't even think that was manufactured, but he gave the song to Dad. Fine. Whatever.

Then Dad dedicated it to him.

That...that was taking a lot longer to get over. We tap danced around the step sibling drama. I thought we'd begun to find a natural rhythm living together. My issues with the other douchebags aside, I'd actually started to let myself forget they were douchebags.

Big mistake.

Huge.

"Can I do anything?" Yvette asked on the phone while I painted my toenails. Aubrey glanced over at me from where she was working on her nails.

"I don't know," I admitted. "Like every single time I think I have a handle on this normal life shit, it just all goes sideways. I talked to Frankie a few days ago and she said that sometimes, life just sucks and you can only push through it, and if I wanted Jake to beat the shit out of the boys, he was in."

"Oh, I vote for that," Yvette said with a laugh. "In fact, I'll come down and help. I'll ask Jean-Paul to come as well."

"Oh, ho," Aubrey pounced verbally. "The mystery man has a name and it's *your* ex-boyfriend?"

Sighing, Yvette said, "Oui. My ex-boyfriend." The mocking tone just made me grin wider. "'Course, he is now my boyfriend again and we have been working on our communication skills and figuring things out. He is attending college here and we ran into each other..."

"And one thing led to another," I said. "Then your clothes fell off."

"Oh no, I threw them off. Jean-Paul has always had a magnificent dick, and to be honest, I did miss it."

Laughter spilled out of Aubrey, and I grinned. "Well, good to know his dick is still good."

"Magnificent," Yvette corrected. "But that is beside the point. As I said, I will volunteer Jean-Paul to help Jake and possibly Ian. He is very protective, too. They can come beat up those irritating boys because how dare they..."

Yeah. How dare they. The douchebags were just— douchebags. Aubrey and Yvette devolved into a debate about how awful the guys were, and I only half-listened while my toenails dried.

My one remaining guitar had come back from the shop "good as new," but it wasn't the same. Even though they'd done a great job of repairing it, it even felt different each time I tried to pick it up.

"Kait," Aubrey said, and I dragged my attention back to the present. "How are things going over here?"

"Fine," I said. "Perfectly polite. He does his thing, I do mine." We were just two step-siblings sharing a suite. We didn't watch shows or share meals, and though he still shadowed me on campus, he kept his distance.

Lachlan and Ramsey had both been there, on the periphery between the dance and spring break. Now I was back on campus and we were looking down the barrel of the end of the year.

Classes were getting tighter, but I cared less. Or maybe I'd just gotten used to it all.

Graduation was coming.

Mid-April turned warm on the campus. Warm, gorgeous skies and beautiful flowers helped me go back to running full-time. I needed it. Mom had emerged from her self-imposed exile to let me know she was considering taking another movie role. That she was ready.

They told her she was ready.

Her guru or whatever. Guilt raked claws through me because I'd kind of tuned her out. Yes, she was still at the Sunshine Retreat, and she'd been there for months. Hopefully, it worked; she sounded happier.

That was something, right?

I'd gotten my speed and my distance back even as I worked on staying focused. Jackie said they were ordering another battery of tests for Pen. We needed to know if this course of treatment had worked.

The fact they weren't sure was making me insane. How could they not know? They figured out the first round of treatments wasn't as effective, but she wasn't that far from a *third* birthday, and we still didn't know if all the treatments were working.

"We want to discuss the terms of a new contract," Teddy said via the conference call. "You will be graduating soon, and you've had a two-year cooling-off period—if you want to get serious about your music again, well, now would be the time to do it."

I glanced at Aubrey and she lifted her shoulders. Neither of us knew what we wanted to do.

We were closing in on finals week and the whole school had turned into a seething mass of chaos and tension. Running kept me sane.

"Ace," Lachlan said as he fell in next to me. I could pretend I had the music cranked up.

But I didn't. "Lachlan."

"You have time to talk later?"

"We're talking now." I managed to even get the words out without huffing.

"You're also running. I was thinking we could sit down—"

"No."

"Ace—"

"I said no, Lachlan. Based on what you did to RJ, I'm going to assume you really do know what the words mean." I slid to a halt and faced him. "So, no. I don't want to talk to you later. I don't want to talk to you at all. In a few short weeks, I'm out of here and we never have to see each other again."

"You're still mad at me."

I just stared at him. Not his brightest moment.

Blowing out a breath, he raked a hand through his hair. "I want to try and explain. Could you maybe trust me a little too—"

"Trust you? The last time I trusted you, I ended up in a room where I not only got to see, but hear a girl being sexually assaulted on a video that *you* set up to punish RJ. I've had nightmares about her cries for weeks, and you want me to trust you?" I stared at him. "I have two words for you, fuck and off."

"Yeah, you're still mad at me. I thought if I gave you some space..."

"Well, you might go back to the space thing. That was working for me." With that, I turned and went back to my run.

Douchebags. They were all douchebags.

Daddy loved them best.

Then again, he was the biggest goddamn douchebag of them all.

"I finished another song," Jonas said, his tone quiet. I hadn't said a word when he came out, just made my coffee. I still made him his. Just like he still brought me food. But we didn't talk.

This was breaking the rules of our armistice or whatever you wanted to call it.

"If I put it on your door, will you look at it?"

Turning to face him, I sipped the coffee. "No."

He blinked.

"I don't want to look at it. If you want Dad to do another of your songs, get him to add the lyrics to it. He used to be good at it." I grabbed the toast as it popped up. "I have to meet Aubrey at the library."

I was almost to the door when he said, "I didn't know he was going to do that."

"Yeah well, you spend enough time with Gibson Crosse and you figure out he's going to do whatever the hell he wants. But enjoy being the favorite," I said and despite all my attempts, I couldn't keep the bitterness out of my voice.

It wasn't Jonas' fault that he was the favorite. Anymore than it was my fault or Bronson's that we'd been born, or any of the members of 'we could have been in a condom'.

Pivoting, I looked into his gray eyes for the first time in weeks. "Be careful with him, Jonas," I told him.

He frowned. "Why?"

"Because he has a way of making you feel like you're the center of the world, then moving on and leaving you spinning. Just be careful—I gotta go."

There, I warned him.

"Your mother is getting married," Trish said and I pulled the phone away to stare at it for a moment then put it back to my ear.

"What?"

"She's getting married, the first week of June, and she wants you to be the maid of honor. I'll send you all the details. Make sure you're free and update me on your measurements so I can get the dress ordered—"

"Trish," I cut into her. I'd heard nothing from Mom in months and she was out of her retreat and *now* she was getting married. "Who is she marrying?"

"Oh, I don't know, honey," Trish said. "I don't really worry about that part. She's had a string of broken engagements, this will probably go the same way..."

"Is it Johnny?"

"No," Trish said with an almost audible wince. "Oh honey, she didn't tell you?"

Of course ,she didn't. "They broke up."

"Yeah, at Christmas." And Johnny hadn't said a word because he was a decent guy.

Fuck.

"Just make sure you're here for the wedding, okay?"

"Sure...why not..."

It was pouring rain when I finished my second to last final for the year. One more. Just one more and I was free. I pushed out of the building with the flow of students on their way toward freedom.

I pulled the phone out of my bag and turned it on to check. The only times I shut it off were for tests. The message on my screen robbed me of all the relief finishing the exam had given me.

JACKIE
Call me.

I went hot then cold as I pressed her contact and hurried away from the other students. I didn't care if I got wet.

"That was fast," she said in an almost too bright tone. "I thought it might take you a little longer."

"Finals week," I told her. "I'm almost done."

"Oh, honey, then go focus on your—"

"Jackie," I said, trying to quell the sinking feeling in my stomach and the hard slap of my heart that seemed too damn loud. "Tell me."

It was bad news.

Her soft sigh shredded me. "The chemo isn't working. They want to try another cocktail, but she's got to get stronger again and right now..."

Heat burned in my eyes. It isn't working. They want to try another. The last couple of rounds had taken a lot of out of Pen. They were worried about the weight loss. She also had a cold. She was back in the hospital.

I angled away from the buildings as Jackie went over everything the doctors said. I didn't care about the hair plastering to my scalp or the rain soaking through my shirt.

"So," Jackie said. "This is where we are. Bronson's already been tested. He's not a match. But you need to be tested next."

"I'll do it as soon as I'm there. Have we checked everyone else?"

"Only Trace is older than you and Bronson. He's not taking calls. Or at least, he isn't taking mine. Everyone else is too young for this, at least right now. We'll just cross the bridge when we come to it."

Trace didn't take a lot of people's calls. "I'll call him. We don't talk as much, but he usually takes my calls. Can you see who I need to talk to about booking the appointment and what I need to do?"

I checked my watch, the pain clogging my throat made it hard to even talk. "My final exam is the day after tomorrow. I'll get flights booked for that evening." I didn't need to be here for graduation. The grand experiment had been a grand fucking flop. "I'll get there as soon as I can. Fuck, I can just blow off the last test and come now."

"You will not," Jackie said firmly. "You will finish the last exam, take a beat, catch your breath, then come home. Even if you got here tomorrow morning and tested as a match, it could be a week or two before they would even move on it."

Oh.

"Sweetheart, I know you're scared. We all are. Bronson's furious he isn't a match. But this isn't anything either of you can control. Penelope is in excellent hands right now, I promise. You'll see that for yourself soon."

I swiped a hand over my face, the water soaking it. My eyes burned so badly. "Jackie..."

"I know," she said with a soft hum. "I know. We're doing everything we can. You'll be here soon. Can you hold on for a little bit longer?"

Did I have a choice?

I swiped at the tears again. It didn't seem to matter. The rain, the tears—the world wavered around me.

"I can," I said, swallowing hard. "I will...I'll call you when I have the flights booked."

We didn't talk for much longer. When we hung up, I just sat down on the steps and stared at the puddles as they jumped and rippled while the rain struck them.

It wasn't fucking fair.

It just wasn't.

Forty-Three

RAMSEY

Finals week was a slice of heaven and hell. As a TA, all I had to do was proctor the exams while keeping an eye on floundering students who might potentially be in danger of harming themselves. It had happened. The exclusivity of the school increased the pressure from the administration, the faculty, and then there were the parents.

As an RA, I had to keep the dorm on target. Curfews were suspended and all-nighters were commonplace. I split my sleep schedule so I could do random checks. My door was always open to students, too. While I had my own exams, I'd made sure to take as many early as I could to free me up for this week.

The week's stressors got to everyone, apparently, even to Lachlan who had spent the last three weeks fucking moping and making me crazy. Before I headed to the gym, I told him to take Jonas out to dinner or a movie or something. Just get him off campus for a break.

"Why?" Lachlan demanded. "He barely speaks to me on a

"

good day lately. And since the Fire and Ice Dance, he's been in a shit mood."

"Exactly, and he has exams this week. He needs to get out of his head. That means we need to keep an eye on him and make sure he is getting downtime." Lachlan wasn't alone in having no idea what happened. The growing closeness between him and KC seemed absent.

It had been evident, even in classes. She was shutting everyone out. The friendships she'd made were all gradually slipping away, as the tide of school and commitments swept them all up.

The only friendship KC maintained seemed to be the one she arrived with. She was leaving everyone—leaving me—even while physically on campus. After Lachlan left with Jonas, I went to the gym. A workout helped, and the rain had turned to a full-on downpour. I tried everything to take my mind off the blue-haired siren, but she was the only thing occupying my thoughts.

My instincts said she was hurting. Whatever went down between her and Jonas piled onto that crap Lachlan pulled with RJ. While the stunt has been effective in getting RJ arrested, as well as banned from the campus, there were no assurances he'd stay in jail.

Combine those incidents with the fire at the start of the academic year and the break-in to her and Jonas' suite... I was impressed that KC hadn't just washed her hands of all of us and left. Impressed and a little grateful.

As long as she was here, I could keep an eye on her. While she might be avoiding my brothers and me, I had spread the word among the other TAs and RAs. We did our best to make sure she was never on her own, even if we weren't physically with her.

Whatever preoccupied her, I kept thinking about the baby in the hospital. If her daughter was struggling, it would explain everything. Daughter. The idea she was a teen mom was hard to wrap my mind around. On the one hand, she just seemed—so self-possessed.

Then again, all the maturity in the world didn't prevent mistakes from happening. Realistically, it was none of my business, but it didn't stop me from thinking about her—I was jogging between the buildings when I spotted the figure sitting on the picnic table beyond the buildings, near one of the trees on the quad most popular in sunny weather for kids catching some rays.

Slowing my pace, I scanned the darkened area. One of the lights kept flickering, but even with the waterproof hoodie on, I was all too aware of the rain and this kid was just sitting there without a jacket...

Fuck.

I altered my route to get them ushered back into a building. If they were one of my residents, I'd look after them...

The soft sobs hit me as I got closer. Then the light flickered, illuminating her slicked down hair and damp face.

"KC?"

She sniffled, lifting her head to look at me. Any cosmetics she might have worn were gone, her eyes were reddened and her face blotchy.

"How long have you been out here?" I glanced around. Where the hell was her friend? Or anyone else for that matter? She didn't say anything, just let out another hiccupping sob as she swiped at her face. It was hardly going to do any good with her crying.

"Kaitlin," I tried her full name, but she didn't stop crying. The soft sounds were gutting me. "Siren? What happened?" I reached out to take her hand, it was ice-cold in mine and she turned those huge, sad eyes on me and the blade sank deep. "C'mon, you're freezing. Let's get you out of the rain."

She didn't fight me, but she didn't get up either. I'd seen

people here before. It was that moment when reality just overwhelmed everything. Hell, I'd been there. Fight or flight wasn't the only thing that kicked in when the stressors grew too much. Sometimes, you just shut down and closed out the world.

Sometimes, it was the only way to survive.

"I'm picking you up," I said, giving her a minute. If I didn't get any verbal responses out of her after I got her in and out of the rain, I'd call for the nurse. I didn't know what happened, but I intended to find out. "Okay, Siren, hold on."

I slid an arm under her legs and another around her waist as I lifted her right off the table. She weighed next to nothing, even soaking wet. The fact she just curled into me and buried her face against my shoulder wrecked me more than I was prepared for.

I'd seen this girl fair beyond measure, feisty, flashy, furious, and funny. This—this sobbing broken mess was not the girl—woman I'd gotten to know over the last couple of years. Every little broken-hearted sound made me want to do violence to whatever provoked this reaction.

Back at the dorm, I didn't waste time taking her upstairs, I just carried her into my suite. Thankfully, Lachlan was still out, so I didn't have to deal with him as well.

I carried her into the bathroom with the towels. When I tried to set her on the counter, she tightened her arms around me.

"Shh, Siren," I whispered against her wet hair. "We need to get you out of these wet clothes and dried off. Okay?" That at least got her to lift her head.

She glanced around the bathroom, but I didn't get the feeling she was seeing it at all. I used the distraction to set her on the counter.

Reaching down, I tugged off her shoes. Her feet were bare, leaving only her pale blue toenails to wink up at me. Even as I urged her jacket off, I reached over to nudge on the heat lamp. She was already shivering.

"Okay, I'm going to turn on the shower and get you something to change into. You get out of those clothes, then into the shower and warm up. I'll be right back, okay?"

Her lack of responsiveness was really starting to worry me. I ducked back into my room, stripped off my wet clothes, and out of the shoes before I dragged on a dry t-shirt and sweats.

Back in the bathroom, she was still sitting on the counter, staring at the shower where the steam was starting to rise. In her hand, she white-knuckled her phone.

"C'mon, Siren," I coaxed. "I need your help here. You need to get out of these wet things, you're cold and you're miserable already. I don't want you to get sick."

"I don't care." Three words came out in a raw, hoarse voice. "Doesn't matter."

"It matters to me," I said, touching a finger to her chin and nudging her gaze up to look at me. "I don't know what happened. You can tell me or not tell me, either is fine, for now. But you need out of those clothes and you need to warm up. Can you do that for me?"

She was trembling so violently. "Why do you care? You hate me. You all do—you think I'm some horrible stuck-up slut who doesn't give a shit about anyone." The edge of misery dipped into a sea of anger.

"No," I said. "I don't. Maybe I did—maybe I was an asshole about it. You know, no maybe, I was. But you are none of those things, Siren, and right now...all I want to do is help you. Can you let me do that?"

"Fine," she huffed, more defeated than defiant. Sliding off the counter, she was already tugging off her tie and then her shirt.

Pivoting, I focused on the shower to give her some privacy. The slap of wet clothes hitting the tile sent a number of inappropriate thoughts dancing through my head and into my blood.

Not the fucking time.

A minute later, she walked around me and I moved so she could still have my back as she got into the shower. Crouching, I collected the soaking wet clothes then stood. Only when I did, I caught sight of her in the mirror. The lean, almost too lean, shape of her seemed so fragile as she stood, one hand pressed against the tile as the hot water poured over her.

The shake of her shoulders, and the near-silent sobbing drove the stakes into my soul deeper and deeper. All I wanted to do was make this better for her. Fix it somehow. Forcing myself to turn away, I left the bathroom and took the clothes into a bag for the laundry later.

When I came back, she was sitting on the floor in the shower. Goddammit, Siren...

Yanking the curtain back, I shut off the water then reached in to pull her out. She didn't protest, just wrapped her arms around me. Soaking my clothes or not, she seemed desperate for contact or maybe just a hug.

That settled it for me, I wrapped her up then sat down in the bathroom with the heater on and wrapped her up in a towel as much as I could while cradling her. When she began shaking with sobs all over again, I stroked her wet hair back.

When she fisted my shirt, I pressed a kiss to the top of her head. Then another. Before I registered what she was doing, she tilted her tear-streaked face up to mine.

"What can I do, Siren?" I whispered. "Tell me how to make this right?"

"I don't know," she confessed, and I found myself cradling her face and swiping away the tears with my thumbs. "It just hurts."

"What hurts?" If I could just fix this for her.

"Everything," she admitted, then she pressed forward and

her lips were on mine. The ferociousness of the kiss caught me by surprise, but it was like dumping kerosene on a fire and all the pent-up frustration, worry, and even aggravation burst into flames.

I devoured her mouth as she fisted my shirt so tight it pulled against my shoulders. Her skin was so fucking soft and smooth under my hands. When she shifted to straddle my lap, I groaned at the pressure of her on my very erect cock.

"Siren," I whispered in between sharp biting scrapes of her teeth over my lower lip and the sweet taste of her thrusting against my tongue. The salt of her tears lingered, but they, too, seemed to evaporate under the warmth of the kiss. The pressure of her breasts against my shirt beckoned. "Siren..."

"I want this," she said, lifting her head to stare at me, and I stared back. Her pupils were blown, her face flushed and still blotchy from her tears.

"Kaitlin," I cautioned. "I'm still..."

"What? My TA? My RA? My fucking stepbrother?" She swallowed hard and the tears shimmered in her eyes again. "I don't need any of those, and in two days—how did you put it? You'll be nothing. Outside of this school? We'll be nothing."

The verbal slap landed. Did I fucking deserve it? Probably. Still, my stomach dropped at the reminder. No.

The third one still applied. Even if it didn't? We would damn well still be *something*.

"Look at me, Ramsey," she said, straightening, and the pressure that put on my cock was exquisite torture. "Look at me and tell me you see a sister."

I swept my gaze over her, from her damp hair to her tear-stained face to the tattoos decorating her arms and shoulders. There were more hidden along her abdomen and one on the curve of her breast. So many tattoos I wanted to map with my fingers and my tongue.

The pretty pale pink of her stiffened nipples beckoned to

me, and there was a hint of blonde hair near her pussy that made me want to spread her out and explore every inch of her.

"No," I admitted. "I just see you, Siren."

"Do you want me?" The naked vulnerability in that question delivered the final blow.

Did I want her?

Fuck, all I'd wanted for two years *was* her. No matter how much I tried to persuade myself otherwise... "Yes," I told her as I pushed up from the floor and carried her up with me. "I want you, Siren."

"Then make me forget," she pleaded. "Just make me forget everything."

No. What I should tell her was no. Call a counselor, find her friend, call her fucking agent if I had to—find someone who could help her. That was what I should do.

Did I do it?

Fuck, no.

I carried her into the bedroom and closed the door to the bathroom. The room had a single low lamp on, and it was suddenly far cozier and more intimate than the too-brightly lit bathroom.

"Are you sure?" I asked, because right now, I was imagining doing everything I could to make her scream before I sank into that sweet pussy. The line I shouldn't cross had been erased a long time ago.

"Yes," she insisted, dragging me downward until our mouths fused. I palmed one of her breasts and she gasped as I teased the nipple, twisting and pulling, then kissed away from her mouth as I set her on the bed.

Rising, I stripped off my shirt and then shoved down my sweats. My cock was already bouncing against my belly, heavy and hard. Pretending I didn't have a hard-on around her was something I'd gotten good at. Imagining fisting that blue hair as I fucked her had been my spank bank material for months.

Even when I couldn't admit it to myself.

Dropping a hand on either side of her, I kissed her gently. "Birth control?"

"Pill," she told me, spreading her fingers over my chest. "And I'm healthy."

"So am I."

But I still hesitated and she nipped at my jaw. The sadness in her eyes was still there, but so was the fight. "I'd say trust me," she whispered. "But we don't do that well."

No. "I have condoms."

"If you want to use one," she muttered, then bit down on my pec. The sharpness of her teeth was going to leave a mark, and it made my cock jump. "Ramsey—I just want to feel you."

"The pill?" I verified. She already had one kid; we didn't need to make another.

"Yes," she muttered, straining upward to capture my lips. She kissed me like she needed me to breathe. Maybe she did. I massaged her breasts, then slid my hands down to her hips, then to her thighs, and finally to her pussy.

It was slick and damp, and I eased a finger into her. Her fierce little muscles clamped down on me as she gasped into my mouth. There was no finesse as we kissed and she writhed against me. She wanted friction and for me to move.

I wanted to give her time to change her mind. When she wrapped her hand around my cock, my good intentions went up in flames.

"Like that," I told her. "Squeeze a little tighter." Then I was thrusting against her palm as I slid two fingers between my lips to wet them before reaching down to massage her clit. She bucked wildly as I increased the pressure.

The urge to come was right there, but I fought it as I dueled tongues with her, then traced wet kisses to her chest. Sucking her nipple against my teeth, I pinched her clit then rolled it with the heel of my hand. She came in an explosive rush of wetness and the little scream was so gratifying.

I didn't give her time to come down from it, I wanted to feel that happy little pussy flexing around me. Shifting her legs wider, I pushed her knees up and then rubbed my dick against her folds.

Pleasure suffused her face, and she gasped as she watched me, tremors shaking her. When I pushed in, there was a resistance and her expression went absolutely pained, and I froze.

"Keep going," she pleaded. "It's supposed to be better after..."

Fuck.

My.

Life.

I wanted to shout and shake her. As it was, I eased back and began to rock into her as carefully as possible. The muscles would stretch, but she wasn't—how the fuck was she a mom? The question floated through the haze of pleasure as I sank into her deeper.

Her soft panting cries grew in intensity, but once I was finally seated, I lifted my head to gaze down at her. "You with me, Siren?"

"It hurts..." But her clenched teeth were at odds with the flushed smile she shot me. "You're pretty big there, teach..."

I growled. "Siren?"

"Hmm?"

"Shut up."

Then I fucked into her again, and it wasn't long before she was digging her nails into my back and our tongues were back to battling. The pain had pushed back on the flutters of her earlier orgasm, but I fought to get her there again.

The rhythm of her cries as I increased my speed and adjusted the angle was going to drive me mad. I waited until she finally began to shake again, her legs flexed around my hips, and then I bit her neck, a stroke of teeth before hitting the juncture of her shoulder and neck.

Just that spark of pain, and she came on a scream. The convulsion of her inner muscles catapulted me past holding my own orgasm off, and I came in hot jets.

She was still shaking when I rolled us over. Cradling her to my chest as cum slid out to soak us both. I didn't care as another splash of a tear hit my chest and I looked down.

"Siren?"

"I can't help it," she whispered. "Pen is so sick, and I don't know if she's going to make it…"

Pen.

The baby in the hospital. The baby that couldn't be hers.

Fuck, I had so many questions.

But now wasn't the time.

"You don't have to help it," I told her, pulling her closer. "I'm here for whatever you need."

If she wanted to bury her grief in orgasms, then we could do that, too.

"Just promise me you'll be here in the morning," I told her. Holding onto her seemed more like trying to cup a raging river and keep it still. The torrent of her life ebbed and flowed even more strongly than I'd realized. "Stay. We'll figure all of this out. Do you promise?"

"We'll figure everything out?" The need for hope in those words clawed me wide open.

"Yes," I whispered, and I meant it. We'd figure it out, but she needed to be *here* for that. This moment was already growing more and more intangible. "Whatever you need. Will you be here in the morning?"

"I promise," she said before she turned her face into my shoulder and cried. I held her, stroking her hair, and when her tears eased off, I went for a washcloth. Then I settled back in to hold her. She finally dropped off sometime around ten, and I fought to stay awake.

Just in case she needed something. A little after two, I woke up when she reached for me. At four, I tugged her back from where she'd migrated across the bed.

At six, she was gone.

The Douchebags Three will return in Party Crashers.

Party Crashers

From the moment I learned she was coming to our school, I had a gut feeling it would end in disaster. Out of all the schools in the world, why did Kaitlin Crosse have to choose ours? Her presence confused my brothers and created tension between them, but I soon realized my initial assumptions about her were completely wrong.

It was me who possessed the flaws of being wild, arrogant, selfish, inconsiderate, and foolish. My bad judgment call in the midst of the school's scandal may have destroyed everything I wanted.

As the world tears Kaitlin apart, my brothers and I find ourselves trapped in a web of lies. Our mother despises her, and even our stepfather's allegiance is uncertain. Kaitlin trusts no one, and who can blame her?

But I refuse to wait for her forgiveness or return. If I want her, I have to take action. Kaitlin needs me, and now, I know I need her too.

All of us do.

Yep. I know. Back to my corner to think about what I've done.

See you soon!
xoxo
Heather

Reader group: facebook.com/groups/heatherspack
Spoiler group: facebook.com/groups/teammadatheather

About Heather Long

I *love* books. Not just a little bit, but a lot. Books were my best friends when I was growing up. Books didn't care if I was new to a town or to a class. They were always there, my trustiest of companions. Until they turned on me and said I had to write them.

I can tell you that my own personal happily ever after included writing books. I've always said that an HEA is a work in progress. It's true in my marriage, my friendships, and in my career. I am constantly nurturing my muse as we dive into new tales, new tropes, new characters and more.

After seventeen years in Texas, we relocated to the Pacific Northwest in search of seasons, new experiences, and new geography. I can't wait to discover what life (and my muse) have in store for me.

Maybe writing was always my destiny and romance my fate. After all, my grandmother wasn't a fan of picture books and used to read me her Harlequin Romance novels.

Friends to lovers, enemies to lovers, friends to enemies to lovers, you name it, I love them and love to write them. I started with Earth Witches Aren't Easy, the first in the Chance Monroe trilogy, but my characters and I have traveled a long way since I created that urban fantasy world.

One of the series I hear my readers recommend the most is the Untouchable series followed in quick succession by the Vandals, and that just delights me. No lie, whenever one of my readers brings up my wolves, I do a little a fist pump.

I'm active on social media, and I love hearing from readers.

Feel free to tag me with a question about any of my books, or just say hi!

Follow Heather & Sign up for her news and updates:
www.heatherlong.net
TikTok

Also by Heather Long

82nd Street Vandals

Savage Vandal

Vicious Rebel

Ruthless Traitor

Dirty Devil

Brutal Fighter

Dangerous Renegade

Merciless Spy

Reckless Thief

Fierce Dancer

Always a Marine Series

Once Her Man, Always Her Man

Retreat Hell! She Just Got Here

Tell It to the Marine

Proud to Serve Her

Her Marine

No Regrets, No Surrender

The Marine Cowboy

The Two and the Proud

A Marine and a Gentleman

Combat Barbie

Whiskey Tango Foxtrot

What Part of Marine Don't You Understand?

A Marine Affair

Marine Ever After

Marine in the Wind

Marine with Benefits

A Marine of Plenty

A Candle for a Marine

Marine under the Mistletoe

Have Yourself a Marine Christmas

Lest Old Marines Be Forgot

Her Marine Bodyguard

Smoke & Marines

Blue Ivy Prep

Problem Child

Mad Boys

Party Crashers

Bravo Team Wolf

When Danger Bites

Bitten Under Fire

Cardinal Sins

Kill Song

First Chorus

High Note

Last Word

Chance Monroe

Earth Witches Aren't Easy

Plan Witch from Out of Town

Bad Witch Rising

Her Elite Assets

Featuring:

Pure Copper

Target: Tungsten

Asset: Arsenic

Fevered Hearts

Marshal of Hel Dorado

Brave are the Lonely

Micah & Mrs. Miller

A Fistful of Dreams

Raising Kane

Wanted: Fevered or Alive

Wild and Fevered

The Quick & The Fevered

A Man Called Wyatt

Going Royal

Some Like It Royal

Some Like It Scandalous

Some Like It Deadly

Some Like it Secret

Some Like it Easy

Her Marine Prince

Blocked

Heart of the Nebula

Queenmaker

Deal Breaker

Throne Taker

Lone Star Leathernecks

Semper Fi Cowboy

As You Were, Cowboy

Magic & Mayhem

The Witch Singer

Bridget's Witch's Diary

The Witched Away Bride

Mongrels

Mongrels, Mischief & Mayhem

Shackled Souls

Succubus Chained

Succubus Unchained

Succubus Blessed

Shackled Souls (Omnibus)

Space Cowboy

Space Cowboy Survival Guide

Untouchable

Rules and Roses

Changes and Chocolates

Keys and Kisses

Whispers and Wishes

Hangovers and Holidays

Brazen and Breathless

Trials and Tiaras

Graduation and Gifts

Defiance and Dedication

Songs and Sweethearts

Legacy and Lovers

Farewells and Forever

Wolves of Willow Bend

Wolf at Law

Wolf Bite

Caged Wolf

Wolf Claim

Wolf Next Door

Rogue Wolf

Bayou Wolf

Untamed Wolf

Wolf with Benefits

River Wolf

Single Wicked Wolf

Desert Wolf

Snow Wolf

Wolf on Board

Holly Jolly Wolf

Shadow Wolf

His Moonstruck Wolf

Thunder Wolf

Ghost Wolf

Outlaw Wolves

Wolf Unleashed